# I Got You, Babe

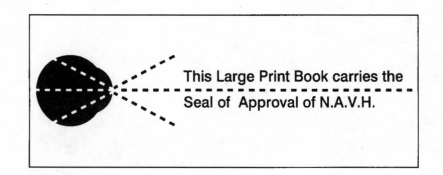

This Large Print Book carries the
Seal of Approval of N.A.V.H.

# I Got You, Babe

## Jane Graves

**Thorndike Press • Waterville, Maine**

$28.95 Gale 11/02

Published in 2002 by arrangement with The Ballantine
Publishing Group, a division of Random House, Inc.

Thorndike Press Large Print Romance Series.

The tree indicium is a trademark of Thorndike Press.

The text of this Large Print edition is unabridged.
Other aspects of the book may vary from the original edition.

Set in 16 pt. Plantin by Al Chase.

Printed in the United States on permanent paper.

**Library of Congress Cataloging-in-Publication Data**
Graves, Jane.
    I got you, babe / Jane Graves.
      p. cm.
    ISBN 0-7862-4808-4 (lg. print : hc : alk. paper)
    1. Female offenders — Fiction.   2. Robbery — Fiction.
  3. Police — Texas — Fiction.   4. Texas — Fiction.
  5. Large type books.   I. Title.
  PS3607.R427 I15 2002
  813′.6—dc21               2002029126

To Linda Kruger,
for always keeping me
on the right track.
Thanks for everything.

# chapter one

Renee Esterhaus peered out of room fourteen of the Flamingo Motor Lodge at the intersection of Highway 37 and the middle of nowhere, shivering a little in the crisp October air. She cast a nervous glance left and right down the sidewalk in front of the other rooms, then turned her gaze to the gravel parking lot and the dense pine forest beyond it. Everything seemed quiet. No suspicious-looking people. No cars she hadn't seen before. No helicopters circling overhead, ready to drop a SWAT team.

Nothing but the evening breeze rustling through the trees.

She slid out the door, leaving it ajar, then scurried to the snack machine in the breezeway between her room and the motel office, telling herself to calm down, that no matter what she'd done, the SWAT team thing was pretty unlikely.

She plugged two quarters into the machine and was getting ready to insert the third when the skin prickled on the back of her neck. She froze, the quarter poised at the slot, then swallowed hard and glanced over her shoulder.

Nothing.

She let out the breath she'd been holding. Her imagination was getting the better of her.

If only her old Toyota hadn't chosen the worst possible moment of her life to fall apart, she wouldn't be stuck overnight in this ratty little motel swearing that someone was looking over her shoulder. She prayed that the mechanic at the Mobil station down the street would keep his promise and have a new fuel pump installed first thing in the morning. Then she'd be back on the road again, one step closer to New Orleans, Louisiana, and one step farther away from Tolosa, Texas.

New Orleans. She didn't know why she'd chosen that city, except that it had a lot of restaurants so she could easily get a job, and the dark mystery that surrounded it meant she could probably lose one identity and pick up another. Of course, she had no idea how a person went about becoming someone else, but she couldn't think about that now. She'd get her car, get on the road, and figure out the rest later.

She shoved the quarter in, pushed a button, and her dinner fell to the bottom of the machine — a package of peanut butter crackers. She leaned over and plucked it out of the slot. As she stood up again, an arm snaked around her waist and something cold and hard jabbed against the underside of her jaw.

"Missed your court date, sweet thing."

In a blinding rush, she felt herself being spun around and slammed against the snack machine. That cold, hard thing — a gun — now rested against her throat. And right in her face was the biggest, ugliest, most menacing-looking man she'd ever seen. He had to be pushing fifty, but not an ounce of muscle had gone to fat. His clean-shaven head, death-theme tattoos, and single gold earring gave him a sinister look that bordered on the psychotic.

"Wh-who are you?" she stammered.

A cunning smile curled his lips. "Max Leandro. Bond enforcement officer. And your luck just ran out."

It took a moment for Renee to comprehend his words, and when she did, a huge rush of panic swept through her. She'd been watching out for cops, who she assumed would announce their presence with bullhorns and bloodhounds. The last thing she expected was to be nabbed by a two-ton bounty hunter who looked as if he could bench-press a Buick.

He shoved his gun into the waistband of his jeans, yanked her wrists together in front of her, and snapped on a pair of handcuffs. He half led, half dragged her around the corner to his old Jeep Cherokee parked on the west side of the motel.

"No!" Renee said, trying to pull her arm away. "Please don't do this! Please!"

"Oh, but I've got to. See, they're holding a party at the county jail, and your name is at the top of the guest list."

"Wait a minute!" She looked back over her shoulder. "What about my stuff? You can't just leave —"

"Sure I can."

He pushed her into the passenger seat through the driver's door, then slid in beside her. He lit up a Camel, shoved a Metallica tape into the tape player, and peeled out of the motel parking lot.

Renee stared at the dashboard, feeling shock and disbelief and a whole lot of anxiety. In less than two hours she'd be back in the hands of the Tolosa police, and they wouldn't be letting her out on bail again.

She glared at Leandro. "How did you find me?"

"By being the best, sweet thing."

*Damn.* Why couldn't she have been chased by a bounty hunter who graduated at the bottom of his class?

She tested the handcuffs with a furtive jerk or two, found them unyielding, then took stock of the rest of her situation. The door handle had been removed from the passenger side of the front seat. Glancing over her shoulder, she could see the back doors had gotten the same treatment. It appeared that plan A — leaping out of a moving vehicle — was not going to be an option.

"You're making a terrible mistake," she told him, putting plan B into action. "I'm innocent. You don't want to take an innocent person to jail, do you?"

He made a scoffing noise. "Innocent, my ass. You got caught with the loot and the weapon."

"Well, yeah —"

"The old lady who was robbed said the perp was a blond woman."

"There are thousands of blondes —"

"She picked you out of a lineup."

"I don't know how —"

"Then there's your record."

Renee sat up suddenly. "How did you know about that?"

11

Leandro gave her a smug look. "I have ways."

"I was a juvenile. Those records are supposed to be sealed!"

"The records *are* sealed. But cops' lips aren't. When you got dragged down to the station on the armed robbery rap, that headful of blond hair of yours spurred a few memories." Leandro grinned. "Shouldn't pour beer on a cop's shoes, Renee. They don't tend to forget that."

*Oh, God.* Renee buried her head in her hands as that nasty little memory came flooding back. She was a bit fuzzy on the details of that night, except that she'd gotten very irate when a certain cop suggested that perhaps she and her friends shouldn't be wandering around downtown at one in the morning, underage and dead drunk. She'd told him what she thought of his assessment of the situation by upending her Bud Light all over his spit-polished shoes. That had bought her a ticket to the county jail. Again.

"How could he remember that?" Renee said. "It was over eight years ago!"

"I guess you're unforgettable, sweet thing. Particularly when you add in the rest of your record. Shoplifting, vandalism, joyriding —"

"I've been clean since then!"

"Once a criminal, always a criminal."

She wished she had a nickel for every time she'd heard that, even though she knew it wasn't true.

When she was seventeen, and had gotten caught riding with her boyfriend in a stolen car, the judge finally decided he'd had enough and tossed her into a juvenile detention center. Her mother had sobered up just long enough to attend the hearing, then went home, pulled out her bottle of Jim Beam, and toasted the judge for finally making somebody else responsible for the daughter she'd barely bothered to raise.

After she'd spent about three months in detention, the pain of incarceration became clear to Renee. But even though she'd seriously started to question the wisdom of a life of crime, she was still way too cool to let them see her sweat.

With her attitude still in question, she'd been invited to spend the day at a "scared straight" program, complete with twelve cussing, hard-core, screaming female convicts whose job it was to convince her and half a dozen other wayward teenage girls that prison was the last place they wanted to be. It had been a lesson Renee had never forgotten, and when they finally released her from the detention center, she promised herself she'd walk through hell if that was what it took to keep from having to go through that experience again.

It had been a long trip up from rock bottom, but she'd managed to make the climb, even when the first step had been a waitress job at Denny's. Her juvenile record was history — or at least, it had been, until some cop with a savantlike memory decided to open his big mouth.

"There's no way I could have committed that robbery," she told Leandro. "I can't stand the sight of guns. How could I possibly —"

"You're wasting your breath. I don't give a damn whether you're guilty or not. I get paid either way."

Renee gave a little snort of disgust. "Yeah. Charming profession you've got there."

"It beats robbing convenience stores."

"I told you I didn't do it!"

He smiled. "That's what they *all* say."

Renee wanted to beat her head against the dashboard. This guy wouldn't know innocence if it bit him on the nose. She turned and stared out the passenger window, watching the miles between her and incarceration slip away like sand through her fingers.

14

On the day the robbery happened, she'd been offered the assistant manager's job at Renaissance, a four-star Italian restaurant with upscale clientele and an honest-to-God wine cellar. About to burst with excitement, she'd called her best friend Paula Merani to celebrate, only to remember that she was away on one of those weekend-for-two packages at a local hotel with her no-good boyfriend, Tom Garroway. So Renee ordered dinner from China Garden and ate it while she flipped around on the tube and thought about all the things she was going to do as assistant manager to help Renaissance get that elusive fifth star.

Then she decided her wonderful new job entitled her to splurge in the finest way possible — with a pint of Ben & Jerry's Cherry Garcia — so she grabbed her purse and headed to the twenty-four-hour Kroger. A cop pulled her over because her taillight was out, and she couldn't believe it when he extracted twelve hundred dollars and a semiautomatic pistol from the backseat of her car. To her utter amazement and subsequent horror, those items pointed to a convenience store robbery in the area only hours before. She didn't have a clue how they'd gotten there. The arresting officer had been unmoved by her profession of innocence, and before she knew it, she'd landed in jail.

She met with the best defense attorney her savings could buy, a munchkin of a man who wore a tie wider than his chest and still had a piece of toilet paper stuck to a shaving cut on his neck. When his message seemed to be, "We both know you're guilty but I have to defend you anyway," Renee had a flashback to the walk she'd taken down a long row of prison cells with those convicts leering and jeering at her. That eight-hour descent into hell was a big part of the reason she'd built a respectable life, and ironically, it was the reason she was running now. Unfortunately, a big, bad bounty hunter with a heart the size of a pea had tracked her down, and innocent or not, she was going back to jail.

Renee glanced around the Jeep. Being driven to jail in this vehicle was like riding to hell in a New York subway car. A dozen cigarette butts littered the floor of the front seat, mingling with a handful of Milky Way wrappers and a copy of *Muscle* magazine. In the back, file folders stuffed to overflowing were scattered on the seat, interspersed with piles of crumpled fast-food sacks. It smelled like a Dumpster.

"This car is a pigsty," she muttered,

hating Leandro's vehicle, hating his music, hating his choice of occupation. Hating *him*.

Leandro took a long drag off his cigarette and blew out the smoke, adding to the carcinogenic cloud already saturating the car. "My cleaning lady didn't come this week. You just can't get good help anymore."

"That smoke is burning my eyes. Think what it's doing to your lungs."

"Turning them black as the ace of spades, I imagine."

"Ever think of quitting that nasty habit?"

"Never crossed my mind."

"Would you mind putting it out?"

"Yes. I'd mind that very much."

Renee knew she was ranting, but she was irritated and scared and she just couldn't stop. "Secondhand smoke's a killer, you know. There was a story about it on *20/20* just last week."

"Gee. Sorry I missed that."

"There have actually been cases where smokers were taken to court for polluting other people's air."

"So sue me."

"You know, that's not a bad idea. I bet there are at least a dozen nasty lawyers in Tolosa just dying to —"

"Oh, for God's sake!" He took a huge, sucking drag off the cigarette, then ground it out in the ashtray. He tossed his half-smoked pack of Camels and his blue Bic into the console beside him and slammed the lid. "There. Happy?"

Not particularly. When it got right down to it, what difference did it make whether she died a slow death from lung cancer or threw away half her life in prison?

Then her stomach growled, which reminded her that she'd eaten next to nothing since she'd left Tolosa, which made her think of the only restaurant they were likely to encounter out here in the boondocks. Dairy Queen. She brightened a bit, not because of the food, but because that might be a dandy place to ditch a bounty hunter. Exactly how, she didn't know. She'd have to figure that out when the time came, assuming she could get him to stop.

"I'm hungry," she said.

"No problem. I hear the food in the county jail is five-star cuisine."

Renee winced. She could see it now: a row of wrinkled old ladies wearing hair nets, slopping swill onto plastic trays.

"Would it kill you to pull through a drive-through?" She glanced into the backseat, crinkling her nose. "God knows it wouldn't be the first time."

"Sorry, sweet thing. Dousing the cigarette took me right to the limit of my hospitality."

"What if I have to go to the bathroom?"

"What if you're trying to get me to stop somewhere because you think it's your only shot at getting away?"

Renee huffed disgustedly. "You're a real jerk, you know that?"

"Yeah," he said, smiling with delight. "I know."

She glared at Leandro, then stared out the passenger window again, trying to hold on to her feelings of loathing and disgust because they were about the only things keeping her from melting into a sobbing, hysterical, emotionally distraught wreck. She wasn't going to get out of this. Innocent or not, she was going to prison, where she'd spend the best years of her life pacing a six-by-eight cell, eating unidentifiable food, and trying to convince large, sexually ambiguous women that she did *not* want to be their girlfriend.

They topped a hill, and Renee saw a railroad crossing ahead. As they approached it, red lights began to flash and the gates started down. Leandro stomped on the gas to run the gates, but the car in front of him — a rusted-out Plymouth with a handicap insignia on its license plate — didn't.

Leandro screeched to a fishtailing halt, practically driving right up the Plymouth's tailpipe. The gates fell into place, blocking the crossing. Renee looked left and right. No train was coming.

"Weave through the gates!" Leandro shouted, as if the other driver could hear him. He laid on his horn. The old guy looked into his rearview mirror, but his car stayed put. Leandro slammed his car into park and stepped out, leaving the door open and resting his arm against the top of the car to survey the situation. Renee glanced at the steering column, and her heart leaped with hope.

He'd left the key in the ignition.

She might not be able to run faster than Leandro, but she was pretty sure she could drive faster. If he decided to go have a word with the guy in the Plymouth, then maybe —

"Move it!" Leandro shouted. "There's no train!" He reached a hand into the car and laid on the horn again. The Plymouth didn't budge.

"Shit. Probably got his hearing aid turned off." Leandro moved away from the car and started to close the door. Renee held her breath, poised for attack. The moment the door clicked shut, she'd leap over the con-

20

sole, punch down the lock —

The door came back open. Leandro reached inside and jerked the keys from the ignition. He shook a finger at Renee. "Stay put. You hear me? I don't want to have to chase you down." He slammed the car door and stalked up to the Plymouth.

Renee slumped back in the passenger seat. What was she going to do now? She had only one way out of this car, and that was the driver's door. But with Leandro looking back at her every few seconds, her window of opportunity was minuscule. If she ran, he'd drop her like a lion would a gazelle. Besides, this was the middle of nowhere, with no place to hide. She saw a little diner about a quarter mile up the road from the railroad tracks, but what good would that do her? Unless she could divert Leandro long enough to get a sizable head start, she didn't stand a chance.

Then, just like that, it came to her. She sat up suddenly, her breath coming faster, her heart beating double time. Leandro's bad habits just might be her salvation.

She dug through the console and extracted Leandro's Bic lighter. She glanced out the windshield and saw him pointing wildly down the track, his mouth moving like crazy. But the old guy was a rock. He just sat there, probably quoting Amtrak disaster statistics, refusing to move an inch.

She reached into the backseat for one of the wadded-up fast-food sacks, the handcuffs straining against her wrists. Judging from the grease stains, Leandro's favorite meal was a triple cheeseburger and a giant order of fries. Perfect.

She held the sack beneath the dashboard and flicked the lighter beneath it, shifting her gaze to Leandro every few seconds to make sure he was still reaming the old guy out. In moments the sack flamed. She tossed it onto the floor of the backseat, then reached for a couple of other sacks and tossed them on top of the burning one. The flames spread.

Renee put the Bic back in the console. At the same time she spied a key. Praying it unlocked the handcuffs, she plucked it out.

Just then Leandro gave up and started back toward the car. She stuffed the key into her pocket, shut the lid of the console, and stared at the dashboard, trying to look nonchalant. Behind her, another sack caught fire, then another, and another. . . .

Leandro yanked open the door. "Old fart," he muttered, climbing into the car. "He coulda made it. But no. He had to park his hemorrhoidal ass at the crossing the minute he saw a few red lights, and now the train's coming. At the rate it's moving, we'll be sitting here for a week."

Renee glanced down the track to see the train finally make an appearance. It chugged along like an overweight asthmatic at about fifteen miles per hour, its cars stretching down the track as far as she could see.

"They ought to jerk his driver's license," Leandro fumed. "If he even *touches* a set of car keys, he ought to be shot. And you can bet your ass I'd volunteer for the job."

The burning sacks cracked and popped, but Leandro was so consumed with his loudmouthed trashing of anyone over age seventy that he didn't notice. Renee waited, her heart beating madly. The flames grew. She waited another second, then another, and then . . .

"Fire!" She let out an ear-piercing squeal and pointed madly to the backseat. "Fire! The car's on fire!"

Leandro snapped to attention and spun around, his eyes flying open wide. He put a knee in the driver's seat, leaned over the back of the seat, and slapped at the burning sacks, only to pull away with a painful hiss, shaking his hand.

He leaped out and flung open the back

23

door. While he was whacking away at the flames with a file folder, Renee scrambled over the console and out of the car — no small task with her wrists still handcuffed. The moment her feet hit pavement, she ran.

"Hey! Get back here!"

He took off after her. She was less than three strides ahead of him, and he made up the ground in a hurry. Alongside the old man's car he reached for her arm and missed. Then he dove at her, his arms around her hips, and sent them both crashing to the road. Renee's knees skidded across the pavement.

Ignoring the pain, she whipped around and smacked Leandro on the side of the head. He recoiled, cursing wildly, then fumbled around and managed to catch her wrists below the cuffs. He hauled her toward him until they were nose-to-nose, his eyes wild with anger and his teeth bared. A little foaming at the mouth and he'd look just like a rabid dog.

Renee smiled sweetly. "How do you like your barbecued Jeep? Well done?"

He spun back around. Smoke was pouring out the back car door. He could hang on to Renee, or he could put out the fire. He couldn't do both.

With an anguished groan, he let go of

Renee and jumped to his feet. He pointed down at her. "Stay there!"

*Yeah. Right.*

As he hurried back to the burning vehicle he hollered at the old man, who gawked out the window of his car with his jaw hanging down to his chest. "Make sure she doesn't get away!"

Renee leaped to her feet again, infused with hope. If Leandro had resorted to deputizing senior citizens, he probably wasn't in complete control of the situation.

The train was less than twenty yards from the crossing. She wove through the gates, and in a single bounding leap, she flew over the tracks and landed on the other side. Seconds later the train filled the railroad crossing. The last thing she saw before it blocked her view was Leandro peeling off his tank top to whack away at the flames. Watching him go nuts over that wreck of a car was a beautiful sight, but she couldn't hang around to bask in the moment.

She pulled the key out of her pocket, fumbled it into the handcuff lock, and held her breath. She twisted it a little and heard a tiny click. The right cuff fell open. Her luck was holding after all. She unlocked the left one, too, then threw the cuffs as far as she could on one side of the road and the key on the other.

Once the train passed, Leandro would be after her again — in his car if he managed to put out the flames, or on foot if it had completely gone up in smoke. Either way, his nasty attitude had already taken a turn toward the homicidal. If he nabbed her again, by the time he dumped her on the steps of the police station they'd have to use her dental records to identify her body.

Her first thought was to hop the train and let it carry her down the tracks, but while it was moving slowly, as trains went, its speed was still too great for such an arm-wrenching experience. If Leandro thought that was what she'd done, though, it might buy her a little time.

She turned and jogged toward the diner, praying some other means of escape would present itself, and fast. No matter what she had to do, she wasn't going back to Tolosa.

No matter what she had to do.

John DeMarco sat at the counter of the Red Oak Diner three miles outside Winslow, Texas, with the front page of the *Winslow Gazette* spread out in front of him and his hands wrapped around a steaming cup of coffee. He took a sip of the thirty-weight liquid and winced, wondering how much more of this stuff he could drink before he overdosed on caffeine.

He glanced out the window. Evening was edging into dusk, filling the countryside with the muted shades of twilight. Soft sizzling sounds came from the kitchen, like raindrops on a tin roof, mingling with the muffled conversation of a gangly teenage boy and his mousy girlfriend, who were sharing an order of fries in a booth by the window.

This place was like a hundred other backwoods multi-purpose establishments — a diner that also carried convenience store items, a small collection of action-adventure videos for rent, and a rack of magazines that centered around four topics — hunting, fishing, hot cars, and sex — aimed directly at the rifle-toting, tobacco-chewing, kick-ass locals on the assumption that they could actually read. Marva Benton served up Texas home cooking guaranteed to clog your arteries, while her husband Harley ran the cash register and shot the bull with the locals. Just about anything you needed to sustain life you could find at the Red Oak, as long as you didn't set your standards too high.

For the past week John had made a valiant

attempt to forget about his job and concentrate only on sleeping late, dressing like a slob, and sitting by the lake with a fishing pole in one hand and a beer in the other.

Easier said than done.

This was the third night in a row he'd come here for dinner. He had to drive twelve miles, but it sure beat cooking, particularly since the cabin he was staying in didn't have a microwave oven. Or an oven, period. Or a television. Or a telephone. A hot plate, a Hide-A-Bed, and indoor plumbing — that was about it. The boredom factor had settled in about fifteen minutes after his arrival, so when he found this diner he considered himself lucky.

*Take my cabin for a week or so*, Lieutenant Daniels had told him. *Do nothing for a while. Just sit. Think. Clear your head.*

What Daniels had really meant was *Get a grip on yourself, and don't come back until you do.*

Harley rang up a *Hot Rod* magazine and ten gallons of gas for a twentysomething cowboy type in skintight Levi's and a plaid western shirt. The guy sauntered out of the store, giving John a territorial stare from beneath the brim of his hat that said *I can tell you ain't from around here, so watch yourself.*

Harley pushed the cash register shut, then

gave John a gregarious grin, displaying brown teeth, gold teeth, and no teeth all in the same mouth. "So, John. How's the vacation going?"

John was already on a first-name basis with the proprietors of the Red Oak, a familiarity that appeared to be commonplace in rural Texas. Back in Tolosa he didn't even know his next-door neighbor's name.

"Slow," John said.

"Well, slow's good if you're lookin' to relax, right? Take a break from the big city?"

*Big city?* John had to smile at that one. Tolosa, Texas, was hardly a major metropolis. But from Harley's point of view, John figured that Tolosa's four movie theaters, two shopping malls, and population of ninety thousand made it look like Tokyo compared to Winslow.

"So what do you do for a living, John?"

He sighed inwardly. Sometimes people acted funny if they knew they were talking to a cop. "Just between you and me, Harley, I'd rather not talk about what I do for a living."

"Which is it? Low pay? Long hours? No respect?"

Harley had just described a cop's life perfectly. "All of the above."

But as irritating as those things were, they

weren't at the heart of John's frustration right now. Nobody in his right mind became a cop and expected to get rich, work short hours, and have people pat him on the back, so he'd been prepared for all of that. But what he hadn't expected were the massive injustices of what was supposed to be the criminal-justice system.

After a month of investigation, John had finally nabbed a nasty little scumbag who'd been beating up senior citizens and then robbing them in the hallways of their apartment buildings. Only one of the victims agreed to testify — a stoop-shouldered, gravel-voiced octogenarian who told John, essentially, that he was mad as hell and wasn't going to take it anymore. Then the day before the trial, the old guy had a myocardial infarction and ended up a vegetable in the coronary care unit at Tolosa Medical Center. Later that day his family pulled the plug, and the prosecution's case went to hell.

Without an eyewitness to tell his story, the defense attorney was able to fill the jurors' minds with a truckload of reasonable doubt about the identity of the perpetrator. John showed up for the verdict, and when the jury pronounced the guy not guilty, his stomach twisted into a tight knot of fury and frustration. He tried to tell himself it was just part of the job. You won some, you lost some. The world went on. But all the while he seethed inside, hating the thought that some bad-to-the-bone, guilty-as-sin loser he'd fought to incarcerate was free to walk the streets again.

Then, as he came out of the courtroom, he saw the little bastard standing in the marble-tiled lobby, grinning like a hyena and backslapping his attorney. As if on cue, he turned and met John's eyes. A slow, cocky smile spread across his lips, joined by a mocking stare that screamed louder than any words could possibly have.

*I win, sucker. And that means you lose.*

John wanted desperately to cross the lobby of the courthouse, back the guy up against a wall, and choke him until his eyes bugged out. As an officer of the law, though, he hadn't been free to exercise that option. Instead he headed to the men's room to cool off. He took several deep breaths and doused his face in cold water, hoping that would do the trick, and when it didn't he spun around and whacked the paper-towel dispenser with his doubled-up fist.

Now that had felt good.

It felt so good, in fact, that he did it again. And again. And again. And all the while he thought about how *wrong* it was that some-body could hurt defenseless people, take their money, then never have to answer for any of it.

Unfortunately, the bathroom fixture John was substituting for the guy's face wasn't in the best of shape, and slug number five dis-lodged it from the wall and sent it crashing to the floor. About that time, two uniformed cops wondered what all the noise was and hurried into the bathroom. To their great amusement, they saw that a certain police detective had gone three rounds with a pa-per-towel dispenser, leaving it bruised and battered on the floor in an uncontested knockout.

By the end of the day, John's battle with an inanimate object was comic legend around the station, leading his colleagues to ask him if he intended to beat up a trash can next, or maybe take on a toilet or two. By then he truly regretted losing his temper, but that hadn't stopped Lieutenant Daniels from calling him in and giving him a twenty-minute lecture on professionalism, impar-tiality, and the inadvisability of dropping by the courthouse for jury verdicts.

*Forget guilt or innocence, DeMarco. Your job isn't to make sure justice is served. Your job is to bring the scum in so other people can make sure justice is served.*

In John's mind, those people were doing a piss-poor job of it, but in light of the circumstances he'd kept that thought to himself.

*An emotionally involved cop isn't worth a damn,* Daniels went on. *They do dumb things. You know, like murder an innocent paper-towel dispenser in the prime of its life.*

The lieutenant had concluded his lecture by handing John the keys to his out-of-the-way cabin on Lake Shelton with the suggestion that he take a little vacation. John had read between the lines. The vacation wasn't optional.

He'd reluctantly taken the keys and started out the door, but Daniels hadn't been through with him yet. He'd mentioned — quite offhandedly, of course — that he'd made his annual contribution to the Joseph DeMarco Foundation to benefit the families of officers killed in the line of duty. And the timing of that remark had really pissed John off.

Eight years before, John's father had taken a fatal bullet during what should have been a routine traffic stop, and it wasn't by accident that Daniels chose that moment to mention the foundation set up in his honor. It was his not-so-subtle way of saying to John, *What would your father think about how you're behaving now?*

If he were alive today, Joe DeMarco, the most by-the-book cop the Tolosa Police Department had ever known, would have plenty to say about what he would deem to be another of his son's frequent lapses in judgment. And he would have said it far more vehemently than Daniels could ever have hoped to.

Now John was forced to vegetate in a backwoods cabin for a week, with the implication that he was to do some serious soul-searching and arrive at an effective means of controlling his temper. But as badly as he hated to admit it, Daniels was right. And his father would have been right, too, if he'd been around to orate on the subject. John knew he'd gone over the edge. Find them, arrest them, move on — that was what he had to do. Other cops seemed to have no trouble maintaining that all-important professional detachment. Why couldn't he?

He finished off the last few sips of his coffee, managing to down it before it congealed into a dark blob of pure caffeine and crawled right out of the cup. Harley filled it again, then checked his watch. He called over his shoulder.

"Hey, Marva! John's been waitin' twenty minutes! Move it on the steak!"

A gravelly, two-pack-per-day female voice boomed out of the kitchen: "You want it fast, or you want it good?"

"I want it today!" Harley growled.

"Shut up, you old coot! You'll get it when I bring it!"

Harley rolled his eyes a little, then leaned over the counter, his expression becoming one of a long-suffering saint. "Thirty-three years I've put up with that. Can you imagine?"

John didn't buy Harley's "poor me" routine for a minute. He knew shtick when he heard it, and this pair had mastered it. If they were smart, they'd start collecting a cover charge for entertainment. When he was younger and a whole lot more naive, John assumed that someday he'd have a wife he could fight with right up to their fiftieth wedding anniversary. But the older he got, the less likely it seemed that would ever happen.

The kitchen door swung open and Marva appeared, a gigantic horse of a woman wearing purple polyester pants and a Hawaiian-print shirt. Her iron-gray hair was swept back in a sweat-soaked bandanna. She slapped a platter down in front of John. The chicken-fried steak lopped over the edge of the plate, dripping gravy onto the counter. It smelled like heaven.

"There you go, sweetie," she said with a smile full of hospitality. "That rotten husband of mine doesn't understand that good things take time." She shot Harley a look of total disgust. Right on cue, Harley sneered back.

Marva turned to John. "Thirty-three years I've put up with that. Can you imagine?"

With a weary shake of her head, she clomped back into the kitchen. Harley glanced furtively in her direction, then reached under the counter. "Hey, buddy. Take a look at this."

He slid a *Playboy* onto the counter and opened it to the centerfold, displaying a healthy brunette in all her naked glory. "Miss October. Ever seen anything like her in your life?"

"Can't say as I have," John said, admiring the photo. Hell, it had been so long since he'd seen a naked woman, he was surprised he still recognized one.

"Didja see Miss September?"

"Sorry. Missed that one."

"Shoo*wee*. She was better'n this one, if you like 'em blond."

Just then Marva reappeared carrying a rack of silverware. She saw Harley's reading material and rolled her eyes. She slapped the silverware onto the counter, then closed the centerfold and the magazine with a definitive *whap, whap, whap.*

"Dirty old man," she muttered. "Didn't I tell you to keep your hands off the smut?"

"I'll show you smut, woman," he retorted, meeting her nose-to-nose. Then the edge of his mouth rose in something that just might have been a smile. "Later."

Marva rolled her eyes. "Promises, promises." She turned to John, talking behind her hand in a loud stage whisper. "Ever since he turned fifty, that's all I get. *Promises.*"

As she headed back toward the kitchen, Harley gave her a smack on her generous rump. She squealed and went on into the kitchen, then looked back out the window of the swinging door, shaking her finger at him before disappearing again.

"Women," Harley muttered. "Gotta keep 'em in line, or they'll walk all over you."

John wasn't sure who was keeping whom in line, but somewhere deep inside he felt a funny twinge of longing. No, he did not want to lose half his teeth, marry a back-woods Amazon woman, and run a shabby diner in the middle of nowhere. But sometimes, in the middle of the night when it was just him alone in a double bed, he wanted *someone* so badly he could taste it. But a cop married to his job made one hell of a poor husband. A cop who had a hard time controlling his temper when faced with the realities of the job made an even worse one.

Maybe he should get a subscription to *Playboy* and let it go at that.

Renee reached the parking lot of the diner, gasping a little at the uphill jog in the cool evening air. She glanced back over her shoulder at the train, encouraged to see that it didn't seem to be picking up any speed.

She thought about ducking into the woods behind the diner, zigzagging in and out of the dense foliage, but the piney woods of east Texas went on forever. She had no food, no water, no coat, and no sense of direction, so sooner or later she'd be buzzard bait. Besides, it was past sunset and nearly dark, and she feared snakes and bobcats and great big spiders almost as much as she feared Leandro. Spending the night hugging a tree and praying a lot didn't seem to be the best solution.

What she needed was wheels.

In the parking lot she spied a tired old Corvette, a beat-up red Chevy pickup, and a forest green Explorer with dark-tinted windows. She took a serpentine route through the lot, nonchalantly scanning each of the vehicles for keys, then realized she was actually considering car theft.

No. She couldn't steal a car. That would be a *real* crime, and she promised herself eight years ago that she'd never commit one of those again.

Well, okay. There *was* the little fire she'd just started in a certain bounty hunter's car. Destroying personal property was a crime. But really, when you thought about it, that car of Leandro's was a rolling fire hazard anyway. It was bound to happen sooner or later. One cigarette butt flicked in the wrong direction, and *poof!* — up in smoke. She'd done nothing more than hasten the inevitable.

Renee took a deep, calming breath. All this rationalizing was making her a little woozy. She needed another plan, and fast. Surely the owner of one of these vehicles could be persuaded to take her . . . somewhere.

She opened the door to the diner and stepped inside. She was greeted by warm air and the smell of deep-fried everything. A teenage kid was taking his change at the register, his arm draped around a dark-haired girl. They probably belonged to the Corvette. It was a two-seater sports car, though, and Renee figured she'd be a little too easy to spot if she rode on the roof.

That left the pickup truck and the Explorer.

She matched the pickup with the overall-clad hayseed standing at the snack-cake rack trying to decide between Twinkies and Ding Dongs. She weighed the possibilities for a moment, then discarded his vehicle in favor of the Explorer with its tinted windows. Perfect for tooling around the countryside incognito. By process of elimination, she decided its owner must be the man sitting at the counter having dinner.

From the back he looked like a standard-issue country bumpkin, with a red-plaid flannel shirt stretched over a broad pair of shoulders, threadbare blue jeans, and boots. His dark hair just brushed his collar in the back, and she'd bet the rent he didn't even own a comb. And he was undoubtedly dumb as dirt.

Okay. She had her target. But what was she going to say to get him to take her anywhere but here?

She couldn't lie and tell him she had car trouble, or that she'd run out of gas and needed a lift. A lift where? To a phone? There was one right here. Back to her car?

She didn't have one. And if Leandro showed up, she couldn't say he was the bad guy and expect anyone to do anything about it. He probably had ID that said he could drag her anywhere he pleased. Besides, he had a very large gun and a face that would scare the average person out of ten years' growth. Asking for protection from him would be like asking someone if they minded pulling you out of the jaws of Godzilla.

If only she had time to think.

Praying a plan would come to her, she slid onto the stool next to the guy having dinner. "Hi, there."

He turned at the sound of her voice. Renee blinked with surprise. This was not Jethro Bodine. This was not L'il Abner. No way, nohow, not in her wildest dreams.

She'd been fooled into thinking he was a local yokel when his back was turned, but she wasn't fooled now. This man didn't belong here any more than she did. He looked to be in his early thirties, but she got the feeling those thirty years hadn't come easily. A few days' growth of beard darkened his cheeks and chin, but it couldn't hide the sharp planes of a boldly handsome face. His skin was still sun-bronzed even in early October, his nose sharp, his jaw well defined. By contrast, his lips looked warm and sensual, a surprising feature on a face that held so much raw strength. His dark eyes regarded her with blatant intensity, as if he were assessing every breath she took and didn't much like what he saw. Somehow he managed, with just a few seconds of eye contact, to make her feel wildly attracted and scared to death all at the same time.

Renee tore her gaze away and glanced around hopefully for the kid or the hayseed, but both of them were gone.

"Is that your car outside?" Her voice came out like a mouse squeak. She cleared her throat. "The Explorer?"

"Yeah. It's mine."

Those eyes again. Staring at her. Staring right into her, as if he could see her brain working. And if only it really were working, she might just find a way out of this mess.

*Think, think, think!*

Adrenaline rushed through her, scrambling her thoughts. *How does a woman get a man's attention* right now?

Her brain cells whizzed through the various possibilities, like a hundred search engines activated all at once. And all of them returned the same solution.

She took a deep, furtive breath, sidled

closer to her target, and gave him a smile, hoping it didn't look as phony as it felt. "Do you live close by?"

"Yeah. For a while, anyway."

She nodded down at his hand. "I don't see a wedding ring."

"That's because I'm not married."

As he moved his fork down to have another bite of chicken-fried steak, Renee ran a fingertip along his arm, raising a trail of goose bumps in its wake. He froze, his fork in midair.

She swallowed hard. "Well, then. Wanna go to bed?"

# *chapter two*

John decided it was a good thing he hadn't taken that bite of chicken-fried steak. He'd have choked on it. Big-time.

"Excuse me?"

She leaned closer and dropped her voice. "You and me. Sex. Your place. Right now. Yes or no?"

John blinked with surprise. She was blond, she was beautiful, and she was throwing herself at him. What was wrong with this picture?

As much as he'd like to think it was his good looks and suave manner that had attracted her, he had to face facts. He had a two-day growth of beard, he was shoveling down a meal fit for a lumberjack, and without looking down he couldn't even say for sure whether his shirt was buttoned right and his jeans were zipped. And he was pretty sure he'd given her his automatic cop look when she first slid onto the stool next to him, a "don't mess with me" expression so ingrained after years of dealing with the lowlifes of Tolosa that he had a hard time keeping it in check. It had scared away more than one woman before, yet this one seemed undeterred.

He took a quick inventory of the way she was dressed. Jeans, sweatshirt, Reeboks. Hardly the animal-print miniskirt, midriff top, and six-inch platform shoes so fashionable among most Lone Star ladies of the evening. And her makeup was practically nonexistent, allowing a healthy glow to shine through. Instead of sultry and provocative, she appeared to be going for cute, fresh, and innocent-looking. He had to admit her marketing strategy had gotten his attention.

"Sorry, sweetheart," he told her, adding more pepper to his steak. "I'm not in the habit of paying for pleasure."

Her eyebrows shot up. Was she expressing disbelief that he'd pegged her profession right away, or offense that he'd think such a thing? Then just as quickly she replaced the look with a provocative smile.

"I'll admit I'd like to get my hands on a lot of things, but your wallet isn't one of them."

This was dangerous. John could feel it in his bones. "Then how about one of Marva's chicken-fried steaks? Best I've ever had."

She laid her hand on his arm. "So that's what you'd recommend for a woman who's *really* hungry?"

John tilted his gaze to Harley, who was leaning his forearms on the counter, watching the scene unfold like a house-bound grandma watching a soap opera. Since he hadn't greeted her by name, as he did everyone else who ventured into his establishment, John assumed she wasn't a local. Back on the job he'd have said she didn't fit the profile of the neighborhood, and that was always a reason for a heads-up.

Still, it had been way too long since he'd been with a woman, and physically, at least, this one pushed all his buttons. Big blue eyes, cheeks tinted pink from the brisk October breeze outside, and a mass of blond hair that was hers by the grace of God and not Lady Clairol. The hem of her blue sweatshirt fell over Levi's that showcased the soft curves of her hips so enticingly that it was hard for him to tear his gaze away.

"Yeah," John told her, sticking to the chicken-fried steak theme. "That's what I'd recommend. And be sure to get a little extra gravy on the side."

He picked up his fork again. She pressed his arm back down to the counter. "You have no idea what you're missing. I can make you forget to eat for *days*."

John extricated his arm from her grasp. "Sorry, sweetheart. See, I just started in on this steak here, and I know Marva would be insulted if I didn't finish every bite."

"Marva'll get over it," Harley said.

John shot Harley a "don't help me" look. Harley held up his hands in surrender and walked down the counter to the cash register. He snagged a roll of Certs and *tap, tap, tapped* them on the counter, his expression suggesting that perhaps John might want to stop being an idiot and reconsider having a date for the evening.

The woman inched closer, her eyes focused intently on him, eyes that were a deep, endless blue that mesmerized him. Then his cop brain kicked in. A beautiful woman didn't just walk up to a man and offer him sex with no strings attached. If he were a betting man, he'd wager this woman had enough baggage to fill a 747.

"Tell you what," she murmured. "Why don't we go to your place and talk it over?" She glanced out the window, then looked back. "Like — right now?"

John didn't want to be suspicious. Not when every man's dream was planted on a stool next to him, offering him a trip to heaven. But while he'd never had a lot of trouble connecting with women if he set his mind to it, even on his best days they didn't just fall into his lap. Usually he had to take at least a few swings before he could hit a home run, but this woman wasn't even making him step up to the plate. Something was wrong here, and if he was smart, he'd never get close enough to find out what it was.

"The fact is, sweetheart, I'm here on vacation, and so far it's been pretty relaxing. I'd like to keep it that way."

Harley rolled his eyes. He pulled a six-pack from the cooler and clunked it down beside the Certs, giving John an admonishing stare. Breath mints and beer. Harley's idea of a really hot date.

She eased closer. "Sugar, the last thing I want is for you to be uptight. All you have to do is settle back and let me do all the work. How does that sound?"

It sounded like heaven on earth, but he hadn't been a cop for eleven years without being able to spot ulterior motives a mile away. "Well, that's a real nice offer, but I'm doing this vacation solo."

Over the woman's shoulder, John could see Harley about to explode with frustration. He gave John a "hey, stupid" look, then reached to a shelf behind him, picked up a beige box, and slapped it down on the counter next to the Certs and the six-pack.

Trojans.

"Whatever one can do," the woman said, "two can do better. And they can do it all . . . night . . . long."

John had a mental flash of tangled, sweat-sheened bodies glistening in the moonlight, then another flash of morning sunlight streaming through a window, illuminating the condom box. The *empty* condom box. Very enticing images. Almost as enticing as the warm palm on his thigh, moving in provocative little circles, inching its way toward his crotch.

John caught her hand, pressing it against his thigh, then fixed his gaze on hers in a no-nonsense stare. "What do you really want?"

Her eyes widened for a moment. Then she raised a single eyebrow. "I think that should be pretty obvious by now, shouldn't it?"

John knew from experience that an obvious explanation and a truthful explanation were rarely the same. But the intensity with which she stared at him, as if she wanted to take him right here on Harley's counter, made him think there couldn't possibly be anything on her mind *but* sex.

"Maybe I didn't make myself clear

enough," she said, her lips only inches from his ear. "I'm talking about sex that makes your toes curl. Sex that makes your hair stand on end. Sex that wears you out and hypes you up all at the same time and makes you wonder where your next breath is coming from. Sex that's so *raw*, so *hot*, so *sinful* that you pray it never ends because there's no way you could possibly experience anything like it again."

Every word she spoke was like a carnal caress, and every time she said *sex* John thought about how long it had been since he'd had any. She teased her fingers over his crotch, and he felt himself getting hard whether he liked it or not. And he liked it. No question about it.

Then her lips grazed his ear, and she dropped her voice to a breathy whisper. "Before it's all over, I'll have you screaming so loud they'll hear you in *Bangkok*."

John swallowed hard.

Maybe, for once in his life, he should take things at face value. She was a woman looking for a good time. He was a man who had all the time in the world to show her one. Harley had provided the only other necessity. What more did he need to know?

Then, before he could open his mouth to say yes, no, or something in between, the woman slid off her stool, spun his stool around ninety degrees, and moved between his thighs. She took his face in her hands, dropped her lips to his, and kissed him.

John was so startled that for a moment he just sat there and let it happen. He'd been kissed by a lot of women in his life, but never by one who put her heart and soul into it the way this one did. Her lips consumed his with an intensity that almost knocked him senseless, and when she slipped her tongue into his mouth and teased it against his, a shudder of pure lust shot through him. Her words had been pretty explicit, but there was nothing like a little mouth-to-mouth contact to let him know exactly what it was she had in mind.

This was lunacy, of course. He'd have to be a complete lunatic to sit in a backwoods diner and let a strange woman kiss him into unconsciousness. He gripped her arms with the intent of pushing her away, only to have her shift closer, her thighs pressing against his and sending a shock wave right to his groin. At the same time she deepened her kiss even more, filling it with honey and fire and the promise of even better things to come, and he decided that lunacy was a delightful state to be in and wondered why he hadn't considered it before. The cop side of his brain saw about a hundred red flags, but the regular, horny-guy side of his brain was blind as a bat. For once in his career-consumed life, the horny-guy side seemed to be winning.

Finally she pulled away, her breath still warm against his lips, her blue eyes hot and hungry.

*Blue eyes. Damn.* He *loved* blue eyes.

He dropped his gaze to her kiss-swollen lips, then met her eyes again. "Was that a preview of coming attractions?"

"Yeah. And it's gonna be a blockbuster. Trust me. Can we get out of here now?"

John thought he actually felt his common sense leave his body, and he wasn't sure he was even going to miss it. He went to the cash register while the woman waited by the door. Harley swept the goods into a sack and handed it to him, waving away his money. "This one's on me," he whispered. "Go get her, buddy."

John escorted the woman out to the parking lot. He looked around, surprised that he didn't see a car that might be hers, even though the diner was way out in the middle of nowhere. The only sign of life was a freight train a quarter mile down the road, disappearing from sight.

"How did you get here?" he asked her.

She looped her arm through his and hurried him along. "I dropped straight down from heaven, sugar."

He decided he was going to believe that. He was going to pretend her headful of golden hair was a halo, and that she was a member of the Angel Adult Recreation Squad sent here to ensure that his vacation was a resounding success. Otherwise he might have to start asking more questions than he ought to and find out things he really didn't want to know.

He opened the passenger door and let her in, then climbed into the driver's seat. He dropped Harley's date-in-a-bag on the floor near her feet, started the engine, then backed out. But as he turned from the parking lot onto the two-lane highway, he was nearly sideswiped by an old Jeep Cherokee pulling in. Smoke wafted out its windows.

He braked quickly and looked back over his shoulder as the smoking car squealed to a halt in front of the store. "What the hell is *that?*"

"Did I tell you I'm wearing crotchless panties?"

John whipped back around to find the woman smiling suggestively. All at once the thought of her wearing nothing but a little scrap of lace was a whole lot more interesting than somebody's smoking vehicle.

"No. I don't believe you mentioned that."

"They're red."

"My favorite."

"Let's get out of here."

"Yes, ma'am."

He stepped on the gas. In a few seconds he reached the speed limit of forty, then nudged the car to fifty and wished it was seventy.

"What's your name?" he asked her.

"Why don't we keep our names out of this?"

Okay. She wanted to play mystery woman. That was fine by him. "Sure, sweetheart. Whatever you say."

Hadn't he had this dream before? An out-of-the-way cabin, all the time in the world, and an anonymous blonde in red crotchless underwear just dying to make his dreams come true?

Maybe Daniels was right. Maybe this vacation was just what he needed after all.

*Good God. What in the world had she done?*

As the Explorer tooled down the two-lane blacktop, Renee hugged the passenger door, her heart pounding like crazy. She had no idea where all that stuff she'd promised this man had come from. It was as if Marilyn Monroe, Sharon Stone, and Madonna had all been whispering in her ear, providing her with seduction language so hot she was surprised the diner hadn't burst into flames. What had ever made her say those things?

*Desperation. That's what.*

Then she had a terrible thought. She sat up suddenly and turned to her getaway driver. "The people in that diner. Do they know where you live?"

"No. Just that I'm on Lake Shelton. Why?"

She settled back onto the seat, wondering how close that information might get Leandro to discovering her whereabouts. "No reason."

"I'm borrowing a friend's cabin. Just for a week or so."

"So you're not from around here."

"Nope."

She nodded, then turned to stare out the passenger window, relieved that he seemed to be a man of few words. The last thing she wanted to do was make small talk. He put a cassette into the player, filling the car with the pleasant sound of soft jazz.

Renee couldn't believe she'd managed to slip out of that diner only seconds before Smokey the Bounty Hunter tore into the parking lot. She glanced into the side mirror every few seconds, relieved that she didn't see Leandro. She was further relieved when the Explorer veered off the main two-lane highway onto a less traveled road. If Leandro were after them he'd have to make a decision about which road to take, and that could slow him down considerably.

Then a few minutes later, he swung the Explorer off the side road onto a narrow gravel road surrounded by thick forest. Instead of feeling relieved at the convoluted path he drove, Renee started to feel a little uneasy. He took one fork in the road, then another, all of them unmarked. Renee tried to maintain some sense of where she was, but pretty soon her warped sense of direction told her they must be in Oklahoma by now, and she knew *that* couldn't be right. Then the gravel road turned to dirt, and she felt a tremor of panic.

All at once it struck her that she didn't know a single blessed thing about the man she'd just propositioned. For all she knew, he could be one of those reclusive guys who stayed in some primitive, out-of-the-way place so he could murder women and bury them under the front porch. After he dismembered them.

She gave him a sidelong glance. His sharp

profile had blurred a bit in the fading evening light, but she hadn't forgotten the way he looked at her in the diner when she had first approached him — as if he could freeze her where she sat with a single glance. She searched for something sinister about him, wondering if she'd traded a bad situation for one even worse. He didn't look like a person who smiled much. Maybe he didn't have much to smile about. Serial killing would do that to a guy.

Looking down, Renee realized her fingernails were leaving little crescent-moon indentations in the door handle. She moved her hands to her lap and took a few furtive deep breaths. She was letting her imagination get the better of her. The worst thing that was going to happen was that she'd be forced to give him what she'd already offered, but even the thought of that made her heart race with apprehension. *Especially* the thought of that.

The car slowed, then came to a halt, and it took Renee a moment to realize they'd reached their destination. At the end of a short, wooded path, a small cabin sat nestled beneath the trees, with a lake practically at its back door. A light shone dimly through one of the front windows, and through a small clearing at the lake's edge the glow of a three-quarter moon reflected off the water.

He turned off the ignition. The silence was so complete she could hear the blood pulsing in her ears.

If only she could dissuade him. If only she could take his mind off of sex. If only she could make him forget all those erotic acts she'd promised him, the sexual heights she'd offered to take him to. If only they could break out the six-pack, maybe turn on the radio, have a nice conversation . . .

And then do each other's hair, bake cookies, and play Twister. *Damn it.* Who was she kidding? After the top-notch sales job she'd done on herself in that diner, the only party game this guy was going to be interested in playing was strip poker.

He grabbed the sack and stepped out of the car, then came around and opened Renee's door. She climbed out, pine needles crunching beneath her feet, the cool night wind lifting her hair off her shoulders. He shut the car door and walked toward the cabin. Renee didn't move.

He turned back. "Coming?"

For a moment she considered fleeing into the woods after all, but her Fear of Forest came crashing back to her.

"Uh, yeah."

Even ten paces away, he exuded a powerful male energy that seemed to fill the space between them, smothering her with thoughts of how big he was and how big she wasn't. He had to be at least six-two, and while she stood nearly five-eight, still he outweighed her by a good seventy pounds. His tall, lean-muscled body made a forbidding silhouette in the near-darkness, and the thought of following him into that cabin made her shiver. A few minutes ago she'd been desperate only to be anywhere Leandro wasn't, but now all she could think about was what she'd promised this man and how desperately she wanted *not* to go through with it. Then she took stock of her situation and realized she might not have a choice in the matter.

Her purse was still sitting in room fourteen of the Flamingo Motor Lodge, which meant she had no cash and no credit cards, which meant she couldn't get a hotel room. She didn't know a solitary soul within two hundred miles. There wasn't a twenty-four-hour anything open in this part of the world she could hang out in, even if she could get him to take her back to civilization. The forest was deep and dark and cold and scary. She had no choice but to stay here tonight, and if he insisted she make good on her promise, there wouldn't be a thing she could do to stop him.

He opened the door to the cabin and stepped aside for Renee to enter. It was the size of an efficiency apartment, with even fewer amenities. A kitchenette lined one wall, which was nothing more than a short counter with a hot plate and a coffeepot resting on it, a stainless-steel sink, and a few knotty pine cabinets with a dull, scratched-up finish. At the end of the counter sat a small refrigerator which was, thank God, not nearly big enough to store body parts.

A stone fireplace sprawled along an adjacent wall, and facing it a sofa in an earth-tone plaid rested on rough pine floors. The room smelled of raw wood and smoke and country air, and despite the obvious lack of tender loving care, under any other circumstances she might have thought it rustic but homey. Now it just looked small. Way too small. With nowhere to hide.

She walked over to the window and stared out into the night, at one pine tree after another standing tall against a pale, moonlit sky. It was the most inhospitable sight she'd ever seen. "Do you have any neighbors?" she asked him.

"Oh, yeah. Lots of squirrels. Maybe an armadillo or two."

"Any two-legged ones?"

"Across the lake."

So they were alone. *Really* alone.

Silence. Then the sound of the sack clunking against the floor. That was a bad sign. A man who didn't refrigerate a six-pack clearly had something more pressing on his mind.

He moved up behind her. She met his gaze in the window reflection, those piercing eyes of his staring back at her with an intent so clear he might as well have spray-painted it on the wall. He closed his hands around her elbows in a gentle but possessive grip. He ran them slowly up to her shoulders, then back down again, and she felt a million nerve endings jump to life. She rested her palms against the windowsill and continued to stare out into the night, afraid to turn around, afraid to do anything that might look like encouragement. No matter what she'd said, she knew nothing about the kind of sex that resulted in broken commandments and global screaming.

She had a feeling this man did.

He ran his fingertip down the length of her hair, blazing a path down her back, then picked up a strand and twirled it around his finger.

"Beautiful," he whispered.

She shivered at the low, velvety tone of his voice. He moved closer and circled his arm around her waist, pulling her against him. Her back met his chest. She felt something rock-hard just beneath the small of her back, proof positive that talking him into having a beer instead of having sex probably wasn't going to be an option.

He rested one hand against her abdomen, and with his other hand he brushed her hair away from the side of her neck. The cool air of the cabin washed over her exposed skin, sending shivers down her spine, which re-warmed instantly when his hot breath fell against her neck.

"Tell me again," he whispered.

She froze. "Tell you what?"

"Exactly what kind of sex we're going to have."

Before John knew what had happened, his hot little blonde had slid from his grasp and flown halfway across the room. It was as if he'd touched her with a cattle prod.

He stared at her, dumbfounded, and she stared back, those blue eyes wide and her mouth hanging open as if she wanted to say something but couldn't find the words.

"Is something the matter?" he asked.

"Uh . . . no. I just . . . I need to go to the bathroom."

John took a deep breath and let it out slowly. He felt like a skydiver on the verge of a free fall who'd just gotten yanked back into the plane.

"It's in there." He pointed to the only separate room in the primitive cabin, and she scurried inside and closed the door behind her. He heard her fumbling with the door handle, probably looking for the lock that wasn't there. Then silence.

John snatched up the sack from beside the front door. He deposited the beer in the minirefrigerator in the kitchen, tossed the Certs on the counter, then stared at the box of condoms. He knew it was too good to be true.

This woman was obviously hiding something. She had no purse, no coat, no car. It was as if she had come out of nowhere. He'd seen all the signs, but he'd chosen to ignore them. He should have trusted his instincts. He should have stuck to naked women with staples in their navels instead of dragging home the real thing.

He tossed the box of condoms into a kitchen cabinet, then collapsed on the sofa, which was a little uncomfortable to do when a certain vital organ of his was inflated to twice its normal size, still trapped inside a pair of jeans that suddenly seemed two sizes too small. As hot as she'd been for him in that diner, when they got into his car he'd expected to feel her hands roaming all over him and seductive words whispered in his ear, and when they made it back to the cabin he'd expected to have his clothes ripped off before he even had a chance to pull out the sofa bed.

Expected it? Hell, he'd *prayed* for it. Instead, for reasons he couldn't fathom, his tigress had morphed into a baby kitten.

She wasn't completely inexperienced. That much he was sure of. She had to be at least twenty-five, maybe older, and no woman could kiss like that if she hadn't been around the block a time or two. Still, while he had no idea what she wanted, he had a pretty good idea it wasn't sex. But she'd sure been motivated to make him *think* that was what she wanted, and it was time he found out why.

Calling her bluff would likely do the trick.

# chapter three

Renee splashed cold water on her face and dried it with a threadbare green towel hanging on a hook beside the bathroom sink. She rested her palms against the sink and bowed her head. She was tired and hungry, her knees ached from the fall she'd taken on the blacktop in her attempt to escape from Leandro, and all she wanted right now was a decent meal, a hot bath, and a good night's sleep. She sighed heavily. Not much chance of any of those things happening, especially the good night's sleep.

Then she raised her head, looked in the mirror, and wondered who the woman was looking back.

According to her, she was an innocent woman who swore from now on she'd control her late-night craving for ice cream. According to the Tolosa police, she was a fugitive from justice. According to the man in the next room, she was a hot, sex-crazed hussy looking for a good time.

Right now, she had to deal with the sex-crazed hussy thing. But since she knew nothing about the man on the other side of that door, she had to face facts: telling him no might lead to worse consequences than telling him yes.

She opened the door slowly, feeling like a mouse coming out of its hole who knows there's a tomcat in the vicinity. He was waiting for her on the sofa, and his hot, hungry expression told her the tomcat analogy was right on target.

"Come on over here, sweetheart."

She inched her way over to the sofa and stood beside it. He patted the cushion beside him. "Park it right here."

She sat down as he requested, but approximately two feet away from the place he'd indicated, cramming herself up against the opposite arm of the sofa. He slid over next to her, draping his arm behind her head and resting the palm of his other hand against her thigh. The look in his eyes — that fiery, almost primitive look — shook her all the way to her toes. She splayed her hands across his chest as he moved closer still, but the solid wall of muscle she felt only heightened her anxiety.

"You never did tell me your name," she said weakly.

"I thought we were keeping names out of this."

"I changed my mind. I'm . . . Alice. And you're . . . ?"

"John."

"John. Nice name."

"My mother thought so."

"Where are you from, John?"

"We're pretty much past the small-talk stage, wouldn't you say?"

"I just thought it might be nice to get to know each other a little."

"That's funny. Back at Harley's place, there was only one part of me you wanted to get to know, and it had nothing to do with my hometown."

"I know. But after all, we did just meet —"

"And I gotta say it was one hell of an introduction." He touched a finger to her cheek, then dragged it along her jaw. "All you really need to know about me is that I'm partial to blue-eyed blondes, particularly when they're looking for a good time."

He brushed her hair away from her shoulder and dropped a gentle kiss to the side of her neck, his touch sending a flurry of shivers down her spine. Then he teased his lips along her jaw, and she felt the scratchiness of his beard.

"When's the last time you shaved?"

"I wasn't aware my personal hygiene was part of the deal."

"Your beard is irritating."

She tried to sound annoyed, but to her dismay, her words came out soft and breathy. Seductive. And she definitely did *not* want to sound seductive.

"Irritating, huh?" He dropped a featherlight kiss on the sensitive spot just beneath her left ear. "It didn't seem to bother you back at the diner."

*Good point.*

She squirmed around, trying to distance herself from him, but she succeeded only in maneuvering herself into a position where his hand crept even further up her thigh. "You know, I haven't had a shower all day. I'm such a mess —"

"A shower? Sounds good. Why don't we take one together?"

*My big mouth strikes again.*

"Well, that's a possibility. But it's a little cold in here, don't you think? Maybe if you started a fire in the fireplace —"

"Not necessary. I'll keep you warm."

He pulled her closer, cradled her head in his arm, and kissed her, and it was as if a nuclear reactor had exploded inside her head. At the diner, she'd been the aggressor out of sheer desperation, but now the tables had turned and he'd assumed command of the situation. Total command. His arms were wrapped around her like a velvet vise, caressing but controlling, allowing her not an inch of leeway in any direction as his mouth engulfed hers.

He slid his hand along her cheek and drew her even closer, twining his tongue with hers in a dance of pure, slow-motion seduction. She knew now that his lips were every bit as warm and sensual as they'd seemed the first moment she saw him. They were beautiful lips. Talented lips. Lips that made resisting him slip farther and farther from her mind. But despite his single-mindedness, she felt an odd glimmer of restraint in his touch, a hint of tenderness she hadn't expected, as if he had no intention of taking without giving.

He kissed her for what seemed like hours, pulling away a little, brushing his lips against hers, then plunging in again. Before long his advance-and-retreat technique was driving her crazy in the very best sense of the word. She'd never felt anything like it. And it was turning her into mush.

Then he eased away and stared down at her. What was he looking for? Surrender? Renee stared back at him, afraid she was about three seconds away from precisely that.

"I could kiss you all night," he whispered.

Her heart leaped with hope. Maybe he'd forgotten she had a body below the neck. Then he ran his hand along the outer swell of her breast, to her waist, down her thigh, and back up again, his gaze following the path of his hand like a moth follows light.

"All over."

*Uh-oh.*

He tugged at the hem of her sweatshirt, easing it upward. When his hand fell against her waist, she gasped softly. He covered the gasp with a kiss, then moved his palm upward until his fingertips brushed the satin cup of her bra. He teased her nipple to a taut peak through the fabric with the pad of his thumb, then traced a fingertip in the hollow between her breasts, setting her adrift in a hazy sea of erotic pleasure she would cheerfully have drowned in.

Then he reached for the front clasp of her baby-pink bra with the white rose at the clasp, the one she'd bought at Victoria's Secret last month, thinking at the time that she'd probably wear it out before a man ever laid eyes on it.

Renee's eyes sprang open. She pulled away, pressing her elbows down to still his hand beneath her sweatshirt.

"What are you doing?" she said in a gasp.

"Trying to get us naked, but I don't seem to be getting a lot of cooperation."

He leaned in to kiss her again, but she turned away, not the least bit ready to let Victoria's Secret out of the bag. "No," she whispered. "I can't —"

"I've got protection, sweetheart, if that's what you're —"

"I said no!"

For several seconds he didn't move. Then his deep, dark eyes that had been hot with desire became hard and probing, his passion melting away like an ice cube on a hot summer day.

Very deliberately, he removed his hand from beneath her sweatshirt and yanked the hem down. Then he gripped her by her arms and sat her upright on the sofa beside him, staring at her with a gaze so sharp it could penetrate steel.

"What are you up to?"

Renee opened her mouth, hoping some brilliant explanation would leap off her tongue. But her luck had totally run out. She clamped her mouth shut again.

"You didn't have a car at the diner. You've got no purse, no coat. Why not?"

Renee remained silent.

"You come on to me like some kind of cheap hooker, then get all uptight when I so much as touch you. You want to explain that one to me?"

He sounded like every cop who'd ever interrogated her, and her heart beat madly. But still she didn't respond.

"I knew this was a mistake." John took a deep breath and let it out slowly, rubbing his hand against his mouth. He got up from the sofa, his stiff gait telling her that the switch from fire to ice had left him a little incapacitated. "Come on. I'm taking you home."

"No!"

She said the word loudly, too loudly, and he looked at her with surprise.

"What do you mean, no?"

Renee just stared at him. She wanted to stay, *had* to stay, but she did not want to have sex. How was she going to convince him to let her have one without the other?

When she didn't respond, he grabbed his coat and headed for the door.

"Wait!"

He spun back around, frustration running wild on his face. "Look. You clearly don't want to do what you came here to do, so it's time I took you home."

"If you'll just calm down —"

"You want me to calm down? Then tell me why you've been jerking me around since the minute you walked into that diner. Tell me *that,* and I'll be the most congenial guy you've ever met!"

She needed a really good lie, but one just wasn't coming to her. "I-I can't."

"You can't? What do you mean, you can't?"

What *did* she mean? "I mean I can't . . . imagine why you're so angry."

John's eyebrows shot up. "Then you haven't got much of an imagination!"

She squeezed her eyes closed, hoping the alley she was heading down wasn't a dead end. "I just wanted to have a nice, leisurely evening. Talk a little. Relax a little. Get to know each other before we . . ." She sighed wistfully. "But it's clear now that no matter how I feel about it, all you want is sex."

John's mouth fell open. "Would you explain to me how *I* got to be the bad guy in this situation? You came on to me like a nymphomaniac, harassing me until I took you up on your offer, and now that I expect you to actually *follow through,* suddenly I'm a sex-crazed maniac?"

"No. Of course not. That's not what I meant at all. It's just that . . . well, I suppose I can see now how you might have gotten the wrong impression —"

"Wrong impression?"

The incredulity in his voice said he wasn't buying, and Renee's nervousness intensified. "Yes. I prefer a more subtle approach to lovemaking —"

John's eyebrows shot up again. "Subtle? You call what you did in that diner *subtle?*"

"That was just to get your attention. Sort of like . . . well, like a peacock spreading her feathers."

*Oh, God. How dumb did that sound?* Renee cringed at her own words, but nothing else had come to her. If she kept talking long enough, saying anything, then maybe he'd calm down, and —

"Pea*cocks* spread their feathers," John said. "Pea*hens* stand back and watch. They *don't* back a peacock up against a lunch counter and promise him a one-way trip to heaven!"

"I was speaking metaphorically —"

"Now, listen up, sweetheart, and I mean listen good. There was nothing metaphorical about your hand on my crotch, so I don't want to hear another word about the mating habits of wildlife. You were pretty clear about what you wanted in that diner, and I'm not a fan of false advertising. We're going to get naked right now, or you're going to give me a damned good reason why not. Otherwise, you're out of here." He jabbed at his watch. "You've got ten seconds. Now *make up your mind!*"

So there it was. Get naked, get truthful, or get out.

Maybe it was the challenging look on his face. Maybe it was the demanding tone of his voice. Or maybe it was just that she was sick and tired of rotten things happening to her when she hadn't done anything to deserve them. Whatever the reason, as she sat on that sofa, staring up at a man who'd issued her the most detestable ultimatum she'd ever heard, something inside her snapped.

She stood up slowly, narrowing her eyes like a backstreet gangster who'd just gotten the upper hand. She planted her fists against her hips and glowered at him. "I can see now why you're not married. There aren't many women who'd put up with such a mean, shallow, arrogant, dictatorial *jerk!*"

She slapped a palm against his chest and gave him a shove. As he stumbled backward, she started for the door, so crazed with anger that she'd have stood up to a grizzly bear before she stayed another minute with this man. But before she had the chance to commune with the creatures of the forest, he grabbed her by the wrist, spun her around, and dragged her back across the room. He put both hands on her shoulders and shoved her down on the sofa. She tried to rise, and he shoved her down again. He sat down beside her and clamped his hand around her upper arm, his gaze boring into her. She set her jaw and scowled right back at him.

"The way I figure it," he said, "you're nothing more than a snotty little tease who gets her kicks from jerking guys around. But I suppose there's a possibility that you just don't have the sense not to mess with strange men who might not be as forgiving as I am. Now, which is it?"

She lifted her nose a notch, refusing to let him see her sweat. "Well, let's see. The 'strange' part. That's accurate."

She tugged her arm from his grasp and stood up, but just as quickly he grabbed her and yanked her back down again. She glared at him. "Oh, so you like it rough, huh? Why didn't you say so?"

She regretted the words the instant they left her lips. He tightened his grip on her arm, an expression of barely restrained fury flooding his face.

"I've never hurt a woman in my life, and I'm not about to start now, even though in your case I'm sure I'd enjoy every minute of it." He leaned closer still, dropping his voice to a gravelly whisper. "And just for the record, I don't like it rough at all. I like it soft, I like it slow, and I like it hot. And above all, I like a woman who knows what she wants. If I ever decide you fit that description, *your* screams are the ones they'll be hearing in Bangkok."

She swallowed hard, never doubting for a moment that he meant what he said.

"Now, why don't you put the bullshit on hold for about five minutes and tell me why you're really here?"

Renee opened her mouth, but nothing came out. She couldn't think of a thing to say that wouldn't get her into even more hot water than she was already in. She figured this was it. This was the moment he was going to hack her up and bury her under the front porch, not because he was some kind of a bizarre serial killer, but just because he'd had enough.

"It was a mistake," she said. "Let's just forget about it, okay?" She started to rise, hoping her semiadmission of guilt would be enough to satisfy him. He jerked her back down again.

And that was when it came to her. The perfect little lie that had been eluding her suddenly filled her mind with the simple grandeur reserved for only the most brilliant of falsehoods. Why hadn't she thought of it before?

She rubbed her arm where he'd grasped it so tightly, then bowed her head and dropped her voice to a near-whisper.

"It was because of my boyfriend, okay?"

He looked at her skeptically. "Your boyfriend?"

"He's the reason I had to get away."

"Get away from what?"

"From him." She sighed, staring down at her hands. "We were out driving, and we got into this terrible argument. He was so angry. Even more than usual. He stopped at the train crossing by the diner when the gates came down, and I jumped out of the car. He came after me." She blinked quickly, as if chasing away tears. "He grabbed me and I fell."

*Physical evidence,* she thought suddenly, and pulled up a leg of her jeans, displaying an angry red wound on her knee surrounded by black-and-blue flesh that looked even worse than she'd imagined it would. And when he stared down at her injury and his eyes narrowed with concern, she knew the tables had turned and she was back on top again. Metaphorically speaking.

Infused with hope, Renee kept on spinning. "I managed to get away from him. I crossed the tracks just before the train got there, but he didn't make it across. The train was moving real slow, so it blocked him until I made it to the diner."

John slumped back on the sofa and expelled a long, weary breath, putting his hand to his forehead and squeezing his eyes closed as if he had a whopper of a headache.

*He's buying it. Every last word.*

"So then you came on to me? What was that all about?"

She shrugged weakly. "I just thought it would be the quickest way to get you to take me away from there before he got to me again."

John looked at her with total disbelief. "Do you know how stupid that was? What if you'd come on to the wrong kind of guy in that diner, and then refused to do what you promised? Do you have any idea what could have happened?"

Renee felt a flush of relief. Even though his brow was all crunched up with annoyance and those dark eyes were skewering her, by telling her she could have come on to the wrong guy he was telling her she'd gotten lucky and picked the right one. A guy who probably wasn't going to hold her to the outrageous sexual activity she'd promised.

"Has he hurt you before?"

His expression remained hard, but the note of compassion she heard in his voice made her a little less proud of the lie she'd fabricated. She sighed. "Yeah."

"Ever put you in the hospital?"

She pondered that one, warning herself not to get too carried away. "Once."

"Jesus." He breathed the word with quiet exasperation. "Why didn't you just tell me what was going on when you came into that diner? I could have —"

"No. You couldn't have. My boyfriend's huge, and he's ugly, and he's got this shaved head and these hideous tattoos, and he's mean. *Really* mean. One look at him and nobody would have helped me, and I wouldn't have blamed them."

John screwed up his face. "And this guy is your boyfriend?"

She had to admit that did sound kind of moronic. She shrugged weakly. "Well, sometimes he can be really sweet, if he sets his mind to it."

"Sweet? *Sweet?*" John sat up on the edge of the sofa, looking as if he wanted to rip his hair out. "What's wrong with some of you women, anyway? You let a man use you as a punching bag, then tell the world how wonderful he is. I swear to God —"

He stopped short, then waved a hand in dismissal. "Never mind. It's none of my business." He got up from the sofa and reached for his coat. "I'm taking you home. Where do you live?"

She sighed, fiddling with a loose string on the sofa. "With my boyfriend."

He stared at her dumbly for a moment, then let out a heavy sigh. "Do you have any friends you can stay with? Relatives?"

"Uh . . . we just moved here. I don't know anybody."

"Well, that's just *great.*" He threw his coat back down on the sofa.

She turned her gaze up to meet his. "Do you think I could stay here tonight?"

"No. No way."

"But —"

"I said no. I don't want to get involved in this."

"You're not involved in anything. My boyfriend has no idea where I am. Let me stay here. Please." She paused, sending him a wide-eyed look of utter helplessness, praying it would be enough to sway him. "I really don't have anywhere else to go."

He rolled his eyes a little, and after several seconds of tight-lipped glaring, he threw his arms up in resignation.

"Oh, hell. Why not? It's a damn fool thing to do, but I might as well stick with the theme of the evening, right?"

She ducked her head submissively. *Mission accomplished.*

"You can stay here tonight. But in the morning I'm taking you to the local authorities."

Renee's head shot up. "What?"

"You're going to press charges."

She felt a surge of panic. She sat up suddenly, shaking her head wildly. "No. You don't understand. I can't press charges. He'll *kill* me if I go to the police —"

"He'll kill you if you don't. That's the deal, sweetheart. Take it or leave it."

Okay. So the world's greatest lie had a flaw or two.

Renee decided she didn't have any choice but to play along, even though she had no intention of getting within ten miles of a police station. At least for now, she was safe. She'd worry about tomorrow . . . tomorrow. After all, if she just flatly refused to go to the police, what could he do? Drag her there?

"Okay," she said. "I will."

John nodded brusquely and rose from the sofa. "It's cold in here. I'll make a fire."

Without another word, he grabbed his

coat and left the cabin. Renee sat back on the sofa, relief spilling through her. She'd just told the most outrageous lie of her life, but her luck had held. Her nose hadn't grown a foot and her pants hadn't caught fire.

Spending the night alone with John still made her a little nervous, but at least now she had a better feel for the kind of man she was dealing with. A few times in the midst of her tragically sincere performance she saw a hint of compassion beneath his tough-guy demeanor, and instinctively knew she had nothing to fear from him.

Unless he found out she lied.

# chapter four

The cold night wind hit John like a slap in the face, and it was a slap he needed badly. He hoped it would clear his head, make him see things more clearly, but as he strode to the woodpile, his brain still felt scrambled. Spending one hour with that woman had been like getting stuck on a roller coaster with no way off.

He glanced back through the window. She was sitting on the sofa, her knees pulled up to her chest and her chin resting on her knees, staring ahead blankly. An unexpected wave of protectiveness swept over him, followed by an even bigger wave of anger. The way she'd looked up at him with those big blue eyes had made him want to beat her abusive boyfriend to a bloody pulp. To make him think twice before he hurt a woman who couldn't defend herself. To render him incapable of even *thinking* of raising a hand to —

*Wait a minute.* Where was all this emotional-reaction crap coming from?

John let out a disgusted breath. All he had to do was look at her and he was back on that roller coaster again.

*An emotionally involved cop isn't worth a damn.*

He wasn't acting in a professional capacity here, but the warning was appropriate just the same. He turned around and headed to the woodpile, cursing himself for going nuts over something that was really pretty routine. Hadn't he seen domestic abuse cases at least a hundred times before? Why was this particular woman making him crazy?

Because he knew what it felt like to kiss her.

The very thought that a man could find it more gratifying to inflict pain on that warm, beautiful body of hers rather than pleasure was completely beyond his understanding. He had a sudden, overwhelming urge to go back into that cabin, take her in his arms, and spend the long hours of the night showing her how a man was supposed to treat a woman. To give her something to think about the next time a bastard like that boyfriend of hers decided to take out his aggression on her. To make her understand that for every guy like that, there were a thousand other guys who'd touch her in ways that fueled her daydreams rather than haunted her nightmares —

He yanked up a couple of logs from the woodpile, cursing himself again. He couldn't believe it. He still wanted her. Even after everything she'd told him, he still wanted her. What did he think he was? Some kind of sexual social worker?

It would be nice to be able to blame this whole mess on her, but he knew he'd been playing with fire back at the diner, and he'd walked right into the flames anyway. This was a perfect example of what happened when he put the cop side of his brain on hold for any length of time. He stopped looking at things rationally and logically.

And started beating up paper-towel dispensers.

With new resolve, he strode back toward the cabin. He'd let her stay here tonight, because at this late hour it would be a pain in the ass to do anything else. Then tomorrow morning he'd deliver her to the local guys and suggest strongly that she give them a statement. Like most battered women, she'd probably refuse, but that wasn't his problem. After that, he'd head back over to Harley's place, see what Marva had cooking, and catch up on the local news of Winslow, Texas.

And if a beautiful woman wandered into the diner looking for a good time, he'd flash his badge like a cross in front of a vampire and suggest she take her sexual appetites elsewhere.

Renee watched as John built a fire, and by the way he thunked the logs into the fireplace, she could tell he was still angry. Well, maybe not angry, but at least annoyed, with a healthy dose of exasperation thrown in. He clearly wanted her out of his life as quickly as possible, and she didn't blame him. In her desperation to elude Leandro and stay here tonight, she'd jerked him around every bit as much as he said she had. Fortunately, he had no idea he was *still* being jerked around, and she prayed he never found out.

"Are you hungry?" he asked her, his voice brusque and impersonal.

Hungry wasn't the word for it. Starving was more like it.

"Uh . . . yeah. A little."

He went to the kitchen, peered into the fridge, then rummaged through the cabinets. He came back with a sack of pretzels and a can of Coke.

"I've been eating at the diner the past couple of days. I don't have much around here."

"That's okay," she said, so hungry she'd have eaten the stuffing out of the sofa if he'd turned his back long enough. He handed her the pretzels and Coke, then mumbled something about taking a shower. He disappeared into the bathroom.

Renee munched on the pretzels, visions of pasta fuma and veal scallopini dancing in her head. Italian food. That made her think of the restaurant where she worked. Or used to work. She sighed wistfully, thinking that if someone hadn't tossed the loot and the weapon from an armed robbery into the backseat of her car, her biggest worry right now would be double-booked reservations, or a substandard bottle of Chianti.

*Stop it. Stop thinking about the life you left behind. It'll only make you crazy.*

She finished off most of the pretzels, then folded the top of the bag down and returned it to the kitchen along with the empty Coke can, promising herself a real meal the first chance she got. She collapsed on the sofa again, blinking slowly, mesmerized by the hypnotizing red-gold brightness of the fire and the muffled sound of shower spray coming from the bathroom.

In her sleepy state, the memory of how John had kissed her swam around in her mind, then oozed into other thoughts, more erotic thoughts, thoughts she'd have quelled in an instant if she hadn't been so incredibly tired and if they hadn't been so incredibly enticing.

She imagined him standing beneath the shower, his naked body surrounded by a surreal haze of steam, his muscles wet and glistening. She followed the bar of soap as he slid it down one arm and back up again, then across a broad chest, bubbles gathering in the smattering of hair there, only to get washed away by a pulsing spray of water. She saw him turning to let the spray massage his shoulders, rolling them once, twice, to ease the tension there. Then she closed her eyes and delved into truly uncharted territory.

She imagined slipping into the bathroom, easing the shower curtain aside, and meeting his startled gaze. She saw him pulling her into the shower in one smooth move, trapping her against the tile wall and kissing her, first ignoring the fact that she was still fully clothed, then remedying that situation in short order. In this particular daydream the hot water never ran out. They stood beneath the shower all night long making love in that glorious way people do when they only have eyes for each other.

Or so she'd heard.

She heard the squeak of the shower knobs, silencing the spray, then the soft clicking of the shower curtain rings as he pushed the curtain aside. A few minutes later the bathroom door opened and John emerged, steam clouding up behind him as it hit the cool air of the main room. She stared at him dumbly, finding it hard to catch a good, solid breath. Where this man's body was concerned, her daydream had been more like a premonition.

He wore a pair of jeans. Only a pair of jeans. His feet and chest were bare. He was towel-drying his hair. And to her surprise, he'd shaved. He'd been handsome before, but something about his clean-shaven face and the fact that he was currently half-naked really got her attention. She compulsively inspected every square inch of his body, from his broad, muscled chest to those rock-solid arms that had been laced around her less than half an hour before, all the way down to his bare feet, which she found inexplicably appealing. His *feet*, for God's sake. She couldn't remember ever thinking a man's feet were sexy, but she sure was thinking it now.

When her gaze traveled back up again, she saw that he'd stopped drying his hair and was staring at her. All at once she realized how long her visual tour of his body had taken, and how obvious it was that she'd been gaping at him. She looked away and ran a hand nervously through her hair. Her cheeks grew warm, and she hoped she wasn't blushing.

John went to a closet, pulled out a worn flannel shirt, and put it on. He tossed the towel back into the bathroom, then buttoned the length of his shirt as he walked over to her.

"That sofa is a Hide-A-Bed," he told her. "The only bed."

Renee had figured as much, since she didn't see a bedroom, but still she'd hoped that maybe this was a remote Holiday Inn and any minute a bellboy would be bringing in a roll-away.

"And I don't think you're any more eager to sleep on the floor than I am."

"You mean . . . you want us both to sleep here?"

"Look, if I'd wanted to take advantage of you, don't you think I'd have done it by now? You stay on your side, I'll stay on mine, and we'll both be comfortable. Any problem with that?"

*Yes.* She had a big problem with it. She'd just been admiring him with the intensity of an astronomer who'd discovered a new celestial body, and now she was supposed to sleep with him? She could deal with her erotic thoughts as long as they were vertical, but horizontally she wasn't so sure.

"No. No problem."

She got up from the sofa. He tossed the cushions aside and pulled out the bed, then got two pillows out of the closet. For its being such a big sofa, she was amazed at how small the bed version of it appeared to be.

John lifted the covers on his side, lay down, and slid beneath them. Renee approached the bed tentatively, then kicked off her shoes and lay down on the other side, thinking that if he was beneath the covers maybe she'd better stay on top.

"The fire will die before morning," he told her. "You'll get cold like that."

She paused a moment, then decided that after everything that had happened it would seem pretty ungrateful to imply that she didn't trust him. She slipped beneath the blankets. He turned out the lamp on the table beside the sofa and lay back on his pillow. Left with nothing but firelight, the room took on a lazy, golden glow. And even though they lay a foot apart, it wasn't long before the heat from John's body mingled with hers.

"Alice?"

John's voice, deep and melodious, broke the silence. It took Renee a moment to realize he was calling her by the phony name she'd given him.

"Yes?"

"Why didn't you tell me about your boyfriend sooner?"

*Because I hadn't made him up yet.*

"I don't know. I guess I was afraid to."

"Afraid? Why?"

Renee paused. "After all that stuff I said to you in that diner, I was afraid of what you'd do if I told you I didn't want to . . . to go through with it."

"What did you think I'd do?"

Renee was silent.

"Did you think I'd hurt you? Is that what you thought?"

She shrugged. "Well, you did yell a lot —"

"That's right. I yelled. Because you were driving me nuts. Because you wouldn't tell me the truth. But yelling's all I did." He paused. "It's all I'd *ever* do."

Renee heard the note of insult in his voice, and all at once she realized he was telling her that no matter how angry he'd gotten, he was nothing like her imaginary abusive boyfriend. And when she remembered how he'd kissed her, like a man who enjoyed giving pleasure as much as taking it, she knew it was true.

"And no matter what you promised me in that diner," he added, "I never would have made you do anything you didn't want to."

*What if I want to now?*

The thought came so clearly into Renee's mind that she was afraid for a moment that she'd spoken it out loud. It was the weirdest thing. Now that she knew he wasn't a sex-crazed maniac, sex with him was all she seemed to be able to think about. She didn't actually want to do it. Well, not all of it, anyway. But she wondered what would happen if she inched closer to him, laid her hand against his cheek, and kissed him. Just one kiss to bring back the memory of how wonderful it had felt. What would he do?

After all the protesting she'd done earlier, he'd probably skip right past the police station tomorrow morning and take her straight to the loony bin.

"Don't let men hurt you," John told her. "You don't have to put up with that."

The concern she heard behind the brusque tone of his voice sent her guilt level soaring. "I know," she said softly. "I won't. Not anymore."

A frustrated sigh escaped his lips, as if he didn't believe a word of it, as if he had vol-

94

umes to say on the subject but realized it was pointless.

"Good night, Alice," he whispered. Then he closed his eyes and was still. Minutes later she heard his soft, rhythmic breathing and realized he'd fallen asleep.

Renee turned to look at him, taking advantage of the first chance she'd had to stare at him all she wanted to without his looking back with anger or pity, or her worrying that he was going to catch her in a lie. The serenity of his face in slumber highlighted by the glow of the fire made him fiercely handsome, and she inhaled the sight of him. As afraid of his touch as she'd been before, that was how consumed she was with the thought of him touching her now.

Every memory of sexual intimacy she had was with a few teenage boys who knew nothing about sex. If the way John kissed was any indication, he clearly did. For a long, seductive moment she let her mind wander again, wondering what it felt like to have a man make love to her. Not a boy, who got it up and got it over with before she even realized it had started.

A man.

She felt a rush of longing so powerful it hurt. She'd had plenty of boyfriends over the years, but when they found out that her no really meant *no,* they hadn't stayed around long.

It wasn't as if she didn't want sex. What she didn't want was the consequences of sex. Not just the pregnancy/AIDS/social disease thing. She remembered the few times she'd given herself to boys who'd given her nothing in return, the shame and loneliness she'd felt, and she was determined never to feel that way again. After her wake-up call eight years ago, she had promised herself that until Mr. Right wandered along, she'd use her body only to hang clothes on and to transport her brain from one location to another. And it was a promise she'd kept. During that fateful summer of her eighteenth year when she'd begun her journey toward self-respect, she vowed that the next man she gave herself to would be a man she trusted. A man she loved.

A man who loved her.

Then she breathed a soft, regretful sigh. Even if she *did* find a man she could trust, a man who wanted more from her than sex on demand, how could she let him love her when she'd be a fugitive for the rest of her life?

She rolled to her side and lay still, trying to put thoughts of tomorrow out of her mind, hoping to get at least one restful night's sleep before she was forced to start deceiving John all over again. Then the glint of something silver on the kitchen counter caught her eye.

John's car keys.

Renee froze. It took her a full five seconds to comprehend the opportunity she saw before her, and when she did, she kicked herself for not thinking of it at a more opportune time. When he was in the shower, for instance. Car theft was a little easier when the owner was preoccupied. Or naked. Or both.

*No.* She couldn't steal his car.

Well, maybe it wasn't exactly stealing. Not if she just used it for a little while, then left it somewhere and called him to tell him where to find it. Car theft involved tearing up steering columns and hot-wiring and generally trashing a car, then taking it to a chop shop, where it would be dissected into an unrecognizable pile of auto parts. *That* was car theft. This was more like, well . . . borrowing.

She figured she'd have to ditch the car pretty fast, though, because if he woke up and found her missing, then found his car missing, he'd call the local authorities and report it stolen. She'd get picked up before she knew what hit her.

*Wait a minute.* He couldn't call anyone. From what she'd seen, the cabin didn't have a phone. The only phone she'd seen was a cell phone in his car. Which she would be driving.

That meant she'd be leaving him out here alone in the middle of nowhere, with no communication and no transportation. For a moment her conscience shouted at her, telling her she couldn't do that. Then she weighed their respective situations. If she took his car, he'd be faced with a ten or fifteen-mile walk back to civilization. If she didn't take his car, she'd probably end up spending ten or fifteen years in prison.

She told her conscience to shut up.

She lay deathly still for a long time, blinking to stay awake. When fifteen or twenty minutes passed and John still hadn't moved, she lifted the covers carefully and sat up, swinging her legs around. The sofa bed creaked, and her heart turned a somersault. John stirred a little, then was still again.

She grabbed her shoes and carried them with her to the kitchen counter. Watching John with every step she took, she picked up his keys as deftly as she could to avoid clinking them together. His wallet sat beside the keys. Wallets generally contained money, and she needed some. Badly.

She sighed inwardly. That stealing thing.

Then again, if she sent him the money back later with interest, it wouldn't exactly be stealing, would it? It would be more like . . . well, like she'd invested it for him. If she gave him, say, a fifteen- or twenty-percent return, how could he possibly complain about that?

She opened his wallet to pull out whatever paper money was in it. But money wasn't the first thing she saw. And when it dawned on her what she was looking at, she had to slap a hand over her mouth to keep from gasping.

A badge.

She tilted it slightly so the badge glinted in the firelight, then read the ID beside it. John DeMarco. Tolosa Police Department.

God almighty, John was a cop.

A sick, sinking sensation swooped through her stomach, and her knees went weak. For several seconds she just stood there as if her feet were fused to the floor. She'd propositioned a cop. She'd walked right into that diner, and with all the intuition of a dodo bird, she'd managed to zero in on the one man who had both the power and the authority to make sure she never saw the light of day again.

She had to get out of here. *Now.*

She pulled all the paper money out of his wallet and stuffed it into her jeans pocket. She walked silently to the door, her heart hammering in her chest. She turned the dead bolt until it clicked softly. When she opened the door, it squeaked a little on its hinges. John stirred. She spun around and held her breath as he turned over, his back to the door, then became still again.

She slipped out the door, pulling it closed behind her. She tiptoed along the tree-lined dirt path toward the Explorer, her warm breath fogging in the cold night air. She clasped her shoes to her chest, trying to avoid big patches of fallen pine needles she knew would crunch beneath her feet. She glanced back over her shoulder. The cabin was silent.

Would he hear her start the car?

It didn't matter. All that mattered was that she got inside the car and locked the doors before he made it outside. Then he'd have no way of stopping her.

She reached the Explorer and slipped the key into the lock, her teeth chattering from the cold. Bits and pieces of prayers ran through her head, promises to God for all the wonderful things she was going to do with her life if only he'd get her out of this one little pickle. If only he'd make John sleep until about ten o'clock tomorrow morning. If only the person who really committed that robbery would step forward, confess, and get her off the hook. If only . . .

As she turned the key, she heard a faint crunch on the path behind her. She whipped around, and all at once she realized the cop sleeping less than thirty yards away was the least of her worries. Her biggest problem had just become the ugly, sneering, tattooed mountain of muscle standing behind her, his single gold earring glinting in the moonlight.

"Hey, there, sweet thing. Going somewhere?"

# chapter five

Renee yanked the key out of the lock and flung the car door open. She leaped into the Explorer and jerked the door shut, but before she could lock it, Leandro yanked it back open. She lunged over the console, heading for the passenger door. But Leandro clamped his meat hook of a hand onto her leg, his fingers digging in like claws. She kicked wildly, her foot smacking him in the chest. He made one of those Batman-like *oof* noises, and she knew she'd knocked the wind out of him. But not enough wind, she realized, when he grabbed her by the waistband of her jeans and hauled her backward.

Renee clung ferociously to the steering wheel. "Let me *go!*"

"Not this time," Leandro said. He peeled her fingers away from the wheel and dragged her out of the car. "You and me got a score to settle."

Renee twisted left and right, kicking and screaming. She knocked an elbow into his ribs and stomped on his toes. Nothing. It was like whacking an elephant with a fly-swatter. He dragged her backward, his arm clamped around her chest. She twisted and fought, clawing at his arm and screaming, knowing the instant he got her into his car she wouldn't stand a chance of getting out.

And then he let her go.

Suddenly and unexpectedly free, Renee spun around to discover that Leandro hadn't released her out of the goodness of his heart. An arm was wrapped around his neck. An arm that belonged to a certain police officer who was no longer sleeping like a baby.

The look of shock on Leandro's face quickly gave way to one of those ugly snarls generally reserved for championship wrestlers. He slammed an elbow into John's ribs. John sucked in a sharp, painful breath and fell away, leaving Leandro free to wheel around and land a solid blow to his face with his doubled-up fist. John recoiled, then countered with a right hook that smashed Leandro's nose, spun him around, and sent him face-first into the dirt. When he hit the ground with a howl of pain and a string of four-letter words, Renee decided she'd seen enough of round one. It was time she headed out.

She leaped into the Explorer, knocking her shoes into the passenger seat, thanking her lucky stars that she'd had the foresight to hang on to the car keys. She clicked the door locks, then started the engine. She glanced back to see that John had evidently paid attention in cop school, because he'd leaped on top of Leandro, his knee between his shoulders and his hand clamped around the back of his neck, shoving his already mangled nose even deeper into the dirt. Leandro squirmed beneath him like a squashed bug. It was a beautiful sight, and under normal circumstances she'd have paid dearly to have a ringside seat. Unfortunately, she had more pressing things to attend to, like getting the hell out of there.

She backed the car around in a semicircle, ignoring her conscience, which was screaming at the top of its imaginary lungs. It was reminding her that the only reason John had come to her rescue was because he undoubtedly believed Leandro was her abusive boyfriend. He was trying to protect her, and she was thanking him by stealing his car.

*No. Not stealing. Borrowing.*

She hit the accelerator and sped down the dark, forest-lined road, intending to put as many miles between her and that cabin as she possibly could. Sooner or later the insane bounty hunter and the enraged cop would stop beating each other senseless and compare notes, and the minute they did, they'd stop going after each other and start coming after her.

Even though John had managed to maneuver himself into a superior position, he wasn't at all sure he had King Kong under control. The guy was rumbling beneath him like a volcano ready to blow.

"Let me *up*, you bastard!"

John felt a little dizzy from the blow the guy had given him to his face, but finally he managed to catch a good, solid breath and inched his knee farther up the guy's back.

"Police officer!" he shouted. "And you're staying *down!*"

The guy went still beneath him. "A cop? You're a *cop?*"

John felt a flush of satisfaction. A certain abusive boyfriend hadn't counted on the law showing up, now, had he?

"You're a *cop*, and you let her get away?"

John froze. *Let her get away?*

"I'm a bounty hunter, you idiot! She's worth a bundle, and you went and screwed it up!"

The guy's words were a little muffled,

since he was still eating dirt, but John could have sworn he said he was a bounty hunter. If he was telling the truth, that meant . . . *Oh, God.*

"Alice is a bail jumper?"

"Alice, my ass. Her name is Renee Esterhaus. She's wanted for armed robbery. And I'd be taking her back to Tolosa right now if you hadn't decided to play Lone Ranger!"

Armed robbery? That pretty little blonde with those big blue eyes? John was paralyzed with disbelief. He'd seen a lot of non sequiturs as a cop, but that topped them all. "No way."

"She got caught with the loot and the weapon, and the convenience-store clerk — who, by the way, she shot and wounded — nailed her in a lineup."

"She shot somebody?"

"Flesh wound. But she didn't think twice about pulling the trigger."

John rose just enough to yank the guy's wallet out of his hip pocket. He flipped it open. *Max Leandro. Bail Enforcement Officer.*

"There," Leandro said. "Satisfied? Now, will you get the fuck off me?"

John got up. Leandro scrambled to his feet, his hand hovering over his bleeding nose. He yanked his wallet out of John's hand and shoved it back into his hip pocket. "Nice piece of police work, ace. While you were busy beating the hell out of me, *she* took off with your car."

John whipped his head around. His car was nowhere in sight. He stared down the road, unable to believe what had just happened. He'd gone after Leandro, thinking he was her boyfriend, trying to *protect* her, for God's sake, and while he was busy playing dueling credentials with a two-bit bounty hunter, Alice — Renee — had made off with his car.

His shock gave way to anger, which rapidly transformed into a burning desire to get his hands on the woman who hadn't uttered a truthful word since the moment she walked into that diner. The woman who'd robbed a convenience store, shot a clerk, skipped bail, then baited a cop and a thousand-pound gorilla into beating each other senseless.

And made the cop look like a fool.

"Stay here." John shot into the cabin and grabbed his weapon and his wallet. He ran back to Leandro. "Give me your keys."

"My keys? I'm not giving you —"

"I'm going after my car. Where are your keys?"

"No way. If you take her in, I lose the bounty."

"You can have her. As long as I get my car back."

Leandro just glared at him.

"Give me your keys! *Now!*"

Leandro reluctantly slapped the keys into John's hand, and John raced toward the car with Leandro hurrying along behind him. As John slid into the driver's seat, a sharp, acrid smell hit his nose. He spun around and glanced into the backseat. It looked like the inside of a garbage incinerator. "Holy shit."

"She's a lunatic." Leandro slammed the passenger door, then hunched down in the seat, grabbing a wad of napkins from the floorboard and pressing it to his bleeding nose. "A fucking lunatic."

All at once it dawned on John what must have happened. "She torched your car?"

"Shut up," Leandro muttered. "Just shut up."

Then John realized this was the smoking vehicle he'd seen pulling into Harley's place. So that was how Renee had gotten away from Leandro. Good God — was there *anything* she wouldn't do?

John started the car, stomped the accelerator, and headed down the dirt road, the headlights slashing through the night. He went as fast as he dared on the winding road, wheeling the car left and right through the dense forest, searching the road ahead for the red glare of taillights. She couldn't have gotten more than a three-minute head start, but he saw nothing but blackness ahead.

"Shit," Leandro said. "Where is she?"

"I don't know. We should have caught up to her by now."

"Step on it, will you?"

"You want me to wrap this heap around a tree?"

"I want you to get my bail jumper!"

"I'm going as fast as I can!"

Leandro made a scoffing noise, then swapped one blood-drenched napkin for another. "So tell me," he said, a mocking tone creeping into his voice. "She obviously didn't let on who she really was, so what did she do to get you to take her away from that diner? Make you an offer you couldn't refuse?"

When John didn't respond, Leandro's face twisted into a speculative sneer. "The old in-and-out, I bet. Was that it?"

John fumed silently, feeling every bit as gullible as Leandro was making him out to be. She wouldn't be the first woman who'd offered him her body to stay out of jail. But it was the first time he'd taken the bait.

"Not that I can blame you for taking her up on it," Leandro went on. "I mean, that's one hot little body she's got, right?" He seemed to ponder that for a moment. "You know, I don't get chicks jumping bail very often. I bet most of them would do just about anything to keep from going to jail."

John imagined the revolting acts a guy like Leandro might expect in return for such a favor, and his hands tightened against the steering wheel.

"Come to think of it, she's just the kind of woman I'd like to get my hands on. Blond hair, blue eyes, nice little ass . . . and how about those lips?" Leandro gave a low whistle. "I knew a girl once who had lips like that. I swear, she could suck the cap right off a beer bottle. By the time she got through with you, you felt like you'd been hit by a Mack truck. Yeah, it might just be worth giving up the money just to see those pretty little lips of hers wrapped around my —"

John slammed on the brakes. Leandro lurched forward, almost going through the windshield and doing his nose in once and for all. When the car ground to a halt, the equal and opposite reaction sent him whiplashing back against the headrest. In the next instant, John took a fistful of his grimy shirt and yanked him halfway over the console. The very thought of Leandro getting within leering distance of Renee made his blood boil.

"If you so much as lay a hand on her, I swear to God I'll arrest you for rape. You got that?"

Leandro's face eased into a cocky smile. "Yeah, Officer. I've got it. It's okay for cops to do the nasty with pretty little fugitives, but bounty hunters gotta be hands-off. Is that right?"

"I didn't know she was a fugitive. And I didn't *do* anything with her! And you're not going to, either!"

Leandro rolled his eyes with disgust. "Shit! Can't a guy think out loud? Do you really think I'd trade that kind of money to get laid only *once?*"

John pushed Leandro away with disgust, only it wasn't just Leandro he was disgusted with. What was the matter with him? Why in the world did he give a damn about Renee Esterhaus? She wasn't a victim, and it was about time he got that through his head, no matter how sweet and innocent she looked. She was an armed robber who hadn't thought twice about putting a bullet in a store clerk. And she was a car thief. A criminal, plain and simple. If she hadn't been robbing convenience stores, she wouldn't be on the run, and Leandro wouldn't be fantasizing about grabbing a little recreation on the side. It was her own fault she was in this mess, and it was time she paid the consequences.

John stomped the accelerator again, and a few minutes later they emerged from the dense woods, reaching the two-lane highway a mile or two down the road from Harley's place. The road was deserted, with no sign of Renee. And John had no idea which way she might have gone.

They were at a dead end. If he kept searching, he could flounder around the countryside going one direction while she'd taken off the other way. He would have much preferred to find her himself so he could take his car back rather than going through all the administrative crap of reporting and reclaiming a stolen vehicle, but it didn't look as if that was going to happen. "Damn," John muttered. "She could be anywhere by now. Do you have any idea where she was heading when you grabbed her?"

"New Orleans."

"Then she's probably heading there now. I'm going to call the local cops, then the highway patrol. With a description of my car, they'll pick her up."

"Oh, that's a great plan, ace. You get your car back, but I lose the bounty because the cops grabbed her instead of me."

"Those are the breaks, buddy."

"This is your fault. We'd already have her in custody if you hadn't jacked around getting out of the woods."

"I was doing fifty on a gravel road!"

"Well, she must have been doing sixty, because I don't see her anywhere. How about you, ace? Do you see her anywhere?" Leandro snorted. "Guess you didn't bother to show up that day at the academy when they covered vehicular pursuit."

A hundred nasty retorts flooded John's mind, and he bit his tongue to keep from lashing out. Why waste time bickering with this guy, when Renee was his real target? Hell, it was probably a good thing he hadn't caught up to her. If he'd gotten exiled to the backwoods of Texas for punching out a paper-towel dispenser, he could only imagine what Daniels would do to him if he went for the throat of a certain conniving little fugitive.

Leandro looked down at the blood-soaked napkins he held, and when the blood kept coming, he flipped on the dome light and pulled down the mirror on the sun visor. A look of horror spread over his re-arranged face, and he let out an agonized groan.

"You son of a bitch! You broke my nose!"

John really didn't see the big deal. What was a crooked nose when it had to live on a face like that? "It'll heal."

"Heal? How? Half my face is on the other half of my face!"

John had no patience with Leandro's whining. Not when he could feel his own face swelling to massive proportions.

"I'm gonna press charges," Leandro went on. "Police brutality. When a jury sees how you've disfigured me, you'll be history!"

John had news for Leandro. Mother Nature had beaten him to the disfiguring thing.

"There's a hospital in Winslow," Leandro said. "Take me there."

"Oh, for God's sake —"

"I'll see a doctor; you call the cops."

John drew a long breath and let it out slowly, wondering how in the hell this had happened. Somehow, in the span of only a few hours, he'd gone from the promise of having hot sex with a beautiful woman to trading insults with the ugliest man on earth. With a sigh of disgusted resignation, he put the car in gear, turned onto the two-lane highway, and headed west toward Winslow.

Renee brought John's Explorer to a halt in a McDonald's parking lot at the corner of Fourth and Taylor in Winslow, her heart still beating like crazy. All the way out of that forest, she'd expected to see headlights in her rearview mirror, but since she hadn't, she could only assume that John and Leandro had no idea which way she'd gone.

The car idled softly. She took a deep, cleansing breath, extricated her clenched hands from the steering wheel, and dropped them to her lap. She pushed the jazz tape back into the tape player, trying to calm herself further so she could think. It looked as if she'd bought herself a little time, but now what?

*Okay.* Priority number one was to ditch John's car, because if he couldn't find her, she was sure his next step would be to call the local cops and report his car stolen. But she had to have some kind of plan before she could give up this car, somewhere to go or some other means of transportation to put as many miles between herself and this town as she could.

What she wanted to do was go back to

that motel Leandro had grabbed her from, get her belongings, then wait there until tomorrow morning so she could get her car. But if Leandro figured out she'd headed back there, she'd be a sitting duck again.

Maybe she should go to the bus station. The money she'd taken from John would probably buy her a ticket to New Orleans. She had no means to disguise herself, though, and John would probably check with the bus station. He could have the highway patrol grab her before the bus hit the Louisiana border.

She decided the worst thing she could do was get on the freeway and head for New Orleans. She'd be way too easy to spot. She squeezed her eyes closed, fighting tears. How in the world had she gotten herself into this mess? She was tired and hungry and scared to death, and she just couldn't think.

Then the aroma of burgers and fries wafted through the car.

*Food.*

Her mouth instantly watered, and it didn't take long for the food-deprived part of her brain to convince the self-preservation part that she should do the rest of her thinking in the drive-through line. She put the car in gear and came up behind a red minivan crammed to capacity with a group of teenagers.

After a moment the line advanced, and the minivan moved to the speaker to place an order. Renee inched the Explorer forward and waited. Two other cars pulled into the line behind her.

Her gaze settled on John's cell phone. She thought of her friend Paula, who was probably the only person on the planet who actually believed she was innocent, and all at once she felt so alone she wanted to cry.

On impulse, she picked up the phone and dialed Paula's number. It rang once, twice. When the line finally clicked and she heard her friend's voice, Renee closed her eyes with relief.

"Paula. It's me."

Paula gasped. "Renee! My God! Where are you? Still at that motel? Is your car fixed?"

"No. The most awful thing happened. A bounty hunter tried to bring me back to Tolosa. A big, ugly monster —"

Paula gasped. "He found you?"

Renee froze. "Huh?"

"A big bald guy, tattoos, looks like a pro wrestler?"

"Yeah . . . ?"

"He was here. He came to my apartment looking for you."

"How did he know to talk to you?"

"I don't know. I think he came poking around our apartment building. Somebody must have told him we were friends."

"And you told him I was at that motel?"

"No! Of course not! I have no idea how he found you!"

"Did you tell *anyone* where I was?"

Paula paused. "Well, only Tom —"

"Tom? You told *Tom?*"

"He didn't tell the guy where you were! I swear! He'd never do anything to hurt you!"

Renee wanted to scream. Ever since Paula had first laid eyes on Tom, she'd been blinded by his blond, surfer-boy good looks and failed to notice that he went through women like most men went through a six-pack. She had also failed to notice that he hadn't bothered to repay the two thousand dollars she'd loaned him when he'd been out of a job last summer.

In contrast to Tom, Paula was cute but ordinary-looking, with dark hair, a pixie face, and about fifteen extra pounds she couldn't seem to get rid of, one of those girls who people always said had a nice personality because physically she was a little lacking. She really *did* have a nice personality, though, and about a thousand other fabulous qualities, and any decent guy would be lucky to have her. But she didn't believe that about herself and always got stuck with guys who were losers. Tom just happened to be a very good-looking loser, and a *very* smooth liar. And sooner or later he was going to break her heart.

"Tom likes you," Paula went on. "He doesn't understand why you don't like him. *I* don't understand why you don't like him."

"Because he cheats on you, Paula! Get a clue, will you?"

"Tom says that has to be some kind of misunderstanding, that maybe you were mistaken —"

"Mistaken about the parade of women I've seen coming in and out of his apartment at all hours of the night? I'm *mistaken* about that? I swear to God, Paula —"

Renee took a deep breath. Good Lord. This was hardly the time or place to discuss Paula's love life.

"I'm sorry, Paula. Really. I've got no right to go on at you like that."

"It's okay, sweetie. You're under a little pressure. That's all. Tom didn't tell that guy where you were. Trust me on that, will you?"

Renee sighed heavily. Maybe Paula was right. Maybe Leandro just had a sixth sense or something, like some kind of bloodhound from hell.

"So how did you get away from him?" Paula asked.

Renee squeezed her eyes closed at the memory of her foray into arson. "Never mind. I managed to ditch him, though, and now I'm driving this cop's car —"

"You're driving a police car?"

"No. His own car. He doesn't know I borrowed it, so I've got to ditch it in a hurry, just in case he —"

"Hold on a minute. Tell me more about this cop."

Renee sighed. *He's drop-dead gorgeous and one hell of a kisser. And if he gets his hands on me again, I'm a dead woman.*

"I'll tell you about him later. But right now . . . right now I just wanted to . . ." Tears welled up in her eyes. "I guess I just wanted to hear a friendly voice."

"So where are you going now? Still to New —" Paula stopped suddenly. "No — don't tell me. Somebody could have my phone bugged." She gasped. "Maybe that's how that guy found out where you were. You called me from that motel, you know."

Renee hadn't even considered that. "Do you think that's how he found me? Oh, God — could someone trace this call?"

"I don't know. Maybe you'd better go. Call me again when you think it's safe, will you? Let me know you're all right?"

"Yeah. Okay. I will."

Paula hung up. Renee held the phone to her ear for a moment, listening to the dial tone. Then she laid down the phone, and her eyes filled with tears again. Even if she got to New Orleans without anyone knowing, even if she assumed a new identity, even if she got a job, met a nice man, got married, and put together some semblance of a life, it would still be a lie.

And she'd still be a fugitive.

A hollow, empty feeling that had nothing to do with hunger settled in the pit of her stomach. It had been so damned hard to finally accept herself as a decent person, after being told by her alcoholic mother her entire childhood that she was a worthless human being. She'd lived up to that assessment for so much of her life that turning herself around had been a struggle unlike any other.

But slowly, over time, she'd built a life in Tolosa, a life she never thought she'd have when she was growing up, a solid, respectable life with a good job, good friends, a decent place to live, and the ability to look people in the eye and not be afraid of what they saw when they looked back at her.

And now it was over.

121

Paula Merani set the phone back down on the table and rested her head against the back of the sofa. She had no idea what was going on with Renee, only that it sounded bad, and she sounded upset. She felt so helpless sitting here, unable to do anything to make things right.

"That was Renee, wasn't it?"

Paula spun around to see Tom standing at the doorway, his hand on the door frame above his head. He wore nothing but a pair of ragged Levi's slung low on his hips, and it didn't matter if nuclear war had been declared, Paula would have stopped to stare. He was tall, with lean, fluid muscles, green eyes, and flaxen hair that glinted like gold.

"Oh, Tom, Renee had a run-in with that awful man! The one who was here last night!"

"The bounty hunter?"

"Yeah. I don't know how he found her, but he did. Somehow she managed to get away from him, but I'm not sure what's happening now." She sighed. "If only there were some way to know who really committed that robbery, she could come home again."

"I don't think that's ever going to happen."

"You do believe she's innocent, don't you?"

"Of course I do. But the evidence is pretty strong against her."

Paula knew what he meant. If Renee went to trial, she probably didn't stand a chance. But Paula didn't want to hear that. She wanted to ignore the truth and believe that somehow everything was going to work out.

"Where is she now?" Tom asked. "Still at that motel?"

"No. But I don't know what's happening. All I know is that she sounded so *upset.*"

Tom brushed a stray strand of dark hair away from her cheek, then pulled her over to lay her head against his shoulder. She had to pinch herself every day to believe that a man as gorgeous as Tom was interested in her. In high school she'd always been the girl who'd been everybody's best buddy and nobody's girlfriend, and guys like Tom had never given her a second look.

Paula didn't know why Renee didn't like him, aside from her misconception about the other women she thought he was seeing. He was nothing like his cousin, Steve, but she didn't think Renee had ever believed that.

Nine months ago, Tom and Steve had moved into an apartment down the hall from Renee. Until a few months before that, they'd played in a band together. They'd finally realized that the local clubs in Tolosa, Texas, were about as far as their act was likely to go, and they'd broken up. Tom had gotten a job and headed for junior college, but Steve had stayed around the club scene, getting DJ gigs at various clubs and gambling most of his paycheck away.

Then Renee had a party and invited them both. At least half a dozen women in the room that night had their eyes on Tom, but Paula was the one he'd invited back to his apartment. He'd played his guitar for her, singing dumb love songs with that incredible tenor voice of his. If she hadn't already fallen for him, that would have cinched it.

Renee and Steve had started to date about that time, too. They broke up within a few months, but Paula's relationship with Tom only grew stronger. For a long time she waited for the ax to fall, for Tom to wise up and realize he was dating a woman who was ordinary when he could have one who was extraordinary. But he hadn't. And now, several months later, she was finally starting to take his word that he really did love her.

Tom had aspirations for something better, even if Steve didn't. Why couldn't Renee see that? Sure, Tom had had a few months of unemployment when she'd helped him out financially, but since he was in college and working toward something better, she'd done it gladly. He'd pay her back some day. After all, they were in love with each other, weren't they?

"Tom?"

"Yes?"

"Have you thought any more about moving in here? If you give up your apartment, you'll save hundreds every month. I know it's hard for you to make the rent ever since Steve moved out."

"No. I know it would be cheaper to give up my apartment, but I just can't do that." He shook his head. "Damn. I *hate* owing you money. I'm just — I'm just having a hard time getting back on my feet again. That's all."

"It's okay. I know you'll pay me back when you can."

"I have this feeling that I might be coming into some money pretty soon. And when I do —"

"I told you not to worry about it. I'll help you as long as you need it."

Tom wrapped his arms around her and pulled her to him, kissing her hair, then hugging her tightly. "Paula?"

"Yes?"

"Do you love me?"

She pulled away and stared at him. "What kind of a silly question is that? Of course I love you!"

"Renee doesn't like me. I'm afraid someday you're going to listen to her."

"She just doesn't know you like I do. That's all."

"But you don't know everything about me," he said, a funny, faraway look on his face. "You might not love me if you did."

"There isn't anything you could do that would change the way I feel about you."

"I know you think that now, but . . ." Tom let out a nervous breath. "There's something I really ought to tell you."

In spite of all his professions of love, Paula had a feeling of foreboding. This was it. She was sure of it. This was the part where he was going to say, *It's been fun, but now it's over. You didn't really think it would be forever, did you?*

"Tom," she said. "Tell me the truth. Please. You're not seeing another woman, are you?"

"Of course not!" He took her face in his hands and fixed his gaze on hers. "Renee is wrong about me. I swear she is. There's nobody but you, Paula. *Nobody.*"

"Then what is it?" Paula said.

He stared at her a long time, those green eyes exuding more power over her than a hypnotist's pendulum.

"Never mind," he said finally. "It's not important."

He kissed her, a sweet, tender kiss that soon evolved into something much deeper and more intimate. She slid her arms around his neck as he pressed her down to the sofa, astonished that in all these months the thrill of his touch had never faded.

Yes, he'd borrowed an awful lot of money from her, but he'd promised to pay it all back. Renee kept saying he was taking advantage of her, but Paula knew that wasn't his intent at all, and if she ever thought it was, it was simply her own insecurity showing. Tom would never do anything to hurt her.

Never.

When John pulled into the parking lot of the Winslow Medical Center, he wondered how the tiny building had the nerve to call itself a hospital. A facility like this generally specialized in treating cases of the flu and sprained ankles. Fortunately for Leandro, a broken nose might be just the kind of challenging case they were looking for.

John veered toward a pay phone in the lobby. As he dug through his pocket for change, he watched Leandro approach the reception window. The receptionist looked up, undoubtedly expecting to see a runny-nosed kid with a cold, or maybe a middle-aged guy with a beer belly and chest pain. She did not expect a bald, six-foot-five, hard-as-steel monster with a face that could make the devil himself run screaming into the night.

Leandro slid the window open, leaned in, and said something to the woman, and by the way her mouth dropped open and her eyes widened, he'd probably told her about some form of bodily damage he intended to inflict on her if he was forced to plant his butt in a waiting-room chair.

She turned and yelled at somebody in the back room. A fortyish Hispanic woman emerged. She had the world-weary look of one of those seasoned health-care professionals who could eat lunch over a severed leg and still want dessert. But when her gaze panned up to Leandro's face, even she looked a little woozy.

John plugged quarters into the pay phone, then watched as Leandro was escorted immediately into an exam room. Strangely enough, nobody in the waiting room seemed inclined to challenge the staff's triage decision.

John started to dial, then had a thought. It was a long shot, but there just might be a way to locate Renee without having to mess with the local cops. It was worth a try, anyway.

He dialed the number of his cell phone in his car.

The phone rang once. Twice. Then three times. This was a crapshoot, of course. Surely Renee wouldn't be dumb enough to —

*Click.*

"Hello?"

He couldn't believe it. She'd actually picked up the phone? Shaking off his surprise, he assumed the nastiest cop voice he could muster and went straight for her throat.

"Now get this straight, sweetheart," he said. "I've already reported my car stolen. Every cop in the area will have his eyes wide open and his weapon drawn, and seeing as how you're already a fugitive, they might not think twice about using them. Ever seen a pissed-off cop, Renee? I mean, really pissed? It's not a pretty sight. Especially out here in the middle of nowhere, where funding is slim and they don't have video cameras on their cars to record their every move like they do on those cop shows. I mean, who's to say you weren't resisting arrest? Are you following me, Renee?"

He paused for a reaction. He could hear her breathing hard, like a teenager in a horror flick right before the knife falls.

"I already ditched your car," she said finally, her voice choked. "I swear."

"And you're still carrying around my cell phone?"

Silence.

"You're a liar, Renee."

"No! Really! I'm not driving your car! I'll even tell you where I left it. You can go there yourself. It's about a mile down the highway from that diner we were at, on the side of the road, the opposite way from Winslow. That's where I left it, with the keys behind the left front tire. I'm not there anymore. I'm . . . somewhere else."

"I'm not buying this."

"And seeing as how I didn't have your car for more than twenty or thirty minutes, and seeing as how I gave it right back, surely you won't —"

"It's *grand theft auto!* Add that to your armed-robbery charge —"

"No! I just borrowed it!"

"Borrowed?"

"Yes! You practically gave me the keys!"

"Gave you . . . ?" John paced back and forth as far as the phone cord would allow, gesturing wildly. "I didn't give you anything!"

"Well, you didn't exactly give them to me, but they were lying right there on the counter in plain sight, weren't they?"

"So that gives you the right to steal my car?"

"*Borrow* your car," she explained. "*Borrow.*"

Astonished by her convoluted logic, John wanted to beat his head against the wall. Once he got hold of her, he'd do the world a favor. He'd wrap his hands around her neck and cut off the blood supply to her scheming, illogical brain. Before long she'd be nothing more than a harmless little vegetable who smiled a lot, looked really pretty, and didn't steal cars. His car in particular. That was what he'd do.

"Tell me where you are, Renee," he said. "Right now. Tell me where you are, or I'll have every cop, sheriff, sharpshooter, bloodhound, and SWAT team within a hundred miles breathing down your neck. *Do you understand?*"

All at once John heard a muffled crackle, followed by a loud, scratchy female voice.

"Welcome to McDonald's. May I take your order?"

A gasp.

*Click.*

John pulled the phone away from his ear, staring at it in dumb disbelief. Had he just heard what he thought he'd heard? A fast-food drive-in window? What kind of car-stealing fugitive stops for a Big Mac?

John slammed down the receiver, thinking fast. In the time that had elapsed since Renee had grabbed his car, she couldn't have made it to any other town besides Winslow. And in a dinky little town like this, how many McDonald's could there be? Surely not more than one. If he called the local guys right now, chances were they could pick her up before she could say "Supersize it." As he grabbed the phone again, though, something caught his eye across the street, maybe half a block down from the hospital.

Golden arches.

# chapter six

The speaker blared again as the woman re-peated her request for an order, but Renee's hunger had vanished in a cloud of sheer panic. Where was John? Twenty miles away? One mile away? Standing right behind her?

The only reason she'd picked up that stupid phone was because she thought it was possible that Paula got the cell phone number off caller ID and was calling her back for some reason. The last thing she ex-pected was to hear John's voice on the other end of the line.

She had to get out of here. Now.

Unfortunately, the minivan was in front of her, at least three cars had pulled in behind her, and a row of carefully pruned holly bushes sat between her and the parking lot. Her panic level took a quantum leap. How was she going to get out of here?

Then the minivan moved up to the window and Renee felt a rush of relief. But relief edged into panic again when the gum-cracking McTeenager at the window started handing food to the driver. Bags and bags of food. And Cokes. And ice-cream sundaes. And chocolate-chip cookies. Renee estimated that in the span of two minutes, enough food went into that van to feed a third-world nation.

Then the driver handed an open cardboard container back to the McTeenager, pointing out something about that particular hamburger that evidently wasn't right. Renee wanted to shout at him, *This is McDonald's, not Burger King! You can't have it your way!*

She gripped the steering wheel until her hands ached. Surely her sense of time was warped right now. This food transference couldn't actually be taking eons.

She leaned her head back against the headrest and closed her eyes, trying to get a grip. What were the odds of John's being anywhere near here? About a thousand to one? Even a hundred to one didn't sound so bad. All she had to do was hug the minivan's bumper, and the second it pulled out, she would, too. Everything was going to be okay. She took a deep, calming breath, then opened her eyes again.

John was coming across the street.

For a moment she sat there, frozen with

disbelief, like the time she'd whacked her finger with a hammer but it took a second or two to feel the pain. Then a big red *danger* sign flashed in her brain, and she slapped her palm against the Explorer's horn in one continuous blare, trying to get the kid to clear out.

He stuck his head out the window and glared at her. "Hey! Keep your shirt on, will you?"

At the same time, three long-haired girls — or maybe boys, she wasn't sure which — plastered themselves against the back window of the minivan and gaped at Renee as if she were some kind of mind-numbing video game.

And John was closing in on her fast.

Renee rolled the window down, stuck her head out, and yelled at the kid, "Move! Please move! *Please!*"

He ignored her, continuing to hog the drive-through as if time were not a factor here, as if the woman in the green Explorer behind him wasn't about to get mauled by one very large and very angry cop.

John leaped over a low hedge at the edge of the parking lot and strode toward her, his face a mask of unmitigated fury. On the verge of hysteria, Renee fingered the door handle, thinking about running. Then she thought again. John was bigger than she was, and certainly faster. She wouldn't stand a chance.

She hit the button to roll the window up, then flicked the door locks. John circled the minivan and headed for the driver's side of the Explorer, his teeth clenched, looking as if he were ready to explode. His left eye was practically swollen shut, surrounded by a Technicolor bruise that made half his face look like something out of a zombie movie.

*Ever see a pissed-off cop, Renee?*

*Oh, yeah.* Now she had.

John yanked at the Explorer's door handle. Finding it locked, hauled a gun from the waistband of his jeans and whipped it around until Renee was looking right down its barrel.

"Police! Put the car in park and turn off the engine!"

Renee gasped at the sight of the gun. She *hated* guns.

"I'm gonna blow a hole in this window!"

From the look on his face right now, she didn't doubt it. She didn't doubt he'd tear right through the door with his bare hands if that was what it took to get to her.

If only the kid in the car ahead of her had the good sense to get himself and his friends away from the raging wild man waving a gun around, Renee might have a shot at escape. But his gaze was glued to the spectacle John was creating as if he were watching an episode of *Cops*.

"Last chance, Renee!"

She was trapped. Maybe it was better to let him in than to have him claw his way in. He'd still mangle her, of course, but maybe he'd actually let her live. She shoved the gearshift into park.

"Unlock the door!"

Renee's finger hovered over the door lock.

"You're resisting arrest! Unlock the door or I'm breaking the glass! *Now!*"

Renee held her breath and flipped the automatic switch. All four locks shot up. John stuck his gun back into the waistband of his jeans and jerked the door open. He clamped his hand onto her arm, yanked her from the car, and spun her around.

"Hands on the car!"

"John, please —"

"Shut up and put your hands on the car!"

She placed her hands on the car like a common criminal, which was exactly what he thought she was. He patted her down, running his hands roughly over her waist, her hips, then down each of her legs. She had a flash of the fantasies she'd had about him less than an hour ago, and not one of them had involved him touching her like this.

"You know I'm not armed," she told him. "I don't have a gun. I hate guns. I don't even like the word —"

"Oh, yeah? The way I hear it, you shot a convenience-store clerk."

"It wasn't me!"

He spun her back around, took her by the upper arms, and pinned her against the car, glaring down at her with an expression that bordered on the homicidal.

"You're a lying, bail-jumping, car-stealing pyromaniac," he muttered. "I ought to —"

"I'm innocent! I didn't do what they say I did!"

"Innocent people don't run! And they sure as hell don't steal cars!"

"I was only borrowing it. Really. I —"

"You have a vocabulary problem, Renee. *Borrow* and *steal* are not the same thing. If I give you something, that's borrowing. You take my keys while I'm sleeping, that's stealing. Now get in the car!"

He shoved her through the driver's door, then got in after her. The minivan still sat in front of them, its occupants glued to the situation as if this were a commercial break and the action would pick up again any minute.

John laid on the horn. The kid's eyes flew open wide. He yanked his head back into the car, stomped the accelerator, and left the drive-through, apparently deciding that John's possession of a firearm gave extra weight to his honking. As John drove by the window, the teenage girl on duty looked as if she'd swallowed her Dubble Bubble.

"You should have told me you were a cop," Renee muttered.

"You should have told me you were a fugitive."

"I'm not a fugitive! I mean, I am, but it's only because —"

"Forget it. I don't want to hear it."

"Where are we going?"

"To give you back to Leandro."

Renee swallowed a gasp of sheer terror. Did he actually intend to throw her on the mercy of a madman? "But you're a cop. Don't you have priority, or seniority, or *something?*"

"Only if I want to exercise it. The minute the bondsman posted your bail, you signed your rights away. He can send anyone after you he wants. Leandro has the authority to bring you in, and since I've had all the fun I care to have for one night, I think I'll step aside and let him do it."

"Please, John! *Please* don't make me go back with him. He's so angry —"

"Why? Because you torched his car? Gee, I can't imagine why that would piss him off."

"You know what he's like. Don't make me go with him. He'll kill me. I swear he will!"

"He won't kill you. They stopped that 'dead or alive' thing about a hundred years ago."

"Please. I want you to take me back. *Please*."

"I said *he* wouldn't kill you. I didn't say I wouldn't."

Renee came within an inch of believing that. She had never witnessed anything like the hard, intense, "I wanna maim somebody" look John was giving her right now, and it was all the more frightening because *she* was that somebody.

"John. Please listen —"

"No. I'm way past listening. Especially when all I hear are lies."

"I'm sorry about that. But —"

"Sorry? *Sorry?* You lie to me, steal my car, and get me into a fight with a thousand-pound gorilla, and all you can say is you're *sorry?*"

That was when Renee knew that this was more than just your average cop-to-fugitive animosity. John was taking this personally. Very personally. She'd made him look like a fool, and there was no way he was ever going to forgive her for that.

A moment later he slowed the car, then swung into a hospital parking lot and came to a halt in a spot near the emergency-room door. Renee looked around questioningly.

"What are we doing here?"

"I told you. I'm giving you back to Leandro."

"He's here?"

"Only for as long as it takes them to shove his nose back into place."

"You actually broke his nose?"

"Yeah. It's standard operating procedure when you're protecting innocent young things from their abusive boyfriends."

Renee winced. If he'd intended to make her feel guilty, he'd succeeded.

John got out, circled the car, then dragged Renee out the other side. "I want you to behave in here," he said, hustling her toward the door of the emergency room. "You step one foot out of line, and I'll make whatever plans Leandro may have for retaliation look like a picnic in the park. Got that?"

Renee fought the irrational urge to yank her arm away and run. What would be the point? She'd never get away from him. She'd just be putting him in an even fouler mood than he was already in.

John dragged her into the waiting room and up to the glass window. A middle-aged Hispanic woman in Snoopy scrubs with a stethoscope dangling around her neck stood behind the glass, flipping through a chart.

John slid the window open with a *thunk* and flashed his badge. "Where's the guy who came in here a few minutes ago? Tall, smashed nose, ugly as sin?"

The woman eyed John's badge. "He's in the back."

"He needs to come to the front. Right now."

"Sorry. He's doped up."

"What?"

"He was complaining about pain, so I shot him up with Demerol. I've got a plastic surgeon on the way."

"Surgeon?" John said with disbelief. "He's having surgery?"

"Yeah. Whoever smacked him really did a number on him."

"When will he be released?"

"Sometime tomorrow."

John closed his eyes and muttered a curse.

Renee felt an enormous surge of relief, an emotion John clearly didn't share. He stuffed his badge back into his pocket with a harsh breath of frustration. "Well, that's just *great.*"

The doctor leaned toward John and dropped her voice. "He's not wanted, is he? Just between you and me, he has a face right off a post-office wall."

"No," John said wearily. "He's not wanted." Then he turned an accusing glare toward Renee, as if it were *her* fault that Leandro was out of commission.

"Pretty wicked-looking bruise you've got there," the doctor told John. "Does your smashed-up face have anything to do with that guy's broken nose?"

"You might say that."

"You want me to take a look at it? You could have an orbital fracture. I can get a facial series —"

"No. It's fine. Got any surgical tape?"

"Uh, yeah. Sure." The woman went to the back room, then returned with a roll of tape and handed it to John.

"Mind if I take this?" he asked.

"No. Go ahead."

John took Renee by the arm again and led her back toward his car.

"So," she said, with as much nonchalance

as she could muster, "I guess you're taking me back to Tolosa?"

He didn't respond. She took that as a yes.

When they reached his car, he pulled Renee's arms around in front of her, crossing one wrist over the other. Before she knew exactly what was happening, he'd wound the surgical tape four or five times around them.

"What are you doing?" she asked, horrified.

"I've got no handcuffs." He ripped the tape off and pressed down the loose end. "And I'm taking no chances."

Renee looked down at her bound wrists, and all at once the reality of the situation came crashing down on her. *How had this happened?* she asked herself for the thousandth time. How had she landed on the wrong side of the law again, when she'd put her heart and soul into becoming the kind of person who would *never* have to worry about being arrested?

As a teenager, she hadn't felt humiliated to be dragged to jail. All she'd felt was defiance, along with that hopeless feeling of not giving a damn because nobody else did, either. The indignity she felt right now was a result of the self-respect she'd managed to gain since then, and a philosophical person might say that her humiliation was a step in the right direction.

She wished she could tell John about the years she'd spent putting her past behind her. About how she'd suffered through demeaning, dead-end jobs just so she could pay her bills. About how she'd finally built a life for herself she was starting to be proud of, only to have it shatter into a million pieces.

She'd seen the man behind the badge. The man with a heart. The man who'd shown her compassion when he thought she'd been abused, then gone to war with Leandro when he thought she was in danger of being hurt again. That was the man she wanted to talk to now.

Slowly she lifted her gaze from her wrists and met John's eyes, but as he stared back at her, she saw that his anger had been replaced by an impassive, stony stare. His jaw was rigid, his eyes cold and unreadable, and that was when she knew. There was only one side of him she was going to see from now on: the cop side.

She held out her wrists. "Please don't do this. Please. I'll go quietly. I promise."

"Tell me some more lies."

"But John —"

"You want your mouth taped, too?"

"No, but —"

"Then I suggest you keep it shut."

He opened the car door and shoved her into the passenger side of the front seat, pushing her head down to clear the opening as she'd seen cops do when they were arresting people on *Real Stories of the Highway Patrol.* He slammed the door behind her. She settled back in the seat, her heart thumping in her chest in a relentless rhythm.

"We're going to the cabin so I can get my stuff," John told her. "Then it's nonstop back to Tolosa."

His words settled on her with heart-wrenching finality, and by the tough, uncompromising expression on his face, she knew she wouldn't be talking him out of this. He was going to deliver her to jail, then turn his back and walk away, believing he'd done his part to incarcerate a desperate criminal. She'd be shuttled through the system and eventually land in prison, sentenced to a life of despair and hopelessness for a crime she didn't commit.

It was official. Her life was over.

Twenty minutes later, John pulled up in front of the cabin, a feeling of déjà vu washing over him like an ocean wave at high tide. Only a few hours ago, he'd been in this very spot, primed for a night of hot sex with a beautiful woman. Now he was dragging that beautiful woman to jail.

*God, what a night.*

Actually, the more he thought about it, the more he decided this turn of events might work out pretty well. This would give him an excuse to return to Tolosa. He could tell Daniels he had had to cut his vacation short to bring in a fugitive. How could the lieutenant argue with that?

Fortunately, Renee had the good sense to keep her mouth shut on the way back to the cabin, because if she'd opened it up and started yapping again about how sorry she was and how she was innocent and all the rest of that crap, he probably would have gagged her, tossed her onto the roof of the car, and tied her to the luggage rack.

But instead of talking, she spent the whole time with her bound hands in her lap, running her fingernail back and forth along the seam of her jeans. And she was still doing it now, her blue eyes downcast, a strand of blond hair falling carelessly across her cheek. She looked so damned innocent that if he didn't know better, he'd think —

John killed the car engine, feeling like the biggest moron who'd ever walked the planet. She'd played him like a fiddle all night, only to start up the music again just by sitting there doing nothing at all.

He yanked the keys out of the ignition, then got out, circled the car, and opened Renee's door. He took hold of her arm and pulled her out of the car. The single flood-light down the path by the cabin door gave off enough light to softly illuminate her face, and when she turned her eyes up to meet his, all at once he felt as if he were manhandling a stray kitten.

*No. She's not innocent. There is absolutely nothing innocent about this woman.*

He flipped the locks, shut the car door, then took her by the arm and led her down the winding, wooded path toward the cabin. She let out a ragged sigh, and he felt as if he'd just *kicked* a stray kitten. *Damn.* This woman was driving him crazy. The quicker he got back to Tolosa, turned her in, and forgot he'd ever known her, the better off he was going to be.

All at once, Renee's head shot up. "What's that?"

"What's what?"

She stopped suddenly and listened. "That noise."

"Cut it out, Renee."

"I mean it!" she whispered, inching closer to John and scanning the darkened forest.

"Someone's out there!"

John stopped and listened, but by his skeptical expression, Renee could tell he thought she was lying. But she was sure she'd heard a rustle of dry pine needles, as if someone were walking through the trees.

John shook his head and started to lead her toward the cabin again, when the same sound filtered through the night air, this time louder. He whipped his head around, his gaze searching the forest, and she could tell he'd finally heard it, too. Slowly he drew his gun.

"Who is it?" she whispered.

"I don't know," John whispered back. "There shouldn't be anyone within ten miles of here."

Renee thought her heart was going to beat right out of her chest. She was sure someone — or some*thing* — was walking through the forest. Unfortunately, the risen moon had faded to a pale amber disk, making it hard for her to see what sharp-toothed animal or ax-wielding human was out there waiting for them.

John led her by the arm into the trees, stepping over a fallen log half-buried in pine needles, dodging a cluster of saplings. Every ounce of self-preservation she possessed told her not to go anywhere near the forest, but then she decided that sticking like glue to the guy with the gun was probably the best course of action under the circumstances.

"Sounds like someone walking through the brush," she whispered.

"Shhh . . ."

"Are we sure Leandro's still in Winslow?"

"Shut *up*, will you?"

John stopped and listened. Seconds passed, filled only by silence. "Hey!" he shouted. "Who's out there?"

Renee heard a mad crunch of pine needles practically at her feet. She looked down, and right in front of her, a pair of red, devil-like eyes glared up at her like a creature from the depths of hell.

With a strangled scream, she yanked her arm from John's grip, whipped around in a blinding one-eighty, and started to run.

"Renee! Stop!"

But her fight-or-flight instinct was in full swing, with the fight part not even an option. Then all at once her ankles hit something hard. She flew through the air, then fell facedown into the dirt, knocking the wind out of her lungs in one big whoosh.

"Renee! It's only an armadil—"

John never finished his sentence. Instead,

the same fallen log that had tripped her tripped him, and he fell in a sprawling heap only inches to her left, letting out a muffled "Oof."

In the span of a single heartbeat, Renee came to two important conclusions: one, she'd just run screaming from one of God's more benign creatures — an armadillo — and two, her way out of a prison sentence lay in a pile of pine needles only a couple of feet beyond her hands.

John's gun.

Without even thinking, she pushed herself to her knees, then lunged for the weapon. She grabbed the gun with her right hand, which was bound beneath her left one, then did a fireman's roll to her right before rising to a sitting position. To John's credit, he was already on his knees, but she'd been quicker in zeroing in on the gun. It felt heavy and dangerous, but despite the awkward position of her hands she clung to it tenaciously, determined not to give in to her gut instinct and run screaming from it, too.

John sat back on his heels, breathing hard. "Give me the gun, Renee."

"No way." Renee got to her feet, her gaze never leaving his.

"There's a big price to pay for shooting a

cop," he told her, easing to his feet at the same time.

"I don't want to hurt you. I just want your car." Assuming, of course, that she could drive with one hand crossed over the other and bound with surgical tape.

"Give me your keys," she said.

He paused for a moment, then methodically reached into his pocket and extracted the keys.

"Throw them down and back away."

He did what she told him to, but even in the near-darkness of the forest, his cold, calculating expression unnerved her. She could almost see his mind working as he formulated a plan to get the upper hand again. He backed away two steps, then three.

"Keep going," she told him, and waited until he was far enough away that when she dipped the barrel of the gun down to pick up the keys, he wouldn't be within tackling distance. Once she was satisfied he posed no immediate threat, she knelt carefully and snagged the keys with her left hand.

She started to back through the trees toward the Explorer, the gun still trained on him. But to her dismay, for every step she took backward, he took one step forward.

"No!" she shouted. "Stay there!"

He kept walking, slowly and steadily. "How many crimes do you plan on committing tonight, Renee?"

"Crimes? I haven't committed —"

He was right. She couldn't exactly quote the statute, but holding a gun on a cop was most certainly a crime, and an even bigger one, she imagined, when the gun was his. Add that to bail jumping, fire starting, car stealing . . . *Good Lord.* How had she gotten herself into this mess when she'd never intended to step on the wrong side of the law again?

"Tell you what," John said, his voice low and even. "Why don't we just pretend this never happened? I'll take you back to Tolosa, and if it turns out you're innocent of the robbery, I'll forget about your stealing my car. I'll forget about your taking my gun. But I gotta tell you — if you shoot me, I'm afraid I'm going to have a pretty hard time forgetting that."

It was a tempting offer. But no matter how reasonable his suggestion sounded, with all the evidence against her, sooner or later she'd be facing a prison sentence. Just the thought of incarceration made her hands shake as if she had some kind of neurological disorder. She took a deep breath, trying to get a grip. Then tears welled up behind her eyes, and she shook even harder. *No, no, no!*

She blinked quickly, but she couldn't stop the tears. She wiped her face against her shoulder, trying to clear her blurry vision. She couldn't fall apart now. Not when she was only a few feet away from freedom.

John held up his palm, still inching toward her. "Now, sweetheart, if you're not careful, you're going to accidentally pull that trigger, and I think you're going to be real sorry you shot me. Isn't that right?"

She was still five yards or so from the car, but all at once she could tell she wasn't going to make it. John was advancing closer with every step, and the minute she had to turn the gun down and away from him to unlock the car door with her left hand, he'd be on her. She had to stop him.

"Don't come any closer, John! I mean it!"

He held out his hand. "Give me the gun. Just hand it over, and I'll forget all about this."

"Oh, yeah. Sure you will!"

"I give you my word, Renee. I'll pretend tonight never happened. But I have to take you back to Tolosa. If I told you anything else, you'd know I was lying, right?"

Renee looked at him warily. He'd probably learned all kinds of negotiating skills in cop school, all of which were designed to keep him from getting shot and make sure she ended up in custody. So how was she to know what was the truth and what wasn't?

"Besides," he went on, "you say you're innocent. If that's true, you don't have anything to worry about."

"Come on, John! With all the evidence against me, they'll just go through the motions. They'll toss me in jail and throw away the key!"

"You'll get a fair trial."

"Oh, give me a break! Do you really believe that?"

"I'm a cop, Renee. What do you think I believe?"

"You didn't answer my question!"

John stared at her, his breath fogging the cold night air. "Of course I think you'll get a fair trial," he said finally, but his response came a bit too late to be believable. She hated the way he was patronizing her. She hated the fact that he thought she was a criminal. And above all, she hated the fact that he was trying to act as though he had her best interests at heart when all he really wanted to do was see her behind bars.

John held out his hand again. "The gun, Renee."

"No! I'm not going to prison for a crime I didn't commit!"

*Prison.*

All at once she was assaulted by the memory of the "scared straight" program she'd been through as a teenager. The harsh, mocking voices of a dozen female inmates pounded inside her head.

*You'll love the food here, blondie. Maggots are one of the four major food groups.*

*Hey, baby, whatcha think of my dress? Pretty snazzy, huh? Get yourself locked up and you can have one just like it.*

*See this scar? Knife's a wicked thing. Didn't even see it comin'.*

*Whatsa matter, chickie? Don't cry. You'll have plenty of friends in here. We'll even introduce you to Big Maude. She just* loves *pretty little blondes like you.*

Renee's stomach churned. The memory of those terrible hours swirled around in her mind like a scene from a horror movie. She couldn't do it. If she let John take her back to Tolosa, her life would become a living nightmare.

The gun felt heavy in her hand, straining the muscles of her forearms until she desperately wanted to drop it. But she couldn't. The weapon she held was the only thing standing between her and incarceration.

She took a deep breath and closed her finger around the trigger.

"I can't let you take me to jail," she said, her voice shaking so badly she could barely speak. "I-I have to stop you somehow. I have to."

She raised the barrel of the gun a notch. John's eyes widened and he held up both palms. "Now, Renee . . ."

She'd never fired a gun before, so she didn't know how it was going to feel. It would be loud, and it would probably knock her right off her feet, so she braced herself, preparing for the worst. She couldn't say John looked panicked, exactly, but there was an unmistakable flash of apprehension in his eyes.

"Take it easy, Renee. Think about what you're doing."

No. She'd thought enough. It was time for action.

"I'm sorry, John."

She took a deep breath, zeroed in on her target, closed her eyes . . . and pulled the trigger.

# chapter seven

"You shot my car?"

John watched, dumbfounded, as anti-freeze-tinged water glugged out of a bullet-sized hole in his radiator.

*"You shot my car?"*

Renee stared down at the gun in her hand. "Uh . . . yeah. I guess I did."

In a fit of angry frustration, John did what he should have done the moment she got her hands on his weapon: he strode over and yanked it right out of her hand.

"What have you got against cars?" he shouted, stuffing the gun into the waistband of his jeans. "You torch one, you shoot another. What's next? A hangman's noose? The guillotine?"

Renee took a tentative step forward, peering at the bullet hole. "I got the radiator, right? Can a car run without one of those?"

"Sure it can! As long as you don't mind overheating the engine and cracking the block!"

158

"Cracking the block. That's bad?"

"About two thousand dollars' worth of bad!"

"So it wouldn't be a good thing to drive the car when the radiator is, well . . . shot."

All at once he understood. So that was why she'd done it. Instead of disabling the cop, she'd disabled his car.

John didn't know how much more of this he could take. He had five shots left, but it would take only one to solve all his problems. After dumping her body into the lake, he could get a good night's sleep, wake to a bright, sunshiny morning, call the auto club, get his radiator fixed, then proceed with his life as if he'd never set eyes on Renee Esterhaus. And she'd spend the rest of eternity making Satan sorry he'd ever bargained for her soul.

*Okay.* So it was just a fantasy. But at least he could do the auto-club part. He took the keys from Renee, then grabbed his cell phone from the car. He flipped it on.

Nothing.

He stared at it dumbly for a moment, then looked back at Renee with an accusing stare.

"Okay, so I made a call."

"I don't give a damn about the call! You left the phone on and ran down the battery!"

A look of sudden understanding came over her face, and her gaze turned speculative. "You can charge it again, can't you? You have your charger, right?"

When he kept on glaring, a subtle yet distinct wave of relief passed over her face that said it all: *I shot your car. I took out your communications. We're not going anywhere, now, are we?*

John tossed the cell phone back into the car and slammed the door, furious with Renee, but even more furious with himself. He was a cop, for God's sake. He'd arrested some of the vilest, most evil people who'd ever drawn breath, yet he couldn't manage to outwit a woman half his size who clearly had a screw loose.

"You think you're real smart, don't you?" he told her. "Well, you're not. You've only delayed the inevitable. If we can't drive out of here, we'll walk. First thing in the morning." He took a few threatening steps toward her, backing her against his car. "And you'll behave yourself every step of the way, or I'll make you wish to God you had."

His words were intended to instill in her a heaping dose of fear and respect. Instead she gave him a stony stare that would have put Medusa to shame. "Well. We'll just see about that."

Her go-to-hell attitude astonished him. She acted as if she were the one being wronged here. As if she didn't belong behind bars. As if he were the absolute scum of the earth for suggesting she not resist arrest.

He gave her a warning stare. "Don't mess with me, Renee."

She stood up straight and pushed herself away from his car, bumping him off balance and forcing him to take a step backward.

"I am *not* an armed robber. I am *not* a car thief. And I don't care what I have to do — I am *not* going to jail!"

Her gaze bored into him, those blue eyes hot with anger. Strangely enough, the hairs on the back of his neck stood up, and he felt that familiar little heart skip that had become his body's way of telling him he'd better watch his back.

*That's crap,* he told himself in the next instant, furious that he'd let her rattle him, even for a moment. "Oh, no. You are going to jail, even if I have to use my last breath to drag you there!"

"Then get your last breath ready, buster. You're going to need it!"

She elbowed past him and started down the path, and John had to fight his gut reaction to reach out and yank her right back around again. What good would it do? Did he really think the bone-rattling shake he wanted to give her would dislodge that smart-ass attitude?

She reached the cabin, fumbled the door open with her bound hands, then went inside and slammed the door behind her. The noise rocketed through the silence of the forest, tripping his anger one more time, and he spewed a string of curse words so virulent the pine trees wilted. What in the hell had he done to deserve all this?

He looked at his wounded radiator. It was going to cost him hundreds of dollars to get it fixed, and it would take him hundreds of years to get reimbursement for the damages. He looked at the dark clouds that obscured the moon and threatened rain, thinking about the miles of dirt road they had to navigate tomorrow on foot. Then he looked back at the cabin. What other tricks did Renee have up her sleeve that would make him wish he'd never been born?

He sighed. Tomorrow was going to be one hell of a day.

Renee never imagined that merely walking along a calm, wooded road could be such an excruciating experience.

The forest was nice enough. In fact, in the

daylight it was downright picturesque. Streaks of bright morning sun shot through the canopy of pine trees, casting cool shadows on the forest floor. Birds were chirping tentatively, as if they weren't quite sure it was safe to venture out again after last night's rain. It was a fairy-tale forest. A weekend-in-the-country forest. A forest this quaint and charming should have a yellow-brick road winding through it, with Dorothy and company skipping along, full of optimistic good cheer as they headed for the Emerald City.

Instead, rain had turned the road into a potholed mud bath, Renee wasn't the least bit optimistic, and she was headed for jail. And Dorothy had a whole lot more congenial company than the man who was slogging through the mud beside her right now. John wore a scowl that had become a permanent part of his face, and he threw off so much negative energy that he practically blew her off the road.

He'd fallen asleep last night before she had, leaving her to shiver in the dark with her bound hands tied to the frame of the sofa bed with a length of twine he'd found in a kitchen cabinet. She'd stared at him in the light of the dying fire, mad as hell at him. At the same time she couldn't take her eyes off him. For a moment she'd imagined he wasn't a cop at all, just the very sexy, anonymous man she'd met in that diner.

*No. Stop thinking about him as a man. He's a hard-ass cop holding a great big grudge, who doesn't care that he might be dragging an innocent woman to jail.*

Yeah, he'd looked pretty good lying there in bed last night, only to wake this morning and turn into Nasty Cop all over again. He hadn't even taken the tape off her wrists to let her go to the bathroom. She'd had to twist herself into a pretzel to accomplish what should have been a relatively simple task, which had forced her to reconsider her natural assumption that all people, even pissed-off cops, were in possession of a heart.

Then he'd gotten all bent out of shape just because she'd used his toothbrush. *Please.* He could kiss her last night, but she couldn't use his toothbrush this morning? If she'd known how much her invasion into his personal space irritated him, she'd have swished his manly extra-strength deodorant stick around in the toilet bowl.

As they walked along the muddy road, she turned to him for yet another plea. "John, will you please take this tape off my wrists?"

"I told you three times already to shut up."

She glared at him. "What's the matter? Did we get up on the wrong side of the lumpy sofa bed this morning?"

"You've already proven you'll do anything to stay out of jail, so why should I take a chance?"

"Because it would be a nice thing to do, maybe?"

"It's not my job to be nice."

"As a taxpaying citizen, I beg to differ."

"Major advantage of prison life, Renee. You won't be paying taxes for long."

She huffed with disgust. "Would it kill you to let me be just a little bit comfortable?"

"The last time you were comfortable, you stole my car."

"I *told* you I had every intention of giving it back to you!"

"Did you also have every intention of giving back the money you stole from that convenience store? And pulling the bullet back *out* of that clerk you shot? Did you have every intention of doing that, too?"

"I didn't shoot anybody! And I didn't rob anybody! How many times do I have to tell you that?"

"I don't give a rat's ass how many times

you tell me. You're going to jail."

What had made her think she could talk him into anything?

She might not have a prayer of escaping jail. Not on John's shift, anyway. But that didn't mean she wasn't going to pour her heart and soul into the fight right up to the moment they tossed her into the cell and clanged the door shut.

"John? How many people do you suppose you've taken to jail?"

"I don't keep track."

"Just an estimate. A hundred? Two hundred?"

"Probably. And before the day's out, I'll be able to add one more to the list."

She really wanted to bite at that one, but she forced herself to remain calm. "Gee, that's a lot of guilty people. Or maybe," she ventured, "some of them were innocent."

"All of them were innocent."

"What?"

"Just ask them. They'll tell you."

A hundred nasty responses swelled through her mind, but she stopped herself before they came rushing out of her mouth. Cops didn't like insults. She'd learned that the hard way once during a Black Sabbath concert at Texas Stadium when she was sixteen. Full of her usual nasty belligerence, she'd told a rent-a-cop to get his fat ass out of the way because he was blocking the stage, and she'd ended up with an even worse view — from the parking lot.

She'd almost forgotten about that night, but now the feeling was razor-sharp again, just as she'd felt it back then. *Cops are the enemy.* Intellectually she knew that wasn't right. Stay within the law, and you had nothing to fear. That was what she'd told herself all the years since then. *You can change. Make a new life for yourself. A life you can be proud of.* But that wasn't right, either, was it? She'd stayed within the boundaries of the law, and look where she'd ended up anyway.

Unfortunately it appeared that John was just like every cop she'd ever encountered. Hard, jaded, don't-give-a-damn kind of guys. Did jerks get into law enforcement, or did law enforcement turn them into jerks?

"How many times do you think somebody's looked guilty," she said, "but they really weren't?"

"Give it a rest, will you, Renee?"

"But it's only logical that —"

He came to a quick halt and faced her. "If you don't shut up —"

"What?" she said. "What are you going to do if I don't shut up?"

He took a few threatening steps toward her. A lock of hair fell over his forehead, bordering his angry eyes and making him look dark and dangerous. She knew that baiting this man was like dangling fresh fish over a shark tank. But instead of maiming her, as his expression said he was considering doing, he merely shook his head with disgust, wheeled around, and stalked up the road.

Renee felt a flush of exhilaration at winning round one. Could it be that the big, bad cop wasn't so big and bad after all?

She trotted to catch up. "John. Slow down."

He sped up again, his long strides taking him several paces ahead of her. She caught up again and strode alongside him.

"Will you slow down a minute and *listen* to me?"

"Not necessary, Renee. I already get the picture. This is unjust. You didn't do it. And I'm a real asshole for doing my job and taking you in. Does that about sum it up?"

No, it didn't. She wanted to take him by the shirt collar, yank him to a halt, and tell him to listen to the whole story or else. Unfortunately, she didn't have an "else" to fall back on. If he kept up this pace, though, she'd be dead by the time they emerged from the forest.

*Oh. Wait a minute.*

She stopped and stood in the middle of the road. She couldn't believe she was being such a fool. Why in the world was she hurrying to keep up? She strolled over to a grassy spot by the side of the road.

And sat down.

John stopped and turned back. "What are you doing?"

She pretended to ignore him. Passive resistance. It had worked for Gandhi, hadn't it?

"Get up," he said. *"Now!"*

When she still ignored him, John stomped over to her. He skewered her with a concentrated gaze of restrained fury — one of those heavy-duty cop looks he'd probably spent hours perfecting in his bathroom mirror.

"Get up," he repeated, his voice frigid.

"Maybe you should sit down with me instead. We could have a nice . . . chat."

"Chat, my ass."

Before she knew what was happening, he'd grabbed her arm and hauled her to her feet. The birds squawked and scattered, their wings making a *whop, whop, whop* noise that echoed through the piney woods. He gripped her by her arms, determination oozing off him like a red-hot aura. "I swear to God, if you don't turn around and walk down this road *right now,* I'll —"

"You'll what? Throw me over your shoulder and carry me out of here? It's only another eight or ten miles, right?"

"You're resisting arrest!"

Renee shrugged indifferently. "Compared to the other charges against me, I'd say that's a drop in the bucket."

Anger flooded his face, but she was on a roll and she couldn't stop now.

"I'm not going anywhere," she went on. "Not until you listen to me."

"Fine," he said, releasing her. "Talk all you want to. While you're walking."

The last thing Renee wanted was to move one step closer to incarceration. But at least he'd be listening to her instead of walking ten paces ahead of her. And he didn't say how *fast* she had to walk, did he?

"Agreed. But only if you take this tape off my wrists."

"No way."

"John . . ." Her voice slid up the scale a few notes, warning him against disagreeing with her.

"No," he repeated. "I am *not* going to —"

She plunked herself down in the middle of the road.

"Damn it, Renee! You are *really* starting to piss me off!"

The last thing John had intended to do was lose his temper, but then again, he hadn't counted on dealing with such an outrageously obstinate woman. How had things gotten twisted around until she thought she was the one calling the shots?

She held up her wrists with a look that said it was her way or no way. He didn't trust her for a minute, but what choice did he have? He could carry her out of this forest and probably die of exhaustion in the effort. He could threaten her again, with absolutely no way to back it up. If he was going to get out of this crappy place and this crappy situation sometime before Christmas, his only choice was to compromise.

He let out a hiss of disgust, then pulled out his pocketknife and sliced through the tape, feeling as if he were turning Godzilla loose to ravage Tokyo. The second she peeled the tape off, he grabbed her by the arm again and hauled her to her feet.

"Get moving," he said, clicking the knife shut and jamming it back into his pocket. "And no stopping until we're out of here."

She turned and started down the road, moving with the speed of a geriatric turtle.

"Get with it," he said, stepping along beside her. "This isn't a walk in the park."

She sped up a little, but at this pace it would be the next millennium before they got back to the main highway.

"You know," Renee said after a moment, "if I'd been that officer, I'd have arrested me, too, with the gun and the money being in my car and all."

Her sudden acquiescence put him on red alert. "Oh, yeah. He deserves a medal for all the intuitive thinking he used to make that arrest."

"And apparently it was a blond woman who committed the robbery."

"So I hear."

"And I don't have an alibi."

"Uh-huh."

"So I guess I look like a pretty good suspect, huh?"

"Damned good."

"But what about motive?"

"What about it?"

"It was the one thing nobody had an answer for. I mean, why in the world would someone like me knock over a convenience store?"

Drugs. Running with a bad crowd. Coercive boyfriend. Being desperate for money. Just plain old lack of conscience. Hell, he had a hundred answers for that one. And not one of them mattered in the least.

"I've got news for you, Renee. If you're standing over a dead body holding a smoking gun, proving motive really isn't necessary."

"I know it *looks* bad. But I had no reason to do it. None. I've got a good job. Why would I rob a convenience store?"

"Do you owe money?"

"Of course. Who doesn't?"

"A lot of it?"

"More than I wish I did, but it's nothing I can't handle."

"Do you have a record?"

She paused. "Of course not."

"You had to think about it?"

"I'm just not used to getting interrogated, that's all."

"Do you do drugs?"

"No! Never! Not even when —" She stopped short, then continued. "I've never done drugs. Period."

"Then I guess you wouldn't mind pulling up the sleeves of your sweatshirt."

She came to a halt and spun around to face him. She narrowed her eyes angrily, then shoved the sleeves of her sweatshirt to her elbows and thrust her arms forward. "Needle tracks? Is that what you're looking for?"

He inspected her forearms. Her smooth ivory skin was as fresh and pretty as the rest of her. Most of the lawbreaking women he encountered were foulmouthed hookers, female con artists, and just plain lowlifes — drugged-up, used-up women who looked forty-five when they were twenty-five. Not this one.

His gaze inched down her forearms to her wrists, where the tape had left pale red welts on her skin. He felt a twinge of guilt, then immediately shoved it aside. The last thing he needed was to feel sorry for her. Any pain she'd suffered she'd brought on herself because of the bad habits she'd recently developed, such as jumping bail, setting fires, and stealing cars.

Still, for some reason Leandro's words lingered in his mind. *That's one hot little body she's got.* It was probably the only thing on earth he and Leandro would ever agree about.

Part of what drew his attention was the jeans she wore, snug in all the right places, and what resided beneath her sweatshirt — a truly spectacular pair of breasts, breasts he'd been within inches of getting his hands on last night. He remembered how he'd kissed her until both of them had practically melted into the sofa, then slipped his hand beneath her sweatshirt until he met warm, soft skin. His purpose had been to call her bluff, to find out why the hell she'd propositioned him in the first place, but somewhere in the middle of that he'd lost his objectivity and wanted nothing more than to see that heavenly little body of hers lying naked on that sofa. Christ, but she'd been soft and sweet. If only she'd been willing —

*Wait a minute.* What the hell was he thinking? If she'd been willing, he'd have made love to a bail-jumping armed robber. If Lieutenant Daniels had seen inside his mind right now, he'd have one more admonition to add to *curb the hot temper* and *stop getting personally involved.*

*Do not get the hots for the women you drag to jail.*

"So you don't shoot up," John said. "There are plenty of other bad habits that require a load of cash to support."

She yanked her sleeves back down. "I don't put anything in my lungs or up my nose, either. I even quit smoking. If you're looking for a drug habit as motive, you're barking up the wrong tree."

"So you're a model citizen."

"No, I'm not. I've got just as many vices as the rest of the world. But that doesn't mean I committed a crime."

"I assume your fingerprints weren't on the weapon."

"Of course not."

"Did they test for gunpowder residue?"

"Yes. My hands were clean."

"What did the victim say? Was the robber wearing gloves?"

Renee paused. "Yes."

"There doesn't seem to be a lot of evidence in your favor, does there, Renee?"

"I didn't do it!"

"Then what was the loot and the weapon doing in the backseat of your car?"

"I don't know," she said with a sigh. "I honestly don't."

She stared down at her feet, her shoulders drooping. The shadows under her eyes said she hadn't slept much last night, and for a second he wondered if maybe he'd tied her so tightly that she couldn't get comfortable.

*Damn.* He had to stop this. Why did he care one way or the other? As long as she had enough energy left to walk out of this forest, that was all that mattered.

"That kind of ignorance will buy you a prison sentence in a hurry," he told her.

"But it's the truth! I don't know how that stuff got in the backseat of my car. My car's old, and the door locks don't work. Anybody could have thrown something in there!"

"Yeah. Any blond woman who'd robbed a convenience store and just happened by."

"I know it looks bad, but —"

"The clerk picked you out of a lineup."

"I know! But I have no idea how —"

"Why did you run?"

"Because I didn't do it!"

"Then you should have stayed around to prove it."

"Even my attorney thought I was guilty. How was I supposed to fight that?"

He shrugged indifferently.

Renee tightened her hands into fists. "Oh, it's so easy for you to shrug it off, isn't it? You're a cop. The guy on the other side. The one who throws people in jail. You've never had to face the prospect of looking at those bars from the inside out!"

"That's right. Law-abiding citizens don't have to worry about that."

"I *am* a law-abiding citizen!"

John snorted with disgust. "I think that's up to the jury to decide."

Renee swept a strand of blond hair away from her eyes and glared at him. "You're a real jerk, you know that?"

"And you're a real pain in the ass. Do you know *that?*"

To his utter surprise, Renee wheeled around and smacked him on the upper arm with her doubled-up fist. He recoiled involuntarily, but when her fist came flying at him again, he lunged at her, caught her by the wrists, and backed her against a tree trunk.

"You just assaulted a police officer," he said. "Add that to the charges you've already racked up, and you're never going to see the light of day again!"

"Tell me, John. Have you ever stopped to wonder if any of those people you lock up are innocent? Or do you just go for the first suspect you see who maybe fits the description, toss him in jail, and think you've done a good day's work? Is that how it is?"

"I'll tell you how it is, sweetheart. I spend my life rounding up the scum of the earth, people who'd shoot their own mother for a fix, people who'd plant a knife in someone's back if it got them what they wanted. *That's* what I deal with every day!"

"So is that what you figure I am?" she said, her whole body trembling with anger. "One of those people? Bad to the bone?"

"Doesn't matter what I think. If I've got probable cause, I pull the scum off the streets. It's somebody else's job to dispose of it."

"So that's how you deal with it? You figure it's not your job, so you don't have to worry about all those poor people serving jail sentences because you got it wrong? How do you live with that?"

"Because more of them are guilty than not, and if they walk, *that's not justice!*"

"Oh, yeah. But it's justice to lock up the innocent ones, just in case?"

John wanted to shake that mocking condescension right out of her. It took a lot of nerve for her to pass judgment on him, as if she had any idea what it was like to do his job. As if she thought he *wanted* innocent people to go to jail. As if he knew who was going to serve time when they were innocent and walk when they were guilty. Judges and juries were insane about half the time and made decisions he wouldn't understand if he lived to be a hundred.

"How can you do it, John?" she repeated. "How can you look people in the eye and —"

"I *don't* look! I've got a job to do, and I don't need that kind of complication!"

"Complication? *Complication?* Looking someone you arrest in the eye makes things complicated? You mean, like, you might actually see that you're making a mistake once in a while?"

John blinked with astonishment at the

words that had tumbled out of her mouth — and his. It wasn't until this moment that he realized the truth — it was the eyes that did him in. That little scumbag who'd gotten off scot-free had those guilty, mocking little eyes that had set John off like a firecracker on the Fourth of July, making him destroy that damned paper-towel dispenser because he hadn't been able to destroy the little scumbag.

And now he was looking at the flip side. At Renee, whose big blue eyes were screaming her innocence. An image slammed into him of her in prison, falsely accused, a nameless, faceless entity shuttled through the system, emerging ten years later a hard, bitter woman, nothing but a shadow of who she was now, a woman whose life had been stolen from her. . . .

*No.*

He looked away. She grabbed his arm and yanked him back. "Don't you *dare* look away!"

He whipped back around, his jaw so tight it trembled. "Okay, Renee. I'm looking. And do you know what I see? I see a criminal who's lying to save her skin. That's what I see!"

"Do you know what I see? I see a man who's so jaded he couldn't recognize the truth if it slapped him in the face!"

His anger surged, pounding inside his head with a primitive rhythm. "You don't know shit about me."

"Oh, but I do." Her voice was low and intense, crawling inside him and setting his nerves on edge. "You're a man who'd like to think the best of people, but you can't do that because you've seen too much of the rotten side of humanity to believe in much of anything anymore. So that means you've lost it, John. You've lost any hope you ever had of spending the rest of your life as an actual human being. Now, I don't know if your life is crappy in general, or if it's just your job that's got you all screwed up, but —"

"Shut up, Renee —"

"— you've got a hell of a rotten attitude. And instead of backing off right now and *thinking* about what you're doing, you're just playing by the numbers no matter what they add up to. And you're too damned afraid to look at me, because you just might see how wrong —"

"I said *shut up!*"

She stopped short and stared up at him, breathing hard, her cheeks flushed red with anger. He needed to back off, yank her away from that tree, and get on down the road again. But the nerve she'd struck was a live one, and all he could do was stare at her, wondering how she'd gotten under his skin. Wondering why he was standing so close to her that a tissue couldn't have separated them. Wondering why, when he needed desperately not to look at her, he couldn't tear his gaze away.

Something John hated to face had welled up inside him — a feeling of uncertainty that rattled him all the way to his bones. He relaxed his grip on her wrists until it became almost a caress. Time seemed to move like molasses as he hovered next to her, and slowly, slowly, her furious expression melted into a plaintive one.

"Look at me, John. Am I guilty?"

Her voice was barely audible now, her words passing her lips on a whispered breath. In that moment he felt all the anger and skepticism drain right out of his body — those critical emotions that were built into cops so they didn't do stupid, reckless things like listen to beautiful blond fugitives profess their innocence.

"The evidence says you are."

"The evidence is wrong."

He stared at her a long time, the cool breeze of the piney woods swirling around them. "Maybe."

*Maybe.*

The moment he uttered that word, he knew he'd crossed a line he never should have gotten within a hundred miles of. There was no "maybe" about this, so how in the hell had he let that word come out of his mouth? It was time to become a cop again, to back away, to clear his head of all this uncertainty. But still he stood so close to her he could sense the rise and fall of her chest as she breathed. This was either one of the biggest injustices he'd ever encountered, or Renee Esterhaus was one of the biggest con artists he'd ever encountered. And the fact that he couldn't tell the difference was eating him alive.

His gaze dropped to her lips, lips that could be telling the truth, or lying to save her skin. The heated anger between them only a few moments ago had faded, and now every second that passed felt blurry around the edges, as if he were walking through a dream.

"I've got no choice," he said. "I'm going to take you in."

"I know," she whispered. She gently pulled her hands from his grip, then flattened both of her palms against his chest. "But just for a minute . . . would you pretend you're not?"

*Holy shit.*

She leaned into him, inching her hands upward until they reached his shirt collar, then moving them across that boundary to ease around his neck. He blinked with surprise, but some force he couldn't fathom kept him from pulling away. For a long, breathless moment he stared at her, knowing exactly what she wanted, and the knowing almost did him in. She moved closer by small degrees until her breasts grazed his chest. Then she touched the tip of her tongue to her lips, leaving them moist and glistening.

One minute he was supercop, taking no crap, and the next minute he was staring at her lips as if he were dying in the desert and they were a cup of crisp, cool water. The last thing he needed was a major complication like this hitting him right between the eyes. If she were to fall backward onto a bed of pine leaves and drag him right down on top of her, God help him, he knew he wouldn't put up one moment of protest.

But as he was pondering the logistics of that, a truth he'd chosen to ignore crept into his mind again, pounding away at him like a native drumbeat spelling out an urgent message.

He'd been here before.

The diner. Last night.

Slowly the memory went from hazy to sharp. In that diner last night, her eyes had been full of lust, her lips full of hunger, her touch full of promise, and her brain full of ulterior motive. He'd been thinking *hot sex* and she'd been thinking *escape*.

In a thunderclap of sudden reason, John froze, allowing his brain time to crawl out of his pants and make its way back up to his head. He couldn't believe what a fool he'd almost been.

It was time to stop her from messing with his mind. To let her know that under no circumstances was he interested in a repeat performance of the kiss she'd given him in that diner, no matter how heart-stopping it had been. To let her know who was the boss here, and it wasn't a pretty blond fugitive with a body that could make a priest toss down his collar and never look back. Coming on to him all of a sudden was nothing more than a ploy to entice him to let her go, and she wasn't going to get away with it.

It was time to fight fire with fire.

In one smooth, quick move, he took hold of her wrists again and pushed her back against the tree. He held her arms firmly at her sides, then inched closer, insinuating his body next to hers, meeting her eyes in a long, languorous stare.

"Now, if I didn't know better, sweetheart, I'd think you wanted me to kiss you."

She stared up at him, her eyes wide with surprise. He moved his lips to within inches of hers. "And I'm thinking that sounds pretty good."

Renee twisted in his grip, but he held her tightly.

"But there are a lot of things besides kissing that sound pretty good, too. How about if I cash in on that promise you made me last night that you never followed through on?"

Her accelerated breathing and widened eyes told him she hadn't counted on this turn of events. John smiled to himself. She'd run scared last night at the mere suggestion that they have sex. The more he poured on the intimidation now, the less likely she was to pull this crap on him again.

"I want what you promised me," he whispered. "And this time I'm not stopping until I get it."

He dragged the words out in a seductive drawl, waiting for her to tell him loud and clear to get the hell away from her so he could claim victory. But all she did was

186

squirm a little in his grip. He tightened his hand on her wrists, then inched closer and placed a feathery kiss on the angle of her jaw. She sucked in a sharp breath at the touch of his lips, as if he'd struck a live nerve, so he followed that kiss with several more, placing them wherever they seemed to generate the most reaction.

"John . . . please . . ."

*Ah.* Now he was getting to her. She shimmied against him, her breath coming faster, but with his hold on her wrists and the tree at her back, there was absolutely nowhere for her to go. He continued his featherlight kisses, letting his hot breath spill over her skin.

Unfortunately, this was getting to him, too.

Every time he touched his lips to her cheek, her neck, her throat, images flashed through his mind of what it would be like to go through with his threat, and it wasn't long before the close proximity he'd created was making him half-crazy with lust. Just because his brain had no intention of following through didn't mean his body had gotten that message, and if he didn't end this pretty soon, he wasn't going to be in complete control of the situation.

*Come on, sweetheart. Say it. Tell me to stop*

*like you did last night. Then I'll tell you that it's your own damned fault for trying to trade your body for a "Get Out of Jail Free" card, and we'll get on down the road.*

He dragged his lips along the curve of her ear. She shimmied against him but he held on tightly, whispering in the most blatantly carnal tone he could muster, "You're not going anywhere, Renee. You started this, and I'm going to finish it. We're going to have sex right here and right now. We're getting down in the dirt, getting naked, and not even coming up for air. And if you think you're getting out of it this time, you've got another thing —"

"Okay," she whispered.

John pulled back and stared at her. *"What?"*

She lunged forward and pressed her lips against his in a fiery, demanding kiss that shocked the holy hell out of him. He let go of her wrists and pulled away, only to have her take advantage of her freedom by winding her arms around his neck and pulling him back again, devouring his mouth with hers.

Somewhere in John's mind, the word *stop* was blinking at him in red neon letters, but those talented lips of Renee's had caused his brain waves to flatline. *Stop.* He knew that word had to be telling him something, but damned if he could figure out what.

And before he knew it, he was kissing her back.

# chapter eight

John pushed Renee backward until she bumped against the tree again, pausing for a few seconds to catch a breath. At the same time he thrust his hands through her wind-tangled hair and turned her face up, and when he met her eyes and saw nothing but sheer, hot desire, he thought he was going to explode right there.

He dove in to meet her lips again, and she opened her mouth to him willingly, her tongue moving with his in a dance of pure ecstasy. Feeling her squirm against him during his testosterone assault had already sent him halfway to heaven, and now all he could think about was finishing the trip.

With a soft groan Renee went on the offensive again, sliding her hands down his chest and around his hips to hook her fingers into his hip pockets. She dragged him hard against her until his groin was pressed firmly against her abdomen. She might not have wanted it last night, but she sure as hell wanted it now, and he didn't stop to wonder why because — *Lord* — he wanted it, too.

He caught the hem of her sweatshirt, nudged his hand beneath it, then went straight for the clasp of her bra. About a hundred times since last night, he'd thought about how that tiny clasp had been just a flick of his fingertips away, and now all he had to do was hold it here, twist it there, and it would open. Just . . . like . . . *that.*

Her bra fell away. He swept it aside, then closed his hand over her breast and squeezed it firmly. She broke off their kiss with a muffled gasp, then dropped her head back against the tree, her eyes closed, breathing wildly, her fingertips digging into his shoulders. He wasted no time pushing her sweatshirt up and over her breasts until they met the cool autumn air. He circled them with his hands, then moved the pads of his thumbs over her tight nipples in a hot, strumming caress.

"John . . . oh, *God* . . ."

The deep, throaty hum of her words sent a jolt of heat spiraling through him. He could tell by the sound of her voice that she wasn't telling him to put on the brakes. She was begging him to hit the throttle and move full speed ahead.

He kissed the ivory column of her throat,

then moved upward to swirl the tip of his tongue against her earlobe, still caressing her breasts, doing his best to drive her crazy at the same time the blood was sizzling through his own veins. The pine forest surrounding them had become strangely unreal, his mind turning hot and hazy and completely beyond his control. Everything about this woman was making him forget who he was and what he was supposed to be doing, because right now he was absolutely sure he was supposed to be making love to her, and he knew that couldn't possibly be right. But anticipation had shoved every other thought from his mind. He wanted her right here, right now, right up against this tree, right down in the dirt or anywhere else he could have her.

She worked her hands in between them and grasped his belt buckle. In only a few seconds she had it undone and was starting in on his jeans, and it was a damned good thing. The way he felt right now, if she didn't rip them off in the next ten seconds he was going to rip them off himself. And then hers would be next.

But as she coaxed his zipper south, slowly it dawned on him that he was only a zip and a tug from standing in the middle of a pine forest half-naked.

A half-naked cop, soon to be all naked, on the verge of making love to an accused armed robber.

When the full force of that mental image hit him, he froze. For the first time he realized that she really did intend to go through with this. She clearly intended for them to get naked in the dirt, just as he'd suggested, just as he'd imagined, just as he wanted so badly he could taste it. And that was when he felt a hard mental slap that knocked his sanity back into place.

Of all the women in the world, he was on the verge of making love to the one most likely to end up in prison. Good God — was he out of his mind?

He leaned away suddenly and took her by the shoulders, holding her at arm's length, fighting to keep his wild breathing and stratospheric body temperature under control. Her hands fell away from his zipper and she looked at him quizzically, her blond hair blowing in the breeze, her cheeks flushed pink with passion. Somehow he managed to grind out the words — the only words that would redeem him from this situation he'd been stupid enough to get himself into.

"Well," he said, with as much nonchalance as he could muster, "I guess we know now just how far you'll go to stay out of jail, don't we?"

Renee stood perfectly still for a moment, his words hanging almost palpably in the air. She opened her mouth as if to speak. Then she clamped it shut again, her expression shifting to a mask of total fury. She slapped both palms against his chest and gave him a hard shove.

"You *bastard!*"

He stumbled backward. She pulled her sweatshirt down and stalked past him, whacking him with her elbow at the same time. She walked up the road several angry paces, then spun around hotly.

"You really think that's why I wanted you? To stay out of jail?"

"Hell yes," he said, buckling his belt as he strode toward her. "And you can give it up, sweetheart. It won't work. I know plenty of cops who can be bought with far less than a hot female body. Unfortunately for you, I'm not one of them."

"Excuse me," Renee said, "but I don't believe I was the only one participating!"

"But you were the only one with something to gain."

"So you didn't really want me. Is that right?"

He gave her a disinterested shrug. Her gaze traveled down his body and stopped at his crotch. "Sorry, John, but your built-in lie detector is telling me otherwise."

He shifted uncomfortably. She had him there.

"Okay, Renee. I suppose there's a lot about you to interest a man, in spite of the fact that you're a fugitive."

"So it was basically a lust thing."

Oh, yeah. Lust had been heavily involved. And so had stupidity. Daniels was right: his objectivity was shot to hell, and he probably needed a month of vacation instead of a week — out alone in the wilderness with no lawbreaking women to tempt him. He'd been thinking with his crotch instead of his head, and that was a very, very dangerous thing to do.

"More like curiosity, really," John said. "You promised me all kinds of interesting things to escape Leandro, so I thought I'd see just how far you'd go to keep yourself out of jail. To tell you the truth, it was even farther than I figured."

"I told you that's not why I did it!"

"Well, then, suppose you tell me the real reason. Because from where I'm standing, it looks like sexual bribery, pure and simple."

Her stance was belligerent, with her fists on her hips and her chin thrust forward, but her angry gaze had faltered a little. She blinked several times, and he was surprised to see tears glistening in her eyes.

"Okay! Fine. You want to know the real reason I wanted you? I'll tell you why. Because where I'm going, I won't have the opportunity to make love to a man again for, oh, say, the next ten years or so. And since kissing you and . . . and other things . . . is not an entirely disgusting experience in spite of the fact that you're a cop, I figured, why not?"

*She's yanking you around again. Tears and all. Don't buy it.*

"Kind of like having that last cigarette before the firing squad pulls the trigger?"

"Well, I could have done without that analogy, but yeah. Kind of like that."

"I see." He shrugged again. "Actually, I suppose kissing you has its advantages. As long as that pretty little mouth of yours is occupied, it can't be telling me lies."

"I've told you the truth! About everything!"

"Are you kidding? You haven't spoken a truthful word since the moment I met you! You've lied to me, stolen my car, *shot* my car —"

"You big, dumb *jerk!* They actually *pay* you to solve crimes?" Her words shot through the forest, then echoed back at him, doubling the accusation. "Think about it, will you? If I'd really been the one who shot that store clerk, I wouldn't have shot your car. I'd have shot *you!*"

Stunned, John just stared at her.

"Now let's get out of here," she said, wiping her eyes on the shoulder of her sweatshirt and sniffing a little. "I'm sick of this damned forest, and I'd just as soon get all that booking and fingerprinting and strip-searching over with, if you don't mind."

She turned and marched up the road, not even bothering to see if he was following. He stared after her, frozen to the spot where he stood.

*I wouldn't have shot your car. I'd have shot you.*

He'd been so furious about his car last night that he'd just written her off as loony, never really stopping to think about the reason why she'd destroyed his vehicle and not him. Why hadn't she shot him when she had the chance? Even a shot in the leg would have rendered him incapable of coming after her. She could have hopped into his car and easily escaped. It would have been hours before he could have gotten out of the woods, and by that time she'd have been long gone.

But she hadn't done that. She'd shot his car instead.

He started walking, staying several paces behind her, suddenly smothered in an avalanche of confusion. He'd seen a lot of things in those clear blue eyes of hers, but God help him, a lie wasn't one of them.

*It's just a ploy. That's all. Take her to jail. Put the bad guys away and you're done for the day.*

This situation was even more clear-cut than most. Renee wasn't a suspect he had to decide whether or not to take to jail. Some other cop had already made that decision, and judging from the evidence against her, it had been a slam dunk. All John had to do was transport her from point A to point B and his job was over. He had a clear, unequivocal responsibility that was as black-and-white as anything could possibly be. So why, when he looked at Renee, did he see all those shades of gray?

Because for the first time, he was actually starting to believe that maybe — just maybe — she was telling the truth.

It took at least twenty minutes after they'd started back down the road again for the fire-red blush on Renee's cheeks to fade. She'd never felt so embarrassed in her entire life. She had never, ever thrown herself at a man the way she'd thrown herself at John. And then to have him turn around and mock her, suggesting that she was trying to bribe him with sex, had been the ultimate in humiliation.

No. The ultimate in humiliation had been when she'd blurted out the whole pitiful truth of why she'd done it.

He'd been standing so close to her, pressing her up against that tree, swearing he was going to take her right then and there, and all at once she'd had a flash of the years of prison that awaited her. Suddenly she'd been desperate to feel something hot and intense and overwhelmingly sexual before they put her away for the best years of her life. All she'd wanted was for John to make good on his threat, to quit being a cop for a few stupid minutes and make her feel the same way she'd felt last night when he'd kissed her. And he had. For a moment. She could still feel his breath warming her neck, his lips engulfing hers, his touch waking up every nerve in her body. Her face got hot all over again just thinking about it.

But at the same time the memory thrilled her, it mortified her, too, because she knew now that it hadn't been real. But even if he had wanted her, making love with him would have been the most foolish thing she could possibly have done. He probably wasn't carrying any protection, and she certainly didn't have anything with her. Would she have done it anyway? Would she have said to hell with all the promises she'd ever made to herself about turning her life around, which included not treating sex as a recreational sport?

*Okay.* There were extenuating circumstances. She was about to be put away in some god-awful prison for the better part of her young life without ever experiencing sex with a real live man. All she'd wanted was for John to give her something she could remember during the long years she was facing inside those prison walls, where a man's touch would be as rare as gourmet meals and bubble baths.

They walked in silence for the next hour and a half, trudging along the dirt road, which soon turned to gravel, then to blacktop. A rusted-out Ford truck passed them once, but even when John waved his arms and practically threw himself in front of it, the driver refused to stop and give them a lift. That had sent John into a fit of grumbling and cussing that used most of the four-letter words Renee had ever heard and added a few new ones to her vocabulary.

It was midafternoon by the time they emerged onto the state highway. Without a word, John turned and walked along the shoulder of the road in the direction of that seedy little diner where she'd propositioned him last night. She had no choice but to walk right along with him.

Soon they topped a hill and the Red Oak Diner came into view. She got dizzy with dread as she realized how close they were to civilization and therefore to jail, and for a minute she thought she was going to collapse right there at the side of the road. As soon as they got to a phone, John could call for help and her fate would be sealed.

She wanted to cry. To run. To beg him not to turn her in. To *help* her, for God's sake, because there was absolutely nobody else on earth she could turn to right now. Instead he walked stoically beside her, his face a mask of coplike purpose, as if things hadn't gotten so hot between them a few hours ago that Smokey the Bear had almost been called into action. She could see now that he was a cop through and through, and he wasn't about to cancel her one-way ticket to jail just because she'd happened to mention approximately a thousand times that she was innocent.

Or because she'd wanted him to make love to her.

They reached the parking lot of the diner, and she couldn't stand the silence any longer. Sarcasm probably wasn't the smartest thing to express right about now, but it was about the only way she could get words out without falling apart.

"So what's the drill now, John? Are you going to find some rope, or tape, or maybe a spare pair of handcuffs lying around so you can subdue your dangerous fugitive again?"

John pulled her to a halt beside him. "When we go into that diner, I want you to sit down at the counter and keep your mouth shut. I mean shut, as in *absolutely nothing* coming out of it. Is that clear?"

She opened her mouth to snap back at him, but then she realized that something was different here. His words were low and intense, but without all the anger and animosity he'd shown her up to now.

What was going on?

He opened the door to the diner and motioned her inside, directing her to sit on a ragged vinyl stool at the counter. They were greeted by the same man who'd been there last night — a balding, fleshy-faced guy with an entire Goodyear steel-belted radial lopping over the waistband of his Wranglers.

"Well, hey, there, John!"

John's face broke into a big, congenial smile. "Hey, Harley."

Renee blinked with astonishment. A smile? From John? She'd assumed his mouth muscles were incapable of moving against gravity, but there it was: a beautiful, dazzling, million-dollar smile that made him look thoroughly sexy and engaging, and she couldn't take her eyes off him. He slid onto the stool beside her with lazy grace, as if he'd just dropped by for a casual cup of coffee.

Harley looked back and forth between John and Renee, flashing them a smile filled with an assortment of teeth in various states of disrepair. "Soooo . . . you kids have a good time last night?"

The question hung in the air for what seemed like hours. Renee waited for the ax to fall, for John to declare that she was a desperate criminal he was in the midst of hauling to jail. Instead, he shifted that gorgeous smile in her direction, this time filling it with so much sexual suggestiveness that she practically melted from the heat of it. He looked back at Harley with a conspiratorial, one-guy-to-another smile.

"A good time?" John slipped his arm around Renee's shoulders. "Well, now,

Harley. What do you think?"

Renee was so stunned she just sat there, her eyes wide, probably looking exactly like what John was making her out to be — a brainless bimbo racking up points toward the Olympic bed-hopping championship.

"I think you're one lucky son of a bitch," Harley replied. "That's what *I* think." He dropped his voice and leaned closer to John. "Looks like she likes the rough stuff, huh?"

John looked at Harley questioningly. Harley pointed to John's bruised eye, smiling as if he thought a little sadomasochism really pepped things up between the sheets.

"Uh . . . yeah," John said, turning to stare pointedly at Renee. "I guess things did get a little rough here and there."

He wasn't kidding about that.

Harley tapped the counter in front of Renee. "Hey, darlin'. Ever consider an older man? Now, I might not be as pretty as John, here, but what I lack in looks I make up for in experience. You and me could —"

*Whap!*

Harley spun around, a little shocked, it appeared, at getting smacked on the back of the head with an order pad.

"Experience *that,* you dirty old man!"

He rubbed his head. "Marva, you rotten

old hag! I oughta —"

"You oughta get your butt into that kitchen and get to work fixin' that dishwasher so you don't have to do 'em by hand later. *That's* what you oughta do!"

Harley muttered something nasty under his breath and slunk into the kitchen. Marva turned to Renee with a kindly smile. "Ignore my husband, sweetie. He's all bark and no bite. Believe me."

Renee turned to John, feeling a rush of hope. He hadn't told them. Why hadn't he told them?

"We had some car problems back at the cabin," John told Marva. "Had to walk out. I'm going to need a wrecker, so if you'll just let me use your phone —"

"Why, sure!" She nodded to the phone at the other end of the counter. "Give Stan a call up at the Mobil station in Winslow. He'll get you fixed right up."

"Thanks, Marva. Hey, something sure smells good. What do you have cooking back there?"

"Beef stew."

"Perfect. Why don't you bring me and Alice some of that?" He glanced at Renee and winked. "We kind of forgot to eat last night."

Alice? Who the hell was Alice?

Then she remembered. That was the fake name she'd given John last night. What kind of game was he playing?

Marva gave John the phone number of the Mobil station. He went to the end of the counter to use the phone while Marva went into the kitchen and returned with two bowls of stew. Renee was so hungry that it was all she could do not to plunge face-first into the bowl.

"So tell me, sweetie," Marva said in a sly whisper. "Was he good?"

It took a moment for Renee to figure out what the woman was talking about. She glanced over to John, who was talking on the phone but watching every move she made. He'd told her not to talk. Until she could get a handle on this situation, she decided it might be best to take that advice.

She turned back to Marva, and in lieu of a verbal response, she gave her a big smile and a provocative little wiggle of her eyebrows.

Marva beamed with delight. "I *knew* it! The first time he walked in here . . ." She fanned herself with her order pad, as if her body temperature had suddenly shot through the roof. "Whew! I'm tellin' you, sweetie, if I was twenty years younger, I'd tell Harley to take a hike and follow that man wherever he wanted to go."

Of course, she'd just smacked Harley on the back of the head for the same kind of pronouncement, but Renee didn't bother to point that out.

John came back and sat down beside her. Renee had no idea what was going on here, except that she'd finally gotten the chance to eat, and not a soul in the vicinity knew who she really was. She gave John a few questioning looks, which he carefully ignored. She felt the faint stirrings of hope. If he'd told these people the real story of what happened last night, he'd be obligated to take her in. As it was right now, though, nobody here knew she'd jumped bail. She wasn't even sure they knew John was a cop.

Did that mean his options were open?

They'd just finished eating when Stan rolled into the parking lot with his wrecker. John paid the tab and escorted Renee outside.

"You didn't tell them," she said, the moment they were out the door. "Why not?"

"This isn't some TV cop show, Renee. I see no reason to disturb a man's place of business any more than I have to."

He spoke with conviction, but his words just didn't ring true. They were the only customers in the place, so they'd have hardly disturbed the man's business. And she had a feeling that if Harley the dentally challenged sadomasochist knew she was a bail jumper, he and Marva would have cracked a beer and sat back to watch the show, glorying in their celebrity status for the next year or so by repeating the story to every redneck within a fifty-mile radius.

So what was the real reason John hadn't told them?

"Are you Stan?" John said, greeting the wiry little grease monkey who got out of the truck.

"Yeah. Where's your car?"

"Back in the woods. Just off Lake Shelton."

"Hop in."

Stan started back toward the truck. John took Renee's arm and followed him. "My advice still holds," John said under his breath. "Keep your mouth shut."

She crawled up into the cab of the wrecker and sat down, hoping that the spring sticking out of the shredded blue vinyl seat cover wouldn't rip a hole in her jeans.

Then she had a terrible thought.

Maybe John was giving her false hope just so she'd behave herself. She'd given him so much trouble on the way out of the forest that he didn't want to deal with any more of it, so he was going to make her think he'd changed his mind about taking her in so she'd do whatever he told her to.

No. That didn't make sense. Now that they were back to civilization, he didn't have to put up with anything. All he had to do was bind her hands, her feet, her *mouth,* if he felt he needed to, then deposit her like so much dirty laundry on the steps of the Tolosa police station.

But that didn't appear to be his plan.

"So what kinda problem you got with your car?" Stan asked, downshifting, then stomping the gas until the engine roared.

"Alice here was doing a little target practice. It got out of hand."

Stan grinned. "She shot your car?"

"Afraid so."

"Tire?"

"Radiator."

"Not smart to give a woman a firearm," Stan said with a sad shake of his head. "Never met a single one of 'em who could hit the broad side of a barn."

*Sexist pig,* Renee thought, then smiled sweetly. "Actually, Stan, I'm an excellent shot."

"You kiddin'?" he said, the words squeaking out on top of a hyenalike laugh.

"You hit a car radiator!"

"I was aiming for the car radiator."

John slid his hand onto Renee's thigh and tightened his fingers against it. "Alice —"

"Because I couldn't bear to shoot . . . the target."

John shot her a quick glance, then turned away again. He loosened his grip on her thigh, but his hand lingered.

Renee dropped her voice to a whisper. "And I think the target knows why."

He flexed his fingers, almost like a caress, still refusing to look at her. "Even if he does," he said softly, "that doesn't take away his responsibility, does it?"

For a moment his words didn't register. When they finally did, Renee felt a horrible sinking sensation in her stomach. All at once the truth of the situation dawned on her. It wasn't just a matter of making John believe her. It was a matter of him also making the choice to protect her over protecting his job and his reputation, and that was never going to happen.

No matter how much she delayed things, no matter how much she pleaded with him, no matter how much she prayed to find a way out of this, she didn't stand a chance. He hadn't told the world she was a fugitive, but that didn't mean he had any intention of letting her go. Maybe it was just his way of allowing her to have some semblance of a normal life right up to the time that cell door slammed shut behind her.

At that moment, she decided that the last thing she wanted was to force John to drag her kicking and screaming into that police station. He was offering her the only thing he had to offer, a little dignity, and she decided she was going to take it.

"I won't give you any more trouble," she whispered. "Just do what you have to do."

Then she turned away to look out the window, staring at the towering pine trees, thinking that she might be forty years old before she ever saw one again. Soon John's hand slipped away from her thigh, taking with it the last shred of hope she had.

It took Stan and his crew nearly three hours to find the proper radiator for John's car and get it installed, which meant that he and Renee were forced to spend the majority of the late afternoon sitting on orange plastic chairs at Stan's Mobil station, breathing in enough car exhaust, brake fluid, and cigarette smoke to cause an instantaneous case of lung cancer. About two hours in, John had sprung for soft drinks for both of them. Since he didn't seem to want to carry on even the most cursory of conversations, about the only words she'd spoken were "diet" and "Coke."

But while John had no interest in interacting with her, still he kept an eye on her the whole time, even to the point of checking out the bathroom window before letting her enter the filthy little room to conduct her business. At the same time, though, he didn't restrain her, and he didn't tell a soul who she really was.

They were on the road again by six-thirty, and by eight forty-five, John had turned his Explorer with its brand-new radiator off the freeway onto the exit leading to Tolosa. Renee's heart thrummed in a hard, painful rhythm, until she wondered if maybe she was having a heart attack. Maybe her short but eventful life would soon be over, saving her from wasting away behind those prison walls.

Unfortunately, her heart kept beating.

The tension radiating from John was almost palpable. She wondered if he felt any compassion toward her at all, but nixed that thought immediately. He hadn't so much as looked at her for the last fifty miles, staring straight ahead at the road, his face tight and expressionless. Even though she felt desperate to say something to break the awful silence, she had the feeling that he wouldn't tolerate so much as a hiccup out of her. Since the last thing she wanted right now was another confrontation, she kept her thoughts to herself.

John turned left onto State Highway 4 from the freeway service road and headed in the direction of the police station. Renee placed her hands on her thighs, then lifted them a little and realized she was trembling. It wasn't cold in the car, so she couldn't blame her affliction on that. She was just scared — pure, grade-A, top-of-the-line terrified.

Darkness had settled over the city. They passed the Tastee-Freez where she and her friends had hung out in high school. It was more like "Tste Frz" now, with several of the neon lights on its sign either broken or burned out. The red paint was peeling, the windows smudged with years of accumulated grime. Renee tried to remember if it had looked that bad when she was in high school. She probably wouldn't have noticed even if it had, since she'd been in an altered state from alcohol most of the time. But when it came to drugs, she'd told John the absolute truth. She'd never done them.

*Well, okay.* There was the pot she'd smoked a couple of times in high school when she was dating Jimmy Calhoun, who was the Will Rogers of addicts — he never met a drug he didn't like. But when she realized Jimmy had fried so many brain cells that he had trouble remembering his own name, neither he nor marijuana had held much fascination for her anymore.

And okay, she'd popped an upper or two. And she'd consumed enough alcohol as a teenager to pickle her internal organs. But it had been seven years since she'd touched anything stronger than an occasional beer while watching a ball game, and that counted for a lot. And no matter what influence she'd been under at the time, she'd never done anything as awful as armed robbery.

She slid her shaking hands beneath her thighs and took a deep breath, which didn't calm her in the least. She knew what it would be like when they reached the police station, because she'd been through this drill before. Of course, she didn't know the last cop who'd booked her, an anonymous, stone-faced guy who'd merely been going through the motions. She hadn't kissed that guy. She hadn't almost made love with him. She hadn't wanted him so badly she'd nearly fainted from the feeling. He'd been a nameless nobody she could easily hate, but when it came to John, her emotions weren't quite that clear-cut.

The light at the intersection of State Highway 4 and Wilmont Street turned yellow, then red, and John brought the Explorer to a halt. Renee caught sight of the police station in the distance, a meticulous little redbrick building with the American and Texas state flags flying out front. Tears sprang to her eyes.

*No.* She wasn't going to cry, and she wasn't going to beg. She hadn't ruled out throwing up, though. Judging from the way her stomach felt right now, that was a definite possibility. She sniffed a little and wiped her eyes on the sleeve of her sweatshirt, but realized immediately the futility of it. So much for holding back the tears.

John was staring straight ahead, his face still impassive, but he was gripping the steering wheel so tightly his knuckles whitened.

"Don't cry."

He said the words harshly, grinding them out through clenched teeth, which only made her eyes tear up more. She felt his anger and really did want to stop crying, but there wasn't much chance of that now.

The light turned green, and Renee's heart lurched.

A second passed. Then two.

John didn't move.

The driver behind him honked, but still John sat there, staring straight ahead, his fingers clenching the steering wheel, releasing slightly, then clenching again. He'd rolled the sleeves of his shirt to the elbows, and the muscles of his forearms stood out in sharp relief with every contraction of his hands.

The driver behind him hit his horn in several more long, droning honks. John acted as if he didn't even hear them.

He looked to his right, down Wilmont Street, then shifted his gaze to Renee, his dark eyes boring right into her. She blinked. A tear coursed down her cheek, and she reached her fingertip up to brush it away before it could fall.

The driver behind them laid on his horn again. John spat out a sudden curse. He stepped on the gas, cut the wheel hard to the right, and swung his Explorer south onto Wilmont Street. Renee grabbed the door beside her as he stomped the accelerator. In seconds he'd blasted past the thirty-mile-per-hour speed limit, pushing the car to forty and beyond. Away from the police station.

"John?"

"Don't say a word."

"But —"

"Do you want to go to jail?"

"Of course not, but —"

"Then don't say a word."

*Okay. No problem.* She'd have her lips sewn shut and her vocal cords surgically removed if it meant not going to jail.

*Not going to jail?*

Renee couldn't believe it. Had he actually reconsidered taking her in? If so, where were they going now?

John drove several miles down Wilmont Street before finally turning onto Porter Avenue and entering Tolosa Heights, an older part of town with aging but tidy storefronts, interspersed with an occasional fast-food restaurant or an office building.

Then he turned onto James Street, a residential area of brick houses that had been built in the 1950s. Even though night had fallen, streetlamps illuminated the calm, idyllic neighborhood. Trees in that flux state between autumn and winter held on to their few remaining leaves for dear life. An elderly couple, bundled against the cool night air, scuffed down the sidewalk, a Boston terrier trotting along beside them. It was a regular Norman Rockwell kind of place. Unfortunately, it was hard for Renee to appreciate it when her insides felt more like Pablo Picasso.

Where in the world was he taking her?

John slowed his car, then reached up to the visor over his head and pulled down an automatic garage-door opener. He swung his car into the driveway at 1530 James Street, a neat little redbrick house with white trim, black shutters, and a row of crape myrtles lining the sidewalk in front of the house.

He hit the button on the remote, and the garage door came up. He drove the Explorer into the garage, lowered the door again, and killed the engine. The silence was overwhelming.

"Where are we?" Renee asked.

"Home."

"Whose home?"

"Mine."

Renee couldn't believe this. John had brought her to his house?

"Why are we here?"

He didn't reply. He escorted her out of the car, unlocked the back door, and led her into the kitchen. The house was in a time warp, with the original cabinets and countertops from the 1950s, both in a creamy shade of yellow. He instructed her to kick off her muddy shoes, and he did the same. She'd barely gotten her feet out of them before he grabbed her arm and led her through the living room. She caught sight of a little bit of updating — refinished hardwood floors, miniblinds, and an area rug or two — before he pulled her down the hall and straight into a bedroom. From the looks of it, it was *his* bedroom, sparsely furnished with a dresser and a bed topped by a solid navy blue spread.

He grabbed something off the dresser. Renee's heart skipped when she saw what it was.

Handcuffs.

Before she knew what was happening, he'd snapped one of them onto her left wrist. The metal felt like ice.

"John. Please. No handcuffs. I promise I won't try to get away."

"Yes, you will. The first chance you get."

He led her over to the bed. He pushed her down to a sitting position, then snapped the other handcuff onto one of the spindles of the headboard.

"Please, John. Not again. Not after being tied to that bed last night!"

"Fine. I'll take you to jail. They have a very nice cot there with your name on it. You won't even have to wear handcuffs."

"Never mind. I don't know what I was

thinking. The handcuffs are lovely."

"I knew you'd see it my way." He started out of the room.

"Wait a minute! Where are you going? You can't just leave me here!"

He left the room and closed the door behind him with a solid *thunk.*

"John!"

His footsteps faded down the hall. Then . . . silence.

Renee looked down at her cuffed wrist, then back at the door again.

What the hell had just happened here?

# chapter nine

John went straight to his kitchen, fished through the cabinet next to the refrigerator, and finally located his megasize bottle of aspirin. He spilled four into his hand and downed them with a glass of water, trying to get rid of the headache that had been pounding his skull ever since he had pulled out of Winslow.

He collapsed on the sofa in his living room, trying to remember exactly what the penalty was for harboring a fugitive. Whatever it was, it undoubtedly took a quantum leap if the person doing the harboring was a cop. As he sat there, he tried really hard to convince himself that it wasn't a damn fool thing he'd just done, but that was one hell of a hard sell.

His descent into bad judgment had started when he hadn't restrained Renee at Harley's when he'd had the chance. He'd sunk lower when he had called her by her phony name. Then he'd hit rock bottom when he made that right turn onto Wilmont Avenue instead of heading to the station.

He had no idea what he was going to do now. If anyone — *anyone* — found out he was keeping her here instead of turning her in, his career was toast. But right now, when he needed to be thinking about taking her to jail, all he could think about was what had happened between them out in the woods only a few hours ago. It had been an experience so hot, so intense, so downright unforgettable that senile dementia would have to set in before the memory would ever dim.

Then he thought of his father.

Without a doubt, Joseph DeMarco was watching him from the great beyond and regretting that the boundary between life and death kept him from collaring his wayward son and beating some good old-fashioned common sense into him. First he'd flipped out over that little scumbag's not-guilty verdict, and now he was keeping an armed-robbery suspect handcuffed to his bed. In either case, the extenuating circumstances wouldn't have swayed his father in the least.

*I don't want to hear your explanations*, he'd heard his father say so many times while he was growing up. *There are no explanations. There's only right and wrong.*

He'd never bothered with an excessive

number of words — he got right to the point, then right to the belt. John remembered the night when he was sixteen years old, when he'd violated his curfew because he'd helped a friend jump-start the dead battery in his car. Late was late, his father said, and John had caught hell for it.

His brothers, Alex and Dave, had found ways to cope with such a narrow definition of right and wrong — Dave by passive resistance and stoic tolerance of whatever punishment he received, and Alex by becoming just like his father so that he rarely got punished in the first place. John had never managed either of those things, spending his teenage years loving and hating his father all at the same time and wondering if the day would ever come when he could live up to his expectations.

So far, the answer was no.

A couple of times John almost decided to march back into his bedroom, grab Renee, and take her in. Then he'd think, *What if she's innocent?* and immediately he'd counter with, *That's not your decision to make.*

No matter how many times he told himself to do his job and get it over with, he finally came to the conclusion that there was only one way he'd be able to take her to jail

223

with a clear conscience. And that was if he was certain beyond a reasonable doubt that she was guilty.

She'd wanted to talk on the way out of that forest. To tell her story. To plead her case.

Maybe it was time to let her do just that.

Renee took stock of her situation, tried to make some sense of it, then gave up. She had no idea what John was up to, but she did feel a tiny glimmer of hope that maybe he believed her, at least a little, or she would be sitting in the county jail right now.

She gazed around the room and saw a typical bachelor's bedroom, with clothes scattered about, bed unmade, and furniture that looked like early flea market. The coating of dust on the dresser told her that housecleaning was at the bottom of his to-do list.

On his dresser she saw several framed photos. Three were studio shots, one of an older couple, one of an attractive, dark-headed woman of about thirty or thirty-five, and another a group picture that had to have been taken some time back because John was in it and he looked at least ten years younger. Surrounding him was a group of smiling people.

Family pictures.

Renee had the weirdest feeling as she looked at them, suddenly realizing that this man with whom she'd been at war for the past twenty-four hours had an actual life. A family. A history. She'd started to believe that maybe he'd just shown up on Earth one day a full-grown cop ready to save Tolosa, Texas, from the bad guys, but here was proof positive that he really was a human being.

She looked at the pictures for a long time, and she found herself wondering if he carried any in his wallet, too. Then she thought about what her own wallet contained, the one that undoubtedly had been confiscated by the manager of the Flamingo Motor Lodge. He might have found her eight hundred and fifty dollars there, but what he hadn't found were photographs. There was that silly one of her and Paula they'd taken in a photo booth at the Texas State Fair a couple of years ago, but other than that, nothing. Wallet pictures were to remind you of your family when you couldn't be with them, but did she want to be reminded of her family, which consisted only of her alcoholic mother? Not likely.

She leaned against a bed pillow, her arm uncomfortably restrained by the cuff, and sighed with exhaustion. That fifteen-mile walk had really taken it out of her. Thoughts of escape filtered through her mind, but fatigue prevented her from forming them into a cohesive plan she could put into action. She'd caught John unaware last night. She wouldn't be getting that kind of chance again.

Sleep. That was what she needed.

She'd almost drifted off when the bedroom door squeaked open. She sat up suddenly to see John's broad-shouldered body filling the doorway.

"Are you hungry?" he asked.

She felt a grumble in her stomach and realized that the answer to that question was yes. "Yeah. A little."

He unlocked her from the handcuff. "I heated up some soup. Come eat."

*Yes.* Eating would be good. Unfortunately, it was all she could do to lift herself off the bed. She came to her feet, wobbling a little, every muscle screaming in agony.

"But first," John said, "here are the ground rules. When you're not locked up, you don't leave my sight. If you do, I'm taking you in. If someone comes to my door, I'm locking you up in the bedroom. If you make any sound at all, I'm taking you in. If you pull *any* of the kind of crap you pulled while we were walking through those woods, I'm taking you in. Simply put, if someone finds out you're here, I could lose my job, not to mention having charges brought against me for harboring a fugitive. I'll do anything to make sure that doesn't happen. *Anything.* Do you understand?"

Renee swallowed hard and nodded.

"And in the event that I do take you in and you mention any of this to anyone, I'll deny every word of it, then do everything humanly possible to ensure that you're convicted of that robbery. Do you understand *that?*"

By now Renee was so shaken by his no-nonsense tone that her heart was thudding like a bass drum. But it was okay. She could do rules. She could do captivity. She could eat worms and stand on her head in the corner if it meant staying out of jail.

"Yes. I understand."

John gave her a curt nod, then led her to the kitchen. With his permission, she washed her hands at the sink, and then they sat down at the table, where he'd set out bowls of chicken noodle soup. It was absolutely surreal, the two of them sitting there and eating as if it were the most normal thing in the world, when Renee had never experienced anything more abnormal in her life. Nothing broke the silence except for spoons clinking against bowls. When they'd both finished, John took their bowls and deposited them in the sink. He returned to the table and sat down beside her again, one bare foot resting on a rung of the chair on the other side of him. This time he was carrying a pad of paper and a pen.

"Okay," he said. "The night of the robbery. I want you to tell me your side of the story."

Renee stared at him with surprise. "You . . . you actually want to hear what I have to say about it?"

He scowled at her. "I said I did, didn't I?"

"Well, yeah, but —"

"All the way out of the woods you wanted to talk, and now suddenly it's a problem?"

"No! No problem. Absolutely no problem at all." She took a deep breath and tried to look innocent, though she wasn't really sure what *innocent* looked like to a cop.

She put her elbows on the table and tried to clear her weary brain to think, wishing she'd had some sleep before he decided it was interrogation time, since this might be her only chance to make him understand that she had no part in that robbery.

"Okay. That night I'd just found out that I'd gotten a promotion at the restaurant where I work. The owner made me the assistant manager. I'd wanted that job for-ever, and when I got it, I felt like celebrating. So I left a little early. I went home and called my friend Paula. But then I remembered that she'd gone to the Hilton for one of those weekend-for-two things with her no-good boyfriend, Tom. So I was stuck celebrating by myself."

"What time did the robbery occur?"

"Apparently it was about ten-fifteen."

"Which convenience store?"

"The Handi-Mart down on Griffin Street. It's only a few blocks away from my apartment."

John made a few notes. "And where were you when the robbery occurred?"

"Home."

"Did you see anybody? Make a phone call? Anything?"

"No. I stayed in my apartment and watched some sappy old movie on TV."

"But then you left your apartment?"

"Yes."

"What time did the cop pull you over?"

"A little after eleven."

John wrote down the time. "What were you doing going out at eleven at night?"

Renee sighed. "Getting ice cream."

"Ice cream?" He looked at her disbelievingly.

"Yes. Ice cream. I know it sounds dumb now, but that's where I was going. Ben and Jerry were the only ones around I could celebrate with."

"So you didn't see anyone from the time you got home after work to the time you left again."

"That's right. Well, except for Steve Garroway."

"Who's he?"

"My ex-boyfriend. We broke up a couple of months ago."

"Did he come to your apartment?"

"No. I saw him in the hall."

"What time?"

"It was almost eleven."

"Forty-five minutes after the robbery."

"Yes. He was coming out of Tom's apartment —"

"Tom?"

"Paula's boyfriend. The one I told you about. Tom lives down the hall from me."

"Does Steve live there, too?"

"No. He used to, but he moved out a couple of months ago. He still lives in the same apartment complex, though, but in a different building. Steve and Tom are cousins."

"So what was he doing at Tom's apartment?"

"Feeding his cat while Tom and Paula were gone. He does that sometimes."

"Did you speak to Steve when you saw him?"

"Yes." Renee stared down at the table. "Or, rather, he spoke to me."

"What about?"

"Do we really have to go into this?"

"No, Renee. We don't have to go into anything. I can take you down to the police station and you can answer their questions instead."

Renee's stomach turned upside down at the mere mention of the police station. At that moment she'd have told John her entire life story if he had asked.

"I'm sorry," she said. "Steve is a very charming man. Smart, attractive, but he's got a character flaw or two that I just can't deal with."

"Such as?"

"He's got no ambition. He DJs at some of those clubs down on Colfax Street during the week when they don't have live bands. He always told me that those jobs were just temporary until he could get a real job, only I figured out pretty soon that the DJ gig was his real job and he had no intention of ever doing anything else. And whatever money he gets hold of he gambles

231

away, so there's no way he'll ever amount to anything."

She hadn't always felt that way about him. She and Steve and Paula and Tom used to get together on summer evenings at Paula's apartment to watch the Rangers play, since Paula had a big-screen TV and made the best nachos on the planet. Renee wasn't the biggest sports fan in the world, but those evenings had been a lot of fun. But then she'd realized that Tom was freeloading off Paula and cheating on her at the same time, and that Steve's main goals in life were to play music and get laid. Things hadn't been quite the same after that.

"Is that why you broke up?" John asked. "Because of what he did for a living?"

"Eventually it would have come to that."

"But that wasn't the reason?"

Renee paused, wondering why any of this was relevant. "No. The real reason we broke up was that after two months he thought I ought to sleep with him. I declined. Once he realized I was serious, he was gone."

John made a note on his pad, and she wondered what she'd just said that he deemed to be noteworthy. That she didn't sleep around? Given the accusations he'd thrown at her out in the woods, he'd probably find that hard to believe.

"So what happened between you that night?"

"Steve started talking to me about getting back together again. I couldn't believe it. He said he'd been a fool, that I was the best thing that had ever happened to him. I knew he was lying, but he sounded so sincere that I almost believed him."

"Almost?"

"Right up to the time he suggested we go back to my apartment and . . . talk about it."

Renee said those last three words with a lilting, suggestive tone, which was exactly the way Steve had said them as he backed her up against the wall and stared down at her, that hungry look in his eyes that said his current girlfriend, Rhonda the drug-addicted bimbo, must have brushed him off that evening, and he was looking for sex wherever he could get it.

"The last thing he wanted to do was talk," Renee said. "He was looking to get laid. He had a lot of nerve thinking that I'd even consider it."

"What did you do then?"

"Let's just say that God gave women knees for a very good reason. He was still bent over double by the time I got on the elevator."

"So you didn't exactly part amicably."

"You could say that. Why are you asking me all this? It has nothing to do with the robbery."

"No, but it has to do with your alibi. I want to know if Steve would be likely to speak positively on your behalf. But after a knee to the groin, I assume he might not be so inclined."

"It doesn't matter. My attorney said Steve can't be my alibi. The robbery occurred about ten-fifteen. I didn't see Steve until almost eleven."

"How long did you talk to him?"

"Only a few minutes."

"You say he lives in a different building. Would he have to cross the parking lot where your car was parked to go into your building?"

Renee thought for a moment. "Yes."

"Okay. If he was coming and going from your apartment building that night, he might have seen something. Somebody in the parking lot. Somebody near your car. Was he interviewed after the robbery?"

"Not that I know of."

"Didn't you tell them he was the closest thing you had to an alibi?"

"Yes, but nobody wanted to listen," she said bitterly. "They had their suspect. And my attorney said it didn't matter anyway, since the timing was all wrong."

"If Steve had seen something, would he be vindictive enough to withhold information?"

Renee shook her head. "I don't know. I mean, we've had our disagreements, but I don't think he'd do anything to deliberately hurt me."

"Even though you gave him a knee to the groin."

"He deserved it."

"That's not the issue, Renee. Would he withhold information? Yes or no?"

Renee sighed, wishing now that she'd gotten her point across with something a little less extreme than a full-frontal testicular attack. "I really don't know."

"Okay," John said. "How do *you* think the stuff got in the back of your car?"

"It's like I told you before. My door locks don't work. Anyone could have put it there. And think about it. What kind of a moron would I have to be to drive around with a gun and all that money in plain sight? If I were going to be an armed robber, don't you think I'd be a smarter one than that?"

John didn't respond. He hadn't really responded to much of anything, except to quietly grill her, and it was driving her crazy.

"Do you know any women who might

want to frame you for a crime? Blond women in particular?"

"Frame me?"

"In other words, Renee, do you have any enemies?"

Rhonda came to mind — Steve's new girl-friend. She had bleached-blond hair and a silicone-enhanced body that screamed *cheap slut* with every move she made. Rhonda had never been able to understand why Steve had once preferred Renee over her, and consequently she still saw Renee as a threat. The truth was that Rhonda didn't have a thing to worry about where Steve was concerned. As long as she continued to give him sex whenever he snapped his fingers and didn't gripe at him about his crappy lifestyle, he was hers forever.

Still, Rhonda's jealousy and vindictive-ness were legendary. When Renee and Steve had been dating, she'd once dropped four red socks into a batch of clothes Renee had in one of the washers in the laundry room, turning all her whites to a putrid shade of pink. But would the little hussy go so far as to commit a crime and implicate her? Renee didn't think so.

"Steve's new girlfriend, Rhonda, doesn't like me. She's still afraid I'm going to want Steve back and she'll be out in the cold. But

I really can't see her doing something as awful as armed robbery and then framing me for it."

"Are you sure?"

"Well, yeah. Isn't that kind of a drastic thing to do to get a romantic rival out of the way?"

"People kill to get romantic rivals out of the way. Is she blond?"

"She's Nice 'n Easy's color of the week."

"Would she have any other motive to commit robbery?"

"You mean, besides the fact that she's a perpetually broke cocaine addict?"

"Casual use, or habitual?"

"She never leaves home without it."

John made a note or two, then looked back up at Renee. "Let's broaden this a little," John said. "Are there any other blond women in the building who might resemble you enough for somebody to mistake you in a lineup?"

"The only ones I can think of are the hookers on the third floor."

John raised an eyebrow.

"At least I think they're hookers. Lots of men come and go from their apartment, and they always leave with smiles on their faces."

"What's the apartment number?"

"Three-seventeen."

Then he asked her for the location of her apartment complex, and she gave that to him, too.

"Do you think they might have had something to do with it?" she asked.

"I don't know."

"You seem to think it might have been somebody in my apartment complex who committed the robbery."

"It's within a quarter mile of the convenience store. Robberies are generally committed by people who live near the place they rob. If it happened as you say and the loot and gun were dropped in your car at that apartment complex, then it's possible the crime was committed by someone who lives there." He paused. "Or it could have been somebody who lives a hundred miles away."

*Or it could have been you.* He didn't say that, but the words hung in the air between them just the same.

John stared at his notes a moment more with intense concentration, as if looking at a puzzle he couldn't quite solve. Finally he blew out a weary breath. "Anything else?"

She heard the real meaning of those words. *Give me some reason why I shouldn't yank you up right now and deliver you to the police station like I should have done an hour ago. Give me some reason to believe you.*

And she had nothing.

"I-I don't know what else to say," she murmured.

He *tap, tap, tapped* his pen against the tabletop. For several long, excruciating moments it was the only sound in the room, with the possible exception of her heart, which was booming so hard inside her chest that seismographs in California had to be picking it up.

"I'm going to ask you one more question, Renee," he said. "And I want the truth."

She waited, her heartbeat reaching 8.5 on the Richter scale. He tapped his pen a time or two more.

"Back at that cabin. Why didn't you shoot me when you had the chance?"

Because she hated guns. Because merely picking one up had scared her to death. Because she couldn't have hurt John, no matter what the circumstances.

Because she was innocent.

"John, if you didn't know the answer to that question," she said, "I don't think I'd be here."

He stared at her long and hard, and all at once she thought she'd made a huge mistake. *Not good enough, Renee,* she heard him saying, and for a few horrible, distressing moments, she pictured him standing up, dragging her out to his car, and heading straight for the police station.

Instead, he tossed his pen down and stood up. "Okay. That's enough for tonight. If you want to take a shower, use the bathroom off my bedroom."

Renee felt a whoosh of relief. "So I'm . . . I'm staying here tonight?"

"Yes. Tonight."

He didn't offer more, and she didn't ask for more.

"Don't get any ideas. The bathroom window's painted shut. And shattering glass makes a lot of noise. I'd be able to hear it even over the shower. And don't lock the door, or I'm breaking it down."

"Okay."

She'd have agreed to anything. After all, she was getting more than she'd ever thought she'd have right now — a place to stay tonight that didn't involve metal bars and nonprivate toilets.

"John?" she said carefully. "What's going to happen to me now?"

"We'll talk about that tomorrow."

"But —"

"Tomorrow."

Renee clamped her mouth shut. *You're*

*here instead of in jail. Don't push it.*

He led her to the bathroom. She looked down at herself, at her dirty jeans and the dead pine needles clinging here and there. "Do you have a washing machine?"

"Yeah. Why?"

"These are the only clothes I have. Would you mind running them through?"

He looked at her with utter disbelief. "This isn't a luxury hotel, Renee."

"Come on, John! Look at me."

He squeezed his eyes closed painfully. "Just hand them to me out the door."

"I'm going to need something to wear when I get out of the shower."

With a heavy sigh, John fished through his closet and pulled out a worn flannel shirt and gave it to her. She went into the bathroom and closed the door behind her.

John waited outside the bathroom door, wondering at what point in time he'd become her personal valet. Bringing her here had been insane enough. Now he was doing her laundry?

A moment later the bathroom door opened a crack and she thrust her jeans and sweatshirt through the opening.

He grabbed them and started to walk away.

"John, wait!"

He turned back to see a pink satin bra and a pair of matching panties dangling from her hand. He just stared at them.

"John?"

She wiggled the undergarments. He watched the satin dance around for a moment, then took the unmentionables from her hand, trying not to think about the fact that this meant she was standing naked on the other side of that door.

She peered through the crack. "Be sure to separate the light stuff from the dark. Don't put the jeans in hot water or they'll shrink so much I won't be able to get into them. And make sure you wash the undies in cold water. There's a lot of static electricity now that it's getting cooler. If you use a little fabric softener —"

"No fabric softener. No separating anything. Your clothes will have to fend for themselves."

"Really, John. How hard is it to —"

He gave her a nasty warning stare.

"Oh, all right." She twisted her mouth with disgust, then shut the door.

He took her dirty clothes and tossed them into the washer, intending to let the cycle go tonight and then dump it all in the dryer in the morning. Then he happened to think about his cell phone. He retrieved it from his car and plugged it in to recharge it. Then he returned to the bedroom and sat on the edge of the bed, waiting for Renee to get out of the shower.

He looked around the room, at the layer of dust on everything, the piles of junk mail on his dresser, his unmade bed. He thought about how his sister Sandy harped at him constantly about the condition of his house, telling him that any woman he dated who came here would throw up and leave, and then where would he be? Forty or fifty years old and unmarried, she said. That was where he'd be.

Suddenly, with Renee here, he felt self-conscious, but he didn't know why. Probably because she was the only woman who'd ever seen the inside of his bedroom. Whenever he dated a woman, he always went to her place when any kind of intimacy was on the horizon because it was a whole lot easier for him to make a hasty exit. And it *always* seemed to come to that.

But Renee wasn't a woman he was dating. Far from it.

He heard her turn off the shower. A moment later a loud whirring noise emanated from the bathroom, and he realized she must have located that old blow-dryer he'd stuck under the sink. A little while later she came out of the bathroom, and his heart just about stopped.

She was at least five-eight, so the tail of his shirt fell only to the middle of her thighs, allowing a good portion of her long, tanned legs to protrude from beneath it. She'd rolled the sleeves up, the bulky fabric at her elbows a sharp contrast to her slender forearms. Her hair was soft and full from blow-drying, a lustrous shade of honey blond that glinted in the dim light of his bedroom.

Since her bra and panties were in the washer, she had to be wearing absolutely nothing under his shirt right now. The thought of her shifting in the night, of that shirt falling away to expose way more of her than he really ought to be looking at, made a little tremor of heat run right up his spine.

He motioned to the bed. "You can sleep here. But I have to lock you back up."

She let out a weak, regretful sigh. "Please, John. I swear I won't —"

He pointed. "Sit."

She came around and sat dutifully on the edge of the bed. He picked up the cuff dangling from the headboard, took her wrist in his hand, and looped the cuff around it. It was such an incongruous sight — that warm, delicate wrist inside the cold metal handcuff. He clicked the cuff shut, reminding himself that she was a prisoner, not a woman he'd invited to spend the night, no matter how attractive she might be. No matter how fresh and pretty she looked. No matter how wonderful she smelled, with fresh scents of soap and shampoo and . . .

And spearmint toothpaste.

"Damn it, Renee, you did it again, didn't you?"

"What?"

"Used my toothbrush!"

She looked at him with dumb disbelief. "You really are anal about that, aren't you?"

"Fine. Consider that one yours. I'll use my travel toothbrush, which, of course," he said, grimacing, "you've already used, too."

"I guess this isn't a good time to tell you I shaved my legs with your razor."

He glared at her. "Just keep your hands off my stuff!"

He stalked over to his closet, grabbed an old pair of sweatpants and a T-shirt, then went into the bathroom and peeled off his dirty clothes. After a quick shower, he took his dirty clothes out to the utility room, then returned to the bedroom and pulled back the covers on the other side of the bed from where Renee lay.

"Are you sleeping here, too?" she asked.

"It's the only bed in the house. I have exercise equipment in the other bedroom."

"So the answer is yes?"

"Do you have a problem with that?"

She shrugged. "No. No problem."

"It isn't as if we haven't occupied the same bed before."

"I know."

"We're just sleeping, Renee," he said sharply. "Nothing else."

"I think you made the 'nothing else' quite clear already today."

"There's not going to be any repeat of what happened out there in the woods. Do you understand?"

"Yes, John," she said, a note of exasperation in her voice. "I get the picture. This is a no-sex zone. I wouldn't think of violating it."

"See that you don't."

She stared at him a long time, then raised a single eyebrow with a look that seemed to say, *Who are you trying to convince, John? Me or you?*

For a moment, John felt positively transparent, as if she could read every thought he had. He crawled beneath the covers with his back to her, then turned out the lamp and settled his head against the pillow, acutely aware that she lay beneath the covers only a foot away — half-naked, blond, and beautiful.

Less than six hours ago, she'd been willing to have hot, steamy, down-in-the-dirt sex if he hadn't called a halt to it. Was that why she'd asked where he was sleeping? Because she wanted to do something more than sleep?

*No, dammit. Get that out of your mind. Where Renee is concerned, it's hands off. Period.*

Several minutes passed. John was hovering on the edge of sleep when he heard Renee's voice.

"John?"

He sighed drowsily. "What do you want?"

A long silence passed between them. Then she shifted a bit and he heard her voice again, floating tentatively to him across the darkness.

"Why didn't you take me to jail?"

That was a really good question. Why was she sleeping here instead of on a cot in the county jail? Why had he brought her to his *house*, for God's sake? Why was he risking his career for a woman he didn't even know who just might be guilty after all?

He would have liked to have given her some coplike answer to shield himself, something like, *The evidence is inconclusive,* or *It's my professional prerogative to get to the truth in any way I see fit,* or even *Just consider yourself lucky and shut up.*

But he couldn't.

He turned to face her. And that was a big, big mistake.

With only the light from the streetlamp outside filtering through the blinds, he couldn't make out the color of her eyes, but their luminescent quality was apparent nonetheless. Had a criminal ever been born who had eyes like that?

The late hour, the darkness, the way she'd whispered the question as if she were terrified of the answer — all those things seemed to make it impossible for him to speak anything but the truth.

"You're here because I have some doubts about your guilt."

"Then you believe I didn't do it?"

"I never said that. I said I have doubts. That's all."

"Enough doubt that you're risking your job?"

"Make no mistake, Renee. If it ever comes down to you or my job, you're going to jail."

He turned his back to her and pulled the covers up over his shoulder in a gesture of dismissal. He didn't need to be looking at her anymore. He was having a hard enough time maintaining his tough-guy demeanor when he wasn't completely sure she deserved it.

She'd told him nothing conclusive to lead him to believe she might be innocent, but he still couldn't get over the feeling that there was something more to this than an open-and-shut case. Could she be the victim of a random drop of the weapon and the cash from the robbery? Possibly. But what about the eyewitness who'd picked her out of a lineup? What were the odds of refuting that testimony?

Despite the overwhelming evidence against her, doubt still lingered in his mind. And he knew the only way to get rid of that doubt was to do a little investigating of his own.

# chapter ten

The first thing Renee saw when she woke the next morning was bright sunlight streaming through the blinds. The second thing was sunlight glinting off the metal bracelet she wore.

Bracelet?

She blinked, trying to focus. No. Not bracelet.

Handcuffs.

She squeezed her eyes closed, and for a moment she couldn't breathe as the events of the past twenty-four hours whipped through her mind. She really was handcuffed to a bed. John's bed. Which she was sharing with John.

She turned over, expecting to find him there. He wasn't.

She glanced at the clock. Ten forty-five. She'd slept until ten forty-five?

No wonder. She'd been so tired after all that had happened, it was amazing she hadn't slept around the clock.

She sat up slowly, looking around. John wasn't in the bedroom, and she didn't hear him in the bathroom. Finally she called out to him tentatively.

No response.

Louder.

Nothing.

She lay back down and closed her eyes, her arm shielding her eyes from the bright sunlight. His absence worried her. Where could he possibly have gone?

"Oh, my *God!*"

The voice out of nowhere made Renee's heart leap right into her throat. She jerked her arm away from her eyes to see a woman standing at the bedroom door.

With a strangled scream, she yanked herself up and scooted against the headboard, hauling the covers up over her with her free hand, her heart beating frantically. Who was this woman, and what was she doing in John's house?

The answer was obvious. Girlfriend.

She looked the part. Tall, long-legged, and amply endowed, with a headful of dark hair pulled into a ponytail at the crown of her head. She wore a pair of jeans, a purple crop top, and flip-flops, and her half-baffled, half-astonished expression was asking a whole lot more questions than

Renee was prepared to answer.

"Wh-who are you?" Renee asked.

"Sandy DeMarco," the woman said, her eyes still big as golf balls. "John's sister."

His sister? Was that better than a girl-friend, or worse? It was *weirder,* that was for sure.

*No.* It was better. A baffled sister was definitely better than an irate girlfriend.

Sandy continued to stare at her with dumb disbelief. "And you're . . . ?"

*Embarrassed as hell? At a total loss to explain this? Going to kill John for leaving me handcuffed? All of the above?*

"I'm Alice. I'm a . . . a friend of John's."

Sandy zeroed in on Renee's handcuffed wrist, looking perplexed, and in that instant Renee knew she couldn't explain this scenario if her life depended on it. Except, of course, to say that she was a fugitive John just happened to have hanging around. What was she going to do now?

Then it occurred to her. There *was* one other way to explain it, but . . . good Lord. Could she actually say it out loud?

"John's a cop, you know," Renee said, her voice shaky. "The handcuffs. I guess it's k-kind of . . . well, you know . . . kind of a . . ." She exhaled. "A turn-on."

Sandy blinked with disbelief. "What?"

*Oh, no.* Did she have LIAR scrolling across her forehead like stock-market figures?

"You're telling me my brother, Mr. Conservative, goes in for the kinky stuff?"

"Uh . . . yeah. I guess he does."

Sandy's perplexed expression slowly gave way to a smile of pure delight. "Well, I'll be damned. There's hope for him yet."

Renee felt a rush of relief. Not only had Sandy bought the idea that her brother was having wild, deviant sex, she applauded it, which meant she probably wasn't going to be calling the Depravity Squad.

"I guess this means he's back early," Sandy asked. "So where is he now?"

"Uh . . . I'm not sure."

Sandy planted her fists on her hips. "You mean he left you handcuffed here and took off?"

"He probably didn't want to wake me."

"Why didn't he take them off last night?"

*Good question.* With only one answer Renee could think of. "He fell asleep."

Sandy rolled her eyes. "Then you should have given him a swift kick to wake him up!" She strode over to the bed. "Where's the key? I'll get those things off you, and then I'll kill him for you when he gets home."

*The key.*

Hope gushed through Renee like water

through a broken dam. If the key was here, this woman could find it. She could unlock the handcuffs. And then Renee could get the hell out of here. Where she'd go, she didn't know. First she had to get free; then she'd think about how to disappear.

"I don't know where it is," Renee said. "Do you suppose you could look around a bit?"

"Sure." Sandy started poking around the bedroom. When it didn't appear to be lying around there, Renee suggested she look in the rest of the house, but after a few minutes of searching, Sandy came up empty-handed. Renee slumped with disappointment. Her best chance for escape was undoubtedly sitting in John's pocket right now.

"I can't believe this," Sandy said with disgust. "He must have the key with him. Do you have any idea where he went?"

"I don't know. To get a newspaper, maybe?"

"He's got you in his bed, and he goes out for a paper?" She made a scoffing noise. "And I thought there was hope for him. I hope you kill him for this, Alice. Or the offer's still open for me to be the hit woman. It'll be no problem proving justifiable homicide, believe me."

Renee would have settled for proving she was innocent of armed robbery.

"Now, don't you worry. I'll keep you company until he gets back. Being handcuffed to a bed all by yourself would have to be a real bore."

*Uh-oh.* This was bad. She pictured the look that would be on John's face the moment he saw her sitting here talking to his sister, and it wasn't a pretty sight.

"No," she said quickly, forcing a smile. "It's okay. I'll be fine by myself. Surely you've got better things to do than hang around here."

"And what if he's gone for another hour or two? I'm not leaving you handcuffed here. What if there's a fire or something? No. I'm staying right here until he gets back." She sat down on the corner of the bed and gave Renee a woman-to-woman look. "I know this sounds kind of weird, but I'm really glad this happened. I don't get to meet many of the women John dates."

This was getting stranger by the minute. Here she was handcuffed to John's bed in the apparent aftermath of a really hot bondage scene, yet Sandy was acting as if they'd just run into each other at the mall. Somehow she would have thought any relative of John's would have been quite a bit more . . . well, appalled.

"Of course, he has to actually ask a woman out before I can meet her," Sandy went on, talking away as if they were chatting over a cup of coffee. "Most of the time he eats, sleeps, and works. That's about it."

"Uh . . . yeah. He seems to take his job pretty seriously."

"Too seriously." Sandy pulled her legs up onto the bed and crossed them, resting her elbow on her knee, her chin in her hand. "So. How long have you two been seeing each other?"

*Ever since he almost arrested me two nights ago.*

"Not long," Renee said.

"Tell me about yourself," Sandy said. "What do you do for a living?"

*Well, if your brother would let me go, I'd have a promising career as a professional fugitive.*

"I work at a restaurant. Assistant manager."

"Perfect! John loves to eat. You're a match made in heaven."

Renee had the feeling that if she'd mentioned she was an undertaker, Sandy would have said John liked dead bodies.

"How about you?" Renee said, thinking maybe she should hold up her end of the conversation. "What do you do?"

"I own a flower shop. I think it's a back-lash against all that testosterone I was around growing up. One father, three brothers, no mother."

"Oh. I'm sorry. What happened to your mother?"

"Cancer. I don't suppose John got around to telling you any of the details of his personal life yet."

Renee knew precisely nothing about John's personal life. But given Sandy's inclination to talk, she was learning more every minute.

"No," Renee said. "He hasn't. His mother's death must have hit him hard."

"Yeah, well, it hit *me* harder. Try dealing with three younger brothers who fought like gladiators and had to be threatened with their lives to pick up their underwear or take a plate to the kitchen once in a while. Even now . . ." Sandy ran her finger tip along the nightstand and held up a fingerful of dust. "Look at this, will you? And that fridge of John's. Alexander Fleming might have discovered penicillin years earlier if he'd had access to that." She made a face of disgust, then brushed her finger off on the leg of her jeans. "That's why I dropped by today. I thought he was still out of town. See, if I don't clean up for him occasionally, any woman he brings around is going to throw up and leave, and when will that workaholic brother of mine *ever* get married?"

*Ahh.* Sandy's goal: to marry off her brother. John's goal: to make sure that never happened.

"I mean, what do you think of this place, Alice? It's a mess, isn't it?"

Actually, it didn't look so bad to Renee. She personally never knocked the dust off anything until she couldn't recognize the shape of the object beneath it.

"I've seen worse," she said.

Sandy smiled. "A forgiving woman. My brother could use one of those."

Renee didn't know how to respond to that, except maybe to laugh out loud at the thought of her and John together. As a couple. The cop and the fugitive. Opposites did attract once in a while, but that was ridiculous.

"Actually, I think John took it harder when our father was killed," Sandy said, jumping back and forth between subjects like a kid playing hopscotch. "He was shot in the line of duty. It happened about seven years ago."

"Your father was a cop?"

"Uh-huh. It was a routine traffic stop. He

had no way of knowing that the guy he pulled over had a dead body in the trunk that he didn't want discovered."

"That's awful. So both of your parents are gone?"

"Yeah. It's just us kids now, and aunts and uncles and cousins. And grandparents."

"Are your other brothers married?"

"Dave was. He lost his wife in a car accident about a year ago, when their daughter was six months old."

"That's terrible!"

"He's doing okay. If anybody can handle it, Dave can. It's a struggle with the baby, but we all help out. He'll get married again. It's just a matter of time. Now, as for Alex, he never has a shortage of women around, but the idea of marriage kind of rubs him the wrong way. And John's too wrapped up in his job to even think about dating, much less getting married." Sandy gave her a sly smile. "But they can't hold out forever."

Renee couldn't help smiling back. The longer they talked, the less weird it seemed, and the more she forgot she was here under false pretenses. Just for a little while it was nice to relax a bit and let herself believe that she was John's sex toy rather than an undercover fugitive. Sandy's nonstop chatter made her feel like one of the family when she hadn't even *met* the family.

As if she ever would.

But even as they talked, John's imminent return was never far from her mind. Where was he, anyway? And what was he going to say when he came back and found her talking to his sister? Surely he'd put on that cop face of his and play it cool until he found out what lie she'd told to cover things up.

Surely he would.

Wouldn't he?

John told himself as he drove to the south side of town that he had one goal, and it was a simple one: he was going to check out the convenience store where the robbery took place. But he wasn't going as a cop, because the last thing he wanted was for word to get out that he was nosing around in this case. Somebody might ask why, and he didn't want anyone to eventually associate him with Renee. He had no business even being back in town right now. If Lieutenant Daniels found out he hadn't finished the term of his exile, he'd pay hell for it.

He decided he'd just poke around a little. Ask a few questions. Talk with the woman who'd gotten shot, if she was there, and find out her take on the night in question. And he was sure that when he was finished doing that, he'd see how mistaken he'd been. He'd see that nobody but Renee could have committed that crime, and once he was convinced of that he wouldn't have a bit of trouble taking her to jail.

Ten minutes later he pulled up to the Handi-Mart, one of those tacky little convenience stores with hand-drawn ads in the window advertising cheap cigarettes and milk for a dollar ninety-nine per gallon. A barefoot woman in a long flowered dress stood talking on the pay phone outside, while a toddler wearing only a diaper and a Cookie Monster shirt hugged her leg.

John went inside the store, bells clinking against the grimy glass door. A geeky-looking Middle Eastern kid wearing wire-rimmed glasses stood behind the counter. According to his badge, his name was Ahmed.

John browsed the store nonchalantly for a moment, then came to the counter with a bag of Doritos and a bottle of 7UP.

"Hey," he said, looking around questioningly as Ahmed rang up his purchases. "Isn't this the store that was robbed a little while back?"

"Oh, you bet!" Ahmed's face broke out in

a huge, toothy grin. "And the owner got shot right in the arm." He made a gun out of his thumb and forefinger. "Pow! Just like that!"

Ahmed had clearly watched one too many action-adventure movies. "An older lady, I hear. That's a shame."

"Nope," he said, shaking his head. "No shame. Mrs. Bunch is a tough old broad. That's what she says."

John heard the shuffle of feet and turned to see someone coming out of the back room, a tiny, gnomelike woman he estimated to be somewhere between eighty and eight hundred. Her sparse white hair lay against her scalp in wispy ringlets, and her face had the deep, fissured look of a dried-up river basin. She wore stretchy pink pants and the same kind of cheap red cotton coat worn by every convenience-store employee in America. Her name tag read *Trudy*.

"Now, Ahmed, you're talking about me behind my back again," she said. "What kind of crap you dishin' out?"

"No crap, Mrs. Bunch," Ahmed said, his hand over his heart. "I tell the truth."

"You tell the truth, huh? Then tell me what you were doing in the bathroom all that time yesterday right after the *Playboy*s came in."

Ahmed gave her a crafty smile. "This is America. Constitutional law. Fifth amendment, you know?" Then he turned his smile to John and added a furtive thumbs-up. "Miss October."

Harley and Ahmed. Appreciation for the naked female form knew no cultural boundaries.

Trudy shook her head. "You're a smart-ass, you know that, Ahmed?"

"Yes," he said. "I am told I have a very smart ass."

"Are you the lady who was the victim of the robbery?" John asked Trudy.

"Yep. You must have read about it in the paper like everybody else." The old woman cackled. "Nothin' like getting robbed to make you famous. I was almost this famous when I got robbed back in '82, but I didn't get shot then. Gettin' shot now that's what really gets people talkin'." She leaned over the counter. "Wanna see my scar?"

Before John could answer one way or the other, she hauled up the sleeve of her red jacket. "Looky here," she said, pointing to the remnant of stitches on her upper arm, circled by a faint ring of black and blue.

John felt as if he'd entered a carnival freak show. He gave a low whistle. "Pretty nasty."

"Yep. Took 'em half an hour to dig out

the bullet, it being deep in the muscle and such."

John nodded with as much awe as he could muster. "I read that it was a woman who robbed you. What did she look like?"

"Well, first off, she was pretty tall."

"How tall?"

"Maybe five-eight. Or ten."

"Wow."

At the expression of awe in John's voice, the old lady immediately upped the ante. "Maybe six feet. Or I don't know — maybe even six-two. It's hard to say."

*Just pick the most impressive number,* John thought, as Trudy added even more credence to what cops generally believed — eyewitness testimony could be some of the flakiest evidence of all. In this case it was especially true. From Trudy's vantage point, just about any woman who walked into her store would look like an Amazon.

"And mean-looking, too," she went on. "She wore these big, dark glasses and all this fire-red lipstick. And she had this deep voice, kinda like Bette Davis in *Dead Ringer*, where she killed her twin sister and assumed her identity. That's what the robber sounded like. Couldn't forget that."

John thought about Renee's voice, middle range, and relatively soft when she wasn't shouting at him about something. But a person's voice was just one of many things that could easily be disguised.

The woman crinkled her nose. "And something else. Now, I know I'm a fine one to talk, being as how I buy most of my clothes down at the Wal-Mart, but that woman had a bit of trouble puttin' a look together, you know?"

"Oh? How's that?"

"She was wearing this god-awful leopard-print blouse. And these black spandex pants. And white shoes. Big white shoes. That woman had some good-size feet on her."

Renee wasn't exactly petite, but her feet weren't in the gargantuan range, either. Another exaggeration? Probably. If Trudy could make her perpetrator grow six inches in six seconds, how accurate was her shoe-size assessment? Also, Renee's fashion sense seemed a bit tamer than animal prints, although there was the matter of disguising oneself to commit a robbery. It wasn't unusual for a robber to dress outlandishly, then dump the disguise somewhere and walk away looking normal to take the heat off.

"And gloves. Black ones. Oh! And her earrings! Huge, dangly things shaped like rainbows. All those gaudy colors with a leopard-print shirt." Trudy's face crinkled like a raisin. "Never seen anything so ugly in all my life."

"You must have a really sharp eye to catch all those details," he told Trudy.

The old lady cackled again. "Nah. Not really. A blind man in the dark couldn't have missed that getup." She leaned toward John and dropped her voice. "Just between you and me, I been having a little problem with cataracts lately. Things are a little blurry around the edges."

John's heart skipped. The woman who'd fingered Renee was telling him she couldn't see? "But the newspaper said you positively identified the woman who robbed you."

She waved her hand. "That was a piece of cake once I saw them all standing there in that lineup, even though none of them was wearin' them ugly clothes. All I had to do was pick out the tallest blonde."

John couldn't believe it. Even the most brainless defense attorney would have this woman discredited the minute she took the stand.

"Pretty smart, huh?" Ahmed said with a smile of admiration. "She picked right, too."

"Yeah," Trudy said. "Found out later

that the one I fingered was the one they arrested. They found her with my money and the gun she shot me with. Am I good, or what?"

Suddenly the open-and-shut nature of Renee's case seemed even fuzzier than before. It had taken him only two minutes of casual conversation to come to the conclusion that this particular eyewitness was loony. Why hadn't the detective on the case made the same call?

"I have a few cop friends who work around here," John said. "Do you remember the name of the officer on the case? The one who interviewed you after the robbery?"

Trudy got a thoughtful look on her face. "Started with a B, I think. Borstad, Botsdorf . . ."

*Oh, God. Not him.* "Botstein?"

"Yep. That's the one. Real nice fella. You know him?"

"Yeah. Good old Botstein."

He knew him, all right. Leo Botstein was a detective out of the South Precinct who'd been counting the days until retirement for approximately the last thirty-two years, and he hadn't put in an honest day's work in the last five. And now he'd finally made the leap. If John remembered right, his retirement party had been last night.

"Hey!" Trudy shouted. "You kids over there! Don't you pick up those magazines unless you're planning on buying them!"

John turned to see two teenage boys standing at the magazine rack, dripping with streetwise attitude. They wore ragged, oversize jeans that hugged their hips and baseball caps turned backward. The shorter of the two shot Trudy a practiced sneer.

"Aw, go to hell, you old bag! We'll read whatever we want to!"

Trudy reached a gnarled hand under her coat and pulled something out of the stretchy waistband of her pink polyester pants. Something that looked suspiciously like a semi-automatic pistol. She leveled it directly at the kid in a two-fisted stance.

"Okay, you little bastard," she said with a snarl. "Just who are you calling an old bag?"

The kid's eyes widened. Clearly he hadn't expected a woman who was the approximate size and shape of a troll doll to be packing enough firepower to blow his head off. He slapped his buddy on the shoulder, yanked the door open, and they peeled out of the store. Trudy stuffed the weapon back into the waistband of her pants. Ahmed gave her a big grin and held up his palm, and Trudy high-fived him.

Then he turned his grin toward John.

"Mrs. Bunch. She takes no crap."

John looked at the old lady, still astonished at her dead-on Dirty Harry imitation. "Now, ma'am, you wouldn't go shooting a couple of kids just for reading the magazines, would you?"

"Aw, heck, no." She snickered. "Sure scares the daylights out of them, though, don't it?"

Looking down the barrel of a gun would pretty much scare the daylights out of anyone, particularly when the person holding that gun appeared to have a very large screw loose.

"You know," Trudy said, "this used to be a really nice neighborhood. Kids had respect. Now they got nothin' but smart mouths, just like Ahmed here."

"Ah, but you would never point a gun at me for reading the magazines. It's what you call a . . . perk?"

"Perk, my ass. If you stay in the john today as long as you did yesterday, I'm blowing a hole right through the door."

John tossed a five down on the counter to pay for the soda and chips. "You know, Mrs. Bunch, that armed robber almost made a big mistake messing with you. She's lucky she didn't get her head blown clean off."

"You can say that again. If I'd been carrying my gun at the time instead of having it under the counter, there woulda been blond-bimbo brains all over the potato-chip rack."

John couldn't wait to dig into those Doritos now. "So what made the robber actually shoot you?"

"I went for my gun. I'm a little slower than I was a few years ago, but I still figured I could take her." She patted the bulge under her coat. "That's where my baby stays these days. I'd sooner walk around without my underdrawers."

John had no desire to dwell on that mental image. "Now, why do you figure someone would want to rob a nice lady like yourself?"

"Probably to get herself some new clothes, considering the ones she was wearing looked like something out of a hooker's garage sale. Course, I guess now she'll have all the new clothes she needs, courtesy of the state of Texas."

Trudy laughed raucously at that, and Ahmed joined in with another high five, and pretty soon all the frivolity was just about more than John could stand.

He left the convenience store and went back out to his Explorer, tossing the 7UP and the Doritos into the backseat. He made a few notes on the pad he'd brought with him, then pulled a notebook out of his glove compartment. He flipped through it, then grabbed his cell phone and dialed Leo Botstein's home number. The man answered with a drowsy, hung-over voice.

"Leo. It's John DeMarco."

A loud, painful groan. "Man, stop yellin' into the phone, will you?"

It appeared that John had remembered right about Botstein's retirement party. Right now even a ticking clock would sound like a jackhammer to him.

"DeMarco," he said. "What the hell do you want?"

"I need some information. You had a rob-bery at a convenience store down on Griffin Street. Elderly lady got shot. Perp was a blond woman. How solid is the case?"

"News flash. I retired seventeen hours ago. That means I don't give a shit."

"Gee, Leo, that must also mean you don't give a shit if I tell everyone about the New Year's Eve incident with the hooker and the Doberman."

Silence.

"You're an asshole, DeMarco."

"Just tell me about the case."

John heard a heavy, drunken sigh. "It's rock solid."

"Who were the other suspects you interviewed?"

"No other suspects. I had the loot from the robbery, an eyewitness, and a smoking gun. I don't go looking for something I already got."

"Motive?"

"Why are you asking me all this crap?"

"It's my aunt Louisa. One of her friends is the daughter of the old lady who got shot. She's been bugging the hell out of me, wanting me to check up." He really did have an aunt Louisa, so at least that part of the story was true. "Who was the case assigned to when you left?"

"Henderson. He'll take it to court."

John slumped with disgust. Oh, that was just *great*. If there was anybody who could beat out Botstein for the Apathetic Cop of the Year award, it was Henderson.

"Assuming somebody finds the suspect," Botstein added.

"She missed her court date?" John said, feigning surprise.

"Yep. Jumped bail two days ago." He coughed a little, then burped. "Shoulda been at my party, DeMarco. Farnsworth sprang for a stripper who could pick up a dollar's worth of quarters with her hoochie."

"Gee, Leo. Sorry I missed that."

"Hell of a table dancer, too."

"And me with all those dollar bills last night, wondering what to do with them."

"Bullshit. When you worked South, I don't remember you so much as going out for a drink after work, much less stuffing a stripper's G-string."

"Crawl back into the bottle, Botstein."

"Get a life, DeMarco."

John hung up the phone. Well, it was pretty clear now that no help would be forthcoming from official sources, even if he could find a way to disguise his real motive for nosing into the case.

He sat there a long time in his car, thinking about Renee's repeated professions of innocence, about the fact that the victim was half-blind and half-nuts, about how a creep like Botstein had held people's fates in his hands for the past thirty-two years. How many cases had he just tossed off because he was too lazy to dig deeper? How many people had gotten screwed to the wall because he just didn't give a damn?

Was Renee going to be another one?

Then John thought about some of the arrests he'd made over the years. Were there times when he'd been so intent on putting somebody away for a crime that when a pretty good suspect presented himself, he put the full force of the law behind the arrest without digging any deeper? Had he been responsible for innocent people going to prison?

Maybe he wasn't so different from Botstein after all.

He told himself that at least his motivation was to see justice done, while Botstein had been trying to do the least amount of work possible and still draw a paycheck. But in the end, the result was the same.

He decided this was one time he was going to make sure that didn't happen. He decided to check out a couple of other suspects — the two women in Renee's apartment complex she thought might be hookers.

A few minutes later he pulled into the parking lot of Timberlake Apartments. The place needed a paint job and some landscaping attention, but otherwise it was clean and neat. He parked his car near the building where Renee's apartment was. As he was getting out, a balding man in a tan windbreaker and brown slacks came from the building across the parking lot and went straight to the late-model Chrysler parked next to him on the left. A cigarette hung out the side of his mouth, the smoke wafting up into his squinty little eyes.

John knew that face. Harold Pinsky, hired heat for a loan shark John had busted in ninety-six. What was he doing here?

John leaned over the Chrysler as Pinsky stuck his key into the lock. The man looked up with surprise, then turned away with disgust.

"Shit. DeMarco. Thought you moved uptown."

"What are you up to, Pinsky?"

"Just visiting a friend. Last I checked, there was no law against that."

"There isn't, unless you break your friend's legs because he owes you money."

"You've been watching too many cop shows. I'm a businessman. Strictly aboveboard."

"So who were you here to see?"

"None of your damned business."

John sighed. "Now, here I ask you such a simple question, and you're having such a terribly hard time answering it."

Finally Pinsky shrugged. "Fine. I was here to see the lovely ladies in 317. Would you like the details?"

Three-seventeen. Just where he'd been heading. Only he'd seen Pinsky coming out of another building across the parking lot. "Would those lovely ladies happen to be working girls?"

"Oh, yeah. They work really hard. Funny thing — the more you pay them, the harder they work. And before you get to thinking maybe you'd like to bust a couple of working girls, you might check out their client list. You wouldn't want to embarrass any of your superior officers."

"You're full of shit, Pinsky."

"Why don't you go see them, DeMarco? I hear they've got a special rate for cops. Maybe they could work the kinks out of that tight ass of yours."

"The day I have to pay for sex, I'll consider it."

Pinsky gave him a "go to hell" look and got into his car, flicking his cigarette butt across the parking lot before closing the door.

Okay. Renee was right. They were hookers. But were they hookers who also robbed convenience stores?

A minute later he was knocking on 317. The door squeaked open and a woman peered through the crack. "Good morning. Do you have an appointment?"

"I hear you take drop-ins."

"Not generally," she said, eyeing John up and down.

"Harry Pinsky referred me."

The door closed. John heard the chain rattle, and then the door swung open again. "Come on in, honey. Harry's one of our best customers."

John entered the apartment, which was furnished in reds, greens, and golds in an unexpectedly tasteful manner. His blond hostess wore a demure negligee of cream-colored lace, and when the other woman came into the living room, she was similarly dressed.

"Nice place you've got here," he told them.

"Only for two more weeks," the first woman said. "We're moving uptown."

The other one smiled sardonically. "And to think our families said we'd never amount to anything."

After a few minutes of conversation, John could tell he'd hit a dead end. With the business these women had going, they could probably turn a couple of tricks in a single night and make far more money than had been stolen from that convenience store, which convinced him that this particular pair of blond hookers probably had nothing to do with the robbery. They also appeared to be independent businesswomen without the assistance of a pimp, which meant they were not under the thumb of anyone who might be directing them to do grossly illegal things. He also learned that Harry Pinsky hadn't been there in over three weeks, which convinced him that there was probably some poor schmuck hobbling around his apartment right now with a broken face or shattered kneecaps.

John gave the women a pair of twenties for their trouble, then left the apartment complex feeling more confused than ever. He'd just eliminated two suspects, which did nothing to help Renee's case, but there was still the matter of the old lady's eyesight problems.

He sighed. If he was out to make himself feel better about taking Renee to jail, he'd just failed miserably.

# chapter eleven

It astonished Renee that she and Sandy talked for over an hour and there wasn't a single lull in the conversation. Sandy was responsible for most of the chatter, her dark ponytail bouncing with animation as she treated Renee to tales about her and her brothers as they were growing up. As the minutes went by, Renee started to see John in an entirely new light. Up to now she was sure he'd been born a cop and would die a cop with nothing in between, so it fascinated her to hear that he actually had a normal life. And even though Renee was sure she had CRIMINAL stamped on her forehead like a tattoo, not once did Sandy say, *And by the way, have you robbed any convenience stores lately?*

But best of all, Sandy's chatter was keeping her mind off the fact that if she didn't go to the bathroom pretty soon, she was going to explode.

Sandy wound down from yet another

story and gave Renee a speculative smile. "So tell me. What do you think of my brother?"

*I think he's going to go berserk when he sees me talking to his sister while I'm handcuffed to his bed.*

"Well, we haven't known each other long, but he seems like a nice guy." Which was at least somewhat true. He hadn't thrown her in jail. That was pretty nice, wasn't it?

"Is he someone you'd like to know better?"

"Uh . . . yeah. Sure."

"Good. But I gotta tell you that that's not going to be easy. Like I said, he's way too wrapped up in his job. He's got this bad habit of getting right up to the point of actually having a relationship with a woman, and then she complains a little about the hours he works, or that he talks about nothing but his job. He hates that, so then he turns around and does something to piss her off just to get her to leave, or he'll find fault with petty things she does and break up with her. He once sent a woman packing just because she used his toothbrush. Can you believe that?"

*Oh, no.* She couldn't *imagine* that.

"He'll pull that nonsense on you, too, if you let him. But if you'll hold out through all the crap he's liable to dish out and let him know that he can't drive you away, he might actually see that a long-term relationship isn't the heinous thing he's always made it out to be, and you'll actually have something together."

Oh, *that* sounded like fun. Kind of like crawling on her belly through enemy territory and praying she didn't hit a land mine. "So it's as simple as that, huh?"

"Okay, so I made it sound like a descent into hell. But let me tell you something, Alice. He's worth it. Even he doesn't know that, but he is. He's a very good man who's just far too focused on the wrong things in life. But I promise you that if you hang on to him, you'll be glad you did."

*A very good man.* Renee felt a little tingle down her spine when Sandy said that, because in the past few days, she'd seen little glimmers of that. The fact that she was here and not in the county jail attested to it. Amid all that yelling and cussing and hard-ass cop pronouncements, she'd seen a few chinks in his armor, and Sandy was widening those chinks with every word she spoke.

Then Renee heard the clink of a key in the front door. Her heart flew instantly to her throat. Unless another family member had decided to drop by, it looked as if John was home.

"He's finally here," Sandy said. "It's about time."

Renee heard footsteps coming down the hall. Quick, heavy footsteps. A moment later John appeared at the door of the bedroom. He saw Sandy and stopped short, a look of utter astonishment on his face. His gaze flitted to Renee, then to Renee's handcuffed wrist, then back to Sandy again.

Sandy zeroed in on John's bruised face. "Good Lord! What happened to you?"

"Uh . . . accident," he murmured.

"Well, I'm gonna screw up the other side of your face if you don't get over here and unlock Alice!" Sandy came to her feet, her fists rising to her hips. "Were you planning on keeping her in handcuffs forever?"

"I know I went along with it last night, John," Renee said quickly, in the sweetest voice she could muster. "And it was fun. Really. But it might have been nice if you'd unlocked me before you left the house."

Understanding appeared to come to him in tiny bits, and she knew the precise moment when he finally realized exactly what lie she'd told to keep them both out of hot water. She thought it impossible, but the big bad cop actually blushed.

"Hey!" Sandy said. "Don't just stand there! Get over here and unlock her!"

John looked so flustered that if Renee hadn't known how furious he was going to be once they were alone again, she probably would have laughed. He extracted a key from his pocket, then took hold of Renee's wrist. With his back to his sister, he gave Renee a wide-eyed *"what the hell has been going on here?"* look that Renee couldn't answer without giving them both away.

He pulled the cuff from her wrist and let it clunk against the headboard. Then he turned back to face his sister, assuming his stern cop voice. "This is not what you think it is."

"Oh?" Sandy's voice held a note of amusement. "Then what is it?"

John grabbed his sister by the arm and pulled her into the hall. Renee could see them through the crack in the door, though, and even though they spoke in angry whispers she could still make out every word.

"Okay," John said. "It's what you think it is. Now will you get the hell out of here?"

"Hey, I'm just thrilled that you have *some* kind of social life, even if it is a little" — she looked back through the crack in the door and grinned — "kinky."

"Sandy, leave."

"Though I must say it's not particularly original, especially with you being a cop and all. Is this your way of mingling business with pleasure?"

"*Out!*"

"Sure, John. I'll go. As long as you promise you'll come to Sunday lunch today at Aunt Louisa's."

"Not today."

"And bring Alice."

"Bring Alice?" He shook his head wildly. "No. No way."

"You haven't been to Sunday lunch in months."

"It hasn't been that long."

"Aunt Louisa only lives three blocks over, you know. It wouldn't have been much of an effort."

"I've been busy."

"The Cowboys are playing today."

"I can watch them right here."

Sandy rolled her eyes. "Come on, John! Would it be so awful to come to dinner and bring a girlfriend along?"

"She's not my girlfriend!"

"She could be."

"That's up to me to decide, isn't it?"

"No offense, but up to now your decisions in that regard have left a little bit to be desired."

"So I need you to tell me how to run my life?"

"Yeah. Sometimes I think you do."

"Drop it, Sandy."

"John —"

"I said drop it!"

There was a long silence.

"Listen to me," Sandy said sharply. "I talked to her. She's nice, she's smart, she's pretty, and I think she'll put up with you. Don't blow it!"

As Sandy disappeared down the hall, John wheeled around and stormed back into the bedroom, slamming the door behind him. He couldn't believe this. He simply could not believe it. He strode to the bed and stood over Renee, glaring down at her. To his dismay, she was regarding him with something less than the abject fear and total respect he really could have used right then.

"What did you tell my sister?"

"Not much, really. A picture is worth a thousand words."

"Does she know anything she's not supposed to?"

"She thinks we had kinky, mind-blowing sex, complete with bondage. Was there another story that would have explained this situation?"

John closed his eyes, trying to quell the

tension he felt rising inside him. He reached for the handcuffs dangling from the head-board.

"No!" Renee said. "Wait! I have to go to the bathroom!"

He slumped with disgust, then motioned toward the bathroom. "Fine. Go."

"You can't lock me up again, anyway. Your sister will think you're a sex maniac."

"She already thinks I'm a sex maniac!"

"No, she doesn't. She thinks you're won-derful. She thinks you work too hard. She thinks you need a wife. And she thinks you finally had a little fun for once. Is there any-thing wrong with that?"

Renee disappeared into the bathroom, leaving John standing there completely and totally dumbfounded. While he'd been gone, they'd been discussing the intimate details of his sex life like a pair of gossipy teenagers. And he hadn't even participated in the sex life they'd been gossiping about. Could he have made a bigger mistake than bringing Renee here? Was there any way he could have made a bigger mistake?

He heard a flush, then water running, and a moment later Renee came out of the bath-room. "And Sandy told me a lot of other things, too," she said, picking up right where she'd left off without missing a beat.

"She told me that when you were six, you tied a bathtowel around your neck and jumped out of a tree. Surprisingly, you did not fly like Superman. You did break your arm."

He was going to kill Sandy.

"She also told me that in the fifth grade your brother Dave used to walk to school three blocks out of his way to avoid a bully, until you went along with him one day and 'kicked some ass.' I believe that was the way Sandy put it." Renee smiled with delight. "And then she told me about the time you saved a kitten from drowning in a sewer drain."

John closed his eyes. That damned kitten story? Again? "I just pulled the stupid thing out of the water before it could go under. I don't even like cats!"

"So that's why you took it home and blow-dried it?"

*No.* Death was too good for Sandy, unless it was a slow, painful one.

"She also told me that you fell in love with Anita Saunders in the seventh grade, and you've been partial to blue-eyed blondes ever since."

"That's crap!"

"So you're not partial to blue-eyed blondes?"

"I'm not partial to my sister yammering on about me to a total stranger!"

Renee grinned. "So she's right."

Oh, boy, was she ever. Anita Saunders had been a walking, talking wet dream who'd gotten imprinted onto his adolescent hormones, turning him into some kind of Pavlov's dog whenever a blue-eyed blonde wandered into his line of sight. Which probably explained why he'd left Harley's with Renee in the first place and gotten himself into this hellacious mess.

But did his sister really think he would have hot, kinky sex with a woman he barely knew?

Yes, thank God, she did, and that was a whole lot better than any alternative explanation.

"Listen to me, Renee. I'm not interested in my sister's warped version of my formative years. We're in deep shit here. If she opens her mouth to the rest of the family —"

Suddenly a loud whirring sound came from the other room. John listened for a moment. It couldn't be.

He yanked open the bedroom door, then wheeled back around and pointed at Renee. "Don't you move *one muscle!*"

He stormed into the hall, and when he turned the corner into the living room, he saw, of all things, Sandy vacuuming his living room rug. He yanked the plug out of the wall.

"What are you doing?"

"This place is a mess."

"But it's my mess, and I don't care!"

"But you know how Aunt Louisa is about dirty rugs."

"What has Aunt Louisa got to do with this?"

Sandy smiled sweetly, then snatched the plug out of John's hand. "Our lunch plans have changed. I called Aunt Louisa. Turns out she'd just be delighted to bring her pot roast over here instead, considering she hasn't seen you in, like, months."

Sandy stuck the plug back into the wall. The vacuum motor whirred. John yanked it out again.

"You call her right now! Call her back and tell her not to come!"

"Sorry, John. She's already out the door, armed with pot roast, that Jell-O salad you hate, and a cell phone to tell the rest of the family what's up." She gave him a smug grin. "I told you I wanted you and Alice to have lunch with us, now, didn't I?"

She plucked the plug from John's hand again, and he wondered if homicide was indeed an option. It would certainly overshadow the fact that he was harboring a fugitive. He eyed his sister's throat for a few calculating seconds, then opted for damage control instead.

He hurried to the utility room, yanked Renee's clothes out of the dryer, then went to his bedroom and tossed them to her.

"Get dressed. We're getting out of here."

"Huh?"

"Sandy invited my whole family over here for lunch. I can't stop them. We have to get out before they get here."

"Get out? Where to?"

"It doesn't matter. Sandy's one thing. The rest of my family is another. We have to get out of here now!"

"But what will Sandy say if we leave?"

"I'll handle Sandy. Just get dressed!"

Renee yanked up the clothes, hurried into the bathroom, and closed the door behind her. John stood next to it, checking his watch every ten seconds.

"Renee! Move it!"

"I can't get into my jeans!"

"What?"

"I *told* you not to wash them in hot water! And you put them in a hot dryer, too, didn't you?"

"Just put them on!"

John waited a minute more, then two, during which time he heard a considerable amount of feminine grunting coming from inside the bathroom.

"Come on, Renee! Hurry!"

"I'm trying!"

Finally John couldn't wait any longer. He burst through the bathroom door. Renee stood beside the toilet, jeans gaping open around her hips, her pink satin panties peeking out. She'd already put her bra on, but not her sweatshirt. He only wished he had time to enjoy the view.

"John! What are you —"

He strode over, spun her around, then took a double handful of the waistband of her jeans and gave it a hard yank. The jeans slid up over her hips, hauling her up to her tiptoes at the same time.

"Ouch! John! For crying out loud!"

He spun her back around, snagging her sweatshirt from the bathroom counter and slapping it against her chest. "Forget zipping them. Just put this on and pull it down over your jeans."

She glared at him, then wiggled into the sweatshirt. He grabbed her by the arm and pulled her out of the bathroom, while she used her free hand to hold the sweatshirt down over her unzipped jeans.

"John!" she whispered loudly. "My shoes!"

"Leave them!"

He took her by the hand, dragged her through the bedroom, and started down the hall, where Sandy was rolling the vacuum cleaner back inside the closet. She spun around, planting her fists on her hips and blocking the way. She glared at John.

"You're not thinking of going anywhere, are you?"

"Alice and I have plans."

Sandy turned to Renee. "Is that true?"

Renee started to answer, but John squeezed her hand and she clamped her mouth shut again. "Sandy, if you don't get out of the way, I'm going to move you out of the way!"

"Nope." She turned to Renee with a confident smile. "He knows better than to mess with me."

"Sandy, I swear to God —"

"Helloooo!"

The voice accompanied the sound of his front door opening. Aunt Louisa. John bowed his head. This couldn't be happening.

"I could use some help with this Crock-Pot, kids!"

"Coming!" Sandy shouted, then turned back to John and shook her finger at him.

"And if you even *think* about slipping out the back door, you move right to the top of my shit list. And you *know* that's a place you don't want to be."

Sandy wheeled around and headed into the living room to greet Aunt Louisa. John peeked around the corner and out his living room window. His worst fear was realized. Aunt Louisa had parked her car in his driveway, blocking his in the garage. Her 1989 Cadillac that was approximately the size of the *Queen Mary*.

He had no escape.

He turned back to Renee. "Okay. You have to play along with this. And make it good. Do you hear me?"

"Yes. I hear you."

"And don't leave my sight for one second."

"I won't."

"Just let me do the talking, and go along with whatever I say. Got that?"

Renee rolled her eyes. "Yes, John. I understand. Do you think I want them to know why I'm really here?"

"And don't even think about slipping out of this house. I've got my car keys in my pocket, and I'm watching your every move."

"Come on. How stupid would it be for me

to run? I've got no car, no shoes —"

"You managed to get away from Leandro with nothing but the clothes on your back, so don't even go there."

"Look, I'm not going to do anything to get you into trouble with your family. It would only get me into trouble, too. Wouldn't that be kind of stupid?"

John inhaled a deep, calming breath and let it out slowly. As long as she didn't proposition his brothers, steal Aunt Louisa's car, or set fire to his house, he was going to consider himself lucky.

"It's no big deal," Renee added. "All we have to do is eat lunch and watch a lousy football game. I don't think it'll be that tough to fool them."

"That's because you haven't met my family."

"I'm sure they're very nice. It won't be any problem just to —"

"Did I tell you my brothers are cops?"

Renee's mouth stopped moving, and she swallowed hard. "They are?"

"Dave's a patrol cop. Alex is a detective."

"Oh, no."

"Oh, yes. And it gets better. My grandfather is a former prosecuting attorney who believes the majority of people have either committed a crime, are considering committing a crime, or wonder what it might be like to commit a crime. Are you getting the picture, Renee?"

Renee teetered a little on her feet, as if oxygen were slowly being sucked from the room.

"Then there's my cousin Eddie, the criminologist, and his wife, Brenda, a member of the SWAT team. Brenda can put a hole through a quarter at two hundred feet, and Eddie can tell you what weapon she was firing when she did it."

Renee looked as if she were going to faint. "Is that . . . all?"

"Yeah. Unless you count my grandmother, who spent twenty years as secretary to the chief of police."

"Oh, God." Renee closed her eyes, then opened them with a hopeful look. "But what about Sandy? She's —"

"She's a florist."

Renee took a breath.

"And the volunteer chairman of the Tolosa Crime Watch Council."

Renee's expression turned positively ghostlike. She opened her mouth but nothing came out.

"I see you're speechless. That's good. The less you say in the next few hours, the better off we're both going to be."

# chapter twelve

As it turned out, a few members of the family were missing, but from what Renee could see, enough law-enforcement professionals came through the door in the next few minutes to man an entire criminal-justice system.

Aunt Louisa was in the kitchen finalizing the meal and Sandy was setting the table when John's brother Dave arrived. The resemblance between John and his brother was striking. They were both tall and ruggedly handsome, with the same dark, watchful eyes. But the intensity that John emanated with every breath was nowhere to be found in Dave. He had a methodical coolness about him, a laid-back demeanor that said life was simply no big deal. Of course, Renee had to admit that the baby girl he was carrying, the diaper bag slung over his shoulder, and his T-shirt that read *Bad Cop! No Donut!* contributed to that image. But he was still a cop. She couldn't forget that, no matter how friendly he seemed.

"It's nice to meet you, Alice," Dave said after John introduced her. Then he turned to the baby. "And this is Ashley."

At the sound of her name, the little girl turned in his arms and gave him a huge, dimpled smile. She was about a year and a half old, with a riot of dark, unruly hair and the biggest brown eyes Renee had ever seen.

"Hi, there, Ashley," Renee said, tickling her arm at the same time. The baby giggled a little. Dave grinned at Ashley, then gave her a big, smacking kiss on the cheek, which made her giggle even more.

From the light in Dave's eyes when he looked at his daughter, she was going to grow up being the center of his existence. As she watched them, Renee felt something stir deep inside her that she thought she'd buried a long time ago — the unbearable ache of loneliness and worthlessness that had shrouded her own childhood. She'd grown up with the feeling that not a solitary soul in the world truly cared whether she lived or died, including her own mother. It had been a long time since she'd dwelled on that, because the road that led her from insufferable teenager to mature, responsible woman was one she couldn't have traveled if she'd allowed the accident of her birth to continue to control her life. Still, as she looked at Dave and Ashley right now, for just a moment the random unfairness of it made the pain feel as sharp as if it had all happened yesterday.

"Come on, Ashley," Dave said, smiling at the baby. "Let's go see what Aunt Louisa's got cooking."

They disappeared into the kitchen at the same time more people came through the front door, this time Brenda and Eddie.

Eddie was a blond, bookish man who looked as if he'd be right at home in the musty back stacks of a nineteenth-century library, poring over English literature texts. The criminologist. Typecasting at its best. But how good was he at his job? Could those sharp, intense, lie detector–like eyes of his see right through her? For a disquieting moment, she expected him to fling the casserole dish he held to the floor, point an accusing finger at her, and declare her a fugitive from justice. Instead, he merely smiled and introduced his wife, Brenda. Central casting had hit the nail on the head again.

Brenda, sharpshooter extraordinaire, was a short, compact woman of about thirty with dominance oozing out of every pore. Her black hair was cut stylelessly short, her unsmiling lips thin and bland, and when she slid her dark sunglasses off her face with a stealthy sweep of her hand, her narrow brown eyes pierced Renee like a pair of bayonets. She looked as if she'd be more at home shoveling in K rations on a marine drill somewhere in the Middle East than eating Aunt Louisa's pot roast. Fortunately, it didn't look as if she was armed, and she seemed no warier of Renee's presence than her husband had been.

Then Eddie introduced their daughter, Melanie, who held Brenda's hand and blinked shyly up at Renee. She was a girl of about five with sea-green eyes and dainty blond hair, who seemed as fragile as dandelion fuzz. Renee glanced at Brenda, then back to the child. She'd never seen such a clear-cut case of a stork screwing up a delivery in her entire life.

After introductions all around, Brenda put a hand on her hip, sizing up Renee. "So you're John's girlfriend, huh?"

"Uh . . . yeah."

She turned to John. "You're getting closer. This one actually admits it."

John gave her a deadpan stare. "There's beer in the kitchen, Brenda. No bottle opener, though. Just gnaw through the cap with your teeth."

Brenda's mouth quirked in an almost-smile. "Like that'd be a challenge?"

Brenda strode into the kitchen, taking the angel child with her, and Eddie followed close behind. Renee turned to gauge John's reaction to Brenda's smart-mouthed retort to his sarcastic remark, but he'd already turned his gaze out his front door again, where Grandma was toddling up the sidewalk clutching a pie plate. John stepped out onto the porch, took the pie from her, then offered his other hand to help her up the steps.

Rosy-cheeked and bespectacled, Grandma wore a dainty rose-print dress and radiated the sweet-faced look of a television grandmother from the 1950s. Renee felt instant relief. She could probably spend her time listening to stories about Black Sunday and the stock-market crash and how they just didn't make presidents like Herbert Hoover anymore, and in doing so she could avoid talking to the rest of the family.

Then Grandma saw Renee and stopped short, that sweet-faced expression falling into a wary frown.

"I don't know you."

"No, Grandma, you don't," John said. "This is Alice."

"Alice? I had a cat once named Alice. Got a skin disease and all her hair fell out."

"That's terrible!" Renee said.

"Nah. Kept her from gagging up hairballs."

Grandma took the pie from John, then toddled through the living room and into the kitchen. *Well.* So much for hiding behind a sweet old lady and her reminiscences.

"I think that's our lineup for today," John whispered to Renee. "Grandpa and Alex are on a fishing trip. We lucked out." In other words, he was relieved that round one was over and they were both still standing.

Under John's watchful eye, Renee ducked into the utility room and finally managed to zip up her jeans, cussing John the entire time. Now she knew what it was like to wear a girdle. A girdle so tight it numbed her crotch. When she sat down, she'd have to have faith in Levi Strauss that the whole back seam wouldn't explode.

The family had gathered in the kitchen, presided over by Aunt Louisa, a woman as tall and upright as the Washington Monument. She wore slacks and a high-necked blouse with a cameo at the collar, her salt-and-pepper hair wound in a tight perm that clung to her head for dear life. She gave firm orders shrouded in sweetness to everyone present, instructing them to mix this or heat up that. Everyone, that is, except Renee, whom she told to sit at the breakfast room table and look pretty because she was a guest. But next time, Aunt Louisa said, she'd have to pull her weight like the rest of the family.

Renee quickly discovered that being in the midst of John's family was like sitting on the tarmac at Dallas/Fort Worth airport — an incredible amount of activity, and a noise level that approached the supersonic range. It was hard to think of them as cops and all that other stuff. They just seemed like people. Nice people. But every time she'd start to relax a little as she listened to their conversation, John would shoot her one of his furtive hard-core cop looks and she'd remember the real reason she was here.

A few minutes later they went into the dining room to eat. John pulled out her chair for her in a most courteous manner, though courtesy had little to do with it. Renee knew he was merely directing her to sit right next to him, where he could keep an eye on her.

"So, Alice," Aunt Louisa said, passing the mashed potatoes. "Tell us what you do for a living."

She'd already told Sandy the truth, or at least what the truth had been before she'd gotten accused of armed robbery, so she had to go with that. "I'm an assistant restaurant manager."

"Oh! How nice! Which restaurant?"

"Renaissance."

Everyone stared at her blankly.

"It's down in the Rosewood Village area."

"Oooh!" Sandy said. "That little Italian place! I hear that's a really nice restaurant. Expensive, too. I saw four little dollar signs beside its review in the paper."

"Hey, John," Brenda said. "You lucked out. You can take Alice someplace nice and get an employee discount at the same time. It's almost like having a coupon."

"Gee, I hadn't thought of that," John said. "Would you like to come along? No, wait — it's not your kind of place. They don't let you shoot your own dinner."

Brenda turned to Sandy. "And you said it was a high-class establishment."

"I hear they recycle the food at restaurants," Grandma mumbled. "If you don't eat it, they take it back into the kitchen and make stew out of it."

"Mother!" Aunt Louisa said. "Of course they don't do things like that! Do they, Alice?"

Well, at a place she'd once worked, she'd seen a waiter drop a steak in the kitchen, then scoop it off the floor, wipe it on his pants, and return it to the plate without missing a beat, but she didn't think that was what Grandma wanted to hear.

"No," Renee said. "Of course not."

"And if you piss off the waiters," Grandma said, "they spit in your food."

"Mother! Please! We're eating."

Grandma shrugged indifferently, then poked around at her mashed potatoes as if she expected to see rat droppings.

"So tell us how you two met," Aunt Louisa said.

Renee looked at John. He cleared his throat. "We met at a diner. She came up to me and . . . introduced herself."

"I like that," Brenda said, whacking her knife through a piece of pot roast. "A woman with balls."

Aunt Louisa patted Renee's hand. "She means that as a compliment, dear."

"Well, he's lucky Alice approached him," Sandy said, "because she'd have probably grown old and gray and died before he'd have bothered to approach her."

Everyone at the table nodded in assent, as if this were a generally known fact, as if John weren't even present. And John was clearly trying to ignore all of it.

Aunt Louisa turned to Brenda. "So how is

Melanie doing in school this year?"

"She's brilliant, of course," Brenda said.

"And her ballet classes?"

"You mean her tae kwon do classes," Eddie muttered.

Aunt Louisa raised her eyebrows. "Tae kwon do?"

"It's one of those kung fu things," Grandma said.

"We decided martial arts would be better for her," Brenda explained. "Girls need to learn how to defend themselves."

"*We* decided that?" Eddie said.

Brenda rolled her eyes. "Learning to dance on your tiptoes is hardly one of life's greatest accomplishments."

"You know, you could try to compromise once in a while."

"Hey! I compromised! I got her a Barbie!"

"Yeah. Military Barbie."

"I said it was a compromise, didn't I?"

"You could think about having a tea party with her once in a while instead of playing Hostage and Negotiator."

"And maybe get her a kitten instead of a rottweiler," Sandy added.

"And take her to the zoo instead of the shooting range," Aunt Louisa chimed in.

Grandma sniffed. "Kid's gonna turn lesbian, if you ask me."

"Oh, all *right!*" Brenda fumed silently for a moment, then turned to Renee. "What do you think, Alice? This is a new century, right? Isn't it time we redefined women's roles once and for all?"

Renee froze. This was definitely one of those "damned if you do, damned if you don't" situations.

"I think," she said carefully, "that Melanie is a very lucky little girl to have so many people who care so much about her."

Silence fell over the table.

"Wow," Sandy said. "Good answer."

In unison, everybody, including Brenda, nodded and resumed eating.

Renee couldn't quite believe what was happening here. Where she grew up, this kind of dinner-table dissension would have plunged her and her mother into the depths of animosity for a solid week. Silence. That was what she'd usually experienced during those rare times when her mother actually made dinner. It got to where she preferred the silence, though, because any conversation usually wound up centering on whatever she'd done that day to displease her mother, and if her mother couldn't come up with anything new, she'd reach back a week or two and haul out something old. Then she'd have another drink and the screaming would start, and Renee would end up leaving the house, slamming the door behind her, and not coming home for days.

But something was different here. These people tossed insults at each other right and left, but the words seemed to be forgotten as quickly as they were said, almost as if they weren't designed to hurt in the first place.

Renee wasn't sure exactly what all that meant, except that nobody seemed to hold on to anger, and everyone was eating as if their appetites hadn't been the least bit affected. Even Melanie seemed totally unaffected by the conversation, her attention turned instead to the task of getting approximately half a stick of butter to adhere to her dinner roll.

And nobody was leaving, slamming doors behind them.

"Well, Alice," Brenda said, "I gotta say you're a cut above the last woman John brought to Sunday lunch. What was her name? Debbie? Gawd, what a brainless little twit she was."

Everyone nodded again. John closed his eyes with a weary sigh.

"She didn't hang around long, did she?" Dave said.

Sandy made a scoffing noise. "She didn't even last through dessert."

"Of course she didn't!" John said, suddenly coming alive. "Not with Brenda telling her that if she wore just a little more mascara, she could be a televangelist!"

Brenda shrugged. "Can I help it if she looked like Tammy Faye Bakker?"

"Her skirt was too tight," Grandma said. "I could see her butt cheeks."

Sandy smiled. "The best part was when Dave started messing with her mind."

"I don't recall her having much of a mind to mess with," Dave said.

Sandy turned to Renee. "Dave asked her if she had any idea why 'abbreviation' was such a long word. Poor woman stopped to think about it and never started again."

"So tell me, Alice," Dave said nonchalantly. "What do you suppose would happen if you got scared half to death twice?"

Renee shrugged. "Got me. I'm still trying to figure out why we drive on a parkway and park on a driveway."

Dave stabbed a green bean. "Okay. She's got my vote."

"Mine, too," Brenda said.

"She already had mine," Sandy added.

John flung his fork down with a clatter. "Well, then. Why don't we just go ahead and make it unanimous?"

"Nope," Grandma said. "I'm still not too sure about the spittin'-in-the-food thing."

"Will all of you cut it out? Whatever relationship Alice and I have is between her and me. Period!"

"Of course, dear," Aunt Louisa told John, then leaned toward Renee and whispered, "He's usually not this cranky. I think he's still upset about the reprimand."

"Reprimand?" Renee said.

Dave grinned. "You didn't tell her?"

John dropped his head to his hands.

"He got all pissed off because some guy he arrested got a not-guilty verdict, so he went into the john at the courthouse and beat the crap out of a paper-towel dispenser."

"Dave?" John said. "You want to shut the hell up?"

"Then he got exiled to Lieutenant Daniels's cabin in east Texas. That's where the lieutenant sends all the bad boys who don't behave themselves."

So that was what John had been doing out in that cabin. It was clearly not the vacation he'd made it out to be. And it was doubly clear that he didn't like anyone talking about it.

"Come to think of it," Dave said, "you're back a little early, aren't you?"

"Yes," John said. "I'm back a little early."

"The lieutenant won't like that."

"The lieutenant doesn't need to know about it, does he?"

"Hey, my lips are sealed, bro."

John looked at Brenda.

"What are you staring at me for? What do you think I'm going to do? Rat on you?" She huffed with disgust. "Personally, I don't think you should have beat up the paper-towel dispenser. You should have saved your energy to beat up the little bastard who walked."

"Of course, there's that little issue of police brutality," Eddie said.

"You bet," Brenda said. "And I'm all for it."

Eddie let out a long-suffering sigh and kept on eating.

"Just lighten up a little," Dave told John. "You win some, you lose some. You've got no control over it, so why let it get to you?"

"I don't need you to tell me how to do my job."

"This isn't the first time you've second-guessed the system. You gotta learn to roll with the punches."

"You're going to have to learn to roll with a few punches if you don't shut up."

Dave shrugged. "Sure. We can go a few

rounds if you want to. Or you can think about what I'm telling you. You've got to quit getting so personally involved. Sooner or later it's going to eat you alive." He eyed John carefully. "Don't give Daniels a reason to slap your hand again. You're too good for that."

John stared down at his plate. Finally he gave his brother an almost imperceptible nod, and Dave immediately turned the conversation to the Cowboys' chances for a victory today.

Renee couldn't believe everything she'd just heard. Now she knew why John had gotten so angry when they were out in the woods. She'd accused him of not caring enough whether justice was done, never realizing that he'd just lost a battle with his supervisor because he cared too much.

All at once she regretted the insults she'd hurled at him, suggesting that he was just going through the motions without a thought as to whether she was guilty or not. Now that she knew better, the strangest feeling came over her, a tingly flush of warmth she hadn't expected. Every moment they spent with John's family knocked one more brick out of the wall that surrounded him, allowing her an occasional glimpse of who he really was. He couldn't

311

stand the thought of a guilty man going free. Would it hurt him just as much to see an innocent person go to jail? How far would he go to make sure that didn't happen?

Aunt Louisa checked her watch. "Everybody about finished? It's almost kickoff time. You boys go into the living room and turn on the game. We girls will do the dishes."

Brenda huffed with disgust. "Louisa. You *know* how I feel about all that girls-do-this, guys-do-that crap."

"Of course I do. Now be a dear and grab that gravy boat, will you?"

Brenda rolled her eyes. She yanked the gravy boat off the table and headed for the kitchen. Renee reached for a pair of dinner plates, but John pulled her aside. "You come with me," he whispered.

"No," Renee whispered back. "It'll look bad if I don't help."

"I don't care what it looks like. I don't want you out of my sight."

"Come on, John. I can't even walk in these jeans, much less run in them."

Brenda and Sandy popped back out of the kitchen.

"Now, Alice," John said for their benefit. "You're a guest. The others can handle the dishes."

"What are you trying to do?" Brenda said. "Deprive your girlfriend of the right to play out her role as a second-class citizen?"

John was forced to comply or look very suspicious. "Alice isn't much of a football fan," he said as he walked away, with a smile that didn't quite make it to his eyes. "Let me know if she tries to slip out the back door, okay?"

"Don't worry," Sandy said with a smile. "We're not letting this one get away."

After they took the dishes to the kitchen and put them in the dishwasher, Sandy washed the casseroles while Renee dried them.

"Don't take it seriously when John blows up like he did at lunch," Sandy told her. "We've been going on at each other like that since we were old enough to talk. John just happens to be one of today's targets. He's not really as mad as he acts. He'll be over it by halftime."

Renee just smiled, knowing halftime wouldn't do a thing toward improving John's mood. "John and Dave are a little different from each other, aren't they?"

Sandy laughed. "Like night and day. And Alex is different from the two of them. Dave's so laid-back he's practically in a coma. But he puts that to good use on the job. He can defuse a lot of situations because nobody sees him as an adversary, even people he's dragging to jail. Alex, on the other hand, has the perp in one hand and a copy of the criminal code in the other. He's nobody's pal if he thinks they've broken the law. Alex was Dad's favorite. Oldest son, you know."

"And John?"

"To Dave, being a cop is a job. To Alex, it's a mission. But to John, it's a passion. He's got this startling notion that justice will always be done. His brothers can walk away at the end of the day, no matter how things turn out. He can't."

Brenda snapped the lid on a plastic container she'd filled with leftover potatoes. "I don't know what's so tough about it. You don't think about the job. You just do it. Can you imagine me zeroing in on a hostage taker and then stopping to wonder whether there are extenuating circumstances before I blow his brains out?"

"No, Brenda," Aunt Louisa said, wiping the countertop with a dishrag. "None of us can imagine that."

"I'm told what my target is, and I take it out. Mission accomplished."

"But there's a big difference between you and John," Sandy said. "See, John actually has a heart."

"True. But he could get over that if he really set his mind to it."

Sandy gave Brenda a look of disgust.

"Oh, all right!" Brenda turned to Renee. "John's a good guy. Really. I'm just saying he makes it hard on himself by thinking he can change the world when the rest of us know that it can't be done. Guilty people are gonna walk, and innocent people are gonna fry. And there's not a damned thing anybody can do about it."

*The world according to Brenda. A very scary place,* Renee thought, particularly since she might be one of those poor, unfortunate people who were destined to fry.

A few minutes later they came back into the living room. The guys had fired up the game, and by the time the seating shuffle was complete, Brenda, Eddie, and Dave had commandeered the sofa while Ashley toddled around the living room. Sandy was sitting cross-legged on the floor with Melanie, Aunt Louisa had taken the chair next to the lamp so she could do her crocheting, and Grandma sat on a dining room chair by the sofa because of her recent back surgery.

John was left alone on his love seat. His very small love seat. On which Renee was required to join him.

She sat down gingerly, and immediately she felt a slight dip between the cushions that tilted her in John's direction. She folded her arms and tried to make herself as small as she could. John seemed to be just as uptight as she was, and if everyone's attention hadn't been focused on the game, she was sure not a soul in the room would have believed they were actually a couple.

There wasn't anything awkward about the rest of the family, though. They shouted, cussed, cheered, made side bets on every other play, cussed, collected the bets, then cheered some more. The whole room seemed to be in motion at once, with smiles and laughter and good-natured insults.

Renee knew her being here was all a sham, but for a long, heavenly moment, she closed her eyes and basked in the feeling of a family surrounding her whether it was hers or not, and suddenly she was so jealous of John she couldn't stand it. He had this wonderful family that she was pretty sure he took for granted, while she'd had nothing but an alcoholic mother who had treated her like crap, and whom she hadn't spoken to in years. The feeling of longing she had was so powerful she felt as if she were going to pass out.

She'd worried about the wrong threat

here today. The problem wasn't that they were all into law enforcement. The problem was that she was liking them all just a little too much. What if she ended up in jail? She barely knew these people, but she couldn't bear the thought of their thinking she was a criminal.

But most important of all — what did John think?

He sat stiffly next to her, not acknowledging her at all. In fact, he didn't acknowledge much of anything. He merely sat with his arms folded, staring at the television, even though Renee could tell he wasn't really following the game. He clearly hated having to pretend she was his girlfriend. And on the few occasions he glanced her way, his expression was laced with suspicion, as if he expected her to go nuts and take hostages at any moment.

As if she'd even consider such a thing with Brenda on duty.

"Alice?"

Renee looked around to see Melanie standing beside her, holding a deck of cards.

"Yes?"

"Wanna play Go Fish?"

"Melanie," Brenda said. "Don't bother Alice when she's watching the game."

"It's okay," Renee told Brenda, then

smiled at Melanie. "I'd love to play. But maybe we'd better go over to the table so we don't bother anybody."

As she stood up, John came to attention, giving her one of the subtle warning looks she'd grown so accustomed to. She nodded toward the dining room table. He settled back on the love seat with an expression that said he didn't much like it but he wasn't going to stop her. Still, as she walked across the room with Melanie she was sure she could feel his gaze boring into her back. She wanted to whip around and shout at him, *It's just a card game, not a prison break!*

But she didn't. Instead she sat down at the table with Melanie and tried to pretend John wasn't even in the room. For a few hours more, she had the opportunity to play a dumb card game and delude herself into thinking her life was absolutely normal, and she decided that was exactly what she was going to do.

John sat on the love seat, drumming his fingertips against the arm, staring straight ahead as if he were focusing on the game. Right now, though, he could barely tell one team from the other, and if his life depended on stating the score, he'd be a dead man. He just wished everyone would get out of his house so he could have time to think, to find a way to fix this mess he'd created. Fortunately, nobody seemed to suspect that Renee was anything other than his girlfriend, which was a good thing.

But did they have to *like* her so much?

He didn't get it. They found fault with every other woman he'd ever introduced them to, even though they supposedly wanted him to get married. Why did they have to choose now to decide Renee was the woman for him?

He was actually relieved when Renee got up to play a game with Melanie, thinking maybe he could turn most of his attention to the football game and the time would pass more quickly. He kicked off his boots and put his feet up on the coffee table, staring at the television, but no matter how much he tried to concentrate on the game, his gaze continuously shifted back to Renee like some kind of high-tech tracking device.

They'd been playing Go Fish for the past half hour. Ten minutes in, Grandma had joined them. He heard snippets of their conversation, Melanie squealing when she got four of something, and Grandma griping that the numbers on the cards were just too damned small to read.

Once, before Renee dealt the cards, she

pointed to one of the clubs and told Melanie all those little black spots were puppy dog feet. Melanie giggled as if that were the most hysterical thing she'd ever heard, practically falling out of her chair in a paroxysm of childhood laughter. Even Grandma smiled at that one. Renee played the game with the energy of a blackjack dealer and the good nature of a favorite aunt who indulges her niece at every opportunity.

And John couldn't take his eyes off her.

He absorbed every nuance of movement and color and light she emanated, from her golden hair that shimmered with every toss of her head, to her long, slender fingers deftly fanning out her cards, to the radiant smiles she showered on Melanie. But on the few occasions when she glanced at him and their eyes happened to meet, her smile would fade. Just for a moment, he wondered what it would be like to be the reason she started smiling rather than the reason she stopped.

What if she weren't a fugitive? What if she really were his girlfriend? Was this how it would feel? As though he never wanted to take his eyes off her?

*Stop it. You're forgetting who she is and why she's here.*

But as the afternoon wore on, the image

of Renee as a gun-toting convenience-store robber slipped further and further from his grasp, and he started to see her as his family undoubtedly saw her — as a beautiful woman who was smart, friendly, and engaging. His brain automatically added *sexy* to that list, which he mentally erased, only to have it pop back onto the list again, this time in bold capital letters.

*Very, very sexy.*

Then Sandy got up from where she was sitting on the rug and headed toward him. He braced himself. No telling what she had on her mind.

She plopped down beside him. "I guess the Cowboys can't count on you for a lot of fan support today, huh?" She grinned. "Alice, on the other hand, can count on you just fine."

"Knock it off, Sandy."

"Look at her," Sandy said, as if he hadn't been doing just that. "She's really good with Melanie, isn't she?"

"Uh-huh."

"Even Grandma seems to be having a good time."

"Uh-huh."

"You're still pissed at me, aren't you?"

"Uh-huh."

"Why don't you just get over it and tell me

that it's been a nice afternoon? Alice got to meet the family. Everybody likes her. That's a good thing."

"I suppose you and Aunt Louisa are going to pick out our china pattern tomorrow."

"No. Silver tomorrow. China on Tuesday." She patted him on the knee. "Now I'm talking seriously, John. She's a good one. Do everything you can to hold on to her, will you?"

An hour later the Cowboys barely squeaked to victory, and John was never so happy to see a game end in his entire life. After the usual standing and stretching and gathering of casserole dishes, his family finally headed for the door. Renee joined him there to say good-bye.

Melanie tugged on John's jeans. He knelt down beside her. "Alice is fun."

"Oh, yeah?"

"Are you going to marry her?"

"Well, Mellie, we haven't talked about that yet."

"I like her. But she's not very smart."

"Oh?"

"I beat her at Go Fish. I never beat Mama."

John had no doubt of that. That would be like pitting Tinkerbell against Rambo.

Melanie skipped out the door. Grandma

approached Renee, her expression guarded. "If I come to your restaurant sometime, will you watch them make my food? Make sure there's no funny business?"

Renee smiled. "I'd be happy to."

Grandma turned to John. "Okay, then. I guess she's got my vote."

She hobbled out the door. Aunt Louisa was next. "It was such a delight to meet you, Alice. Hopefully Alex and Grandpa will join us next time and you can meet the whole family. How would that be?"

Renee smiled again. "I'd like that."

Dave came next, holding Ashley. "Please don't judge all of us by John. He might not be worth a damn, but his family's really something." He gave her a quick hug. "Don't be a stranger," he said, then followed Aunt Louisa out the door. Even Brenda offered a perfunctory but genuine good-bye before whipping out her dark glasses and making her eyes disappear.

As Renee stood at the door and waved good-bye, John remembered Sandy's words: *Do everything you can to hold on to her.* Now that was all he could think about. Holding on to Renee. For hours on end. Maybe all night long . . .

How had this happened? How, in the span of a few hours, had his perception shifted so dramatically that he saw not a woman accused of a crime, but a woman he wanted in so many ways — to talk to, to touch, to hold, to make love to. . . .

He blinked away that thought and watched out the window as the last car disappeared around the block. After the pandemonium that had taken place all afternoon, the house was suddenly so quiet he swore he could hear his own heartbeat.

"Well, it looks like we pulled it off," Renee said. "They never knew, did they?"

"No," he said, still looking out the window. "They never knew."

"I was afraid they'd ask me something and I'd screw up and say the wrong thing. I didn't, did I?"

John closed his eyes. "No. You didn't."

"Did I say too much? Not enough?"

"It was fine, Renee. They liked you."

"Then what's the matter?"

He turned around slowly. Thanks to her, his family had never suspected she was anything but his girlfriend. And that made it even harder to do what he had to do. But he had no choice. None at all.

He glanced toward the bedroom, where the handcuffs still dangled from the headboard. That small shift of his gaze was all it took for Renee to understand. Her words came out in a hoarse whisper.

"You have to lock me back up."

He paused. "Yes. I don't want to, but —"

"Duty calls?"

He expelled a harsh breath. "What am I supposed to do, Renee? Tell me. What am I supposed to do?"

"Let me go, maybe?"

"You know I can't do that."

"John —"

"Don't make this hard for me."

Her hand crept to her throat, as if she were suddenly having a hard time breathing. "I guess I should have known, but I guess I thought . . . after everything . . ." She looked at him plaintively. "I-I just can't believe you're going to do this."

They stared at each other a long, shaky moment. God, he hated this. But there was absolutely nothing else he could do. He was hovering in a terrible limbo — in good conscience he couldn't take her in, and in good conscience he couldn't let her go.

"I won't try to get away, John. I promise. Please. Just for a few more hours at least . . ."

Her voice trailed off, and the plaintive look in her eyes made John realize just how much he wanted that, too. He wanted this situation to become normal, where she wasn't an armed robbery suspect and he wasn't a cop, and words like *responsibility* and *duty* and *obligation* never even had to enter his mind.

"For just a few more hours," she whispered.

*Damn it.* Why was she doing this to him? He was in a hell of a position here. Why couldn't she see that?

"We can do this one of two ways," he told her. "Either you can walk in there, or I can drag you in there."

Tears sprang immediately to her eyes. "Damn you! I did what you asked me to, and this is how you treat me?"

"You're still a fugitive. You seem to have forgotten that."

"How could I forget? You won't let one minute pass without reminding me!"

"I'm just doing my job!"

"No, you're not. Your *job* would have been to take me to the police station. Instead, I'm here. And now you don't know what to do with me. You could take me to jail, but you know what will happen if you do, and you can't live with that!"

In a fit of frustration, John clamped his hand onto Renee's arm. He dragged her down the hall and into his bedroom, then sat her down on the bed.

"No, you don't, John. *No!*"

She started to stand again, but he shoved her back down. She tried to yank her wrist away, but he was too quick. He snapped the dangling handcuff around it.

Renee glared at him. "Why did you bring me here in the first place? If all I'm going to do is sit here in handcuffs, I might as well be in jail!"

"Don't push me, Renee!"

"You can't do it, can you? You can't take me to jail. Because you know I'm not guilty. You know I didn't rob that store. You know I didn't shoot that clerk. But still —" She held her cuffed wrist up defiantly, then dropped it back to the bed, the chain rattling against the headboard. "*Still* you're acting as if I did it!"

The tension crackled between them with an intensity that practically lit the drapes on fire.

"I'm asking you one more time, John. Do you think I'm guilty? Or am I an innocent woman who was in the wrong place at the wrong time?"

"There's no evidence —"

"Damn it! Would you forget the evidence for five seconds? I don't want the cop version. I want *your* version."

He turned away, desperately needing to

walk out of this room, to *stay* out of this room, until he felt more in control. But then she spoke again, her voice soft, with a tenderness to it that caught him off guard.

"I realized something today," she said. "I was wrong out there in the woods. Your problem isn't that you don't care. In fact, sometimes you care so much that it tears you up inside."

He needed to get out of there. Right now.

"You know the truth, don't you?" she said. "You *know*."

He turned to face her, which was his first mistake, and his second one was thinking he could maintain any objectivity at all where she was concerned. She eyed him with such intensity that he felt as if she were looking right inside him. He turned away again, knowing he was on the verge of stepping over a line he'd never intended to cross, and once he was on the other side of it, there would be no going back.

But she was right. He knew the truth. How could he deny it any longer?

"The cop side of me says you're guilty," he told her. "And that part of me wants to take you straight to jail and be done with it. But still there's something. . . ."

He paused, then slowly turned back and met her eyes, those clear blue eyes that had captivated him since the moment he met her.

"Even though I haven't got a shred of evidence to base it on, for some reason I still believe you're telling me the truth."

# chapter thirteen

In that moment, Renee felt as if every bone in her body had melted with relief. She'd wanted John to believe in her innocence — *needed* him to believe in her innocence — but what he'd just said meant something more. It meant she wasn't alone in this any longer.

But as welcome as his admission was to her, she could tell it had taken a toll on him.

He sat down on the edge of the bed and stared at his hands, his shoulders hunched, his face tight and drawn, and for the first time she saw that he wasn't supercop at all. He was just a man — a man with some very tough decisions to make.

"What's going to happen to me now?" she asked.

"I don't know."

A long silence ensued. Finally John rubbed his hand over his mouth, then shifted around to face her.

"I talked to the woman who owns the convenience store that was robbed. Your eyewitness is a flake. She can barely see her hand in front of her face. Even a crappy defense attorney will discredit her in a heartbeat."

Renee sat up suddenly. "That's wonderful!"

"Don't get your hopes up. It doesn't prove you didn't do it. It only proves she can't positively identify you. It's pretty meaningless in light of the physical evidence."

"But it's something, right?"

"It's . . . something. And you were right about the ladies in 317. They're hookers. But they've got a pretty lucrative operation going, and I think we have to discount them as suspects. Another negative is that the original detective on the case has since retired. The guy who's taking it over is worthless. We're not going to be able to count on any help from official sources. They've got their suspect, and they won't be looking for another one."

"You actually checked all this out?"

"Yes."

Renee couldn't believe it. That was where he must have been this morning. While she'd been handcuffed to this bed, he'd been out investigating the crime.

"Do you think it's possible that we could

find out who really committed the robbery?" she asked him.

John shook his head. "No. I don't."

"But that's the only way —"

"No. It's not. We don't necessarily have to find the person who did it. All we have to do is find enough evidence to put reasonable doubt in a jury's mind that *you* did it. If we can do that, you'll be acquitted."

"And if I'm not acquitted —"

"You'll go to prison."

*Prison.* Just the word made Renee's stomach churn with anxiety. "John. Please listen to me. Please. I can't go there. If there's even a possibility —"

"Our best hope is to come up with a piece or two of compelling circumstantial evidence. You say you didn't see Steve at the right time that night to establish an alibi, but it's close timewise, so it might make a jury think twice. Your eyewitness can easily be discredited. A defense attorney can use those things to instill reasonable doubt in the minds of the jury members."

The thought of being thrown on the mercy of the criminal-justice system was just about the most frightening thing Renee could possibly imagine. But somehow it didn't seem quite so ominous with John beside her, now that she knew that he'd been checking things out, going out on a limb for her when he could have done the easy thing and taken her straight to jail.

Sandy had been right about him. So very right.

"But I've got to tell you, Renee. This could still end badly, no matter what I do."

He didn't define *badly*. He didn't have to. If he didn't find enough evidence to support her innocence, she could still go to jail. And because she was still locked up, even though he believed she was innocent, she knew there would come a day when he'd be forced to take her in and let the court decide what to do with her. Luckily, today didn't appear to be that day.

Then she had a terrible thought. He'd just told her he believed in her innocence, even though he had nothing to support that belief. But what if he discovered evidence that pointed to her guilt? How would he feel about her then?

When they were walking through the woods, he'd asked her if she had a record. She'd told him no.

What if he found out about her juvenile record? Would he understand that she wasn't that person anymore? That the adult woman she was now didn't so much as toss a gum wrapper down on the sidewalk? That the memory of the terribly misguided girl she'd been was so painful she didn't even like to think about it?

*No.* She couldn't risk telling him. The records were sealed, and they wouldn't be brought into evidence at a trial. He'd never know.

Then again, it wasn't the trial she had to worry about.

Leandro had known about her juvenile record because some cop couldn't keep his mouth shut. How likely was it that John wouldn't find out about it, too? If he ever discovered she'd lied to him — about anything — he'd never trust a word she said again.

"John?"

He turned.

"There's something I have to tell you."

Her hands actually started to tremble. She closed her eyes for a moment, trying to gain a little bit of control. "You asked me out in the woods if I had a record. I told you I didn't, but . . ."

His eyes flickered with surprise, then immediately narrowed with suspicion.

"It was a long time ago," she said quickly. "Juvenile. Five arrests, six — I don't even remember. But I've been clean since then. I swear to God I have."

His expression changed again, this time displaying the one thing she'd never wanted to see on his face again: doubt. And it just about killed her.

"Why didn't you tell me this before?" he asked sharply.

"Because I was afraid you'd think I couldn't possibly have changed since then," she said, trying to keep her voice sure and steady and failing miserably. "I was afraid if I told you I had a record, any kind of record, I didn't stand a chance of staying out of jail. But I'm not that person anymore. Just because I did a little shoplifting and joyriding as a teenager doesn't mean I committed armed robbery."

"Shoplifting and joyriding, huh? Anything else?"

"Uh . . . maybe a little vandalism here and there. And public intoxication. I only got arrested once for that, and I think the cop might have let me go if I hadn't poured beer on his shoes. But that's it, John. I swear it is."

"You poured beer on a cop's shoes?"

"It was light beer."

"Jesus, Renee." He dropped his head to his hands and blew out a long breath. Then he started to get up off the bed. She reached out quickly and grabbed his arm, clutching it desperately, praying he wouldn't leave.

"I did those things when I was a kid, John. I was just a dumb teenager with a bad attitude who didn't give a damn about —"

"Just a dumb teenager? Where do you think adult criminals come from, Renee? They used to be dumb teenagers."

"I know I lied to you. But I never will again. Never. Please, *please* don't let this change things!"

He expelled a breath of disgust.

"There's more. Please let me tell you everything."

He stared down at his hands. At the wall. Anywhere but at her. But at least he didn't get up and leave.

"When I was seventeen," she went on, "I got caught riding around with my boyfriend in a car he'd stolen, and the judge threw me in a juvenile detention center for three months. God, how I hated that. *Hated* it. I'd never really understood until then what it would be like to be locked up, and I was starting to think seriously about my future, about how stupid I'd been and how I needed to make some changes. But I was still way too cool to let anyone know that, so I got a special invitation to a 'scared straight' program at the state prison."

She paused, the memory so awful she

didn't even want to think about it, much less talk about it. But she had to. John had to know everything that had happened to her back then or he'd never understand where she was coming from now.

"I didn't think it would be any big deal. See, I'd been through all the drug- and alcohol-awareness stuff in high school, where they have a former addict or alcoholic come and tell his story and tell you not to do what he did. I guess I expected more of that. I was radiating my usual screw-you attitude, just daring them to slap my hand one more time.

"Then one of the women got up and started talking. No, actually she started screaming, like a boot-camp sergeant. I remember my heart was beating about a thousand times a minute."

Renee paused again, the memory so vivid that even now it put her on the verge of tears.

"Then one of the women looked me up and down in this leering kind of way and ran her fingers through my hair. She told me not to worry, that a pretty girl like me would be *real* popular in prison. It was awful. I mean, *awful*. It was as if I were already in that prison, feeling every horrible moment of what my life would be like if I didn't straighten up. And that's when I finally made the decision to change. No matter what, I was never going to step foot in a prison again. Just the idea of going back to a place like that terrifies me." She lowered her voice, trying to keep it from trembling. "I'll do anything to stay out of jail, John. *Anything.*"

He didn't respond. He merely stared straight ahead, his face tense and immovable, and she could tell he was still reserving the right to leave the room at any time and slam the door behind him.

"It was hard as hell after that," she went on, "but I scraped myself off rock bottom. I got a waitress job at Denny's. Polyester, sensible shoes. The whole ugly thing. After a while, though, I got better jobs. The night of the robbery, like I told you, I'd just gotten the assistant manager's job at Renaissance. I'd wanted that job forever, and then I got it. I was so excited. I thought my life had finally turned around for good. And then . . ." She sighed. "And then this. I'm not that rotten teenager anymore, John. I didn't rob that store. After what I went through at that prison, just the thought of taking one step outside the law makes me break out in a cold sweat. You *have* to understand that."

He faced her. "Is that all?"

His voice had faded into a monotone, and

she couldn't read him. She couldn't tell what he meant to do next. He'd put on that stoic cop face again, and she just couldn't tell whether he believed she wasn't that dumb, screwed-up kid anymore.

*Everything. You have to tell him everything.*

"When I was in that prison, one of the women asked me if I screwed around. I told her no, but of course, that was a lie. I'd seen the backseat of every jacked-up, souped-up teenage hot rod in the city of Tolosa. And suddenly all I could think about was how lucky I was that in all those times I hadn't gotten pregnant, because not one of those guys would have taken responsibility for anything."

And then she thought about how all those encounters had made her feel, as if she needed to take a shower after every one to wash away the shame. Why was it that when John had touched her she hadn't felt that way at all?

"What I said out there in the woods was true," she told him. "I wasn't trying to bribe you. All at once I thought about being locked up for years and never seeing a man, touching a man, and I remembered the way you'd kissed me in that cabin, and I wanted to . . . to feel that way again, feel *more* than that, just once, before . . ."

Frustration welled up inside her. "It's not that I wanted it one last time, John. It's that —" She closed her eyes and exhaled. "I wanted it for the first time."

He looked at her with surprise. "But you said —"

"I know. I'm not a virgin. Not technically. But high school sex by the dashboard lights doesn't really qualify."

He looked at her with surprise. "How old are you, Renee?"

"Twenty-six."

"You mean, in the past eight years —"

"That's right. I haven't."

He stared at her, trying, she knew, to make some sense out of this mess he'd found himself in, trying to make some sense out of the way he felt about her. His dark eyes seemed deep and endless, and caught in his gaze now, she felt as if she'd only seen a tiny glimmer of the man he really was. His help was more than she ever could have hoped for. *He* was more than she ever could have hoped for. It wasn't just any man she wanted so she could feel the heat of passion before the coldness of prison surrounded her.

It was John.

"You told me once that you like a woman who knows what she wants." Renee spoke the words softly, singularly, her gaze never leaving his. "I know what I want."

"What's that?"

"You."

He stared at her a long time. "Why me?"

"Because I trust you."

"You might want to think twice about that."

"Why?"

"God, Renee — don't you know there's only so much I can do where the evidence is concerned? I can't guarantee —"

"When I say I trust you, I don't mean just about that."

Understanding seemed to come to him slowly, and when she saw in his eyes that he knew what she was talking about, she felt embarrassment creep in. But she wasn't about to turn away now.

"I don't know what it's like to have a man make love to me, John. I want him to be you."

"If this is about gratitude —"

"Yes. It's about gratitude. And a whole lot more."

Seconds passed. She couldn't imagine what he might be thinking, and for a moment she regretted everything she'd said. Then, slowly, the tension that had kept his body rigid and defensive seemed to melt away, and the wariness disappeared from his eyes. Very deliberately, he reached over to the nightstand and picked something up.

The key to the handcuffs.

"No matter what Sandy thinks," he said, "the kinky stuff has never really appealed to me."

He took her hand in his, then slid the key into the lock of the handcuff and twisted it. The cuff clicked open. Slowly he slid her wrist free, then disengaged the other cuff from the headboard and laid them on the nightstand. When he glanced back at her, she saw it in his eyes.

He wanted her, too.

At that moment, it was as if the very air in the room changed, became electrified, molecules dancing between them, drawing them together, and she could barely breathe for the anticipation she felt. For the first time she felt free to look at him, to stare at his handsome face without fear of his looking back at her with anger or recrimination. She focused on the purplish bruise that still ringed his eye, a reminder of how quickly he'd jumped to her defense when Leandro had grabbed her. She touched his face.

"I never wanted you to get hurt," she whispered. "I'm so sorry."

"It'll heal."

He leaned toward her, moving slowly and deliberately, and when she realized he intended to kiss her, she literally stopped breathing. When he finally touched his lips to hers, he did it so softly she wasn't quite sure he'd even made contact. Then he pulled back a scant inch, waiting several long, excruciating moments before kissing her again — a gentle kiss that was only a faint whisper of what she ached for. She waited for him to kiss her hard and deep as he had out in the woods, but he didn't. He slid his hand up and down her arm in slow, mesmerizing strokes, just firmly enough to make her realize he was actually touching her and just softly enough to drive her crazy. Still he was kissing her, always kissing her, every touch of his lips and his hands incredibly slow and endlessly erotic. It should have relaxed her. It didn't. She grew edgier and edgier, her body sizzling, every nerve humming with anticipation.

Then he leaned away, and it was all she could do not to take him by the shirt collar and drag him right back. His gaze drifted down her face, to her throat, to her breasts, and back up again.

"Take off the shirt."

His voice wasn't demanding. Instead, it was full of desire, and the very sound of it sent a wave of excitement sweeping through her. She wanted this. God, how she wanted it. So why was she still sitting there, frozen in place?

He watched her intently, waiting, she knew, for her to do as he asked, to take off her shirt, to initiate a far deeper intimacy with a man than she'd ever experienced before. But she remembered how things had been out in the forest, when she'd wanted him so much, only to feel shock and humiliation when he'd suggested she had an ulterior motive. He didn't feel that way now. She knew he didn't. But still she couldn't get it out of her mind.

She swallowed hard. "You first."

He gave her a tiny smile. "A show of good faith?"

"I'm sorry, John. It's just that —"

"It's just that this has been a game between us up to now, and you want to make sure the games are over."

She turned away, feeling totally transparent, wondering how he could have known exactly what she was thinking. Was he thinking, too, about how she told him she trusted him, and now she was acting as if she didn't?

He caught her chin with his fingertips and eased her back around. "It's okay," he whispered, then got up off the bed and stood beside it, reaching up to unbutton his shirt at the same time. Inch by inch he revealed himself, until finally he tugged the tail of the shirt out of his jeans, unbuttoned his cuffs, and pulled it completely off, revealing a lean, muscled chest that flexed sharply with every move he made. She remembered how she'd stared at him when they were out in that cabin, after he'd taken a shower and had been naked from the waist up. He'd noticed her staring, and she'd felt so embarrassed. Now that she could look at him all she wanted to, she took full advantage of the opportunity. *Gorgeous.* That was the first word that came to mind to describe him, followed by *strong* and *sexy* and a dozen more adjectives of total appreciation.

He tossed the shirt to the floor. "Okay, sweetheart. Your turn."

It was now or never. And no matter how apprehensive she felt, *never* just wasn't an option.

She took a deep breath, then grasped the hem of her sweatshirt and pulled it off over her head, her long blond hair swooping through the neck. She held it up against her for a moment, then dropped it to the bed beside her. She leaned back against the pillow, trying desperately to be cool about this; at the same time her cheeks were so hot it felt as if they'd caught fire.

It wasn't as if he hadn't seen her bra before, or even her bare breasts, but they weren't in the middle of something hot and wild and mindless now as they had been out in that forest, moving so fast she couldn't get her bearings. This was slow and sensual, his eyes taking in every square inch of her exposed skin. She'd never felt so naked in her entire life, and she wasn't even naked.

Yet.

"Your turn," she said, barely able to speak, because she knew what his *next* was going to be.

He reached for his belt and unbuckled it. She watched his dexterous fingers at work, her pulse skittering wildly. He pulled the belt out of its loops, moving slowly — so slowly that either her perception of time was really warped right now, making her feel as if every second were an hour long, or he was deliberately teasing her, making her want it. Making her want *him*.

If so, it was working.

Finally he dropped the belt, its buckle clinking against the hardwood floor. She waited for what came next, but he just stood there expectantly.

"Your turn," he said.

She blinked with surprise. Technically she guessed the belt qualified as an item of clothing removed, but fair or not, it put her in a precarious position.

She reached down and touched the button of her jeans, then changed her mind and fingered the clasp of her bra. John's gaze followed the path of her hands, attentive to the tiniest movement they made. His breathing had quickened slightly, and there was a look in those dark eyes that said patience really wasn't one of his virtues. She wavered back and forth between the two options, either of which would leave her nearly naked and completely vulnerable.

Suddenly she had a flashback to the teenage boys she'd had sex with, who'd been so hell-bent on getting her to hike up her skirt and pull down her panties that they'd say anything, do anything, to make it happen. And then had begun the frenzied thrusting, the grunting, the sweating, accompanied by the hollowness she felt inside because she could have been a blowup doll for all they cared about her, and when it was over, it was over. Oh, the more chivalrous of them might have offered her a cigarette, or maybe a ride home, but that had been about it, and she felt shame rise up inside her as she remembered how easily she'd sold herself for a few minutes of something resembling closeness to another human being. Only somehow she'd always been left feeling even emptier than before.

She swore she'd never feel that way again.

She fumbled around on the bed and finally grasped her sweatshirt, pulling it up in front of her. "I'm sorry, John. I wanted to do this. I thought I *could* do this, but I can't. Please don't be mad. *Please.*"

He sat down on the bed beside her, running a calming hand along her thigh. "Now, why would you think I'd be mad?"

She looked away. "When we were in that cabin, and I told you no . . ."

Her voice trailed off. When she finally dared to look back at him, he was shaking his head. "Sweetheart, a lot has happened between us since that night out at the cabin."

He reached up and took hold of the sweatshirt, carefully extracting it from her hands and dropping it on the floor. She folded her arms across her chest, amazed she could want him so much and feel so vulnerable all at the same time.

"You're shaking," he whispered.

"Yeah."

"Cold?"

"Scared."

He skimmed her cheek with his fingertips. "You don't have to be afraid."

"Do you have . . . protection?"

"Yes," he said. "You're not a teenage girl anymore, Renee. And I'm not a teenage boy."

At least part of that was true. He was a man. All man. But where sex was concerned, she was still stuck at age eighteen.

"I-I'm not going to be very good at this."

He smiled. "Sweetheart, there's no way you could possibly be bad at it."

He hooked his finger into the silky strap of her bra and pulled it down until it rested against her upper arm. He kissed the place where it had been, at the same time running his fingertip along the swell of her breast.

"Take your bra off for me," he whispered against her ear. "I want to see you."

He leaned away and stared down at her. He could have removed her bra himself, and her shirt, too, but something had changed from that encounter they'd had in the forest. He wasn't taking what he wanted from her in a wild, heated moment. He was asking her to give it to him.

She moved her hands to the clasp of her bra, his gaze following every nuance of the path they took. She unhooked it, paused a moment, then took it the rest of the way off and let it fall to the floor. She leaned back against the pillow that was propped up against the headboard, and as the cool air of the bedroom spilled over her naked breasts, she resisted the urge to fold her arms and hide herself from his view.

Why was this so hard? Was it because she was twenty-six years old and barely knew what sex was? Or was it because she was afraid of being a disappointment to a man she wanted so much to please?

He curled his hands around her rib cage beneath her breasts, his eyes shimmering like black diamonds as he stared down at her. For a moment she felt self-conscious again, but then he leaned in to kiss her, coaxing her lips apart and sweeping his tongue against hers, and she practically melted into the pillow. At the same time he circled her breasts with his hands, caressing them, teasing her nipples with his fingertips and sending currents of electricity pulsing through her. Boys had touched her breasts before, but not like this, never like this, and when he bent his head to swirl his tongue around her nipple, the onrush of pleasure she felt was so great she thought she'd die from it.

He kissed her again, but his hands were never still, finding erogenous zones she'd never even known existed. She moaned softly and clutched his shoulders, wanting this to go on forever, but the longer she reveled in the touch of his hands and his mouth, the more she felt a harsh, persistent pulsing between her legs she just couldn't ignore.

"John . . ." she said softly, squirming against him, her fingers digging into his shoulders. She didn't know what to say to put it into words, but somehow he knew. He trailed his hand down her stomach to the fly of her jeans. He unbuttoned them, then slid the zipper down. He tried to tug them off, but they stayed stubbornly up over her hips.

"I swear to God I'm never doing your laundry again," he murmured.

"Cold water," she said on a breath. "Air-dry."

"I'll remember that."

He took her hand and pulled her to her feet beside the bed, and somehow, despite the fact that the jeans couldn't have been tighter if they'd been painted on, and despite the fact that it meant she'd be standing in front of him wearing nothing but a scrap of pink nylon, she managed to wiggle out of them. He nudged them aside with his foot, then pulled her into his arms. His strong hands moved down her back, and as his lips descended on hers again, he slid his hands beneath her panties and cupped her buttocks. She gasped a little as he squeezed and kneaded them, urging her closer, so close she could feel his erection hard against her abdomen, straining against the fly of his jeans.

Then he backed away and sat down on the bed, pulling her along with him. He leaned against the headboard, and before she knew it, he'd turned her around and positioned her so she was sitting between his legs, her back to his chest. It felt awkward for a moment, but then he kissed her neck, sending shivers down her spine, and slid his hands around from behind to touch her breasts, strumming her nipples until they grew even hotter and harder than before.

He splayed his palm against her abdomen, then hooked his bare foot around her calf and eased her leg outward. Slowly he moved his other hand downward, pressing it against her panties, finding the tender, sensitive spot at the apex of her thighs. His touch was so unexpected and so intimate that she gasped and tried to twist away. But with his other hand pressed against her abdomen, he held her in place.

"Relax, sweetheart," he whispered, his

breath warm against her ear. "Trust me on this."

He began to stroke her, but his touch felt so acute, so invasive, so embarrassing that she was on the verge of begging him to stop. Instead she tolerated it, and after a moment she felt the strangest little swirl of pleasure. It flared gently, like a match against kindling, and any objection she'd thought about voicing slipped her mind. She relaxed against him, letting him hold her and touch her the way he wanted to, his hot breath spilling across her neck and shoulder. Soon the pleasurable feeling grew stronger, and she felt a sudden compulsion to move her hips in sync with his strokes, wanting, *needing* him to do it harder, faster. . . .

Then suddenly he stopped. Before she could cry out in protest, he slipped his hand deftly beneath her panties and delved his fingers into her slick, moist cleft. She froze, gasping with surprise, but he held her tightly, whispering calming words in her ear, then began stroking her again. It wasn't long before she was moving against him in cadence with his strokes, desperate to reach that indefinable *something* she trusted would be there if only she gave herself completely to it.

To him.

She gripped his hand where it rested against her abdomen, barely able to catch a breath. As the flame inside her flared more brightly, she moved in tempo with his strokes, pressing harder against him, reaching . . . reaching. . . .

"John . . . *please* . . ."

More words wouldn't come. All she could do was moan deep in the back of her throat, a strangled, needy sound that caused him to tighten his hand against her abdomen and increase the pressure, the rhythm, until she thought she'd go out of her mind.

"I know, sweetheart," he whispered, his voice deep and ragged. "Let go. Come for me."

The moment he uttered those words, something swooped together inside her, then broke apart, bursting with the brilliant intensity of a thousand stars. She clutched his hand and dropped her head back against his shoulder, rocked by wave after wave of pure pleasure.

"Yes," he murmured, enveloping her in his arms as she spiraled downward. *"Yes."*

The sensations pulsed through her with a wild, sensual rhythm, then slowly, slowly wound down. It seemed that a very long time passed before the last contraction faded away and she could breathe again.

But still she clung to him, feeling so warm and safe that she never wanted to let him go. This was so different from anything she'd ever experienced before. This was John, whom she'd gone to war with for the past two days over a terrible situation neither one of them had asked for, only to realize he was the one man in the world she trusted her life to.

John wrapped his arms around Renee and held her tightly, feeling a rush of emotion he couldn't put a name to, but it was so powerful it nearly knocked him unconscious. Up to now, she'd shown him just how tough she could be, from escaping Leandro, to fighting him all the way out of that forest, to keeping her cool through Sunday lunch with his family. Only there was nothing tough about her now. She was a soft, sweet, vulnerable woman who'd just dissolved in his arms, who clung to him so tightly and so trustingly that he wanted to hold her and protect her forever.

Then she turned in his arms and met his gaze, and the sight of those beautiful blue eyes glazed with passion just about sent him over the edge. She shifted around, draped her arms around his neck, and kissed him, and he kissed her back with every bit of enthusiasm he had to give. He would have sworn she wouldn't have had a bit of energy left, but here she was, moaning softly against his lips and pressing herself against him, as if she were getting hot all over again. She might not have a lot of experience in lovemaking, but everything she was doing was making him want her desperately. Could he ask for more than that?

"I've got to get out of these jeans," he whispered harshly. She rose from his lap. He came to the edge of the bed, but before he could stand she gently pushed him onto his back. In seconds she had his jeans open. She slid them down his thighs, taking his underwear with them. She got them down to his knees, then she glanced back up and froze.

"My God," she said, her voice choked.

"Don't stop now, sweetheart."

She pulled his jeans the rest of the way off, staring at what lay beneath with an expression of total awe. And he couldn't ask for more than that, either.

She dropped his jeans to the floor and stood there, her eyes wide, and he knew she wasn't quite sure what she should do next. He sat up and held out his hand, coaxing her to sit down on the bed. Then he went to his dresser and fished around in the top drawer. He found one of the plastic packets he was looking for, ripped it open, and slid its contents into place, astonished to see that his hands were actually trembling. He hadn't been this shaken up over the prospect of sex since he was a teenager.

*Take it easy,* he warned himself. *She's looking for a man, not a kid. A man in control of himself.*

He only hoped he could live up to that.

He was dying to rush right over and plunge himself deep inside her, but he knew he couldn't. She'd had enough of that kind of behavior years ago, when she'd let herself be used by any horny teenage kid who'd been persuasive enough to talk her panties off her. She'd never forgive him if he acted like that. He had to take it slowly, even if it killed him. And it just might.

He turned back around and was surprised to find her lying on the bed, her arm tucked behind her head, staring at him. She'd taken her panties off. His heart skipped a beat at the sight of her totally naked, and when she pulled one leg up and dropped it to one side, then ran her hand sensuously over her inner thigh, his mouth went bone-dry.

"John," she whispered. "Hurry."

*Thank God.*

By the time he got to the bed, she'd dropped her other knee to the mattress, too, and was reaching out for him. He moved between her legs and sank into her.

He froze suddenly, gritting his teeth, the intensity of being inside her so great that he was afraid of losing control right there. But she refused to let him pause, even for a moment. She pulled his face down to hers and kissed him deeply, wrapping her legs around him and thrusting her hips upward to take even more of him. He moved inside her, trying to take it slow in spite of her enthusiasm, trying to make this last longer than he'd been able to at age eighteen, but she was so hot and so tight that he knew he didn't stand a chance of that.

She ran her hands over his back and whispered his name with increasing urgency, and he thrust harder and faster, his body throbbing, aching for release. He'd been so afraid of moving too fast with her, but here she was capturing his rhythm and moving right along with him, any shyness or fear she'd expressed earlier only a distant memory.

"John!" she cried out. "Oh, *God* . . ."

He stopped, thinking he'd hurt her. "Renee?"

"No!" she said. "Don't stop! *Don't stop!*"

She pulled his hips toward her and arched to meet him, and as he buried himself deep inside her again, he realized, unbelievably, that she was teetering on the brink of orgasm right along with him. It was such an incredible turn-on to know he was taking her there again. No way would he be able to hold back now. He had to, though . . . just enough . . . just long enough . . .

Then she cried out his name again, clenching hard around him. He knew she was coming, *felt* her coming, and that was all it took to send him over the edge, too. He shuddered as pulse after pulse of white-hot electricity shot through him. For several seconds they clung to each other, breathing wildly, riding out the last few ripples of sensation together.

Slowly the intensity of the moment gave way to relaxed euphoria. John rolled to one side and pulled Renee into his arms. She laid her head on his shoulder, her warm breath tickling his chest. He held her tightly for a long time, so tightly she couldn't possibly take a good, solid breath. She clung to him just as tenaciously, as if breathing were only a secondary priority and being wrapped in his arms were number one.

John couldn't believe how he felt right now — as if he'd die if he ever let her go. With all the other women he'd ever known, he'd started planning his escape almost from the first moment he touched them. Why was Renee so different? For the first time in his life, he wanted more than *right now* with a woman. How ironic was it that she was a woman who might not have a future to offer him?

When she had first told him about her juvenile record, his belief in her innocence had wavered. But her story about her time in juvenile lockup and her "scared straight" experience rang true. Those kinds of things were very effective with some kids, and clearly they had worked with Renee. They had terrified her so much, in fact, that he was sure she couldn't possibly have committed that robbery.

Had it terrified her enough that she'd still consider running?

The moment that thought entered his mind, he felt a jolt of apprehension. *No.* Surely she wouldn't do that. Surely after what they'd shared tonight, she'd trust him to help her.

But what if he couldn't help her? What if she realized that the possibility of his amassing enough evidence to give her a chance with a jury was very small? What then?

*Just the idea of going back to a place like that terrifies me,* she'd told him earlier, her eyes awash with dread, as if she were reliving every moment of the experience she'd had as a teenager. *I'll do anything to stay out of jail, John. Anything.*

A terrible feeling of foreboding overcame him. If he closed his eyes and went to sleep right now, would that be the last time he ever saw her? Would he wake up to find the bed beside him empty?

He couldn't let that happen. No matter what he had to do, he couldn't let that happen.

# chapter fourteen

Renee lay in John's arms, in complete and total awe of what she'd just experienced. She'd never felt such an assault on her emotions, never believed for one moment that making love could be anything like what they'd just shared. Lying here with him now, she could almost forget the awful situation she faced and pretend, just for a little while, that everything was absolutely normal in their lives, that they were free to explore just how far a relationship between them could go.

God, how she wanted that.

Maybe it would happen. He was going to help her. Already he'd discovered that the testimony of the robbery victim could be discredited. What other evidence could he discover that might lead a jury to find her innocent? She took a deep, calming breath and let it out slowly, feeling her worries slip away. With John on her side, she could almost allow herself to believe that everything was going to be all right.

She laid her hand against his chest and felt its rise and fall, soft and measured, and she wondered for a moment whether he'd fallen asleep.

"John?" she whispered.

"Yes?"

"I thought you were asleep."

"No. I'm not asleep."

A long silence ensued. She felt a twinge of apprehension, then decided maybe he was just tired. She certainly was. What the walk out of that forest hadn't taken out of her, making love with him had.

Then she realized how tense he seemed. Or angry. Or both.

She rose on one elbow and looked down at him. He closed his eyes and looked away.

*Oh, God.* She'd done something wrong. But what?

"John? What's the matter?"

He didn't respond. She felt a rush of panic. This was just what she'd been afraid of. Somehow she'd disappointed him.

All at once it was as if her rose-colored glasses had been ripped off, and she was looking at their lovemaking in an entirely different light. Her cheeks grew hot with embarrassment. He'd given her so much, and she'd responded like some kind of self-centered nymphomaniac, giving him next to nothing in return.

"I'm sorry, John," she said, feeling as if she were on the verge of tears. "It'll be better next time. I promise."

Instantly she knew she'd said the wrong thing. He'd never said there would be a next time. Maybe she'd made too much out of this. Maybe he had no intention —

"Better?" he asked, his voice incredulous.

"It's like I told you. I-I don't know what to do . . . you know, how to please a man. The way you touched me . . . I know I should have done something for you, but I just didn't know —"

"Renee."

She stopped and stared at him. He rested his palm against her face, stroking it with his thumb.

"It couldn't have been any better, sweetheart. I enjoyed every minute of it, and I'd do it a thousand times more if I could."

"Then what?"

He sighed softly, his hand falling away from her face. "You know there's a chance I'll never find enough evidence to help you."

Renee closed her eyes. "Please don't talk about that now. *Please*."

"We have to."

*No.* She didn't want to hear it. She wanted to slap her hands over her ears and beg him to let at least this night pass without reminding her of the terrible situation that had brought them together. Just for tonight, she wanted to pretend —

"I just want to make sure you understand that the time will come when I've done all I can. You'll have to turn yourself in and hope for the best. Are you going to be able to do that?"

All at once Renee realized she'd been deluding herself. She'd let herself assume that as long as John was on her side, everything was going to be okay, but now he sounded so unsure of things that she felt apprehensive all over again. All at once the cold, hard reality of the situation struck her — the reality she didn't want to face: she could still end up in prison.

*If* she turned herself in.

"I-I don't know, John. If the time comes . . ." She exhaled, shaking her head. "I just don't know." Then she looked at him hopefully. "But I don't think it's going to come to that. We'll find some evidence. I know we will. Maybe we'll even find the person who did it. You say it's not likely, but it's possible, isn't it?"

He shook his head. "I don't think so."

"I thought you were going to help me!"

"I am! But there's only so much —"

"Don't you understand? I can't go to prison, John. I just can't!"

"Are you telling me you'd run again?"

She swallowed hard, her voice coming out in a raspy whisper. "Are you telling me you'd stop me?"

As soon as she said the words, the air between them filled with tension, and silence stretched on endlessly as she waited for his denial. It never came. Instead, he turned and pulled the handcuffs off the nightstand.

At first her sex-numbed brain didn't comprehend what was happening. Then all at once the fragile cocoon of warmth and safety she'd felt only moments before shattered into a million pieces.

She sat up suddenly. He reached for her wrist, but she yanked her arm away.

"After all this?" she shouted. "After everything that's happened between us tonight, you're handcuffing me back to the bed?"

"It's for your own good."

The betrayal cut right to Renee's soul. "It's because I told you about my juvenile record, isn't it? Now you think I really *did* commit that robbery!"

"No. I don't think that at all."

"Yes, you do! You wouldn't be doing this if I hadn't told you!"

"Listen to me, sweetheart. I know now just how scared you are of going to prison, and why you're scared. I can't say for sure you won't run, not because you're guilty, but because you're afraid, but if you do, your life will be over. Do you understand that?"

"I'm not going to run! I swear I'm not!"

He took hold of her wrist.

"Don't do this to me, John. Don't do it!"

She tried to yank her wrist free, but he held it tightly.

"I trusted you!"

"You can still trust me."

"Like *hell* I can!"

"Renee," he said softly. "Please."

She pulled hard against him, her teeth gritted. He merely held her in a persistent grip until she was forced to stop fighting him. The moment she relaxed, he pulled her arm over and snapped the cuff around her wrist. Tears burned behind her eyes.

"Damn you!"

He closed his eyes for a moment, as if waiting for the insult to pass over him, then opened them again. "I just don't want to wake up and find you gone."

Then, to her surprise, he held up his own

wrist and snapped the other cuff around it.

"Just stay with me tonight, Renee, and we'll get through this somehow. I promise."

*I promise.* Why was he making promises? Didn't he know that the minute he reached for those handcuffs, she'd stopped believing a word he said? *Stay with me.* As if she had a choice in the matter?

He rested his head back down on the pillow. Still sitting up against the headboard, she yanked the covers up over her naked body and turned abruptly away from him.

"Renee," he whispered. "Lie down."

"Go to hell."

A long silence passed between them. She didn't look over at him, but she knew he was still awake. How could he do this to her?

"I know you don't understand," he murmured. "But I'm doing this because I care about you."

"No. You're doing this because you're a cop who doesn't believe people can change."

"If that were true, you'd be on your way to jail right now."

Renee fought her tears tenaciously, determined to show no more weakness in front of him. She'd bared her very soul to him, and clearly that meant nothing. Suddenly she felt as if they were a million miles apart, when only a few moments ago she'd felt closer to him than she'd ever felt to a man before.

Finally she lay down, but only because sitting up all night wasn't an option. He reached for her. She flinched and moved away to the extent the handcuffs would allow. He expelled a breath of frustration.

"Just trust me," he whispered. "Please."

"I did trust you, John. Right up to the time you snapped this cuff on my wrist." She paused. "I won't be making that mistake again."

"Aren't they *ever* going to leave?" Paula whispered to Tom as she pulled yet another plate of nachos out of the microwave. "I thought they were going home after the game. It's nearly nine o'clock!"

Tom sighed. "Do you want me to say something to Steve?"

She knew Tom would do that, if it was what she really wanted. But as usual, guilt set in. Steve and Rhonda were about to drive her nuts, but he *was* Tom's cousin. It was the one thing — the *only* thing — that she and Tom had ever disagreed about. She'd tried to be understanding, though, knowing that Steve was the only family Tom had.

Actually, Steve wasn't so bad. It was his cheap blond bimbo who drove her nuts.

Paula sighed. "No. It's okay. How much longer could they possibly stay, anyway?"

"Oh, look!" Rhonda squealed from the living room. "*The Creature from the Black Lagoon* is on! It'll be so *cool* on the big-screen TV!"

*Oh, God.*

Paula had the sudden feeling that Steve and Rhonda were never going to leave her apartment, that they'd be here through the rest of eternity, flopping on her sofa, eating her food, and hogging her TV remote. Occasionally Rhonda would get up to head to the bathroom, where she'd blot that fire-red lipstick of hers with toilet paper and leave it lying on the counter, then envelop herself in a fog of that cheap perfume she wore. Then she'd come back out, flop onto the sofa, and start the process all over again.

"I'm sorry," Tom said. "Do you think you can put up with them a little while longer?"

Paula sighed with resignation. "Sure. I love *The Creature from the Black Lagoon*. Really."

Tom smiled. "You're a really bad liar. But I love you for it." She picked up the plateful of nachos and they went back into the living room.

Steve was sprawled out on the sofa beside Rhonda. He was almost as handsome as Tom, but not quite, his hair more sandy than blond, his features not as sharply defined. But when it came to personality, they were on opposite ends of the spectrum. Steve was quiet and brooding, while Tom was upbeat and friendly. Still, Steve was a handsome man, who would have been even more handsome if not for the bruise on the side of his face, the laceration on his cheek, and the split lip. When Tom asked him how it had happened, he'd said he'd gotten smacked around trying to help break up yet another bar fight. Paula had wanted to scream. If he had any pride at all, he'd be working somewhere nice instead of in those disreputable clubs. Then again, if he had any pride at all, he'd be dating somebody besides Rhonda.

"Here you go," Paula said, setting the plate down on the coffee table with a forced smile. "More nachos."

Rhonda flicked her coarse, pseudo-blond hair over her shoulder and looked down at the plate, huffing with disgust. "Did you *have* to put beans on them this time?"

Paula stood very still. "I didn't know you didn't like beans."

"Well, now you do."

"Come on, Rhonda," Steve said, his gaze never leaving the TV screen. "You're too picky. Just eat the damned nachos."

She gave him a dramatic eye roll. "Fine. I'll eat them." She picked up a nacho, then proceeded to disengage every single bean from it, leaving them in a pile on the plate, before stuffing the half-naked nacho into her mouth.

Incensed, Paula turned around and went back into the kitchen, wondering if she'd be a bad hostess if she shoved every one of those beans up Rhonda's nose.

Tom followed, holding up his palms. "I know. She's a pain in the ass. But I think a lot of it is the withdrawal, you know? Steve says she's going cold turkey. Once she gets off the stuff —"

"Gets off it? Are you kidding? She did a line of coke in my bathroom ten minutes ago!"

Tom slumped with resignation. "Okay. So maybe it's the coke that makes her cranky."

"Breathing makes her cranky!"

"Just try to tolerate her, okay? Steve will come to his senses pretty soon, and he'll dump her. I know he will."

Tom inched closer to Paula. He wrapped his arms around her and gave her a kiss that made her knees weak. Not only did she suddenly feel inclined to tolerate just about anything out of Rhonda, she was having a tough time even remembering who Rhonda was.

Tom nuzzled her neck, sending little shivers of delight racing down her spine. "Why don't we continue this in the bedroom?"

"Now? With them still here?"

"They'll barely notice we're gone."

He took Paula by the hand and led her back to the living room. "Hey, Steve. Paula and I are going to bed. You and Rhonda watch whatever you want to and lock up on your way out."

Rhonda ignored him completely, still focused on her systematic nacho dismemberment. Steve merely grunted.

Tom led Paula by the hand into the bedroom. She closed the door behind them. "Why do I get the idea that they only love me for my big-screen TV?"

"Come on, Paula," Tom said with a smile. "This isn't like you. You always give everyone the benefit of the doubt. Even sleazy, drug-addicted smart-asses like Rhonda."

Paula couldn't help smiling back. He was right. She'd always been one of those excessively optimistic people who tried to see the good in any situation. But lately, since Renee's arrest, she'd had the feeling that maybe things didn't always work out for the best.

"Do you remember how we used to watch the Rangers last summer?" she asked Tom. "You and me and Steve and Renee?"

"I remember."

"I had this crazy idea that we'd all be together forever." She sighed with regret. "I wish that had worked out. Not that I would have wanted Renee to stay with Steve, but —" Paula stopped short, then expelled a breath of frustration. "I'm sorry, Tom. I don't mean to put Steve down, but —"

"It's okay. I know Steve has his shortcomings. I'm just hoping someday he gets smart enough to find someone like Renee rather than someone like Rhonda."

Paula sighed. "I miss Renee so much. Do you think she ever made it to New Orleans?"

"I don't know. Maybe she'll call soon."

"But she can never come home. She's the closest thing I've got to a sister. I don't know what I'm going to do without her."

"Will you stop thinking about Renee? It only makes you crazy."

Tom sat her down on the bed and

grabbed his guitar from where it rested in the corner of her bedroom. She settled back against the pillows, sighing with pleasure as Tom sang for her. He had such a beautiful voice, and every time he shared it with her she felt like the luckiest woman in the world. She closed her eyes, letting the sound of his voice flow over her like a gentle tide on a deserted beach, washing away all her worries. . . .

"Hey! You people wanna keep it down in there? We're trying to watch a movie out here!"

Paula's eyes sprang open. Rhonda. Shouting at the top of her coarse, vulgar lungs.

Tom's fingers froze on the strings. Then he smiled at Paula, and in spite of Rhonda, or maybe because of her, they started to laugh. Tom set his guitar aside and took Paula by the hand, pulling her around until she fell onto her back on the mattress. They laughed harder, and then he was kissing her as only Tom could, and she wondered how she'd ever gotten through life without him.

From the living room, she heard the rumblings of *The Creature from the Black Lagoon*, laced with Rhonda's theatrical squeals of fear.

"Hey!" Tom called out. "You wanna

keep it down out there? We're trying to have sex in here!"

"Tom!" Paula said.

He gave her a wicked grin.

"You're *so* bad."

"Actually, no. I'm good. Very, very good. You want me to show you?"

And then he kissed her again, and she saw that he wasn't exaggerating in the least. But as he started to make love to her, Paula felt the old doubts come creeping in again. No matter how good things were between them, Renee's warnings were always in the back of her mind.

*He cheats on you. Get a clue, will you?*

Tom had always had a reasonable explanation in response to Renee's accusations — a friend dropped by, or maybe some woman had come to the wrong apartment and was just leaving. And Paula believed him. She loved him. How could she not believe him?

*When does he plan on paying back the money you've loaned him? Like, never?*

Paula refused to think about that anymore. After all, hadn't they talked about it just a few days ago? And what had Tom said?

*I have this feeling I'm going to come into a little money pretty soon.*

Paula didn't know exactly what he meant by that, only that he hadn't forgotten he owed her, and he had every intention of paying her back. And in the end, that was all that really mattered.

When Renee awoke the next morning, she felt disoriented, and it was a hazy moment before she remembered where she was. Then she turned and saw John. His head rested against the pillow, a stubble of a beard on his cheeks and chin, his dark hair sleep-mussed. She had a sudden, intense flash of how incredible things had been between them, how she'd felt things with him she'd never felt with anyone before.

Right before it had all fallen apart.

She looked at their wrists bound together by the cuffs, and she had to swallow hard and grit her teeth to keep from crying. How could he have done this to her? How could he have made love to her, then handcuffed her again, as if what they'd shared together had meant nothing?

Because he didn't believe she was innocent. Oh, he said he did, and that this was for her own good, but when it came right down to it, telling him she had a juvenile record had changed the way he looked at her. For all she knew, she'd be in jail before the day was out.

She lay back against the pillow, tears coming to her eyes. Turning to gaze at the sunlight peeking in through the blinds, she wondered if this would be the last sunrise she'd see as a free woman. Then she glanced at the nightstand.

And saw the key.

She stared at it for several seconds, her heart going crazy. The key to the handcuffs lay only an arm's length away.

She glanced back at John, who still lay sleeping.

In the next breath she realized what she had to do, and her heart turned somersaults.

Just like that moment out at the cabin when she'd spied John's car keys on the kitchen counter, she knew she was looking at her only means of escape. And she had to take advantage of it now, before any more sunlight spilled through the window and woke him up.

She slid the key off the nightstand, turned back over, and waited, clutching it in her fist. Still John slept.

She looked quickly around the room and spied her jeans and sweatshirt. Forget her underwear. She just needed something to cover herself until she could get out of town.

In her mind, she mapped out the shortest route to grab each piece of clothing. Her strategy in place, she slid the key into the lock and turned it. The resultant click sounded like an explosion to her ears, but John kept on sleeping. Slowly, slowly she pulled the cuff away from her wrist, her heart beating like a jackhammer.

She started to lay the cuff down on the pillow beside his wrist, when he stirred beside her.

*No, no, no . . .*

He shifted, turning his head on the pillow until he was facing right toward her. His eyelids fluttered. She gripped the handcuff, frozen with panic. He was waking up. She wasn't going to make it. He was going to see her trying to escape.

John blinked. Still groggy, he didn't focus on her right away. In a mindless rush, she did the only thing she could think to do. She wrapped the handcuff she held around the spindle of the headboard and clicked it shut.

At the sound of that tiny click, John's eyes flew wide open. He lunged for her, but she was quicker, scrambling naked out of the bed and backing against the dresser. He hit the end of the cuff, swinging his other arm in a wide arc, trying to intercept her. He missed.

"Renee! Get back here!"

She quickly scooped up her jeans and sweatshirt and held them up in front of her. He eyed the handcuffs with total disbelief, then gave them several hard yanks. When they didn't budge, he whipped back around.

"Renee. You can't leave. It won't solve anything!"

"Yes, it will! It'll keep me out of prison!"

"You'll be running forever. Is that what you want?"

"If it means I won't go to prison, then yes! That's what I want!"

He bowed his head in frustration, then snapped it back up again. "Look. You've got a chance of getting out of this if we can just hunt up a little more evidence in your favor."

"But you won't help me. Not anymore. Not when you think I'm guilty."

"I never said that!"

"No. You let your handcuffs do the talking for you."

John held up his palm. "I know you're scared, sweetheart. But I told you I'd help you, and I will."

"You think I'm guilty! You wouldn't have handcuffed me last night if you didn't!"

"That's not true! Damn it, Renee! Will you listen to me?"

"I have to go."

She wiggled into her jeans, sucked in hard and zipped them, then put on her sweatshirt. She grabbed the car keys out of his jeans.

"Renee. You're not going to go to prison. Not if I can help it. Unlock me, and we'll talk about it."

She started for the door.

"Renee! Stop!"

She turned back, hating the indecision she felt when she knew this was the only thing she could do, hating the fact that he was sitting there so gorgeously naked, a life-size reminder of how wonderful last night had been. She knew she was doing the right thing, but that didn't stop the tears from forming behind her eyes or a feeling of intense regret from welling up inside her that threatened to tear her apart.

"No, John," she said, her voice quavering. "It's better this way. For both of us. You don't have to make a decision about taking me to jail. It's out of your hands. You can blame me for escaping, and your conscience will be clear."

"Damn it, Renee! Don't do this!"

She wanted to stay. Desperately. She was right on the verge of believing every word he was telling her, because she had absolutely nothing else to believe in. But she couldn't. The handcuff she'd worn last night said he didn't trust that she was innocent, no matter how much he argued to the contrary.

If only she could go back to those few precious moments they'd spent together last night, when the rest of the world had disappeared and he'd shown her just how incredible lovemaking could be. She'd never known. She'd never even had a clue it could be like that. And all she'd wanted afterward was to fall asleep next to him, then wake up this morning by his side and have him tell her one more time that he believed in her and he was going to help her, and that maybe, just maybe, her whole life wasn't going to hell.

Then he'd destroyed it all by clamping that cuff onto her wrist.

"I won't leave you here like this," she told him. "I'll call Sandy later and tell her to come over."

John closed his eyes. "Oh, that's just great."

"I'll tell her we had a fight or something, and that I got so mad I handcuffed you there and left. She'll believe it."

"No, she won't. She likes you, Renee. She won't believe —"

"I'll make her believe it. And I'm sorry

about your car, but I'm going to have to take it. I know that makes me a car thief, but I don't have any choice. I'll get it back to you soon, though. Somehow. I promise."

She started out the door.

"Renee."

This time his voice was soft, pleading, reaching right inside her and wrapping around her heart. She stopped, her back to him, her hand on the door frame, and wished to God this could have ended any other way.

"Didn't last night mean anything to you?" he said.

*Don't do this to me,* she begged him silently, tears starting down her cheeks. *Just let me go and forget you ever knew me.*

She wiped the tears away with the back of her hand, then turned and met his eyes.

"It meant everything to me, John. I just wish it had meant something to you."

She walked out of the room. She heard him curse loudly and bang his fist against the headboard. She flinched hard at the sound, stopping to put her hand against the wall because she wasn't sure her knees were going to hold her up. Taking a deep, shuddering breath, she collected herself again and grabbed John's car keys off the kitchen counter, laying the handcuff key in their place.

She had to get to Paula's apartment, borrow some money, then get the hell out of town.

# chapter fifteen

Twenty minutes later, Renee pulled into the parking lot of Timberlake Apartments. As she drove down the east side of the complex, she remembered how excited she'd been the day she moved in. It had been such a step up from the vermin-infested rat hole she'd just moved out of, the only place she'd been able to afford at age eighteen on the meager salary and tips she earned at Denny's. This apartment had a built-in microwave and mini-blinds and carpet with no stains, and even though the other tenants weren't the cream of society, at least they weren't trying to sell her drugs in the lobby or throwing up in the hall.

Now, six years later, she could see that it really wasn't the palace it had felt like back then — the parking lot was potholed, the trim needed paint, and the awnings along the front of the complex were tattered and faded. But still she loved it, because it had been the first tangible proof she'd ever had that hard work paid off.

But as of today, she'd never be coming back here again.

She parked John's car as close to Paula's apartment as she could, then checked the area for any signs of life. Fortunately, the only activity she saw was a stray cat peeking out from behind a shrub and a flock of starlings chirping in the branches of a nearby live oak tree.

She got out of the car, slipped through the lobby door, and trotted up the back stairs. She knocked softly on 214, praying that Paula was home, because she had no idea what she was going to do if she wasn't.

Finally, after so much time had passed that Renee had almost given up hope, Paula opened the door. The moment she saw Renee, her sleepy eyes snapped open wide.

"Renee!"

They fell into each other's arms, hugging the breath out of each other. Then Paula took her by the shoulders. "You should be in New Orleans by now! What happened?"

Renee shook her head. "You wouldn't believe me if I told you."

"No! You have to tell me. I've been so worried about you. I have to know what's been going on."

Renee sat down and gave Paula the

*Reader's Digest* version of what had happened since they'd last talked, when Renee had been on John's cell phone, sitting in that McDonald's drive-through. Paula's eyes grew bigger and bigger as the story progressed, especially when she told her about John taking her to his house. Renee related the story as matter-of-factly as she could, leaving out the part about how John had made love to her and then proceeded to slice her heart into ribbons. That wasn't an issue now. It was over, and she refused to think about it anymore.

"Wait a minute," Paula said. "You left this guy handcuffed to his *bed?*"

"I had to. He would have ended up taking me to jail. You know where I'm coming from, Paula. I couldn't let him do that."

"Are you sure he won't help you anymore?"

Renee felt a twinge of uncertainty, and for a split second she pictured herself going back to him, slipping into his arms, and feeling warm and safe all over again. . . .

*No.* That was impossible. He didn't believe her. Not anymore. Her only chance of staying out of jail was to get out of town.

"I'm sure," she told Paula. "But you can help me. I need money. I don't have my purse, my credit cards — nothing."

"Of course! I think I've got at least a few hundred dollars." She grabbed her purse from the kitchen counter, pulled out her wallet, and fished through it, looking confused. "I thought I had more than this — oh! I forgot! I paid for groceries with cash. I've only got about thirty dollars!"

Renee slumped with disappointment. She was going to need a lot more than that.

"Renee?"

Renee spun around, and her heart leaped crazily. Tom was standing in the doorway between the hall and the living room.

She turned back to Paula. "You didn't tell me Tom was here!"

"Now, calm down," Paula said. "He won't tell anyone you're here."

Tom ventured into the room, wearing nothing but a pair of blue plaid boxers. He had a drowsy, quizzical look on his face, his surfer-boy blond hair standing up Don King–style on top of his head, making him seem even taller than his usual six feet.

"We need to get some money together for Renee so she can get out of town," Paula told Tom.

"What's she doing *in* town?"

"That's none of your business," Renee said sharply, shooting Paula the evil eye so she might actually consider *not* telling him the whole ugly story.

"Hey, take it easy, will you?" Tom said. "It's just that I thought you'd be in New Orleans by now."

Renee let out an exasperated sigh. Why had Paula told Tom her destination? The more people who knew, the more danger she'd be in.

"Renee, it's okay," Paula repeated. "Tom, do you have any money with you right now? Anything at all?"

He frowned. "I don't know. Maybe a few bucks."

"Do you mind loaning it to Renee?"

"Sure. I'll see what I've got."

Tom retrieved his wallet, and it was no surprise to Renee when he produced a paltry nine dollars. Paula gave him an approving smile, as if it had been nine hundred dollars he'd handed over.

As Renee took the cash, Tom sighed with disappointment. "I'm sorry it's not more," he said, and for a moment Renee believed he really would have given her nine hundred if only he'd had it.

"Renee?"

When she heard yet another voice behind her, Renee wheeled around, and her jaw dropped when she saw who was standing there.

"Steve!" Paula said. "What are you doing here?"

"The movie ran pretty late, and you've got a spare bedroom. I didn't think you'd mind." He turned to Renee. "Shouldn't you be in New Orleans by now?"

Renee shot Paula a look of total exasperation. "Is there *anybody* who doesn't know where I was going?"

"What do you think I'm going to do?" Steve asked. "Tell the cops?"

Renee wasn't so sure he wouldn't. Especially after that little matter of her knee in his groin.

"Of course he wouldn't," Paula told Renee, then turned to Steve. "Renee needs money. Do you have any?"

"Sorry. I'm all tapped out."

Renee let out a breath of disgust. "What's the matter? Did you pick the wrong horse last night and lose everything but the fillings in your teeth?"

Steve actually got a hurt look on his face, though it was hard to tell through all the cuts and bruises. It wasn't the first time Renee had seen him looking like that. Bar fights again, no doubt. When was he ever going to get a real job?

"Look," Steve said. "I know you're under a lot of pressure here, but do you have to be that way? I really would like to help you. I just don't have any money on me right now."

To Renee's surprise, he sounded absolutely sincere, and she felt a sudden flash of guilt. Both he and Tom were being nice to her when she needed help, and all she'd done was snap at them. Right now she could use all the friends she could get.

Renee let out a frustrated sigh. "I'm sorry, Steve. I just . . . I just can't believe I'm in this mess."

"I can't believe it, either," Steve said. "If only I'd seen you sooner on that night, I could have been your alibi and you'd never have gotten arrested in the first place."

She was surprised by the sincerity in his voice. "There's nothing we can do about that now."

"If it ever comes down to it, I'll testify for you. You know I will."

"It wouldn't do any good, Steve. But . . . thanks."

"Hey! What the hell is *she* doing here?"

Renee whipped around once again to see a cheap-looking woman standing in the doorway. A faint shadow of mascara ringed her eyes, and her chemically altered blond hair was scattered over her head like a Halloween fright wig.

Rhonda.

This couldn't be happening. That hallway of Paula's was like one of those little cars at the circus that clowns keep piling out of — just when you thought another one couldn't possibly be in there, out he came.

Rhonda flounced into the room wearing nothing but a midriff T-shirt, a pair of bikini underwear, and a hateful sneer. Renee slumped back onto the sofa, wishing she had a handful of aspirin and a good, stiff drink. "Is there anyone left on Earth who doesn't know I'm here?"

"Renee, it's okay," Paula said. "We're all your friends. We know you didn't do it."

"I'm not so sure she didn't."

Four pairs of angry eyes turned on Rhonda.

"Well, I'm not! I mean, the evidence said she did it. Who are we to think otherwise?"

"Rhonda!" Steve said.

She thrust her chin in the air. "I'm entitled to my opinion." She turned to Renee. "And why aren't you in New Orleans, anyway?"

Renee buried her face in her hands, her exasperation hitting an all-time high. She might as well pass out United States maps with her picture stuck to it and a big red circle around New Orleans.

"I mean, if you're gonna be on the run,

you need to do a better job of it than this."

"Shut up, Rhonda," Steve said.

"She makes a lousy fugitive, don't you think?"

"I said shut up!"

Rhonda's eyes narrowed with anger. "I should have known you'd take up for *her!*" She spun around and stomped back into the bedroom, slamming the door behind her.

"I'm sorry, Renee," Steve said weakly. "Rhonda's really not all that bad. She's just a little jealous."

They all looked at each other in a way that said Steve had understated both issues. Rhonda was a *lot* jealous, and she really *was* all that bad.

"She thinks Steve is still in love with you," Paula explained.

"That's ridiculous," Renee said, but when she glanced at Steve, his expression said maybe it wasn't so ridiculous after all.

"That night of the robbery," he said. "If only you'd have stayed to talk to me, none of this would have happened."

What he really meant was *if only you'd given in to me.* But she refused to have any regrets about that. Steve had been pushy and obnoxious that night, and keeping her distance from him had been the right thing to do. It was just too bad that it had to make everything else turn out wrong.

"Steve, I really don't want to discuss that."

"I just wanted you to know how I feel. After all, I may never see you again."

She'd assumed that Steve would never forgive her for planting her knee in his groin. But here he was acting as if none of that mattered, even offering to testify on her behalf, and it made tears come to her eyes. Not that she'd ever want Steve again, not like that, but she was glad to feel some of the old animosity fade away. Maybe she was even wrong about Tom. He seemed to make Paula happy, and wasn't that the most important thing?

Now, Rhonda was another story. For the rest of eternity, she intended to remember her for exactly what she was — a sleazy blond drug-addicted bimbo.

"Wait a minute!" Paula said. "What am I thinking? I can get money from an ATM!" She grabbed Renee's arm. "I'll go there with you right now. It's too early for the bank to be open, but I'll squeeze all the money I can out of the machine. It should let me have five hundred, at least."

"Oh, Paula," Renee said. "Thank you."

"Which one are you going to?" Steve asked. "The one on Eighteenth and

Meadowlake seems to always break down. I've had better luck with the one by the drugstore on Harris Avenue. The one in that strip shopping center."

"Okay, we'll go there," Paula said, then turned to Renee. "Are you ready?"

"Yeah," she said, sniffling a little as she stood up. "Thanks, guys. For everything."

"I'd better go see about Rhonda," Steve said, looking as if that were the last thing in the world he wanted to do. He gave Renee a hug, then looked at her sadly. "Good-bye," he murmured. "And good luck."

He headed off toward the bedroom, but at the last minute he veered into the kitchen instead. Renee didn't blame him. He probably wanted to get a cup of coffee under his belt before facing that shrew again.

Ten minutes later, Renee pulled up in front of the strip shopping center and parked John's Explorer next to an aging blue Chrysler. Paula pulled up next to her in her car, and they both got out. Renee was dismayed to see that despite the early hour, two people were in line ahead of them for the ATM.

They stood over to one side, Renee shivering a little in the cool morning breeze. Paula fingered her card nervously, while Renee merely tried to look inconspicuous.

She was anxious to get on the road, because she needed to be a long way from Tolosa before she got Sandy to turn John loose. She didn't want him to be in those cuffs any longer than he had to be.

*That's because you still care about him.*

It was true. She couldn't deny it. But as sharp as the feeling was now, it would fade, and the pain would go away. It was just a matter of time.

Finally, after what seemed like hours, the last man grabbed his receipt and walked away. Paula and Renee hurried up to the machine. Paula stuck her card in, punched a few buttons, and a moment later the machine spit out five one-hundred-dollar bills. She scooped them out of the cash tray and gave them to Renee, then tucked her card and receipt into the pocket of her purse. Renee gave her a big hug.

"Thanks, Paula. I don't know what I'd have done without you."

"Just give me a call when you get where you're going, okay? I want to know you're all right."

"It may be a while."

She looked at Paula a long time. Her warm hazel eyes had filled with tears, and Renee wondered if she'd ever have a friend like her again — somebody who accepted people for who they were and loved them, anyway. Tom was probably the luckiest man in the world, and Renee hoped to hell he knew it.

Finally she backed away. "I have to go now."

Paula nodded.

Renee got into John's car and pulled out of the parking space, refusing to look back at Paula, keeping her mind on getting out of town instead. When she got to the street, she turned right and headed for Highway 4, which would take her to the freeway. Tears clouded her eyes. She blinked rapidly, then wiped her eyes on her sleeve, trying to clear her sight. The last thing she needed was to be blinded by tears and end up wrapping John's car around a telephone pole.

The light turned red at Harris and Twelfth, and she pulled up behind another car and waited. She leaned her head back against the headrest and closed her eyes, trying to get a grip on her frazzled nerves. By the time she made it to the freeway, she'd be calmer. She'd be able to decide which way she should go. Everything was going to be all right. As long as she kept her cool, everything was going to be all right.

Then, for some reason, she got that prickly sensation along the back of her neck that made her feel as if she were being watched. She turned her gaze to her left, to the car that waited at the light beside hers — a brand-new red Blazer, hot off the show-room floor. Behind the darkly tinted glass, she could just make out the figure of a man, a very large man, staring in her direction. Then his front passenger window came down and she saw his face clearly — that hideously ugly nightmare of a face with a big white bandage slapped across his broken nose.

"Hey, there, sweet thing," he called out. "Long time no see."

# chapter sixteen

Renee stared at Leandro's revolting face, paralyzed with disbelief that he could have caught up with her again. What was he, anyway? Some kind of bounty-hunting savant?

She had to get out of here. *Now.*

But how? A car sat in front of her, blocking her way. And the light was still red. She laid on the horn, but the driver in front of her merely shrugged and pointed to the red light.

And Leandro was getting out of his car.

*No, no, no!*

She threw the Explorer in reverse and almost floored it, only to hit the brake again when she looked in the rearview mirror and realized that a bread truck had pulled up behind her.

She was trapped.

Leandro circled around the front of his car and headed straight for her. She flicked the door locks and laid on the horn again, but the guy in front of her merely turned around and gave her a disgusted look while he waved his arm at the opposing traffic. She knew the door locks would keep Leandro at bay only so long, but all she needed was a matter of seconds.

*Change, light! Change!*

Leandro came up beside the Explorer, that bald head of his glinting in the morning sunlight, his tattoos standing out in sharp relief on his huge biceps. And that was when she saw the baseball bat.

Without missing a beat, he whacked the bat against the driver's window, shattering the glass. Renee recoiled and covered her face as safety-glass beads rained down on her. Leandro reached into the car, pulled up the lock, and yanked the door open. He jammed the car into park, then clamped his hand onto her arm and hauled her out of the driver's seat.

"Let me go!"

He dragged her toward his car. She kicked and screamed, desperate for somebody who was watching this spectacle to help her. But who in his right mind would even consider going toe-to-toe with a huge, ugly, bat-wielding monster like Leandro?

"Hey!" she shouted. "You can't just leave my car in the middle of the street!"

"Not my problem."

Leandro shoved her through the passenger door of his Blazer, and when he slammed it behind her, she saw he hadn't yet removed the interior door handle on the passenger side as he had on his other car. A rush of sheer panic made her fling the door open again, intending to make a run for it. But he doubled back, slammed the door, and shook the bat at her threateningly, and she was forced to reconsider.

He circled the car, tossed the bat onto the back floorboard, then folded himself into the driver's seat. Just sitting within touching distance of him again made Renee quiver with disgust. She hated his smug expression, and she desperately wanted to smack his surgically altered nose right off his face. But she had no doubt that if she got the least bit physical, he'd turn her into SPAM.

She couldn't believe this. John's car had to be cursed. Every time she drove it, she got trapped somewhere with large, angry men coming at her. How could Leandro have found her? Tolosa wasn't a huge town, but it wasn't microscopic, either. How bad must her luck be?

Then she had a terrible thought. Could he have known she was at John's? Could he have followed her from there?

No. Surely if he'd known she was there, he'd have barged right in and ripped her out of his arms. Maybe she'd just been right the first time about him. He was a bloodhound from hell.

"How did you find me?" she asked.

"I told you before," Leandro said with a self-satisfied grin. "I'm the best."

The light turned green and he peeled out, tires squealing, and Renee strapped herself into the shoulder belt out of pure self-preservation.

"I got no cuffs with me," he told her. "But being an invited guest the way you are, I'm sure you'll want to mind your manners." He added a warning look that said if she didn't adhere to Emily Post's rules of fugitive apprehension, he'd break her in half.

Renee felt as if she were sitting outside her body, watching each terrible moment unfold. She thought about how she could be back with John right now, in his bed, and she wanted to cry. She wanted to be in his arms again, having him tell her once more that he really did believe she was innocent. Maybe it was true; maybe it wasn't. But she'd have given anything to hear him say it one more time, to have him tell her he was going to do everything he could to help her.

But there wasn't anything he could do to help her now.

Leandro floated through a stop sign, then turned down Fifteenth Street, passing through a rural-looking niche of the city with a cow pasture on one side of the road and a cemetery on the other. He lit up a Camel and dragged hard on it. He started to toss his Bic on the dashboard, then shot Renee a quick glance and stuck it into his jeans pocket instead.

"So how do you like the new car?" Leandro said, stroking the steering wheel. "Pretty hot, huh?"

"Not nearly as hot as your last one," Renee said.

"Now, that's real funny, sweet thing. Maybe you should be a comedian. Right after you spend the next ten years in prison."

Renee's stomach turned upside down, and she seriously wondered if she was going to throw up. That wouldn't be a good idea. She'd already incinerated his last car. If she barfed in this one, he'd rip her to shreds.

He shoved a CD into the player, and something very loud with only a faint resemblance to music blasted out of the speakers.

"Now, there's a sound system," he said, tapping his fingers against the steering wheel as he drove, the bass rumbling through the car. "Shoulda upgraded years ago. I was long overdue for new wheels. This baby's got it all — cruise control, keyless entry, airbags, power everything. Extended warranty, even. And I got a hell of a deal. That pussy of a salesman never knew what hit him."

*No kidding.* He'd probably taken one look at Leandro and handed him the keys — no charge.

*Wait a minute.* What did he say about airbags?

All at once Renee's mind was buzzing like crazy. Could she actually *do* that?

"So it's got airbags, huh?" she said, then made a scoffing noise. "I doubt that's plural. Knowing you, you've only got one on the driver's side. To hell with anyone riding with you. Right?"

"You got it, sweet thing. Because it's usually fugitives from justice such as yourself occupying that seat. Why spend the extra couple hundred bucks to protect someone I'm dragging to jail?"

"You know, in theory that makes sense, but in practice, I think it could get you into trouble."

"Trouble?" Leandro snorted. "What kind of trouble?"

Renee grabbed the steering wheel and gave it a hard downward yank.

"Hey! What are you —"

The car veered hard to the right and jumped the curb. The impact sent the airbag whooshing out, whacking Leandro right in the face and stuffing any words he was about to say right back into his mouth. The airbag deflated instantly and his mouth opened again, this time to emit one long, horrendous howl of pain.

The car traveled a good twenty yards with its left-hand tires on the street and its right-hand tires up over the curb. Its right front bumper whacked a lamppost, slowing the car considerably; then it veered over, hopped the curb the rest of the way, and struck the cemetery's brick fence, coming to a huge, jolting halt. The impact sent Renee hard into the shoulder belt, her head whipping forward and then recoiling back, but still she had the presence of mind to get out of the belt, yank open the door, and hit the ground running. To her undying relief, the impact had wrapped the fender of Leandro's car around the right front tire. He wouldn't be driving it anywhere for quite some time.

The last thing she saw as she glanced over her shoulder was Leandro with both hands over his face and blood running down his arms, and she felt a deep-seated sense of satisfaction knowing that his surgically repaired nose was destined to take another trip through the operating room.

Fortunately, they'd traveled less than half a mile, and the adrenaline pumping through Renee's body helped her cover that ground in a hurry. She prayed the whole time that nobody had called the police to tell them there was an abandoned car in the middle of the street.

Several minutes later she came around the corner onto Harris Avenue, and if she hadn't been gasping for breath, she'd have shouted for joy.

John's car was still there.

She crossed the traffic and opened the driver's door. She raked a couple of handfuls of shattered safety glass out of the front seat, then hopped inside. The keys were still in the ignition, and it was still running. She was lucky no real criminal had seen it and decided he needed it worse than she did.

With her hands still shaking, she put the car in drive, then made a U-turn at the intersection and chose a new route to Highway 4 — one that wouldn't require her to pass by Leandro's wreckage.

Five minutes later, she saw the freeway in

the distance. She pulled the car onto the shoulder of the road and brought it to a halt. It was decision time.

New Orleans was out. The entire population of planet Earth and possibly some nearby galaxies knew that it had been her original destination. So where was she supposed to go now? East or west?

The engine idled softly as she clutched the steering wheel, her mind spinning with the possibilities. She had five hundred and thirty-nine dollars in her pocket. How far could she go on that?

*Think. Think.*

Las Vegas? Everybody was shady and possibly a little criminal there, weren't they? She'd fit right in. Or maybe she should go someplace squeaky-clean where nobody would suspect she was running from the law, like Santa Claus, Indiana, or Cherryvale, California, both of which sounded a lot like Mayberry or Walton's Mountain. Their law-enforcement staffs would consist of three or four Barney Fifes who wouldn't know what to do with a fugitive even if she were right under their noses.

She checked her watch. It had been less than an hour since she'd left John handcuffed to his bed.

Naked.

*No. Do not think about John naked. Think about geography.*

Maybe she could go to Arizona, dye her hair black, and mingle with an Indian tribe. Or head to New York, where nobody thought much about armed robbery — it was merely part of the local color. Or San Francisco. Everyone was so weird there that a fugitive on the run from an armed-robbery accusation would be positively bland by comparison.

Or she could think about John.

She closed her eyes for a moment and imagined him sitting in that bed, fuming as only he could fume, thinking about how stupid he'd been to trust her for even a minute.

Thinking about how she must be guilty, or she wouldn't have run again.

Renee clasped the steering wheel, her stomach churning, wishing there had been some way for her to leave without his assuming she was guilty. From now on, when he thought of her, he'd think not of the night they'd spent together, but of the guilty woman he'd been crazy enough to try to help.

She blinked her eyes open again, trying to scrape together a little determination. She had to get out of here now, because sooner or later Leandro would be on her tail again, and if he'd been angry before, he'd be in a delirious rage right about now.

But he probably wouldn't be half as mad as John.

She couldn't help it. Raw, hot memories of the hours they'd spent together last night flooded her mind, sending a warm shiver down her spine like an erotic caress. She folded her arms on the steering wheel and dropped her head against them, willing the memories to go away.

*Impossible.*

She'd be calling Sandy soon, and she'd go over there and turn John loose. He'd never live that down with his family. Never. It wasn't as if Renee could call 911, though, because that would be fire rescue or something, and undoubtedly one of those guys would know him or know somebody who knew him. He'd be a laughingstock either way.

*It's you or him.*

She raised her head slowly, astonished that it had come to that. Or had it?

She could go back.

Just as quickly as the thought crossed her mind, she drove it away again. If the worst happened — if John took her to jail and she was convicted of armed robbery

— her life would be over.

But if she ran, she'd be looking over her shoulder for the rest of her life.

It was a prison either way.

The engine idled, waiting for her to put it in gear, but her mind was so fuzzy that she just couldn't think. Her whole life seemed to flash before her eyes, and she wondered how everything she'd tried to make right all these years could suddenly have gone so wrong. She saw those long days in juvenile detention that had taken her freedom away. She saw the leering faces of those horrible inmates, taunting her with the realities of life behind bars. She saw endless miles of interstate ahead, without a friendly face in sight.

She saw John's face, asking her not to leave. Pleading with her to trust him.

She dropped her head to the steering wheel again, overwhelmed by the emotions bombarding her from all sides. She had to decide where she was going. Now.

And once she did, there would be no turning back.

Being on the captive end of a pair of handcuffs was an experience John had never imagined he'd have to deal with, and he wasn't doing a very good job of it.

In the first five minutes after Renee left, he'd torn up everything within the radius of his reach, looking for something to use to saw through the spindle of the headboard. Nothing. In the next five minutes, he sat against the headboard and fumed, furious with her for leaving him here like this. And for the next hour, he alternated between wanting to throttle her and wishing to God she were back in his arms again.

*She's guilty, or she wouldn't have run.*

He kept shoving the thought aside, hating to believe it, but it kept coming back until he was forced to acknowledge it. Guilty people ran. Innocent people stayed and fought.

She'd run.

Only a tiny thread of belief remained inside him, and it was growing thinner by the minute. He held on to it, though, trying to keep believing she was innocent, because if he believed anything else, he was going to have to regret making love to her, and he couldn't imagine living the rest of his life with a memory like that.

Then he heard a key in his front door.

He closed his eyes. Well, here it came. Facing his sister while he was handcuffed to this bed — naked — was going to be just about the most humiliating experience he could imagine. She'd never let something like this go without squeezing as many laughs out of it as she possibly could, quite possibly for the rest of eternity.

He decided he wouldn't say a word. Whatever story Renee had concocted to get her to come over here . . . well, he'd just let Sandy think that, then stay away from family lunches for the rest of his life.

He heard footsteps in the hall, and someone appeared at his bedroom door.

He blinked. It couldn't be.

Renee.

She paused at the door a moment, then walked over to the bed. Her eyes were red and puffy, as if she'd been crying. She was holding the key to the handcuffs.

To his utter astonishment, she sat down beside him. Her hands were trembling, so she had to take three stabs at getting the key into the cuff. After a shaky twist of her fingers, it fell away from his wrist.

The moment he was free, all of John's pent-up frustration was released in a sudden blast of action. He grabbed Renee by the shoulders and pushed her backward onto the bed. He held her by her upper arms, pressing her into the mattress, hovering over her. She squeezed her eyes closed as if she expected some kind of onslaught —

verbal, physical, or maybe a little of both, and right about now, he wasn't ruling out anything. A dozen different emotions swam through him, and he didn't know which one to address first. Finally the frustration he'd felt for the past hour came rushing out in a torrent of anger.

"What's the matter with you?" he shouted, giving her a good, solid shake. "Don't you know that leaving here was the stupidest thing you possibly could have done?"

She swallowed hard, staring up at him and looking terrified.

"What the *hell* were you thinking?"

Still she didn't respond, as if her vocal cords had suddenly been stolen away. Anger and frustration still raged inside him, but as he looked down at her, the emotion that finally took over was one he hadn't counted on. Relief. Sudden, overwhelming, almost incapacitating relief that she was back.

"Are . . . are you going to take me to jail?"

She stared up at him with those tear-filled blue eyes, and the last of his anger drained away.

*Innocent people stay and fight.*

He couldn't believe she'd actually come back, risking the prison sentence she was so terrified of. In that moment he knew that no matter what happened, no matter what his job told him he was supposed to do, there was no way on earth he'd be able to turn her in.

He relaxed his grip on her arms. "No," he told her, his voice a weary whisper. "I'm not going to take you to jail."

"Not now? Or not ever?"

How had this happened? How, in the span of only a few days, had everything in his life turned upside down, changing his priorities until his job wasn't the number one thing in his life anymore? Until it wasn't even a close second?

"Not ever," he said.

"Do you still believe me?"

"I don't think I ever stopped believing you."

Relief washed over her face, and he felt her go limp beneath his hands. "Oh, God, John. I was scared. I was so *scared* to come back. I just didn't know —"

He sat down on the bed, pulling her up and into his arms. She wound her arms around his neck in a desperate hug.

"Shhh," he whispered, as she sobbed against his shoulder. "You did the right thing, sweetheart. You don't have to be afraid anymore."

*What a lie.* There was one hell of a lot she had to be afraid of. He knew he was making promises he couldn't keep, and that a dozen more were liable to spill out his mouth and he wouldn't be able to stop those, either. But the moment she'd shown up at his door something gave way inside him, unleashing a flood of protectiveness he'd never felt before.

"I thought I'd never see you again," he said.

"I was almost out of town. But I couldn't leave. I had to come back. I realized I couldn't run forever, and . . . and after last night —" She pulled away and stared up at him. "I know you must have been with a lot of other women, so it was probably nothing special to you. But to me . . ."

Her voice faded away, and he saw color rise on her cheeks. Nothing special? How could she even think that? Making love with her had awakened something inside him that he hadn't even known existed, a feeling he wished he could hold on to forever.

"It meant everything to me, too, Renee."

She closed her eyes with a sigh, as if those were the very words she needed to hear to get her through this awful situation. Then she looked back up at him, her blue eyes wide.

"John?" she whispered. "What's happening between us?"

In spite of everything, the question blindsided him. Yes, they'd made love. And yes, he'd been terrified at the thought of never seeing her again. And yes, the possibility that she could still end up in prison was intolerable. But what in the hell did all that mean?

"I'm not sure," he murmured. "All I know is . . . I don't know what I'd have done if you hadn't come back."

He touched his lips to hers in a tender, bittersweet kiss that bound them together more powerfully than a pair of handcuffs ever could. Then he eased her back down to the mattress again, her hair fanning out in a honey-gold cloud around her head. He lay alongside her, resting his hand along the curve of her waist. She touched his cheek, staring up at him as if she were seeing him clearly for the first time.

"I've never known a man like you," she murmured. "A man who does what's right instead of what's easy."

"I'm not the only one, Renee. I know how hard it was for you to come back here. But I promise you it was the right thing to do."

There he went again with the promises. He just couldn't seem to stop himself, even though their shadowy future loomed ominously in his mind. What would he do if he couldn't find enough evidence to sway a jury in her favor? Continue to carry on a relationship with a woman who was running from the law?

He closed his eyes, refusing to think about it. She'd come back to him. And right now, that was all that mattered.

"Make love to me," Renee whispered, and for the next few hours, that was exactly what he did.

# chapter seventeen

Shortly after noon, Renee waited at John's kitchen table while he went to the front door and paid a delivery guy for the Chinese food he'd ordered. Her neck ached from the collision in Leandro's car, but the pleasant exhaustion she felt from spending hours in bed with John made the pain seem like nothing at all.

When she'd returned and unlocked that cuff from his wrist and he'd reacted so violently, she'd cursed her decision to come back, thinking surely he was going to take her to jail. But then he'd swept her into his arms and held her so tightly, and in that moment all her anxiety had fled. She realized how wrong she'd been to ever think she couldn't trust him.

As they dug into the moo goo gai pan and sweet-and-sour chicken, John asked her about what had happened this morning when she left his house, and she spilled the story of how she'd gone to Paula, who'd loaned her money, and then gotten nabbed by Leandro.

John froze at the mention of that name. "He grabbed you again?"

"Yes."

"How did you get away from him?"

She related the story. John looked at her with total disbelief, his fork hovering in the air.

"You set off the airbag? Right in his face?"

"Uh-huh."

"And wrecked his car? And smashed his nose again?" He looked at her with total incredulity. "How do you do it?"

"Uh . . . I'm afraid his car wasn't the only casualty."

John's eyebrows shot up. "Are you talking about my car? What did you do to my car?"

"When I saw Leandro, I locked the doors, but he had this baseball bat, and, well . . . the driver's-side window . . ."

"Is in a million pieces." John closed his eyes and shook his head.

"It kind of got caught in the cross fire. I'm really sorry."

He held up his palm. "It's okay. It's not your fault. And it beats a bullet hole in my radiator any day."

"I'm sorry about that, too."

"Don't be. That beat a bullet hole in *me*."

"You know I never would have shot you!"

"I know," he said with a smile. "But I think I'll keep the guns out of your reach just the same."

She grinned. "You've got to admit I'm a pretty good shot."

"Sweetheart, you were shaking so hard I thought you were going to take a bird or two out of the treetops." He laid down his fork and shoved his plate aside. "Okay. This means that Leandro knows you're back in town, and he'll be gunning for you. And he's going to be more pissed off than ever. Any idea how he found you this time?"

"None at all. But this town's not that big. Maybe he just got lucky."

"Maybe." John looked unconvinced. "Did he recognize my car? He saw it out at that cabin, you know. If he ties you to me —"

"No. I don't think he remembers. It was pretty dark out there that night. And he's such a jerk, I know he would have mentioned it if he did recognize it."

"Still, he'll be on the lookout for you, so I don't want you leaving this house. If he and Paula are the only ones who know you're back in town, you should be safe."

"Uh . . ."

"What?"

"They're not the only ones. I saw a few other people."

"A few? How many is a few?"

"When I went to Paula's apartment, Tom was there. And Steve was, too." She paused again. "And Rhonda."

"Steve's new girlfriend? The one who hates you?"

Renee sighed. "That's the one."

John rubbed his hand over his mouth. "The more people who know you're back in town —"

"But they all believed I was on my way out of town."

"Nobody knows you were coming back to my house?"

"No. Absolutely not. Not even Paula."

"Do they know my name? Anything to connect you to me?"

Renee thought for a moment. Even though she'd told Paula the whole story, she hadn't mentioned John by name. "No."

"Then you should be safe here. Just don't step foot outside."

He got up and retrieved the pad and pen he'd used the other night. He sat back down next to her, so close their thighs brushed against each other, and already she wanted him again. He turned and met her eyes. She gave him a suggestive smile, and the way he smiled back at her made her body temperature shoot through the roof.

"Business first," he told her, as if he'd read her mind.

*And then pleasure,* she added mentally, knowing he was thinking the same thing.

"Okay," John said. "Let's go over what happened the night of the robbery one more time."

For the next half hour, Renee stepped back through the events of that night, and when she'd already gone over it three times, John made her go over it again. Then he told her the specifics of what he'd discovered when he'd questioned the victim, and when he got to the part about her description of what the robber was wearing, Renee crinkled her nose with disgust.

"The robber was wearing *what?*"

John consulted his notes again. "A leopard-print blouse, black pants, white shoes, black gloves. And, let's see . . . 'huge dangly earrings shaped like rainbows.' "

"Well, that clinches it. I'm innocent. I'm not exactly a fashion plate, but white shoes with a leopard print? Really. And no self-respecting woman would ever venture out in white shoes after Labor Day."

"If this were a self-respecting woman, she wouldn't be robbing a convenience store."

John stared at his pad some more, shaking his head. "There has to be something we're missing. There *has* to be." He tapped his pen on the table. "Tell me about Rhonda again. You saw her this morning. Is there any way she could have robbed that store?"

"It's possible, I guess. But you said the victim emphasized that the robber was tall. Rhonda isn't."

"She could have been wearing high heels. And the victim is about four-foot-zero. Anyone would look tall to her." He put a question mark beside Rhonda's name.

They went back over some of the events again, but eventually they realized they were talking in circles and not gaining any ground.

"I know you're assuming the robber is someone who lives in the vicinity," Renee said. "But couldn't it just as easily have been somebody totally anonymous who lives on the other side of town whom we'll never find?"

"Statistics don't bear that out."

"But it's possible."

"Yes. But something tells me that if somebody threw the stuff in your car, there's a connection to you, however small."

"Well, I'm not aware of any women who live around there with taste in clothing that's as bad as that," Renee said, still reeling from the fashion nightmare John had described. "Even Rhonda's a step up from leopard prints and white shoes. I just can't imagine any woman —"

She stopped suddenly, feeling a sharp tingle race down her spine, followed by a current of excitement that made every nerve ending in her body come alive. She put a hand against John's arm.

"Unless it isn't a woman."

"What?"

"Maybe it's a man."

A glimmer of understanding entered John's eyes. "A man?"

"Yes." Renee was almost afraid to say it out loud — afraid it would sound too outlandish when in her brain it was starting to sound very logical. "Maybe a man dressed as a woman. The robber was tall, right?"

"The victim said so."

"With big feet?"

"Yes."

"Deep voice?"

"Yes."

"Doesn't it make sense, then, that —"

"Yes," John said. "Perfect sense."

There was a long silence, with enough mental energy shooting back and forth between them to electrify the entire state of Texas.

"I think you may be on to something," John said.

"But it doesn't get us any closer to finding the culprit."

"Sure it does. There are far fewer guys dressed in drag in this town than there are blond women." John made a few notes, then looked back up. "Okay. I'll call Dave and get him to check the crime computer to see if there have been any other robberies in town where a male dresses in drag as part of his m.o."

"Won't Dave ask why you want to know?"

"No. He doesn't spend a lot of time wondering about other people's business. He'll just assume I've been thinking about a case I'm working on, and since I'm not supposed to be back in town yet, I can't go in to check something out myself. Now, Alex is another story. He practically makes a career out of sticking his nose into everybody else's business."

"I'm glad he was away on a fishing trip, then."

"That makes two of us." John made a note on his pad. "Then later this evening I'll go to Colfax Street and hit a few of the clubs down there that cater to, shall we say, the gender nonspecific."

"Gender nonspecific?"

"Sorry. Is my police sensitivity training showing?"

Renee rolled her eyes.

"I'm hoping," John said, "that somebody's wandered around down there wearing those clothes and that somebody else remembers."

Renee frowned. "That's a long shot, isn't it? If you're going to rob a convenience store, would you run around in public in the clothes you did it in?"

"Probably not. But maybe he went out in them sometime before the robbery and somebody will remember."

"And maybe we're totally off base here, and it really was a woman, and all this is just a waste of time."

"Maybe. But right now we haven't got much else to go on."

Renee stared down at the table. John slipped his hand against her thigh.

"Don't worry. We're not beaten yet."

She wished she could feel that optimistic. Telling her not to worry right now was like telling her not to breathe.

John went to the phone and called Dave, leaving a message for him since he wasn't in. As he hung up the phone, she started to ask him what was going to happen if a few days passed, or a week, and still they'd found no solid evidence either supporting her innocence or somebody else's guilt. But in the end, she decided not to ask, because she wasn't sure she wanted to hear the answer.

She followed him to the back door. He must have read the concern on her face, because he stopped and pulled her into his arms. "Hey, didn't I tell you not to worry?"

"I can't help it, John. If I go to prison, I'll be losing more than just my freedom." She melted into his embrace, resting her head on his shoulder. "I'll be losing you, too."

He held her tightly, running his hand along the length of her hair in soothing strokes, and she wondered how in the span of only a few days things could have changed so much. The man who had been her captor had become her ally. Her friend. Her lover. And the thought of being taken away from him was more than she could bear.

"You know I'm going to do my best to get you out of this," he said.

"I know," she whispered, but she couldn't help wondering if his best was going to be enough.

Several years had passed since John had worked the streets on the south side, and he found that nothing much had changed, except that the storefronts and sidewalks were a little rougher around the edges. It was a little after seven o'clock when he parked along Colfax Street, the epicenter of Tolosa's alternative-lifestyle crowd. At least three clubs in the area — Queen's Court, the Chameleon, and Aunt Charlie's — catered to people who hopped across gender boundaries like fleas from one dog to another.

He got out of the car, knowing he was going to stand out in these places like a full moon on a clear night just by looking normal. He'd never get any answers by engaging in casual conversation the way he'd done with that old lady at the convenience store. Many of the people down here flirted with the edge of the law, so they could make a cop in a heartbeat. He had no choice but to flash his badge and hope somebody was in a talkative mood.

He entered Aunt Charlie's and headed toward the bar, and in no time he was approached by a tall man wearing a long black wig and a short black dress, holding a thin brown cigarette between manicured fingers. He looked like Cher on steroids. If not for the Adam's apple, the five-o'clock shadow, the hairy arms, the knobby knees, and the size-thirteen feet, he might have actually resembled a woman.

"Hello, there," he said with a guarded smile, eyeing John up and down. "I'm Samantha. The assistant manager. And you are . . . ?"

John flipped out his ID. Samantha gave it a quick, offhand glance, then slid onto a bar stool, resting his arm against the bar. He crossed his legs, then flicked his cigarette into a nearby ashtray and gazed at John warily.

"What can I do for you, Officer?"

John laid a fifty on the bar, and Samantha's mascara-laden eyes widened with interest.

"I'm looking for a guy who might be one of your customers. Last time he was seen he was wearing a leopard-print shirt, black spandex pants, black gloves, and white shoes."

Samantha raised a deadpan eyebrow. "White shoes with that ensemble?" He took a drag off his cigarette and blew out a ring of smoke. "Are you sure you're not the fashion police?"

"And big, dangly earrings that look like rainbows."

"Oh, dear. Is this everyday wear, or Halloween?" He stabbed the cigarette out in the ashtray. "To tell you the truth, that could be one of two hundred people who come in and out of this place every night."

"This guy is maybe five-ten, maybe six feet. Probably wearing a long blond wig."

"Blond. They all want blond. What is it with that, anyway?" He brushed his phony waist-length hair over his shoulder with a preening flick of his hand. "There's no mystery to blond. It's nothing more than somebody jumping up saying, 'Me! Me! Look at me!' " He rolled his eyes with disgust. "Self-absorbed, self-conscious. That's what it is. It takes class to go brunette. To stop letting your hair talk for you."

As if his wasn't singing, "Gypsies, Tramps and Thieves" at the top of its hairy lungs.

"Do you have a photo?" Samantha asked.

"No," John said. "Just hoping the clothes might ring a bell."

Samantha eyed the fifty-dollar bill, clearly trying to figure out what he could do to earn it.

"Tell you what." He reached over the bar and nabbed a pink flyer from beneath it and handed it to John. "Tomorrow night we're having a talent show. Every cross-dressing, sexually ambiguous gender-bender in town will be here. You can probably find the person you're looking for."

John eyed the flyer, noting that the grand prize was one thousand dollars, with the runner-up receiving five hundred. A show like that could draw a considerable crowd.

He folded the flyer up and stuck it in his coat pocket, then grabbed a cocktail napkin. He wrote his phone number on it, then slid it along with the fifty down the bar toward Samantha. "I'm sure you'll call me if you see anyone before then who fits that description."

"Well, certainly, Officer. You can bet I'll be on the phone right away." Samantha snagged both items and tucked them into his phony cleavage. "And if you find who you're looking for, try not to bust the place up, okay? The owner will have my ass if you do."

John left the club and ventured across the street to Queen's Court. The owner and manager were nowhere to be found, and the bartender zipped his lip so tightly when he saw John's badge that he knew something illegal had to be going on somewhere in the vicinity. But unless that illegality was being committed by a man wearing a leopard print, right now John wasn't interested. One look from the bartender, though, and the patrons at the bar clammed up, too, leaving him no chance to get any information at all.

He walked a block and a half south to the Chameleon, where business had started to pick up a little. He hung out there for half an hour, watching people come and go. He talked to several employees and even a patron or two, but nobody remembered the clothes or the earrings.

John went back outside and stood on the street corner, wishing he had better news for Renee. It wasn't as if he'd expected a guy wearing leopard print and rainbow earrings to walk right up to him and confess, but at least he'd hoped for some kind of recognition on somebody's part.

Still, the talent show was something he hadn't anticipated, and it could very well draw the person he was looking for. Right now, it was about the only hope he had.

But what would happen if it turned up nothing?

*Don't think about that now.*

He shoved his hands into his pockets and headed back down the block to his car. For the next twenty-four hours, his task was clear: he had to keep the world from finding out Renee was with him until he could get to the talent show tomorrow night. With luck, a certain badly dressed man who robbed convenience stores would be out for a night on the town, never dreaming that there would be a cop in the crowd who was looking just for him.

When John got home, he found Renee curled up on his sofa waiting for him, her legs tucked up next to her and her long blond hair spilling over her shoulders. He'd been coming home alone to an empty house for so long now that he didn't know what it was like to do anything else, and he felt an unfamiliar stirring of warmth as he looked at her. What would it be like if she were here when he got home every night?

He shut the door, and Renee rose to meet him. "What did you find out?"

"Not much," he said, tossing his wallet and his car keys on the dining room table. "Nobody I talked to remembered anyone in clothes like the ones I described. But I did come up with this." He handed her the flyer. "There's a talent show tomorrow night at a club called Aunt Charlie's. It should draw a big crowd that'll be full of just the kind of people we're looking for. I'm planning on being there."

"Do you think you'll find something?"

It was a long shot, but he couldn't bear the thought of telling her that. "I think there's a good chance I'll come up with something."

Renee eyed the flyer, then looked up at

him with a cautious expression. "What are we going to do if you don't?"

He could tell she desperately needed him to give her an answer, but the truth was that he didn't have one. Right now he had no other leads to follow. If they turned up nothing tomorrow night, all she would have going for her would be a very shaky eyewitness, an almost-alibi, and an absence of motive. He knew firsthand that juries sometimes made incredibly dumb decisions. Under those circumstances, how could he ever suggest that she should turn herself in? By the same token, how could they carry on the way they'd been with no resolution to the situation at all?

"Let's take this one step at a time," he told her. "Let me go to the talent show tomorrow night and see what that nets us. We'll go from there."

She looked as if she wanted to say something else, but she didn't. Finally she just nodded. He knew his answer hadn't satisfied her. Hell, it hadn't satisfied him, either.

"It's nearly eight-thirty," John said. "Are you hungry?"

"Yeah. A little."

"How about a pizza? Sausage and black olives?"

"Sounds good."

Renee sat back down on the sofa again while John ordered the pizza. When he went back to the living room he found her sitting on the sofa, her legs tucked up beside her again, staring off into space. He knew she needed some reassurance, but he just didn't know what to say. So he simply sat down beside her and slipped his arm around her. Instantly he felt how tense she was.

"Renee? Are you all right?"

She laid her head against his shoulder. "Yeah. I was just thinking about my mother."

"Your mother?"

"Yes. She still lives here in Tolosa, but I haven't seen her in almost two years."

"Why not?"

"Because she hates me."

"But why? It looks like she'd be proud of you for putting all your teenage problems behind you."

Renee sighed. "My mother's an alcoholic. She didn't want me around when I was a kid because I was too much trouble when all she wanted to do was drink. And she doesn't want me around now because I remind her that people really can change, and she doesn't want to believe that, or she'd have to do something about herself."

John couldn't imagine what it must be

like to grow up with that kind of nonstop negative bombardment. Renee had suffered through it for years, yet still she'd been able to rise above it.

"I got up the nerve to visit her two years ago," she said. "I thought it might be time to mend some fences. I'd become a rational adult and I thought maybe she had, too."

"What happened?"

"She greeted me at the door with a drink in her hand. It was nine o'clock in the morning. Things went downhill from there. Within fifteen minutes I was reminded of what a rotten kid I'd been back then and what an ungrateful daughter I was now."

"Ungrateful daughter?"

"Oh, yeah. She told me that after all she'd done for me, I should be able to give her a few bucks once in a while now that I had a good job at a fancy restaurant. Apparently she was running low on booze, and her welfare check hadn't shown up yet."

John heard the catch in Renee's voice, as if she were on the edge of tears. He took her hand and held it tightly.

"Before I left her house," Renee said, "I went back into the bedroom that used to be mine. It was as if I'd never left it — the unmade bed, the concert posters I'd stolen from a music store, the broken dresser mirror I'd once slammed my alarm clock into in a fit of rage. I just stood there staring at all that, at the evidence of what my life used to be like, and I told myself that it was the last time — I was never coming back there again."

"Good. Stay away from your mother. You don't owe her anything."

"I know. I just feel cheated sometimes, you know? Other people have these wonderful families, and I've got nothing but an alcoholic mother who doesn't give a damn whether I live or die." She sighed softly. "To tell you the truth, if I end up in prison, she'll probably be thrilled, because then what she always said will finally be true."

"What's that?"

"That I'd never amount to anything."

She said the words matter-of-factly, but John knew the magnitude of the pain behind them. If only he had the power to sweep those memories from her mind so she'd never be haunted by them again, he'd do it in a second.

"I tried to do everything right," she said. "So why is everything turning out so wrong?"

"There's no answer for that. And if you go looking for it, you're just going to make yourself crazy."

"Did you know that, except for Paula, you're the only person I've ever told about my past? I can't bear the thought of anyone else knowing. I'm always afraid of what they'll think of me."

"It's over. You don't have to be ashamed of it anymore."

"I was beginning to believe that. I really was. And now . . . this."

"It'll all be over with soon and you can put it behind you."

There he went again, making more promises. He had no business promising her anything. But just the thought of her pulling herself out of the dark hole of her past only to get shoved over the edge again was more than he could stand, and he'd say anything to take that sad, wounded look off her face.

"Is there a movie or something on television?" she asked. "I could use a distraction until the pizza gets here."

He reached for the remote and flipped on the television, and he found he welcomed the distraction as much as she did — something to get their minds off the problems they faced. They watched an episode of an old sitcom, and finally both of them relaxed enough to start laughing at a few of the jokes.

He pulled her close, tucking her into his

arms as they watched, and soon her body seemed to dissolve into his. He thought about how flawlessly they fit together, how warm she felt against him, and how wonderful her hair smelled even though she'd washed it with nothing more than the cheap shampoo he used every day. He wished there were a way to stop time, a way for them to stay in this little niche of life they'd found together without having to worry about mingling with the outside world ever again.

Then the doorbell rang.

John rose reluctantly to answer the door, leaving Renee sitting on the sofa. Looking out the peephole, he saw a man holding a pizza box. He swung the door open.

"Twelve-fifty," the guy said.

John put his hand to his hip pocket, then realized he'd tossed his wallet on the dining room table. He left the door open and went to retrieve it.

"If you ordered this pizza with black olives, I'm gonna be pissed."

John froze. He couldn't have just heard what he thought he heard.

His brother's voice.

He spun around. Alex was standing at his front door.

At nearly six-foot-four, his brother towered over the pizza-delivery guy, who stared up at him a little nervously. Alex swiped the pizza out of his hand and flipped open the box, then turned to glare at John. "When are you going to learn that there are some food items that do *not* belong on pizza?"

John's gaze flicked over to Renee. She sat frozen on the sofa, her eyes wide, and unless Alex backed out the door right now and went away, he couldn't possibly miss seeing her. And now that he had his hands on a pizza, he'd never leave.

"Alex," he said, trying not to sound as uptight as he felt. "What are you doing here?"

"Heard you were back in town. Thought I'd come by." He nodded down at the pizza with a satisfied smile. "Great timing, huh?"

John gave the delivery guy a ten and a five and closed the door, his heart beating double time. There was no way out of this. No way.

Alex started toward the kitchen, then stopped short when he saw Renee sitting on the sofa. He gave her an appreciative smile. "Hey, John. You should have told me you had company."

"Uh, Alice," John said, "this is my brother, Alex."

Alex smiled broadly. "Ah. So this is Alice. The one Sandy couldn't shut up about." He glanced back at John. "The one she said you're not good enough for."

"Sandy has a big mouth."

"But she speaks the truth, unless she's talking about me." Alex walked over, swapped the pizza to his left hand, and held his right hand out to Renee. Renee rose from the sofa and shook his hand, a somewhat terrified expression lurking right beneath her shaky smile.

"Hear you made it through Sunday lunch with the family," Alex said. "Good for you. That's the first hurdle out of the way."

"Uh . . . what's the second one?"

"Me." He eyed her up and down, then turned to John with a guy-to-guy grin. "She passes. Flying colors. Now let's eat."

As he carried the pizza into the kitchen, John whispered to Renee, "I'll get rid of him as fast as I can."

"We'll just do what we did with the rest of your family," she whispered back. "It'll be okay."

When they got to the kitchen, Alex set the pizza down on the table. "John's always getting those damned black olives," he told Renee. "I hope you break him of that. Make him see that pepperoni —"

He stopped suddenly and stared at Renee. His eyes narrowed, and he tilted his head in that way that said there was something he didn't quite understand.

"Alice?" John said. "Can you get us some plates?"

"Uh . . . sure."

Renee walked over to the cabinet beside the refrigerator, and Alex turned to follow every move she made. His expression grew more hard-edged as the seconds passed. When she turned back around, she stopped short, obviously sensing that something was terribly wrong. Then John glanced back at Alex. His questioning gaze had become an accusing glare.

"Alice?" he said. "I don't think so. It's . . . Renee, isn't it?"

# chapter eighteen

Renee felt light-headed, and for a moment she was sure she was going to pass out. Renee? Had he just called her Renee? How did he know?

Alex turned to John. "Don't you know who this woman is?"

The room went deathly still. John didn't move. He merely stared at his brother, keeping his cool, but she knew it was a hard-won battle. She held her breath, trembling with apprehension, because she knew his back was against the wall. What would he tell his brother?

"Yes. I know who she is."

"No, I don't think you do," Alex said. "She's an armed robbery suspect. She skipped bail days ago."

"I told you I know who she is," John said sharply.

"Then what the hell is going on here?"

"Renee," John said, his gaze never leaving his brother. "Go to the bedroom."

"John —"

"I said go. Now." His voice was low and intense, with a commanding quality to it that said she didn't dare disobey. She set the plates down on the countertop and left the kitchen, but instead of going all the way to the bedroom, she stopped halfway down the hall and leaned against the wall, where she could hear everything the two men said.

"Let me get this straight," Alex said. "You know she's an armed robber, and yet—"

"*Alleged* armed robber."

"Don't dump that semantics crap on me, John. This is the woman you sat down with your family at Sunday lunch, knowing who she was?"

"I didn't ask for that. That was Sandy's doing."

"But you didn't think twice about lying to everyone, did you?"

"You don't know the whole story."

"I know all I need to know. I was there the night they brought her in on that armed-robbery rap."

John's voice held steady. "She's innocent, Alex."

"You think so, huh? Well, maybe you'll think twice when I tell you this. When I saw her that night, I happened to remember a certain little juvenile delinquent I arrested several years ago on a public-intoxication charge. How could I forget her? She dumped beer all over my shoes."

Renee bit back a gasp. Was it possible? Had John's brother been the patrol cop who had picked her up all those years ago? He was a detective now, but he wouldn't have been back then, and he clearly remembered the incident. . . . *Oh, God.*

He was the one. And he was John's brother. She didn't remember seeing him the night of the robbery, but she'd been in such a daze when they brought her in that she didn't recall much of anything.

"She has a juvenile record as long as your arm," Alex went on. "Public intoxication was the very least of it. Then I looked up, and there she was again. Little Miss Bad Attitude, all grown up."

"I know about that too," John said, his voice escalating. "But I don't care what she's done in the past. She didn't commit that robbery."

"Don't you get it? It doesn't matter if she's guilty or not. She jumped bail, you're a cop, and she's in your damned house! *That's* the problem!"

Several seconds passed before Alex spoke again, and when he did, his voice took on a no-nonsense quality that made Renee shudder.

"Let me tell you something, John. She didn't just have a bad attitude back then. She was one of the scary ones. She truly didn't give a shit whether she got thrown in jail or not. People like that don't change. They may hide it for a while, but it's always there, waiting to surface. I don't know if it's genetic, or if it's beaten into them from the time they're old enough to talk, but it's there, and you just can't get rid of it."

Alex's description of the person Renee had once been was so accurate that she winced at every word. But that stupid teenage girl didn't exist anymore. How would John ever convince him that she was dead and buried, and the woman who rose in her place would never even consider breaking the law?

"It doesn't always happen like that," John said, his voice quavering a bit. "People change."

"Christ, John, haven't we both seen it? Kids who were rotten to the core, who grew up and looked okay on the surface, only to end up in jail one more time because it's all they know?"

"Renee's not like that!"

"Oh, she's not? Do you think it's just a coincidence that she's accused of armed robbery? It's *never* a coincidence. They're

446

always running around with the wrong people. They never break that habit. Then they end up acting it out all over again, committing bigger and bigger crimes. It never ends."

Renee slid down the wall and sat on the floor, her knees tucked up to her chest, wanting desperately to cover her ears against Alex's accusations. But she couldn't. She had to know what she was up against. What *they* were up against.

*Please, John. Please don't give in. Please...*

For several seconds neither man spoke. Renee hugged her knees against her chest and waited, her heart thudding in a sluggish, heavy rhythm. As long as John stood by her, everything would be okay. She could take anything. She could walk through hell doused in gasoline if only he stood by her.

"Listen to me, Alex," John said. "I talked to the victim. She's half-nuts. Her positive identification of Renee is a crock. She'll be discredited right off the bat. But something she said gave us a lead to find the real culprit."

He went on to tell Alex about their speculation that the robber was actually a man. He told him about the talent show at Aunt Charlie's, and about his plans to go there to look for someone who met the description that the victim gave them. Alex protested a time or two, but John cut him off, telling him it was their best hope of finding the person who actually committed the crime, and that he intended to go there tomorrow night.

"First of all," Alex said sharply, "that's such an incredible long shot that no cop in his right mind would chase it. And second of all, you'd be pursuing it in an unofficial capacity while harboring a fugitive. Do you want *that* coming down on your head?"

There was a pause. Too long a pause. And when John spoke again, she could feel his conviction slipping away. "I've got to try, Alex."

"Come on, John! You've never been one of those spineless idiots who'll throw away his entire career for a few hot rolls in the hay. You've always been above all that crap. You, me, Dave — we all have. So what's going on now?"

John didn't reply. Alex lowered his voice. "Look. We're all entitled to a bout of really bad judgment at least once. We'll consider this yours. Just do the right thing, and we won't have a problem here."

"A problem? What are you saying?"

"You've got twenty-four hours. If you don't take her in, I'm going to."

"Are you telling me you'll take her right out of my house?"

"I'm telling you I'm not going to have you ruin your career because of some hot little felon who's got you wrapped around her finger!"

"It's *my* career! This has nothing to do with you!"

"The hell it doesn't! Think of the family. It's not just you we're talking about here. You get caught doing something like this, and it'll come down on all our heads. What do you think Dad would say if he saw how you're behaving now?"

Suddenly Renee remembered something Sandy had said about Alex, that he was the one who'd followed in their father's footsteps. But she got the impression that their father had practiced his own no-extenuating-circumstances brand of justice, and that John had never lived up to it.

Renee slid her hand to her throat, feeling hot and breathless. Why wasn't John telling Alex to go to hell? Why wasn't he saying something more in her defense? Could it be because he cared more about his family's opinion than he ever let on?

Could it be he was starting to believe Alex and not her?

It was Alex's voice she heard next, and

449

every syllable he spoke reverberated like a cell door clanging shut.

"Twenty-four hours, John. If you don't do the right thing, I'm going to."

She heard footsteps leaving the kitchen, the front door opening, then closing sharply. The noise sliced through her like a cold wind.

Then . . . silence.

She heard nothing from the kitchen. Absolutely nothing.

She sat in the hall, mentally begging John to come to her, to tell her that everything was going to be all right.

He didn't.

All at once she felt as if she were drowning in a sea of desperation, and every second that passed added to the deluge. She didn't know how much time passed — maybe three minutes, maybe four, but finally she got up off the floor and inched her way toward the kitchen.

John sat with his back to her, his elbows on the table and his hands clasped in front of him. She walked over tentatively and sat down beside him, resisting the urge to reach out, to touch him, to connect with him somehow, when she sensed things were going terribly, terribly wrong.

He wouldn't look at her. Renee knew

what that meant. She'd seen enough legal shows on television to know that when the jury didn't look at the accused, it meant the news wasn't good.

"I heard everything," she said.

"Alex will be back in twenty-four hours. He wasn't joking, Renee. You'll go to jail."

"Only if you let him take me."

"I can't stop him."

"You can't? Or you won't?"

"Don't you understand? He knows. He knows you're a fugitive, and now . . ." He paused, shaking his head. "We can't go on like this. Not with Alex knowing."

"Do you still believe I'm innocent?"

He paused. "Yes."

"But that doesn't matter to you anymore?"

"Alex is right, Renee. This isn't about whether you're innocent or not. You shouldn't even be here in the first place."

She grasped his forearm. "I'm here because you know what will happen to me if I stand trial. They'll convict me, John. They'll put me in prison. They'll take away my life for something I didn't do. And even when I get out, I'll have to carry that with me for the rest of my life!"

He spun around to face her. "Don't you think I know what you're facing? Do you think I want you to go to prison?"

"Then tell your brother to go to hell!"

"I can't do that!"

An icy chill trickled down Renee's spine. "Does this mean you're going to take me to jail?"

He stared at her a long time, and she felt a rush of panic. *Don't let it end this way. Please. Not this way.*

"No," he said. "I'll never do that, no matter what my brother says."

Renee put her hand to her throat, feeling relief because of that at least. "But Alex —"

"Alex doesn't make idle threats. If you're here tomorrow night, he'll take you in."

"Then I won't be here," she said, trying to interject a note of hopefulness into her voice. "I'll go somewhere else. Then you can go to the club tomorrow night and find the person who committed that robbery."

"No. Alex was right. We're never going to find the person who did this."

"But when you came home tonight you said it was a possibility. You said you thought we had a good chance —"

"I was dreaming. We both were."

"It's my only hope!"

He just shook his head.

"Why don't you try to talk to Alex again tomorrow?" she said. "After he cools off.

Maybe you can make him see —"

"No," John said sharply. "Even if I could talk Alex out of taking you to jail, as long as you're here, we still have only two choices. Either you eventually give yourself up and risk going to prison, or we carry on as if you're not an accused criminal and I'm not a cop, waiting for the day when we slip up and you end up going to prison, anyway. Now, which of those two do you think we ought to pick?"

Renee felt as if she were walking through a nightmare where nothing was real anymore, and behind every word, every phrase, every look John gave her was something grim and heart-wrenching.

"What are you saying?" she asked.

"You have to leave. Tonight."

Renee's whole body quivered with disbelief. He was slipping away from her. A feeling of hopelessness built up inside her until she wanted to scream.

"Just one more night, John," she said, her voice choked. "Just let me stay tonight, and then —"

"There's a motel up the road. I'll take you there. It'll give you a chance to think about what you're going to do. Then tomorrow —"

"No!" she shouted. "I don't want to go to a damned motel!"

His jaw tightened, his eyes drifting closed. "I know how you feel, but —"

"No! You *don't* know how I feel! If you knew how I felt, you'd never be able to do this!"

He pushed his chair away from the table and stood up. She caught his arm. "John."

She held on tightly, waiting until he looked down at her. She swallowed hard, trying to keep her tears at bay. "I thought there was something between us," she whispered. "Was I wrong?"

For just a moment she saw a tiny shaft of light in his dark expression, something that told her that no matter what he said, she still had his heart. But just as quickly as she'd seen the light, it disappeared, and his expression fell into shadow once again.

"No. You weren't wrong. There was something between us. And it was all based on a fantasy. We've got no future, and we were crazy to think we did."

Every word he spoke in that cold, emotionless voice ripped her open a little bit more. He slid his arm from her grasp and strode out of the kitchen, leaving her sitting at the table, tears streaming down her face.

How could he do this? How could he abandon her now, when she needed him the most?

★ ★ ★

John took Renee to the motel he'd told her about, a cheap but decent establishment ten minutes from his house. They didn't speak the entire time he drove, and the silence allowed Alex's words to bombard the inside of his head over and over again.

*It doesn't matter if she's guilty or not. She jumped bail, you're a cop, and she's in your damned house.* That's *the problem!*

The longer Alex had talked, the more John's eyes had opened to the reality of the situation, a reality he hadn't wanted to face. He'd been going along these past few days, thinking that if he wanted Renee badly enough, somehow things would work out all right. Listening to his brother, though, he'd realized the truth.

He'd screwed up. Royally.

Then he remembered what Dave had told him. *You've got to quit getting so personally involved. Sooner or later it's going to eat you alive.*

Dave was right. His lack of objectivity was a cross he'd borne since he first became a cop. It had gotten him exiled to east Texas, and it had gotten him into this situation now.

He didn't look at Renee. He didn't even glance at her, but he'd become so involved with her that he could feel every breath she took. He could feel her anxiety. Her fear. And it had clouded his judgment to the point that he didn't even know what professional objectivity was anymore.

*What do you think Dad would say if he saw how you're behaving now?*

Alex's accusation had been right on target. If their father were here, he'd be wearing that expression that was so familiar, that look of disgusted disappointment that said John hadn't lived up to his expectations. He never had, not from the beginning, and certainly not now. He'd always been the one to ask questions when their father's word was supposed to be law. He'd been the one to challenge authority and get slapped down for it. He had the eeriest feeling that his father was looking down from heaven right now, and he didn't much like what he saw. And the mere thought of that sent a chill down John's spine.

It wasn't as if he had any delusions about his father. Joseph DeMarco had been ruthlessly strict and heartlessly demanding, insisting that his sons live up to unreasonable standards. So why was he still beating himself up every time he fell short of his father's expectations?

Deep down, he knew the answer. Because

his father had died before he could do that one thing that would make the old man proud.

He pulled into a parking space near the garishly lit motel lobby and put the car in park. He shouldn't have brought her here tonight. He should have waited until the light of day, when things wouldn't have looked so desolate to her. But he'd been afraid that if she stayed with him one more night, she'd end up in his arms again and he wouldn't have been able to bring her here at all.

He was going to catch hell from Alex tomorrow night when he showed up and found Renee gone. But no matter what his brother had told him to do, he couldn't be the one to turn her in. As much as he wanted to right the wrongs he'd committed, taking her to jail when he knew she was innocent would haunt him forever. This way, at least he could hold on to the hope that maybe she'd managed to escape somewhere and live a halfway decent life.

She reached for the door handle.

"Renee," he said. "Wait." He pulled out his wallet.

"I have money," she said quietly. "Paula let me borrow five hundred dollars."

He held out a handful of bills to her. "Take it anyway."

"I don't want anything from you."

He held the money out a moment more, but when it became clear that she wasn't going to take it, he stuffed it back into his wallet and tossed it onto the dashboard. He desperately wanted to do something for her, knowing all the while that what she really needed from him he just couldn't give her.

"So what happens when Alex shows up tomorrow and I'm gone?" she asked. "What will he do to you?"

"He won't do anything to me. He won't like it, but if you're gone, it'll all be over with."

"For you, maybe. Not for me."

She put her hand on the door again, then stopped. For several seconds she didn't move. Then slowly she turned back around, her eyes filling with tears again, shimmering softly in the dim light.

"I'm so scared."

At the sound of those faint, whispered words, John had to fight the urge to pull her back into his arms, to make more promises he couldn't keep, to tell her everything was going to be all right when he knew that nothing was ever going to be right for her again.

"What should I do?" she asked.

"Run."

She swallowed hard. "I haven't got any way to run. I don't have my car, or —"

"Call Paula. She'll help you."

"Is there any way, if I turn myself in —"

"No. Right now the evidence is overwhelming, and if you're arrested, you'll go to prison. If you stay in town and Leandro catches up to you, after what you did to him this time, he may decide to take his own revenge." He paused, feeling an overpowering desire to kiss her tears away instead of causing more. "Run as far and as fast as you can."

"Maybe I'll call you. When I get where I'm going. Maybe —"

"No. Don't call. Don't write. I don't want to know where you are. It's —" He stopped, then expelled a weary breath. "It's better for both of us."

She nodded slowly. "Do you want to hear something crazy?" she asked, with a small, humorless laugh.

"What's that?"

"I think I was starting to fall in love with you."

John closed his eyes, wishing to God she'd never said that. How was he going to spend the rest of his life knowing she was out there somewhere, remembering him as the man she might have loved if he hadn't turned his back on her?

She opened the door, slipped out of the car, and walked away. She never looked back. And she was never going to know that maybe, just maybe, he was starting to fall in love with her, too.

He watched her approach the desk in the brightly lit lobby and ask for a room. He waited until he saw the clerk hand her a key, then jammed his car into gear and left the motel parking lot, thinking what an incredible fool he'd been the night he'd turned away from the police station and gotten involved with her in the first place. Thinking how cold and lonely that house of his was going to feel without Renee in it.

Thinking that there wasn't any possible way he could hate himself more.

# chapter nineteen

Renee lay on the orange flowered bedspread in that ugly little motel room, staring at the cracked ceiling, crying until she didn't have a tear left to shed. It was as if a hole had opened up inside her with nothing to fill it, and the pain it caused was excruciating. She'd thought she knew what kind of man John was, but a few angry words from his brother and he'd turned his back on her, depositing her at this crummy motel as easily as taking out the trash.

Her head pounding, she reached for the phone and called Paula. Twenty minutes later, they were sitting on that ugly orange bedspread together, and she was telling Paula the whole story. She told her about how she'd gone back to John and he'd pledged to help her, and how they thought maybe the talent show might hold the key to finding the real culprit, and then how Alex had shown up and John had turned his back on her.

She'd intended to leave out the part about making love with him and about how she'd come to trust him so much. But when she got to talking, those tears she thought had left her for good came back with a vengeance, and suddenly she was spilling everything. Through it all, Paula nodded sympathetically, letting her tell the story without passing judgment, which was what Paula did best and why Renee loved having her for a friend.

"I think he forgot for a while that he was a cop," Renee said, wishing her headache would go away. "His brother reminded him."

"Oh, sweetie, I'm so sorry you had to go through all that."

Renee sniffled, and Paula got her another handful of tissues from the bathroom.

"I can't tell you how he made me feel," Renee said, dabbing her eyes. "Like nothing could hurt me. And then . . . this."

She wanted to hate him. She wanted so desperately to hate him so she could replace the pain she felt with anger, but she couldn't. Every time she tried to picture slapping him, she pictured kissing him instead.

*Stop it. If he cared about you, you'd be in his arms right now and not in this tacky motel room.*

"So what are you going to do now?" Paula asked.

Renee thought about the life that lay ahead of her, and she had no idea which way to turn. "I don't know."

"So you really think the robber was a man?"

"It's possible."

"So what about the talent show?"

"What about it?"

"Do you think the person who committed that robbery will be there?"

Renee blinked. "It's possible, I guess."

"So are you going?"

She thought about that for a moment, about how John and Alex had both decided it would be an exercise in futility. Then she thought about how neither of them was facing an armed-robbery accusation, and if they were, they just might see things a little differently.

The longer she thought about it, the more she realized that it was the only chance she had to get out of this mess without running for the rest of her life. She had absolutely nothing to lose.

"Yes," she said suddenly. "I'm going there."

"You are?"

"Yes. The talent show starts tomorrow

night at nine o'clock, and I'm going to be there." Her conviction gained momentum as she spoke. "And I'm going to find some answers."

"Good for you!"

"Will you come with me?"

Paula froze, her excitement deflating like a popped balloon. "Uh . . . me?"

"Yes. I could use another set of eyes, not to mention the moral support."

Paula's expression got a little shaky. "Won't we, you know . . . look out of place?"

"We shouldn't. We look like women, don't we?"

"Right. We look like women. We don't look like men trying to look like women. They might not even let us in the door."

"Good point." Renee thought about that a moment. "Okay. I've seen transvestites and cross-dressers on those sleazy talk shows. Most of them overcompensate. Shorter skirts, flashier clothes, bigger boobs. Maybe we just have to show a little bad taste and a lot of Cottonelle."

The prospect of stuffing her bra did nothing to improve Paula's mood. "This is crazy."

"Paula. I need you."

"Come on, Renee! This sounds like

something Lucy and Ethel would do. Lucy would come up with something goofy, like wanting them to dress up like men who dress up like women, and Ethel would tell her uh-uh, nope, not gonna do it —"

"And then she'd do it anyway."

Paula sighed.

"Because she loves Lucy."

"You're killing me, Renee."

"It's my only shot at getting out of this mess. You have to help me."

"I know, I know." Paula closed her eyes. "Bad taste, huh? Okay. I guess I can do bad taste."

"Go to my apartment and get that red dress of mine. The one with the slit all the way up the thigh. And get the black one with the sequins for you."

"I can't wear that dress! You're two sizes smaller than I am!"

"It's stretchy."

"A fabric hasn't been made that's that stretchy. And I'm not exactly the sequins type."

"Trust me. It'll be fine. We'll wear the highest heels we've got, and maybe stockings with seams. Do you have a feather boa?"

Paula looked at her pointedly.

"Okay. Forget the boa. But find us some

hats. I've got to hide this hair of mine. And dark glasses. I don't want anyone recognizing me."

"Come on, Renee. How many people do you know who go to places like that?"

"I don't want to take any chances." Renee eyed her friend carefully. "Paula? Are you with me?"

Paula sighed and buried her head in her hands. "Tom would die if he knew I was doing this."

"But Tom's not going to know, is he?"

"He has an evening lecture at school tomorrow night. We're not even planning on seeing each other."

"Promise me you won't tell him."

"Believe me — this is one thing I'd just as soon he not know."

"Good." Renee took a deep breath. Her headache had subsided a bit, and she didn't feel like crying anymore. Those were definitely steps in the right direction.

But then she leaned back against a pillow, and all at once she pictured lying not in this bed, but in John's. Hazy images played through her mind — images of his hands and his mouth and the feel of his softly spoken words fanning against her ear, and she desperately wanted to go back a few days in time and experience it all over again

— right up to the time Alex had barged through the door.

Paula patted her arm. "You'll get over him, sweetie. It just takes time."

Renee started to protest that she wasn't thinking about John at all, but Paula knew her too well.

She sighed softly. "Do you know I've never been in love before?"

"Never?"

"No. Not really."

"But you were in love with him?"

It seemed so silly now, but just for a while, when they'd been together . . .

"I think I could have been. If he'd been the man I thought he was."

Renee knew that Paula, being that glass-half-full kind of person, wanted to tell her that everything was going to be all right. Instead, she just patted her hand again and gave her a bittersweet smile.

"You look tired. Get some sleep. I'll stock up on what we need and come back tomorrow night about seven o'clock."

She gave Renee another hug and slipped out the door. Renee locked it behind her and collapsed on the bed again, trying not to think about how thin the thread of hope was that she was hanging on to, because if she thought about it, she'd go crazy. Then she decided it was less painful to think about that than it was to think about John.

She might be able to prove her innocence tomorrow night. But nothing she did would ever bring John back.

At eight-fifteen the next evening, Paula pulled her car into a parking space along Colfax Street and killed the engine. She turned to Renee, an expression of abject terror on her face.

"You look . . . great," Renee told her.

"No. I look like a cheap hooker. A hooker so cheap she can't afford to buy new clothes when she outgrows the old ones. That's what I look like."

"The hat's nice."

"I have a peacock on top of my head!"

Renee patted the fashion statement on her own head. "I said you could wear this one if you wanted to."

"Purple satin with pearls? Now, there's a choice. I can either look like a big-tailed bird or Barbara Bush at a state dinner."

Renee couldn't help smiling. Tension really brought out the sarcasm in Paula. "Where did you say you got them?"

"The thrift store down on Market Street. They had lots of hats. These were the attractive ones." She took a deep breath and let it out slowly. "Tell me again about how we're going to find the guy who committed the robbery and get you off the hook."

"It's my only hope, Paula. And I'm eternally grateful to you for putting on that god-awful outfit to help me, even if you wouldn't stuff your bra."

"Okay, then. Let's get this over with."

They simultaneously slid their sunglasses on, and Renee had visions of a high-security undercover operation. Which she guessed was pretty much what it was.

They got out of the car and approached the club. Even standing on the sidewalk outside, Renee heard the music pulsing inside, and when she opened the door, it took a minute for her eardrums to accept the assault and stop rattling around inside her head.

Once inside, she glanced around and saw a window that looked like a box office. It appeared there was a cover charge. They went to the window, where a guy clad in a blue-sequined dress and big hoop earrings sat behind it counting money. His blond-tipped black hair stood out from his head like a mutant dandelion.

"Ten dollars, ladies," he said, in a voice a few octaves higher than the one he was born with. Paula stood over to one side to avoid even looking at the guy. Renee handed him twenty dollars to cover both of them, then gave Paula a little smile. They were in.

With a mutual sigh of relief, they turned to walk through the door leading to the main room.

"Wait just a minute!" the guy at the window shouted.

They froze, casting sidelong glances at each other. Renee waited for him to fly out of the booth, clamp a hand on each of them, and drag them back out the door, telling them they had the wrong plumbing to be admitted to a place like this.

Slowly they turned around, and the guy motioned to Paula with a crook of his finger. Renee saw her swallow hard, as if a Ping-Pong ball were lodged in her throat. She took a wary step or two back toward the booth. The guy leaned out the window, his eyes narrow and intense.

"Where did you get that *marvelous* hat?"

Paula stood there frozen, her mouth hanging open. Renee came up beside her and gave her a nudge.

"Uh . . . the thrift store down on Market Street."

"Damn! Then it's one of a kind!"

"Afraid so."

He shook his head. "The great stuff

always is." He gave them a big smile. "You're lucky you're here a little early so you get a good table. Enjoy the show."

Renee literally had to drag Paula by the arm to a table along one wall, where they had a good view of the entire room. The place was already in motion, with the strangest assortment of gender-questionable people roaming around that Renee had ever seen. Up front was a large stage draped with a thick maroon curtain. The music throbbed as multicolored lights swarmed around the room, and so much cigarette smoke hung in the air that breathing was a chore. A cocktail server came immediately to their table and took their drink order.

"See, we made it," Renee said. "That wasn't so hard, was it?"

Paula's face was still ashen. "I think I wet my pants."

"Just be cool," Renee said, dropping her shades down her nose a bit and furtively scanning the club. "And stay on the lookout. If you see anything suspicious, we'll take a closer look."

John sat on his sofa, the television turned on but muted, staring ahead at nothing. He missed Renee. God, how he missed her. Compounding that was the guilt that had been eating away at him since the moment he'd left her at that tacky motel last night and watched her walk away. He hoped she took his advice and ran far and fast, because the very thought that she could end up behind bars amid the scum of the earth was just about more than he could tolerate.

He remembered the look on her face as she'd stepped out of his car — that lost, lonely expression that said she'd trusted him to help her, and he'd let her down. Now she was going to spend the rest of her life wishing she'd never laid eyes on him.

He checked his watch. Eight-thirty.

The talent show started in thirty minutes. It was possible that the person who committed that robbery would be a part of that crowd, the person who'd either accidentally or deliberately framed Renee and was going to walk away a free man.

But maybe they'd been one hundred percent wrong, and the robber was some anonymous person he'd never hope to find in a million years. After all, how many crimes in this town went unsolved every year? This was probably going to be one more.

He tossed the remote down to the coffee table and rested his head against the back of the sofa. He'd done the right thing by making her leave. He knew he had. So why did it feel so wrong?

Then he heard a hard, rapid knock on his door that sounded like machine-gun fire.

Alex.

John stayed on the sofa for a moment, willing him to go away, only to hear another knock, this one more intense than the last. And he would continue knocking until John let him in.

He finally got up and opened the door. Alex stepped inside, glanced around the room, then looked back at John.

"Where is she?"

"Gone."

"You took her in, right?"

"To tell you the truth, I don't know where she is."

Alex glared at him accusingly. "You let her go?"

"Yes. I let her go. She was innocent."

"You don't know that for sure. And even if you did, it doesn't make a damned bit of difference!"

"Christ, Alex, she was going to spend years in prison for something she didn't do! Doesn't that mean anything to you?"

"Listen to me, little brother," Alex said, pointing a stern finger. "Once you start down this path, there's no going back."

"What path?"

"The one where you think you're above the law. The one where you start second-guessing everything instead of doing your job."

"Don't you understand? I knew what was going to happen to her if I took her in. You know as well as I do that the system doesn't always get it right!"

"Listen to me," Alex said. "I know what she was like back then. They never change. Never. If she gets thrown in jail, believe me, there's a good reason for it."

How could Alex know that? How could he know that a woman like Renee couldn't decide to make a better life for herself?

Alex huffed with disgust. "I can't believe this. I can't believe that you've made a fool out of yourself over a woman like her."

*A woman like her.*

John felt a sharp burn of anger start in the back of his throat and spread through him like wildfire. Suddenly it struck him that Alex didn't know a thing about Renee. He knew about some girl who existed eight years ago, who'd just as soon spit in a cop's eye as look at him. But that girl was gone. The woman he wanted to protect was someone else entirely.

Someone he was in love with.

He'd felt it last night when she'd gotten

out of his car at that motel, but he'd instantly shoved it aside, guarding his heart against the possibility that he could have fallen in love with a woman he'd never see again. But now the truth leaped into his mind with such force and such clarity that he couldn't help but acknowledge it.

He was in love with Renee.

But how could it be? How could he be in love with her? The situation was too crazy. He barely knew her.

But was that really true? The pressure she'd been under these past few days had revealed more about her than if they'd known each other for years. She had faced her biggest fear and had trusted him to help her through it.

*Yes.* She'd trusted him to help her, and he'd turned his back on her. How could he have done such a thing?

Because he was afraid of screwing up his career, afraid of what Alex thought, afraid of what his family would think. Hell, he'd even been afraid of what his dead father was thinking as he stared down at him from heaven. How foolish could he possibly have been?

All this time he'd been berating himself for his failure to become the man his father thought he ought to be, for his inability to reach that place in his life where he could finally do that one thing to make his old man proud.

Then Renee had come along, and in just a few days he'd finally understood something that had eluded him for as long as he could remember. He didn't need his father's approval. He needed to live according to his own rules and not give a damn what his father thought.

As of right now, he didn't.

He felt a surge of energy, accompanied by a sudden, overwhelming need to right the wrongs that his misconceptions had caused. He could feel his brother gearing up to berate him some more, but all he could think about was Renee. Right now he was the only thing standing between her and either a life on the run or a prison sentence.

He knew what he had to do. He had to get to that club.

He turned to his brother. "I did something really stupid last night, Alex."

"Damn right you did."

"I didn't throw you out of my house when I had the chance."

Leaving Alex standing there with his mouth hanging open, John went into his bedroom and grabbed his gun from his closet and his cuffs from the dresser. He stuck the gun into the waistband of his jeans at the small of his back, then returned to the living room and grabbed his coat from the front closet. He put it on, then stuffed the handcuffs into his pocket.

"Where do you think you're going?" Alex asked.

"Aunt Charlie's. Renee is innocent. And I'm going to prove it."

He started toward the door. To his surprise, Alex stepped in front of him. "You're not going anywhere."

John blinked. "What did you say?"

"I said you're not stepping foot out of this house."

Alex folded his arms over his chest, his legs spread wide, like a bouncer in a particularly bad ass bar. John couldn't believe it. Did his brother mean to physically stop him?

"Get out of my way, Alex."

"If you want out that door, you're going to have to go through me first."

John had expected Alex to be belligerent and unreasonable. He'd been that way ever since they were kids, lording his superior size and strength over his brothers every chance he got. But John had never expected this.

As tall and muscular as John was, Alex

was taller, and he outweighed him by at least twenty pounds. For all his talk about throwing his brother out of his house, in a bare-knuckles brawl, John knew there was a strong possibility that he could come out on the losing end.

Time was short. He had to get to that club, but his brother was not one to make idle threats — if John decided to leave, Alex would be all over him.

"So you think you can take me, huh?" John said.

Alex scoffed. "With one hand tied behind my back."

"Bullshit. You'd be lucky to bench-press three hundred."

"Kid, I was bench-pressing three hundred while you were still in diapers."

"Prove it."

"What?"

"If you can do ten reps at three hundred, I won't leave the house. Deal?"

Alex smiled. "Your negotiating skills stink. I can do ten reps at three hundred in my sleep, and you know it."

"Then how about you get in here and show me?"

John started toward his spare room, where his exercise equipment resided. Alex paused only a moment before striding after him, his intensely competitive nature allowing him to do nothing else.

John slid a hundred and fifty pounds on either side of the bar. Alex gave him a snide look and added ten more to each side. He lay down on the bench, and John watched in awe as Alex lifted the weight as if it were a bagful of feathers. He knew his brother was pretty powerful, but any minute he expected him to start twirling the barbell like a baton.

Good thing he hadn't expected to win this battle with brawn.

John slipped the handcuffs out of his pocket, and as Alex raised the bar to full extension, he clamped one of them around his left wrist. Alex caught on instantaneously, but he was holding a three-hundred-pound barbell, and in the time it took him to return it to its resting place, John had slapped the other cuff around the bench.

Alex dropped the barbell with a clatter and lunged for John. John managed to sidestep him, getting out of the way just as Alex hit the end of the cuff. His brother glared at him with a look of unbridled fury that said that if he ever got loose, John was a dead man.

"You son of a bitch!" he shouted, his voice thundering through the room. "What the hell do you think you're doing?"

"I thought I made that clear. I'm going to that club."

Alex started after John, dragging the weight bench after him with surprising speed, its legs making a hideous scraping noise across the hardwood floor. John managed to make it out the door with Alex only inches behind him. Then the weight bench hit the door with a clatter, too wide by a few inches to clear the space, and Alex hit the end of the cuff with a loud curse.

"John! Get back here! You get your ass back here and get me out of these cuffs! Now!"

"Sorry, Alex. I've got things to do."

Alex yanked at the cuffs so hard that John thought for a moment that he might actually succeed in breaking them. After all, they might be a little worn by now, since they'd practically seen more action in the past three days than they had in his entire career.

"Do you have *any* idea what I'm going to do to you when I get my hands on you?" Alex shouted.

Oh, John knew. Thank God for plastic surgery and dental reconstruction. After six months or so of recuperation, he might actually resemble a human being again.

Alex was still screaming at him as he went

out to the garage, but that didn't sway him from his mission. He had to get to that club, find the real culprit, then find a way to bring Renee back home to him again.

"The show's getting ready to start," Paula said. "This really ought to be something."

Renee couldn't have cared less about the show, except that the standing-room-only crowd gave her a lot more suspects. But pretty soon all the people kind of melted together into a sea of cosmetic excess, big hair, and plus-size glitz, and she was having a hard time sifting through it all.

The lights dimmed. Renee heard a drumroll, then a crescendo of introductory music. The emcee slithered onto the stage in a short, black, barely-there dress, fishnet stockings, and a long black wig, introducing himself as Samantha. If Sonny Bono had walked out from the other side of the stage and met him in the middle, the look would have been complete.

"Uh-oh," Paula said.

Renee whipped around. "What?"

"We're in trouble now." She pointed toward the DJ booth. "Steve's here!"

Renee blinked with disbelief. Paula was right. Steve was in the DJ booth, taking care of the music for the evening.

*Damn.* Of all the nights for Steve to be working at one of these clubs, why did it have to be tonight? Why couldn't he be gambling his paycheck away instead of earning one?

Paula whipped back around. "I can't let Steve see me! He'll tell Tom!"

"I don't want him to see either of us," Renee said. "Just take it easy. He obviously hasn't seen us so far, and now that he's busy, he won't notice us."

"I knew this was a bad idea," Paula said, taking a big swig of her wine spritzer. "A *very* bad idea."

Renee spent the next half hour scanning the crowd. Once she thought she saw somebody wearing a leopard print, so she got up to take a better look. But before she could get to the guy's table, he headed toward the hall that led to the bathroom and the pay phones at the back of the club. She ripped off her sunglasses and followed him, but halfway there she realized it wasn't a leopard print at all — just a lot of gold spangles on a black background.

Disappointed, she turned to go back to their table, at the same time glancing toward the DJ booth. For a moment she thought Steve's gaze had met hers. She shoved her sunglasses back on and turned away, scurrying through the crowd and sitting back down at their table. When she finally gathered the nerve to turn back, she saw that Steve's attention appeared to be on his job and not on her. She breathed a sigh of relief.

"Any luck?" Paula asked her when she returned.

"No. It wasn't a leopard print after all. I thought for a minute that Steve saw me, though, but he's not looking this way. I think we're in the clear."

"Are you sure?" Paula asked.

Renee looked back toward the DJ booth, suppressing a gasp when she saw Steve lay down his headphones and step out the door. But instead of walking toward them, he trotted back toward the hall, probably taking a quick bathroom break before the performer onstage finished his act.

"I'm sure," she said.

"Okay. Good." Paula let out a sigh of relief and took another sip of her drink. "You know, this is actually a pretty good show."

Renee wondered if the wine spritzer had gone to Paula's head. Which act had she enjoyed the most? The ballet number with the guy in the pink tutu, or the guy who stuck a pillow under his dress and sang, "I'm Just a

Girl Who Can't Say No"?

The more Paula relaxed, the more uptight Renee became. As act after act came and went, she started to realize that nobody here was wearing anything like what the man had worn to commit that robbery. Not even close.

If it had even been a man at all.

Hopelessness slowly crept in, and soon the futility of what they were doing here tonight became clear. It had been sheer speculation that the robber was a man, speculation based on what a crazy old lady had told John about what she saw that night.

John had been right. They'd been dreaming. She'd been foolish even to think of coming here, because even if she did find somebody wearing something suspicious, what was she going to do? Walk right up and accuse him of armed robbery? She could find out his identity, but then what? Without John to help her, how was she going to investigate any further?

As she watched a guy clad in yellow chiffon singing "The Yellow Rose of Texas" while a bunch of drunk men in dresses stomped and shouted, she realized the only thing she'd accomplished this evening was to risk being seen by somebody she knew, a danger even greater now that Steve was here. And she'd dragged Paula into the situation right along with her.

She couldn't do this anymore. She couldn't sit here in this strange place any longer hoping for the impossible.

She leaned toward Paula. "The show's almost over. Let's go."

"But you haven't found who you're looking for!"

"And I'm not going to, either. I was crazy to think I could. Can we just go? Please?"

Paula sighed. "Okay. If you say so."

Renee tossed money on the table, and they walked away amid a flurry of applause for "The Yellow Rose of Texas." The emcee announced the next contestant. Renee glanced back to see a performer coming out onstage looking a bit uncomfortable, wearing a short dark wig, snug blue pants, and an oversize blue silk top. He sat down on a stool in the middle of the stage, microphone in hand. Even at this distance, Renee could see that the crowd was in for a Judy Garland imitation, which was probably going to make poor Judy turn over in her grave.

Renee glanced toward the DJ booth. Steve's attention was on the show, making it easy for them to slip out the door unnoticed.

She wanted to go back to that ugly but quiet little motel room, feed herself a dose of reality, and plan her escape. By this time tomorrow, she needed to be well on her way to somewhere else.

Then the music started, and the performer onstage began to sing. Softly. Mournfully. A beautiful rendition of "Somewhere Over the Rainbow" in a voice not that different from Judy Garland's.

"Oh!" Paula said, turning back. "I love that song!"

"Paula, *please*. Let's get out of here!"

But Paula stopped. Stared.

"Paula. Will you come *on*?"

"Renee?"

"What?"

Paula pointed toward the stage. "Did you see his earrings?"

It was a long way up to the stage, but still Renee could see large earrings dangling from the guy's ears. Large, multicolored earrings. She whipped off her sunglasses.

Multicolored earrings? "Somewhere Over the Rainbow?"

Could it be?

She started back toward the stage, pushing her way through the crowd. She got jostled back and forth and almost fell off her four-inch heels, but finally she managed to get within several feet of the stage. She could go no farther. The crowd at the edge of the stage was like a solid wall of beads, sequins, satin, and lace, and she just couldn't squeeze her way through. She kept leaning right and left to see around people's heads, trying to make out the shape of the performer's earrings. She thought maybe they looked like rainbows, but she couldn't be sure.

Glancing to her right, she saw four steps leading up to a curtain, which looked as if it led backstage. If she hurried, she could catch the guy coming offstage and get a really good look. She inched her way around a redhead in a purple beaded gown and started toward the steps.

And ran right into John.

He caught her by the shoulders. She stared up at him with total shock. A heartbeat later recognition lit his eyes. "Renee?"

*He's here to arrest me.*

It was the first thought that entered her mind. Suddenly she was sure that Alex had convinced him that he shouldn't have let her go. John had checked her motel room, found her gone, then decided she might have come here. And now he was going to take her to jail, just as he thought he should have done in the first place —

"The earrings!" he shouted to her over the roar of the crowd. "That man onstage! I think those are the earrings!"

Renee almost collapsed with relief. He'd been looking for the culprit, just as she had, and he'd seen the earrings, too. He wasn't here to arrest her — he was here to help her.

Judy Garland was wrapping up his performance, sliding up to that high note at the end of the song and holding it while the crowd went crazy with applause.

John grabbed Renee's hand and wove through the crowd, then ran up the steps that led to the backstage area. He swept the curtain aside. Renee saw Judy Garland coming off the stage, accepting congratulations on his performance from another contestant.

John strode over, spun the guy around, and backed him up against a wall. He yanked one of the clip earrings off his ear.

"Hey!" the guy shouted. "What are you doing?"

John held up the earring, and Renee's heart slammed against her chest. It was a rainbow. No doubt about it. Just as the old lady at the convenience store had described.

Renee was sure this was the guy who'd committed the robbery. She didn't know what it was going to take to prove it, but she knew for a fact that they had their man.

Then he turned and met her eyes.

Renee stopped suddenly, sensing something familiar about that heavily made-up face. She stepped closer to get a better look, and when she realized who was behind those false eyelashes and that ruby-red lipstick, her jaw dropped so far it practically hit the floor.

"Tom!"

# chapter twenty

Tom's blue-shadowed eyes sprang open wide, a panic-stricken look on his face. "Renee! What are you doing here?"

Renee stared at Tom, paralyzed with disbelief. This couldn't be. This simply couldn't be. Tom had dated more women than there were stars in the sky, yet here he was dressed like one?

Then all at once it made sense. Now Renee knew who all those women were whom she'd seen coming out of his apartment. They weren't women Tom was cheating with.

They were *Tom*.

"You can't tell Paula," he pleaded. "You can't. She has no idea about this. She'll hate me, Renee. She'll leave me. Please, *please* promise me you won't tell her!"

Renee was still so stunned that for a moment the truth of the situation didn't hit her.

And then it did.

He was wearing the earrings. He was the one.

"You *bastard!*" She hauled off and whacked him with her doubled-up fist, then did it again and again, until he had to throw up his arms to ward off the blows.

"Renee! Stop! Renee!"

She continued pummeling him until finally John grabbed her and pulled her away. She squirmed in his grip, but he held her tightly.

"It was him, John! Tom robbed that store, and he was going to let me take the fall!"

Tom's eyebrows shot right up to his artificial hairline. "What are you talking about?"

"Don't play stupid! You're wearing the earrings!"

"Earrings?"

"The robber was wearing rainbow earrings. Big ones. Just like yours. It was *you!*"

"No! It couldn't have been me! I was with Paula that weekend at the Hilton, remember?"

"How can I be sure of that? How do I know you didn't slip away to rob that store?"

"I was with Paula all night. I swear I was!"

Then Tom looked over Renee's shoulder and groaned loudly. She turned around to see Paula walking toward them in slow motion, teetering a bit on her high heels, her peacock-feather hat slightly askew. She pulled her sunglasses off slowly, disbelievingly. "Tom?"

"Paula!" Tom said, horrified. "What are you doing here?"

Paula just gaped at him.

"Is that true, Paula?" Renee prompted. "Was he with you that whole night? Tell me!"

Paula continued to stare at him, shock freezing her face into a mask of total disbelief. Finally Renee shook her arm to get her attention.

"Paula! Was he with you all that night?"

"Y-yes. All night. Dressed . . . as a man."

"I'm straight, Paula," Tom said, his voice pleading. "I swear to God I am. I just have this thing about" — he expelled a long breath — "women's clothes."

Paula moaned and buried her head in her hands.

"But I can sing, you know, and Steve told me about the talent show. I thought maybe if I won the thousand dollars, I could pay you back at least part of the money I owe you."

This had to be scrambling Paula's brain. Renee wished she could stop to offer a little sympathy, or whatever one offered in situations like this, but she still believed a connection existed between those earrings and the robbery, and she had to find out what it was.

"Wait a minute," she said to Tom. "You said Steve suggested you compete here to-night. Does that means he knows all about" — she waved her hand up and down in front of him — "this?"

Tom closed his eyes. "Yes. But he's the only one. And he knows only because we roomed together and he found my stuff once."

"Your earrings," John said. "They're exactly like the ones the robber wore. Did you loan them to anyone?"

"No! Of course not!"

"This is just too much of a coincidence," John said to Renee. "If he didn't loan them to anyone, then who could have gotten his hands on them?"

The question hung in the air for several seconds. Then Renee had a thought that was so preposterous that she almost couldn't form the image in her mind.

She pointed to the wig Tom wore. "Is that the only wig you have?"

He gave Paula a cringing glance. "No."

"Do you have a blond one? A long blond one?"

"Yes."

"A leopard-print shirt?"

"Yes."

"White shoes?"

Tom's face crinkled with disgust. "Well, yeah, but not with the leopard print."

Maybe it wasn't so preposterous after all.

She raced to the curtain leading back out to the club. The others hurried after her, standing behind her as she looked out over the crowd. She zeroed in on the DJ booth near the bar. Steve was standing inside it, headphones on, still tuned in to the emcee wrap-up of the show.

"Renee?" John said. "What are you doing?"

Her mind was spinning too fast to respond. She was crazy even to think it, wasn't she?

Then her attention was drawn to the front door of the club, and her heart just about stopped. Someone was coming in. Someone about six feet, five inches tall. Someone with more tattoos than brains. Someone with a bald head that glinted under the neon lights.

"That's Leandro," John said. "What the hell is he doing here?"

Renee watched as he strode straight over to the DJ booth and started talking to Steve. Then both of them turned and scanned the club, and her stomach dropped through the floor. They were looking for someone.

They were looking for her.

She wheeled around to face Tom. "Did you tell Steve I was out at that motel in east Texas? Before the bounty hunter found me?"

Tom squeezed his eyes closed.

"Tell me!"

"Uh . . . I may have said something to him."

A slow, boiling anger rolled through Renee, an anger fueled by the horrible days she'd spent since her arrest wondering if her life was going to be over. Now she knew precisely what had happened that night. She knew who was to blame. And she knew that the reason she couldn't shake a certain bounty hunter was because he had an informant — an informant who had a motive to make sure she landed in jail. If she took the fall for the crime, he wouldn't.

She whipped the curtain aside and stomped down the steps.

"Renee! Stop!"

John started after her, but the whole place was on its feet applauding again, and she quickly lost him in the crowd. She stormed through the club, weaving among the tables, driven by a single-minded fury unlike anything she'd ever felt before.

Leandro turned as she approached, and when it dawned on him who the woman was in the bright red dress and the purple, pearl-studded hat, a malicious grin spread across his repugnant face. He squatted a little in anticipation, curving his arms away from his body like a pro wrestler ready to do battle. His nose was taped yet again, with blue and purple bruises extending two inches beyond it on either side.

Full of fury, Renee never missed a beat. She yanked a tray from a nearby cocktail server's hand, sending the drinks crashing to the floor. Leandro snarled, his hands curling into hooks, ready to sink right into her. What he had on her in sheer bulk, though, Renee made up for in speed. She took the tray in both hands, reared back, then swung it around in a wide arc and smashed him right in the face.

He stumbled backward, his hands flying to his nose. He let out an excruciating howl of pain like a wounded moose wailing through the wilds of the Yukon.

Then she zeroed in on Steve.

She leaped over the counter of the DJ booth, which she should never have been able to do in four-inch heels, but she was experiencing a surge of power greater than that of a mortal woman. When her feet hit the floor on the other side, she went for Steve's throat. He stumbled backward and fell. Renee landed on top of him, her hands wrapped around his neck.

"Hey!" he said, his voice choked. "What the hell —"

Renee tightened her hand on his throat and inched forward until her knees were on his shoulders. He stared up at her, gagging, his eyes almost popping out, and when she thought about how he was going to let her go to prison for a crime he committed, it was all she could do not to keep squeezing until he turned blue.

Instead, she spotted a bottle of Jim Beam on a lower shelf of the booth. She took it by the neck and smashed it against the floor. Glass flew in all directions, followed by a tidal wave of golden brown liquid. She was left with a nifty little weapon of razor-sharp glass shards still clinging to the neck of the bottle. She rested it against Steve's throat with the points pressing into his skin, feeling like Wonder Woman, Supergirl, and Xena, Warrior Princess, all rolled into one.

"You scum-sucking bastard. You set me up!"

"Come on, Renee!" he said, coughing. "I don't know what you're —"

She pressed the glass to the side of his neck, and he let out a gaspy squeak. "Hey! That hurts!"

"You haven't even begun to hurt, you slimy little toad! Now tell me the truth!"

When Steve didn't respond, Renee pressed her knees even harder into his shoulders and dropped her voice to a malevolent growl. "Ever hear the phrase 'going for the jugular'? One little flick of my wrist, and you're history."

"You're crazy!"

"Damn right I am! I've got nothing to lose! They already think I shot a store clerk, so what's the big deal about drawing a pint or two of blood from a slimy little DJ?"

"Renee, please —"

"I know you dressed in Tom's clothes. I saw you leaving his apartment after the robbery. I know you're the one who's been sending Leandro after me. You even told Paula and me which ATM to go to so he could find me!"

She pushed the glass harder against his neck. "Say it. Tell me you were the one who robbed that store!"

"I can't breathe!"

"Then you'd better hurry!"

He gagged a little more, and then the words came spilling out. "I didn't mean for you to be involved! I swear! What were you doing going out at eleven o'clock at night, anyway? I tried to stop you from leaving. I tried! If only you'd stayed home, I'd have been able to get the stuff out of your car and none of this would have happened!"

"Why did you do it? Tell me!"

"I owed money. A lot of it. I didn't have it, and the guy I owed was demanding a down payment or he was going to kill me. I swear he was, Renee. He'd already come to my apartment and beaten the hell out of me more than once. That's the only reason I robbed that store. But I *never* intended to implicate you!"

All at once she heard the door to the booth swing open behind her. John reached in and lifted her off of Steve, then pried the broken bottle out of her hand and let it fall to the floor with a clatter.

"He's guilty!" she shouted. "Did you hear him? He confessed! He's the one who did it!"

"I heard, sweetheart. Every word. But let's not add murder to the charges, okay?"

He pulled Renee out of the booth, then went back in after Steve and hauled him out. Suddenly she realized that everyone in the place had turned their attention from the stage to the guy getting arrested. The emcee shoved his considerable bulk through the crowd, wondering what was going on, and John asked him to call 911. Then he dragged Steve out the front door, calling to Renee over his shoulder and telling her to stay put.

By now a big crowd had gathered around the DJ booth, with everyone staring at Renee as if she'd grown an extra head. For a moment, all she could do was stand there, stunned.

Then she remembered Paula.

*Oh, God. Poor Paula.* Where had she gone? This was one of those pill-popping, wrist-slitting situations that some women just wouldn't be able to handle. She knew Paula was a whole lot more stable than that, but what must she be feeling right now?

Renee shoved her way through the crowd and finally saw her sitting at a table by herself, a lost, confused look on her face. Renee had no idea what to say to her. Even Hallmark didn't have a card for "sorry your boyfriend wears women's clothes."

She started to walk over, but then she saw Tom approaching Paula. She stopped and thought about the situation for a moment, wondering if Paula needed her, then decided that maybe it was best to let them work it out for themselves.

She went to the bar and sat down to wait for John. So many emotions were spinning around inside her head that she couldn't see how she'd ever sort them out.

Paula and Tom weren't the only ones who had some talking to do.

# chapter twenty-one

Paula shoved aside two beer bottles and an ashtray full of cigarette butts, then rested her elbows on the table and dropped her head to her hands, feeling as if her entire world had just collapsed. She couldn't believe Steve had committed that crime, then let Renee take the fall for it. After what he'd done, she was glad he was going to jail. She was glad he was finally out of their lives.

*Their* lives?

Hers and Tom's.

Only there wasn't the two of them anymore. How could there be, when he was more of a woman right now than she was?

"Paula?"

She turned to see Tom standing behind her, minus his dark wig. But still he wore the dress, the makeup, the false nails —

"Don't, Tom. I can't handle this. Please go away. Please!"

He pulled out a chair and sat down beside her. "I'm not going anywhere. Not until you listen to me."

"I don't understand any of this! How can you —"

"It's complicated. And it'd be impossible to explain in just a few minutes, so I'm not even going to try. I just want you to know two things. This does not mean I'm gay, and —"

"You're wearing a dress, Tom!"

"I know. Not everybody who does this is gay. It's still me under here. The same me you've always known."

She gave him a sidelong glance, then turned away again. She couldn't deal with this. She just couldn't.

"Don't you want to know the other thing?" he said.

"What?"

"I love you."

She closed her eyes, feeling the tears coming. *Damn it.* She was *not* going to cry.

"With other women this wasn't an issue — I never got close enough to them that I thought I'd ever have to tell them. And then you came along. I've dated a lot of women, Paula. But you . . ." He paused, shaking his head. "I know you think you're plain and all that nonsense, and sometimes you wonder why you're the one I want, but the truth is that I've always been afraid that I'm the one who's not good enough for you."

And then she really did cry, tears pouring down her face, and she felt so dumb sitting there in that weird, weird place, crying her eyes out. Tom put his arm around her shoulders. If she kept her eyes closed, she could almost believe that he was the Tom she knew so well. The one who looked like a man.

"Do you remember what you told me?" Tom said. "That there was nothing I could do that would make you stop loving me?"

Of course she remembered. Every word. But how was she to know he meant something like this?

Still, when she looked at him now, his beautiful green eyes stared back at her the same way they always had — with complete and total adoration. Was he still there? Underneath the false eyelashes and the too-bright lipstick, was he still the man she loved?

"I'm not asking you to say yes or no right now," Tom said. "I know we have a lot of talking to do. I'm just asking you to keep the door open."

She looked at him plaintively. "Are you sure you're not gay?"

"Remember the last time we made love?"

"Yes?"

"Now ask me that question again."

She couldn't help smiling a little. *Good point.*

"So all this time Steve knew about this?"

"Yes. When we roomed together, he found my stuff one day. He said he'd never tell anyone, but I could never be sure." Tom sighed. "Every time I'd get a little money together, thinking I could start to pay you back what I owe you, Steve would get in hot water with his bookie and hit me up. He never said it directly, but I was always afraid that if I didn't do whatever he wanted me to, he'd tell you about . . . this."

Paula couldn't believe it. Steve had been holding this over Tom's head? Was that why Tom had tolerated his cousin, and his cousin's nasty girlfriend? Because he was afraid of his secret being revealed?

"Steve did a terrible thing to Renee," Tom said. "And I'm going to do everything I can to make sure he pays for it. I knew he'd been into my things that weekend the robbery occurred. Stuff was moved around. He denied it, but he was the only one who knew about me, and he'd been there that night. I had no idea his messing with my stuff had anything to do with the robbery, though, or I'd have told the police right away. Even if it meant the world knowing about me. I wouldn't have let Renee take the fall, Paula. You've got to believe that."

"Of course I believe that," she said. "So you're going to tell the police what you know?"

"Yes." Tom's expression grew grim. "Steve has always had a rotten streak, from the time we were kids. I held out hope that maybe he'd change, but obviously he never did. It was such a good thing when he started dating Renee. I thought finally he'd found somebody nice. And then he went and screwed that up, too."

"Why didn't you just tell me what was going on?"

"And risk losing you? How could I?"

Paula closed her eyes, feeling those tears coming again. "I love you, Tom. I think I always will. But I'm not completely sure I can get over this."

He brushed a lock of dark hair away from her forehead, then slid his hand down her arm and took her hand in his. "I know. Just promise me you'll try."

She nodded, then managed a tiny smile. He smiled back, taking that little bit she gave him and not asking for more. But even as she expressed her concerns, she knew the truth. She couldn't imagine spending the rest of her life without him.

So he had one little flaw. She'd once dated an IRS auditor who never used deodorant and believed he was abducted by aliens every Halloween. This was a definite step up from that, wasn't it?

"I love 'Somewhere Over the Rainbow,' " she told him. "Why haven't you ever sung it for me?"

"I will. Every day from now on, if you want me to."

This was all very strange, and more than she could absorb all at once, but he was still Tom, and she still loved him. She didn't know how, but she had the feeling that sooner or later everything was going to work out all right.

When Renee glanced toward the door of the club and finally saw John coming back in, her heart fluttered wildly. She took a deep, calming breath, reminding herself that just because he was here now didn't mean everything was all right between them.

He made his way through the crowd that remained and sat on a stool next to her. She sensed he wanted to be closer to her, to touch her, but she turned away and stared down at the bar.

"Steve's on his way to the station," John

said. "I talked to the detective on the case. He's going to meet me there in an hour to get a formal confession."

"What if he changes his mind about confessing?"

"The clothes he wore in the robbery can be used as evidence. Hair samples in the wig, that kind of thing. We can prove he wore the clothes, that he was coming out of Tom's apartment that night, and that he had strong motive to commit the robbery. Gunpowder residue on the gloves will prove whoever wore them fired a gun. Considering what we know now, the D.A. will forget about you and go after Steve. But it won't come to that. I'm betting he'll confess. Then the charges against you will be dropped."

"It's over, then?"

"Not officially, but I don't think you have anything to worry about."

Renee nodded, emotions tugging at her from all sides, the most overwhelming of which was relief that it was over and she was free again. She knew she should feel happiness, too, because John was here, because he'd come to help her. But something still nagged at her that she just couldn't ignore.

John stared at her, his face full of concern. "How about you? How are you doing?"

"I'm fine. A little tired."

There was a long silence between them. Finally he turned her around on the bar stool until she was facing him. "Renee? What's wrong?"

Didn't he know? Did he think he could just walk back in here after what happened last night and everything was going to be fine?

"After the number Alex did on you last night," she told him, "my first thought when I saw you here tonight was that you were going to arrest me."

"What?" He shook his head. "I told you I'd never take you to jail, and I meant it!"

"Before last night, you told me you'd do everything you could to help me, too. But you didn't mean *that*, did you?"

He closed his eyes. "Renee —"

She felt the tears coming, and she was *not* going to give in to them. "You have no idea how it felt to have you turn on me the minute your brother snapped his fingers. And then you dumped me at that motel, telling me you never wanted to hear from me again. I'm going to have a hard time forgetting that, John."

He bowed his head. "I know. I'm sorry. I never should have done that." He took her hand in his, his thumb rubbing hers in gentle, mesmerizing strokes. "But I'm here now. Doesn't that count for something?"

She pulled her hand from his grasp. "You came here tonight only because you could do it on the sly. If you were successful, fine. If not, well, who was to know you'd even tried in the first place? But when it came to standing up to your brother face-to-face and fighting for me, you refused. So what happens the next time it comes down to me versus your job or your family?"

His eyes narrowed thoughtfully. "We need to talk. Come back to my house with me."

"No. We have nothing else to talk about."

"Renee, if you'll just listen —"

"Alex already knows I have a record. Remember how big that went over? Imagine telling it to the rest of your family. I'm sure they'll be equally thrilled."

"I don't care what they think."

"On the contrary. You care very much what they think, or you wouldn't have sent me away last night."

"Things have changed since last night."

"Oh, really? So you think now that you can tell your family I'm innocent, you can slip the juvenile record past them and maybe they'll overlook it?"

"Renee —"

"Well, I've got news for you. None of them are going to overlook anything. Alex is going to think I'm a criminal until the day I die. And what about Dave? How's he going to feel about having an ex–juvenile delinquent hanging around? Oh, hell, what am I saying? What about Brenda? If I show up at a family lunch, she's liable to haul along an automatic weapon and blow my brains —"

"Renee!" John shouted. "Will you shut *up* for a minute?"

She glared at him.

"You're coming home with me."

"I don't think so."

"I'm not asking. I'm telling."

"Oh, really?"

"Really."

Before she knew what was happening, he'd stood up, grabbed her arm, and hoisted her over his shoulder. A few seconds of sheer astonishment gave way to a surge of anger. She kicked and screamed, but he held on, his arm wrapped snugly around her thighs. He walked her through the club, past the prying eyes of every cross-dresser in town, giving them an unobstructed view right up her microminiskirt that probably made it quite clear that she really was here under false pretenses. He hauled her out the front door and strode down the street, then

511

deposited her by the passenger door of his Explorer. He unlocked the door and yanked it open.

"Get in."

"Forget it."

"Renee —"

"I said no!"

He took a step toward her, backing her against the car, then took her face in his hands and slammed his mouth down on hers.

It happened so quickly that Renee didn't even get a chance to take a breath. She'd thought about him kissing her again a hundred times since last night, just like this, hot and hard, his hands taking command of her body while his mouth devoured hers. The jolt of ecstasy she felt as fantasy became reality was almost too powerful to bear. She knew she should yank herself away and ask him how he *dared* kiss her after everything that had happened. She couldn't let him get away with sweet-talking her, sweet-*kissing* her, because she knew she could never trust him when the chips were down.

Then she realized, as her brain started to feel woozy from lack of oxygen, that she really had no choice in the matter. He was going to kiss her until he decided to stop or she died of asphyxiation, whichever came first. Soon any inclination she'd had to fight him melted right out of her, and all she could do was let the feeling overtake her and hope she survived the experience.

Finally he pulled away, his breath still burning her lips. She took a huge, gasping breath, teetering on her high heels, her brain so fuzzy that she thought she just might pass out.

"Get in the car."

Still a little woozy, she plopped herself down in the passenger seat and he closed the door behind her. He climbed into the driver's seat and started the car, yanking it sharply into gear and heading for his house. He pushed the limit all the way home, saying nothing, just staring straight ahead with a man-on-a-mission expression that made her very, very nervous.

Then all at once she had a flashback to the time he'd first dragged her to his house instead of to the police station. He'd led her through the kitchen, into his bedroom, and then . . .

*Oh, no.* Surely he wasn't thinking of that. Was he?

"John?" she said weakly, knowing he was a whole lot stronger than she was, and if he chose to do this, she'd never be able to stop him. "Where are your handcuffs?"

He turned to her with a small, wicked smile. "You'll see."

Renee looked at him with a mixture of disbelief and dread. Was she destined to live out the rest of her life handcuffed to this man's bed?

He pulled into his garage, then dropped the automatic door behind them. He escorted her into the house, much as he had that first night, only this time, the moment they hit the door she heard shouting coming from one of the bedrooms. A lot of very angry shouting laced with profanity that just about peeled the paint off the walls.

She looked at John quizzically.

"Alex paid me a visit tonight, just like he promised."

More shouting. More creative profanity in strange and startling combinations. More threats of extreme physical violence, all of them against John.

What was going on here?

Renee moved quietly down the hall toward John's spare bedroom. Then she turned the corner, and she couldn't believe what she saw.

Alex was handcuffed to John's weight bench.

She blinked, thinking maybe she was seeing things. But there he was, his face all red with anger, looking like a bull ready to charge. Fortunately, he could charge only as far as the handcuffs would allow.

"He was going to stop me from going to the club tonight," John said, coming up beside Renee at the door. "So I persuaded him to allow me to go after all."

"Persuaded, my ass," Alex muttered. "Of all the low-down, rotten things to do to your own brother —"

Renee stared at Alex in dumb disbelief. The implication of what John had done came to her in small bits, until finally she realized the truth: he'd put his neck on the line with his brother, his family, his job. For her.

She stood there, staring at Alex, feeling like the biggest fool alive. After everything she'd said to John at the club about not standing up to his brother, what was she supposed to say now?

She put her hand to her forehead, overcome by the feeling of her own stupid misconceptions flying right out of her brain. If only John had explained. If he'd just explained all this to her, then maybe she wouldn't have prattled on, saying all those rotten things to him. But then again, she hadn't given him much of a chance to explain, had she?

"What's going on here?" Alex said.

"Renee is innocent," John told him. "We found the guy who robbed that convenience store."

Alex looked back and forth between them. "No way."

"He's in jail right now."

"So she really didn't do it?"

"Nope."

Alex looked all red and flustered, as if he didn't quite know how to respond to that. "Well, you were still wrong last night. You should have taken her in. And you sure as hell shouldn't have done this. *Now get these cuffs off me!*"

John let out a reluctant sigh. "I guess I can't leave him locked up forever," he told Renee, extracting the key from his pocket. "Get ready to call 911."

He unlocked the cuff. The moment it fell away, Alex whipped around, coming to his feet as if they still had a score to settle. Renee wedged herself between them.

*"Stop!"*

Her top-of-her-lungs command halted Alex in his tracks, his eyes flying open with surprise. "Wait just a —"

"No, *you* wait," Renee said, jabbing her finger at his chest. "You're not going to lay one finger on him!"

Alex stared at her, dumbfounded.

"Now, listen up. You may be twice my size, but if you so much as *touch* him, I'll make you sorry you were ever born. I'll find ways to torment you that you can't even imagine. I'll make your life miserable. Death will seem like a *relief* after what I'm going to do if you touch *one hair* on his head. Do you understand?"

Alex leaned away from her slightly, a look of utter astonishment on his face. He turned his gaze to John, then back to Renee. Finally he rubbed his wrist and let out a breath of disgusted resignation.

"Jesus, John," he muttered. "She's as insane as you are."

John glanced back at Renee, who was still huffing from her attack on Alex. That microscopic red dress made her look like a little blond devil who'd risen up from the underworld to give his brother holy hell. She was actually an angel in disguise, but it was going to take Alex a while to figure that out.

"We can consider this matter closed, then," Renee said, her angry gaze still boring into Alex. "Is that correct?"

"Oh, all right," he muttered, then glared at John. "But I swear to God, if you tell a solitary soul what happened here tonight, nothing will be able to save your ass. Not even your crazy girlfriend."

John smiled. "I wouldn't think of it."

"Yeah, I'll just bet you wouldn't." He started toward the door, shooting them both nasty looks. "I've had to pee for the last hour. If you'll excuse me?"

He left the room, and John turned slowly to face Renee. "Does this mean I'm forgiven for last night?"

She walked over and slid into his arms, and John felt such an outpouring of relief that he could barely contain it. He held her so tightly he was almost afraid of hurting her, but when he thought about how close he'd come to losing her, anything less just wasn't enough. He couldn't believe they'd actually found the person who committed that robbery. He couldn't believe she was back here with him again.

He couldn't believe she'd stopped Alex from murdering him.

"Thanks for sticking up for me, sweetheart. If you hadn't, you just might be taking me to the hospital right about now."

"Nah. He's not so tough."

*No, he's not. Not compared to you.*

After what she'd been through in the past several days, still she managed to go to that club tonight to try to prove her innocence, and he felt nothing but shame that he hadn't stood by her. That was a mistake he intended never to make again.

John heard the bathroom door open, and then Alex stomping down the hall toward the living room. The front door opened, then slammed so hard the pictures rattled on the walls.

"I guess he's still a little mad, huh?" Renee said.

"He'll get over it." John took Renee's face in his hands and kissed her gently. "I need to go to the station. Make sure we get that confession out of Steve. You'll stay right here until I get back, won't you?"

She leaned close and whispered in his ear that yes, she would, and precisely where in his house she'd be, and that it had just become and would forever remain a no-handcuff zone.

When John returned home an hour and a half later, he found Renee asleep in his bed. That hot little red dress was tossed on his dresser, along with those pink undies of hers, and the purple hat was in the trash can. He sat down on the bed beside her. She stirred and turned over, and that was when he realized that she hadn't bothered to put on one of his shirts. She hadn't bothered to put on anything.

A very nice surprise.

He touched her shoulder, and her eyes blinked open. She smiled up at him.

"Everything's okay, sweetheart," he said, brushing a strand of blond hair away from her cheek. "Steve confessed."

"He did?"

"Yeah. He wasn't too sure he wanted to, but then Tom came down to the station and added a little extra persuasion. You're off the hook."

She took a deep breath and let it out slowly, her body going limp with relief.

"I owe my life to you," she whispered.

He felt a shiver when she said that, thinking about how anything in the past few days could have taken a wrong turn and maybe they wouldn't have discovered the truth. Renee might have run so far that he never would have found her, or she'd have eventually gotten caught and he'd have had to live with the knowledge that she was inside prison walls and he hadn't been able to do anything to stop it.

"Come on, sweetheart. You were the one who took out a rabid bounty hunter and extracted a confession from an armed robber. You didn't need me."

"Yes, I did. I needed a man who couldn't

take me to jail when he knew I was innocent, no matter what the rest of the world said." She laid her palm against his cheek. "I love you, John. I know that's hard to believe after so short a time, but I do."

He didn't realize until this moment how desperately he'd wanted to hear her say that. But still he felt uneasy. "Are you sure it isn't just gratitude?"

He'd asked her that once before, when they were on the verge of making love for the first time, and that same doubt was creeping in again. He was afraid to ask the question. Afraid to find out it wasn't really love on her part, because he'd fallen so hard for her that if she didn't feel the same, he wasn't sure he'd ever pick himself back up again.

"No," she whispered. "It's not just because of what you did. It's because of who you are. It's because you were willing to risk everything that's important to you. For me."

She lay back against the pillow, smiling sleepily. "Now, will you please take off your clothes and come to bed?"

She didn't have to ask twice.

# epilogue

Renee had survived a false criminal accusation and three run-ins with a bounty hunter who was out for blood, then single-handedly choked a confession out of an armed robber, but going to Aunt Louisa's house the next Sunday for lunch was still one of the most nerve-racking experiences of her life.

Even though John assured her that he'd told his family the whole story, Renee still felt uneasy.

"This is so weird," Renee whispered to John as they took their places at the table.

"Relax," he whispered back. "I told you everything's fine."

"Alex is giving me the evil eye."

"That's the way he looks at everybody."

"Are you sure they want me here?"

"Trust me, sweetheart. Everything's okay."

The family had greeted her in a perfectly gracious manner, but now that they knew everything about her, she couldn't help but think they'd never again look at her as favorably as they had the first time they'd met her. Did they still think she was the woman for John? Or did they hope he'd eventually come to his senses and dump her?

Everyone stuck their napkins in their laps, and Aunt Louisa started the mashed potatoes around. Brenda picked up the platter of fried chicken, took a couple of wings, then handed it to Alex.

"Hey, Alex," she said offhandedly. "Been meaning to ask you. Where did you get that bruise around your wrist?"

Alex froze for a moment, then grabbed three or four chicken legs and deposited them on his plate, saying nothing.

"Yeah," Dave said. "I was looking at that myself. I cuffed a guy once who was resisting arrest. He flipped out. When I finally turned him loose, his wrists looked just like that."

"Handcuffs?" Sandy said, looking bewildered. "It couldn't be. I mean, when's the last time you saw a cop in handcuffs?"

"I'll be over tomorrow evening to help you fix that door frame," Eddie told John. "It's a shame it got beat up that way. What did you say happened again?"

"Oh, all *right!*" Alex turned to glare at John. "You couldn't keep your mouth shut, could you?"

John shrugged. "Something may have slipped out."

"Thanks one hell of a lot," Alex muttered. "Now I suppose the whole world is going to know about it."

"Nope," Sandy said. "If we tell everyone you were outwitted by your brother and spent three hours handcuffed to his weight bench, we'd also have to say *why* you were handcuffed to the weight bench, which means we'd have to tell the world what was going on with John and Renee, and we're not going to go there, are we?"

"But that doesn't mean it can't become family legend," Brenda said.

"Of course not," Sandy said. "We reserve the right to give him a hard time about it at every family gathering from now until the end of time."

"Especially the part about Renee wearing the purple satin hat when she slapped Alex down," Brenda said. "I *love* that part."

"With pearls," Sandy added.

"Of course," Brenda said.

The tight knot of anxiety Renee had felt since she walked in the door slowly unfurled, exposing a sense of belonging she'd wanted desperately to feel. She glanced at Sandy, then Brenda, and they both smiled at her. She smiled back. Furtively, of course. It wouldn't do for Alex to see that she was enjoying this.

"Well, we're certainly glad to have Renee with us again, aren't we?" Aunt Louisa said.

Everyone nodded. Enthusiastically, even. Well, almost everyone. She thought Alex kind of twitched a little, but she couldn't be sure.

Then Aunt Louisa got a bewildered look on her face. "But you know, John, you told us something about Renee growing up, something about when she was a teen-ager. . . ."

Renee frowned, feeling all that anxiety crawl right back inside her again.

"But for some reason," Aunt Louisa went on, "I just can't seem to remember what it was." She shook her head. "I suppose I'm just getting old. Do you remember, Sandy?"

Sandy pondered that for a moment, then shrugged. "Seems to have slipped my mind, too. Dave?"

"Sorry. I don't remember either."

"Me either," Brenda said, then turned to Alex with a pointed stare. "How about you, Alex?"

Alex's mouth twisted with disgust. Brenda kicked him under the table.

"Can't remember a thing," he muttered.

Then Grandpa and Eddie voiced the same memory loss that, tragically, appeared to run in the DeMarco family. Only Grandma looked around the table with a perplexed expression.

"What's the matter with you people?" she said. "She was a rotten little juvenile delinquent with a rap sheet so long you could measure it with a yardstick."

The whole family froze, then turned their gazes to Renee. She knew she should be mortified, and a week ago she might have been. But now she just couldn't help it. She smiled. Then Brenda smiled, too, and Sandy snickered a little. Then everybody else joined in, and before long the walls were shaking with laughter. Grandma looked at everyone as if *they* were nuts, and Renee realized it had been a very long time since she'd laughed so hard her sides hurt, and it felt *good*.

When the laughter finally died down, Alex gave everyone a roundhouse glare. "So where's everybody's selective memory loss when I need it?"

"Renee left all that stuff behind her when she was a teenager," Sandy said. "You, on the other hand, were a jerk just last week."

Everyone nodded again, then resumed munching on Aunt Louisa's fried chicken.

They speculated about how well the Cowboys might hold up against the Steelers this afternoon, and soon a heated discussion erupted, with one person quoting quarterback statistics, another reciting injury lists. And Renee couldn't believe how wonderful it felt to be part of the family rather than an outsider looking in.

"Renee," Alex said.

She froze at the sound of Alex's booming voice. The casual chatter at the table fell silent as he skewered her with a sharp stare. That evil eye again.

"Yes?"

"Are you still a beer drinker?"

"Uh . . . yeah. Sometimes."

"Do you think you can keep it in the bottle, where it belongs?"

Renee smiled just a little bit. "I think maybe I can. I'm not nearly as clumsy as I was eight years ago."

"Then I think we're going to get along just fine. Now, will somebody pass the peas?"

Renee ducked her head, that tiny smile still playing across her lips. She picked up her fork and started to take a bite of potatoes. Then suddenly she had the strangest feeling, a tightness in her throat as if maybe she was going to cry. She set her fork down, tossed her napkin beside her plate, and went into the kitchen, where she grabbed a paper towel and dabbed her eyes. She heard footsteps behind her and turned around, and as soon as she saw John, the floodgates opened.

"Renee? What's wrong?"

"I-I don't know," she said, falling into his arms and sobbing against his shoulder. "It's so dumb to be crying, because I'm happy. I really am."

"Is this about the beer, sweetheart? I'll handcuff Alex to something and you can pour a whole bottle on his shoes if you want to."

Renee burst into laughter. It felt so weird to be laughing and crying at the same time. "Oh, John, this is all just too much for me."

"You'll be fine. You just haven't had a lifetime of experience dealing with them the way I have." He smoothed her hair away from her cheeks. "I should tell you, though, that it wasn't the easiest thing in the world to spill all our secrets to them."

"Oh, really?"

"Yeah. They slapped me around a little for taking such a risk with my career. Then they got all huffy that I lied to them about your identity. And you should have seen the looks on their faces when they heard about your juvenile record."

Renee slid her hand against her throat. "Why didn't you tell me that?"

"Because it would have scared you to death before you even showed up today, and in the end it didn't matter, anyway."

"Why not?"

"Because I told them we were a package deal. I told them I loved you, and they'd better get used to it. You'll notice they got used to it pretty fast."

"John! Renee!" Dave shouted from the dining room. "Get in here! Brenda and Alex are going to arm wrestle!"

"And now you're going to have to get used to them."

Renee laughed and fell into John's arms again, and as he hugged her close, she realized how lucky she'd been. She'd propositioned a dangerous-looking man in a backwoods diner to escape a bad situation and ended up with the best situation of all. She'd fallen in love with a man she could trust her heart to, and she intended to proposition him every night for the rest of their lives.

The employees of Thorndike Press hope you have enjoyed this Large Print book. All our Thorndike and Wheeler Large Print titles are designed for easy reading, and all our books are made to last. Other Thorndike Press Large Print books are available at your library, through selected bookstores, or directly from us.

For information about titles, please call:

(800) 223-1244

or visit our Web site at:

www.gale.com/thorndike
www.gale.com/wheeler

To share your comments, please write:

Publisher
Thorndike Press
295 Kennedy Memorial Drive
Waterville, ME   04901